GIFT OF THE GODDESS

The mysterious lady at the inn had been gener-
ously and graciously loving, but only when she
named the gift she would bestow on him—and
the return she would require of him—did Herewiss realize her identity.

For the flask of Soulflight—the potion that
freed the self from the body—could not have
been purchased by the massed fortunes of an
empire. With it Herewiss could seek in the Middle Kingdoms that lay beyond mortal sight the
secret of his crippled Power . . . and of the
ancient guilt that burdened him.

Supremely human and splendidly womanly
though her love had been, Herewiss now knew
her for the Goddess Herself. . . .

The Latest Science Fiction
and Fantasy from Dell Books

IN THE OCEAN OF NIGHT   Gregory Benford

BINARY STAR #1*:
DESTINY TIMES THREE   Fritz Leiber
RIDING THE TORCH   Norman Spinrad

THE ZAP GUN   Philip K. Dick

THE COLD CASH WAR   Robert Asprin

AS ON A DARKLING PLAIN   Ben Bova

RENEGADE OF CALLISTO   Lin Carter

STAR RIGGER'S WAY   Jeffrey A. Carver

THE FAR CALL   Gordon R. Dickson

THE ICE SCHOONER   Michael Moorcock

STILL I PERSIST IN WONDERING   Edgar Pangborn

VISIONS AND VENTURERS*   Theodore Sturgeon

FIRESHIP   Joan D. Vinge

THE PERFECT LOVER   Christopher Priest

COSMIC KALEIDOSCOPE   Bob Shaw

BINARY STAR #2*:
THE TWILIGHT RIVER   Gordon Eklund
THE TERY   F. Paul Wilson

*Illustrated

THE
Door
INTO
Fire

DIANE DUANE

A Dell Book

Published by
Dell Publishing Co., Inc.
1 Dag Hammarskjold Plaza
New York, New York 10017

Dell ® TM 681510, Dell Publishing Co., Inc.

ISBN: 0-440-11874-3

Printed in the United States of America

First printing—February 1979

This first one is for David, who took me up into a high place at sunset and showed me the view—

for Steve and Kathleen, who yelled "FLY!!!" and kicked me off—

and for the Unknown Pro from Dover, Khávrinen's wielder, who turned a nothing Tuesday evening in July into Opening Night and gave me the greatest gift of a lifetime.

> To him,
> my brother,
> and to you three—
> the best I have:
> my book;
> my love.

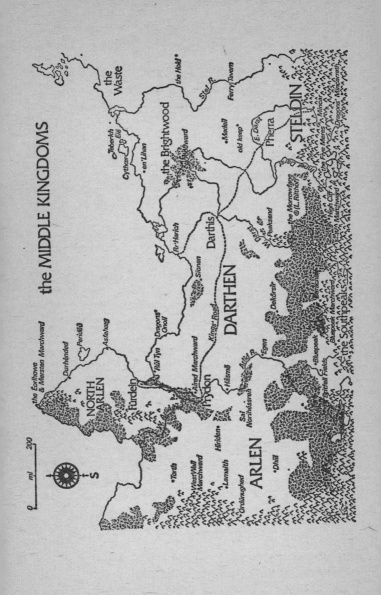

AN OVERTURE
BY DAVID GERROLD*

My first meeting with Diane Duane occurred at a *Star Trek* convention in New York City in 1975.

There were fifteen thousand rabid Trekkies in attendance at that convention, and Saturday morning, I was chased up three flights of stairs and then down again by twelve nubile young females, who—when not in training for the Olympic decathlon—worked as acrobats and contortionists for Ringling Brothers, all of whom wanted to rip the clothes off my strong young limbs and then perform a variety of grotesque, vile, perverse and otherwise disgusting acts of a sexual nature all over my body—none of which I was averse to, you understand, but these particular nubile young females were all under eighteen. (If that description sounds a wee bit like wishful thinking of a sexist nature, I have more than enough reliable witnesses to verify the incident; otherwise I would never, not even in my wildest flights of fantasy, dare to report it, even at this late date.)

I managed to elude my pursuers only by hiding out

*This was supposed to be an introduction, but I'd rather make overtures to Diane Duane than introductions.

—D.G.

in the one place they could not possibly follow: the men's room of the Grand Central Station, which was connected via the third level of that structure to the catacombs of the Commodore Hotel, where the aforementioned *Star Trek* convention was being held.

As an after-effect of that exercise, which was more physical exertion in one wind-sprint than I had performed in the entire previous decade, I came down with a pseudo-asthma attack. I say "pseudo" because I am not, never have been, and have no intention of ever becoming an asthmatic on either a regular or a temporary basis; but no matter, at that point in time, I was having an asthma attack, which began slowly and then continued to worsen throughout the day, so that one hour before the costume masquerade, which I was supposed to help judge, I was in no condition to do anything more than lie on my bed and groan. (I have it on the best authority that I can be very good at groaning when I put my mind to it.) After a while, realizing that this was not the best state of affairs, I was able to corner one of the more responsible convention gofers ("Gofer this, gofer that."), an elf named Lise Eisenberg, and by a complicated series of grunts and pantomimes, imparted to her the information that she should find the hotel doctor and have him come up to my room. She went mumfling and merfling off down the hallway, passing one Diane Duane heading in the opposite direction. At the sound of an elf mumfling and merfling things that sounded like: ". . . mumfle, mumfle . . . doctor . . . merfle . . . paramedics . . . CPR . . . mumfle, mumfle . . . iron lung . . . Mayo Clinic . . . merfle . . ." Diane Duane's super-sensitive radar-like antennae twitched, and triggered her slender lithe body into throbbing action: a reflex known in medical circles as the *Nightingale Syndrome*. Grabbing the elfin Eisenberg in a vise-like grip, she lifted the small one off her feet and up to eye level. "I," announced Diane Duane to the startled short person, "am a night-roving nurse! Dressed in

8

my special black cape, I roam the streets of this great city, searching for the tired, the poor, the wretched, the ill, the homely, and I heal them—often, whether they want to be healed or not! Also, I am an anti-vampire. I sneak up on people and give them blood. Now, what's all this about a doctor?"

Lise pointed Diane in my direction and neither her life nor mine have ever been the same since.*

First, Diane held my hand until such time as the hotel doctor chose to make his appearance. She not only held my hand, she predicted the doctor's diagnosis and prescription with a degree of accuracy that should be investigated by both the AMA and the Rhine Institute. All I remember of the doctor at the Hotel Commodore, by the way, was that when he finally did show up, his fly was open, and I spent the entire physical examination wondering if he had remembered to wash his hands when he finished. The doctor prescribed Valium, and disappeared back into the night.

By then it was time to go down and help judge the masquerade; another gofer, one not quite as alacritous as the elfin Eisenberg, went off to find a pharmacy to fill the prescription. As usual, the masquerade started right on time: an hour and a half late. During this waiting period the prescription did not arrive, although we did receive several updates on the gofer's position as he/she/it struggled to find a way out of the hotel—this being the sum total of entertainment during the wait for the masquerade to begin. Because this was a *Star Trek* convention, there were one hundred and forty-three Spocks, nine thousand giant tribbles, fourteen hundred "Captain's Ladies" in search of their Captain, five swarms of Klingons of varying temperament, and a pre-Reform Vulcan in platform

*I don't think I have ever thanked Lise properly. Lady, bless you forever!

—D.E. Duane

shoes: in other words, the usual, all of them waiting impatiently for their moment onstage.

While we were watching the conventioneers milling about, and while we were waiting for the errant prescription, I started sipping at a glass of Scotch—for purely medicinal purposes, you understand—trying to bring a measure of relaxation to my tortured and still-aching lungs. When the Valium finally did arrive a couple of eons later, without thinking, I popped one into my mouth—which immediately set off a chorus of horrified shrieks and yells—"Pills and booze! Pills and booze! David Gerrold's trying to kill himself again!" (Again?!!) The only one who didn't panic in all this hysteria was the formidable Diane Duane, all ninety-nine pounds of her (44.9 kilograms for those of you who have already gone metric), who rose majestically like Venus from the sea and announced that we were retiring to the twenty-second floor, there to have a picnic, and also write a marching song for the suicide club we were forming—

I know that all of the above sounds a little manic—but this is the way I remember it. The fact that as a result of the pills and booze I was on one of the best benders of my life had very little to do with it—*Star Trek* conventions are always a little manic. The big ones are even more so than this description implies. (Or they *were*; I haven't been to one in almost three years; I haven't the slightest idea what they do at them now—although I have heard stories about ritual sacrifices of small animals before a 7-foot Advent Videobeam television.)

—a word here about the windows in the late (but undeservedly now-defunct) Commodore Hotel: *no screens*. You can open them up and jump out, if you've a mind to.

I didn't have a mind to, but that open window was giving me a very hard time. You see, if the truth be known, I'm an acrophobia-phobic—that is, while I am *not* afraid of heights, I have a fear of being afraid of heights. I also have a fear of being afraid of small enclosed places (claustrophobia-phobia) as well as a fear of being afraid of fear (phobia-phobia-phobia), a direct result of over-exposure to Franklin Delano Roosevelt in my formative years.

—none of which is important, but when you are on one of the best benders of your life you tend to babble about all sorts of things. Diane Duane was delighted to sit and take it all in like an avid audience, never once letting me know that in her real life, she was employed as a Registered Nurse with special training in Clinical Psychiatry and she was in her own mind trying to decide whether to humor me or merely stuff me into a barrel of sour pickles, that being the approved remedy at the time.

Anyway, eventually various baskets of food arrived and we had a picnic—Diane, myself, and a few close friends, all of whom had been privately coached that if I got too close to the window, they were to form a flying wedge and pile on top of me so as to prevent me from falling, jumping, or flying out of it.

Her analysis, by the way, was that I was sane—or if not sane, then at least compulsively rational. This fact has been a great disappointment to me—it means that whatever goals I might someday achieve, I will have to do so by dint of hard work alone because I cannot depend on the kind of inspiration that is a by-product of schizophrenia to occur in my day-to-day life as a writer.

The point of all this is that from that moment on, I have been forever indebted to Diane Duane: you see, after she finished convincing me that I was really Chinese and had only been raised by the couple I had thought were my real parents, and who had never had the courage to tell me I was adopted, she then told me of the ancient Chinese tradition that after you save someone's life, you are responsible for them forever after, and that now she was going to be responsible for

11

me; something like a fairy godmother, but a lot more ballsy.

There were a lot of other adventures that happened after that, but we don't have space to discuss them here—that would require another book. At some point in those adventures though—I think it was the day she tripped while crossing in front of my silver Stingray, presenting me, still sitting in the driver's seat, with a grotesque view of what a shark sees as the swimmer disappears into its mouth—Diane mentioned to me that she wanted to be a writer too.

My response was a reflex action. I couldn't help it. Even if I had wanted to, I could not have prevented it: my upper lip curled into a sneer, a weary sigh of resignation escaped my lips, my eyes clenched tightly shut in pain—

This is a protective reflex. All professional writers have it to some degree or other. It is a way to try to discourage beginners, because if you *can* be discouraged then sooner or later you will be, so you might as well quit now and save yourself a lot of trouble—and on the other hand, if you can't be discouraged, then seeing a professional writer sneer at you will only make you angry enough and determined enough to go out and prove that bastard wrong, that you *can* write! Which is exactly what happened to Diane Duane. Even before the sigh had finished escaping my lips, she got angry with me. She didn't show it though. She listened to my weary protest that I was tired of hearing from would-be writers about all the great books they plan to write—"Real writers don't talk writing," I said. "They go home and *write*."

Diane didn't say anything. At least, not out loud. Inside, she was saying, "I'll show this ******* bastard!" She filed the decision in an appropriate place in her head and I didn't hear about it again for two years, because that is the way Diane Duane is.

I will gloss quickly over the two years between that decision and its fruition. I will skip the story about

Diane and the bear who came to dinner, and the one about Diane and the falcon in the spaghetti, and even the one about Diane and the flying dog; suffice it to say that after a while, Diane loaded all of her worldly possessions into the Conestoga, hitched up the mules, and headed west to begin a new life in the rough frontier town of Northridge, California, where she has taken up duties as the faithful Indian companion to yours truly, David Gerrold (who by day pretends to be your average ordinary science fiction writer and hot-shot TV scripter, but who by night dresses up in flashy leotard and cape and steps into his real identity as a person who likes to wear flashy leotards and capes).

What I have not yet told you is that Diane Duane is a far more complex individual than all of the above suggests. She is an unlicensed helicopter pilot, a better-than-average graphicist and map-maker (she also drew the map for this book and would have painted the cover too, if they would have let her), a very cunning linguist, a black-belt in various oriental arts of mayhem and violence—including the little-known ones of Kabuki and Karezza, a not-too-bad motion picture director's assistant, an accomplished tree surgeon and horticulturist, a classical music analyst (specializing in Wagner and Anna Russell), one of California's ten best falconers, and also, a pretty good Quantum Mechanic. How much of the above you want to believe is up to you—but those who have met Diane Duane personally do not doubt any of it. In point of fact, there are depths to Diane Duane that I am prohibited by law from revealing; it would endanger national security, the sanctity of the confessional, and quite possibly, the stability of the San Andreas Fault. I can tell you, however, that she is an organist of such proficiency that she has been required to register her hands as dangerous weapons in thirty-seven states.

It also pleases me no end to report that she is a terrible cook. Not only is she living disproof of the male-

13

chauvinist belief that all women are naturally good cooks, but it also allows me the vanity of knowing that there are at least two things that I can still do better than her. Diane Duane's cooking is so bad that we could scare away the mountain lions with it, except that in our area of Northridge, there are no mountain lions any more—some of the other wildlife lurking in the nearby hills have eaten the last of them. Whatever that wildlife is has not yet been identified, but it leaves footprints large enough to park Volkswagens in. Periodically it comes down into the inhabited part of the valley and rummages through our trash cans—God only knows what it's looking for. One morning, while replacing the scattered remains of the previous evening's revelry back in the trash can, I came across the following piece of manuscript:

TUPPERWARE/Duane—118

her creamy-pale, scantily clad body against him so that he almost dropped the chicken.

"I cannot!" he gasped as her hands moved over him, slowly stroking downward. "I have a quest!"

"For *what?*" she demanded, tossing back her mane of fire-red hair imperiously. "For the Rooster of the Gods? That creature is no more: Datril the God of Premature Ejaculations wrung its neck long ago, in the Time Before. Come, hero, forget such foolish *aij*-chases and turn your mind to something more worth your attention. See," and she bent her body back away from him a little, "am I not beautiful?"

"Well," he began, his eyes wandering down her throat past her cleavage and toward the enticing shadows below. "But—but the Dark Swordsman warned me—!"

"Will you listen to the rantings of a crazy old man who lives in a cave in the desert," she purred, drawing him closer and beginning to unlace his jerkin, "or will you not rather take what I offer

14

you—pleasures unimaginable? Men have fought to the death for a night with me, and after the winner has died of pleasure, I have brought *both* corpses back alive. . . ."

He strained to remember the words of the Swordsman, but she pulled his face down to hers, and the long-ago warnings faded to nothing, washed away by red torrents of desire. He groped about with half-closed eyes for somewhere to put the chicken, and then with one motion stripped the garment from

Upon confronting Diane Duane with this incriminating evidence, she broke down and confessed that yes, indeed, she *was* trying to write a book. I told her that, based on this scrap, it wasn't dirty enough to please a mass audience and she should go back to her typewriter and try again.

She thereupon produced the following:

TUPPERWARE/Duane—134

to scorn *me!*"

There was not even enough slack to rattle the chains in defiance. He hung there, bruised, beaten, helpless, as she advanced on him slowly. Her face had the look of a cat about to pounce.

"All that has gone before was nothing more than preparation," she purred. "The elephant, the eighty-eight virgins with the mousetraps inserted, the giant leeches, the Little Stretcher, the deaf-and-dumb slaves with the, ah," she chuckled, "specially augmented equipment, the nose dildoes, all the other hardware—all of that was just to keep you entertained." She smiled sweetly. "Now you have me to deal with. I will, of course, allow you to beg first."

He mouthed a particularly vile Alij obscenity and spat on the floor.

"Commendable," she said. "And you?"

The chicken, hanging upside down in its chains, was only able to squawk feebly, but there was red death in its eye.

"Well then," she said. "Time to resort to more potent measures. *Aliquot qed nyarlathotep telefunken!!!*" she cried.

An eldritch darkness fell over the smoky room, and before they understood the import of the words, the change was completed. Out of the shadows heaved the glistening, sickly-wet bulk as it crawled obscenely toward them, drooling nameless secretions. The giant vagina clicked its teeth and

Neither of the above two excerpts actually appears in this book—Diane eventually decided that they were too tame and deleted the whole section that required their inclusion, although you might watch for them in the upcoming sequel.

When she finally finished the manuscript, at that point still untitled, she presented it to me and asked if I would read the beast. I was reluctant: I gnashed my teeth, screamed and yelled, jumped up and down, and held my breath till I fell over on the floor unconscious—I was *very* reluctant. Diane promised to return my children unharmed. I told her I didn't have any children. She said she was going to borrow some in my name. I said, "Not with *my* reputation!" And that was the end of that.

She passed the manuscript on to some other friends instead: Dorothy Fontana, Steve Goldin, Kathleen Sky, all of whom are professional writers of extensive credential and with far better manners than myself, not to mention a greater degree of tolerance for aspiring beginners. When the first few positive reports began filtering back—"Gosh! Wow! Whoopeee! Oh, boy! This is fantastic! I can hardly wait for the sequel! This is really gonna blow some minds away!"—I went

16

to Diane and asked her plaintively, "When do I get to read it?"

She said, sticking it to me where I so obviously deserved it, "I thought you weren't interested in a beginner's first effort."

"Well . . . maybe I was wrong. . . ."

She brought the manuscript into the house and laid it before me like the number three wife asking her Lord to accept a newborn son . . . I placed the manuscript carefully on the kitchen table and began a calculated period of indifference, three weeks long. The manuscript and I eyed each other warily every time I passed.

It sat there on my kitchen table, gathering dust, waiting. I knew I was going to have to sit down and read it, but I hated the thought of actually doing so. I knew it was going to be awful, I just *knew* it. All beginners' first novels are awful—no matter what the reviewers say. And I knew, if it was awful enough, I'd have to help Diane correct its faults; I'd have to carefully phrase my criticisms so as not to hurt her feelings, yet at the same time I'd have to ruthlessly point out to her all the myriad ways she could make this into a better book. I hated the thought of beginning such a heart-rending process—it would be as much a strain on her as it would be on me.

But finally, one afternoon, after a particularly vile threat on her part ("I'll erase all of your Three Stooges video-tapes.") I actually forced myself to sit down with the manuscript and begin reading.

Ten pages into it, I got up, got my red flair-tip pen to mark a grammatical correction and sat down again. Two hours later, I had to throw that pen away because the tip had dried out—from *not* being used. There wasn't *anything* wrong with the book! I liked it!

Look, I'm not supposed to review this book—I'm not even supposed to tell you how good it is, because you're about to find that out for yourself; but this

17

novel, this book that you are holding here, is the first novel that I have read all in one sitting since I don't know when. It's exciting, magical, intelligent, heart-warming, thrilling, scary, all of that good stuff, and in all the right places too—best of all, it has that rare, elusive quality called *sense of wonder*.

The book is so good, it's terrifying.

I knew when I finished it that I was going to have to kill Diane Duane. She was *too* good.

I mean, who needs competition like this?

In fact, I was even to the point of choosing my murder weapon when I realized something purely awful—if I killed her, I wouldn't find out what happened in the next three books in this series, and that thought was even more unbearable; so I did the next best thing: I told her that I would help her find the right market for the book—a person who does this is called an "agent"—and we would *both* get rich. (I know a good thing when I see one.)

Diane rewrote two pages to clarify one minor plot point, made some minor grammatical corrections, and handed me the final draft to pass on to the good folks at Dell Publishing: Don Benson and Jim Frenkel. I remember how much pleasure it was to tell them what a terrific and special book this was. It was an equal delight to see their editorial faces light up in anticipation—or perhaps they could sense my enthusiasm, I certainly made no secret of it. Two weeks later—an unprecedentedly *short* response time for a publisher—they telephoned to tell us they agreed, the book *was* special, and they were willing to pay a lot of money (well, not all that much, but a lot for a first novel) for the privilege of bringing it to you, the reader.

I insisted on the privilege of introducing not just a special and magic book (and the series it inaugurates), but the author as well, who is equally a special and magic person.

If I've been a little bit irreverent here, it's because—well, that's the way Diane is. When I tell her life back to her in my own inimitable way, her face lights up like the front window of the *Millennium Falcon* going into hyperdrive and *I like to see her face all lit up like that,* and when I showed her what I'd written about her, I was nearly blinded by the glare. (Now I know what Roy Neary saw when he walked up into the mothership.) It's the kind of relationship we have, okay?

One extra bit of truth—I knew I was going to write the introduction to Diane's first novel, no matter whether it was a stinker or a gem—because Diane herself is a gem and it would be a way for me to tell her so in public and probably embarrass the both of us—but it is a special pleasure in itself for me to be able to write this introduction, because this book, *The Door Into Fire,* is a beautiful book indeed. It is more than just a gem, it is a whole bloody treasure! And I am delighted to be associated with it even in this small way.

I make no claims to being Diane's mentor (no matter what she might say) and lest there be those among you who suspect that I had a hand in the writing of this book, I wish I could say I had—it would be an honor to be a part of this work; the truth is that I was the last person to read the manuscript—but I will *not* be the last to applaud Diane's triumph; it is *her* accomplishment and hers alone and that is the way it *should* be. My part of the triumph is to be allowed to help rave about it.

This book is also a promise of a great deal more to come that should be every bit as special and magic too.

And if Diane doesn't follow through, rest assured that I will also be the first to thrash her soundly for not living up to her potential.

Read. Enjoy. Tell friends.

—David Gerrold
Northridge, CA
March, 1978

Herewiss Hearn's-son might very possibly have grown up to be just another Lord of the Brightwood, ninety-second of his line, ninety-third in descent from the Eagle, a Prince of Darthen by gift and decree. He probably would have ruled wisely, passed on the Lordship of the Wood and the sword Fänderë to his son or daughter when the child came of age to rule, and lived out the rest of his life quietly with his loved until the Mother came for him. In that time, no one would have thought such a life unusual. Many felt that the great days of the Middle Kingdoms were a thousand years past, the heroes dead, the Lion and Eagle gone without intent of return, the Dragons silent, even the blue Fire of the Power cooling or being taken for granted.

But as it was, Herewiss had four things that made this impossible. He had a hero's talent for being in the wrong place, with the wrong people, at the wrong time. He had the Goddess' own knack for bringing victory out of defeat, light out of darkness, life out of death. He had Freelorn of Arlen for his loved. And he had the Fire.

It was all he needed to change the world.

"Aye, night commes and Hee risith from the Flame;
Lyoun and Eagle loudlie cry His name:
The Phoenix that schall spurn the shatter'd Spere.
Hys Fire shall fede upoun his darkest Fear:
But nott yntil the Starres fall owt the Skye,
Dawn coms up Blue, and our Daye be past by . . ."

(rede fragment, Héalhregebócan, IV, 6-12)

A BRIEF NOTE ON LINGUISTICS AND PRONUNCIATION

Darthene and Arlene are both outgrowths of the same root language, which dates back at least as far as the post-Worldwinning migrations northward from the Highpeaks. The Oath of Lion and Eagle, the Great Road from Prydon to Darthis, and other such stimulants to exchange of goods and information, have worked to lessen the linguistic changes that might occur when two nations are so large and sparsely populated. Vocalic and consonantal shifts tend to filter back and forth across the borders as they happen, though very isolated towns often keep pronunciations of words that are centuries-gone elsewhere. Differences in accent are usually due to this kind of isolation. Freelorn's remark about Herewiss' ridiculous Southern accent was prompted by the fact that the Brightwood dialect of Darthene is almost unchanged since the days of the migration, and is something of a humorous anomaly in the cosmopolitan North. At the other extreme, in the country on either side of the Arlid, the two languages are so intertwined that it's almost impossible to tell them apart. "Pure" Arlene and Darthene exist, like "classical" Latin and Greek, as primarily written languages: the two tongues use a common set of runes, though diacritical marks and cursive ligatures differ.

22

Nháired is a subdialect of Darthene, full of anachronistic forms of words, odd rules for rhythm and scansion, and "denser" abbreviatory forms than those occurring in orthodox Darthene. The involved rules for speaking the language suggest that it was originally intended strictly as a vehicle for poetry; learning to scan Nháired is the work of years, and making magic in it is another business entirely. In Herewiss' time, it is the preferred language for the working of serious sorcery, and as much pride is taken by the artist in the poetic flow of the spell as in the effects after it is spoken. There is a saying in Darthene: "Half of poetry is magic: half of magic is poetry."

Where a "foreign" language appears in the text, it is Nháired; it is considered both unartistic and unwise to translate it. Some of the proper names of places and things in the book are in "regular" Arlene or Darthene.

The proper names of people, however, I have usually translated into equivalents, using Latin, Greek, Coptic, or Anglo-Saxon roots. I have tried to convey the feeling that those names give the people in the Arlene/Darthene cultures who hear and use them—a feeling that a given name is rooted in one's own language, though an older form perhaps. "Herewiss," to me, has a more familiar, analyzable sound than "Aerphrárdë," which is his name in Darthene; and the roots of the Anglo-Saxon form, meaning "battle-wise, crafty, brilliant," translate the original well.

Accents fall, for the most part, on the next-to-last syllable of a word. Exceptions are indicated with diacritical marks, and umlauts (··) are used to warn against letting vowels, especially terminal ones, fall silent or short. Outside of these restrictions, the reader is encouraged to pronounce the words any way she/he likes.

—D.E.D.

ONE

Smiths and sorcerers come both from the same nest.

Chronicle of the White Eagle,
XII, 54

Herewiss sat crosslegged on the parquet floor, his back braced against the wall, his eyes closed, and concentrated.

Part of the problem was that he couldn't stop thinking of the thing resting across his upturned hands as a sword; a noisy feeling of weaponness trickled through him from it. *It* knew that it was a sword; that was the problem. It was good Darthene steel, folded on itself in its forging the required sixty times, and sealed with the Mastersmith's hallmark down on the rough tang of the metal. It knew that it was destined to be a killing weapon, an elegant, finely polished thing, soft of back, hard of edge, with the Mastersmith's distinctive forging-pattern embedded like waves in water within its silver blade. It knew what it was for— woundings and death, the abrupt soft parting of flesh beneath its stroke, the sudden crunch into cloven bone. The taste of pain, like wine. It lay there across his hands, and waited to be presented with slayings as a banqueter waits eagerly for the first course.

No, dammit, Herewiss said to himself, and pulled away from the perception. *Sometimes I wish I weren't so sensitive. How the Dark can something dead know so well what it's for? —This is ridiculous. I should be*

25

able to impose my will on a piece of steel, *for Goddess'* *sake. Maybe this way . . .*

He took a moment to clear his mind out, and then concentrated on seeing the thing in his hands, not as a sword, but as a great number of particles of metal that just happened to be arranged in the long, rough bar-shape he held. If it was filed down, it would be just so much steel-dust. *See it that way,* he told himself. *A thousand thousand glittering points of steel, bound together only loosely—soft, porous enough for a sorcery to pass through them—*

It took him a while, but he achieved the perception. The metal fought him, trying again and again to become a killing instrument. It knew what it was for, and Herewiss couldn't say as much; but he was alive and concentrating, and that gave him a slight edge. Finally the blank presented itself the way he wanted to see it, as countless tiny brilliances, sparkling metallically as they danced about one another, shining like dust in sunlight.

All right. Now, then—

Holding the image in mind, he began to construct the sorcery he had planned. It was an old formula, one of the very few sorceries that had any power over life at all—a binding used to prevent the dying soul from leaving the body temporarily. However, Herewiss had made certain changes in the formula, since the soul he planned to slip among the glittering points of metal was not anywhere near death. The words of the spell were hard and dull like black iron in the back of his mind as he linked them one through another like chain mail, the stress on the last syllable of each word sealing each ring closed. He sang the poem softly over and over inside him, adding link to link, until the spell surrounded the bright bar of metal like a wide sheath.

Herewiss had some small trouble finishing the spell, welding the two sides of it together—like most circular spells, it wanted only to go on and on, building itself back inward until it had trapped the sorcerer inside its own coils and choked the life out of him. But he prevailed, and sealed the spell shut, and pulled himself away from it, inspecting it for flaws and undone links. There were none.

Now for the interesting part, he thought.

Sorcerers and Rodmistresses had been speculating for as long as anyone could remember on the question of why the Science and the Art killed their practitioners so young. Many people believed that sorcery chipped away slowly at the soul, so that when the soul became too small to support the body, the body died; and the blue Flame, of course, since it had power over both the giving and taking of life, as mere sorcery did not, had the same effect but more quickly. Herewiss' mother had been a Rodmistress, and he could remember hearing her laugh about the idea some years before. "Your soul is as big as you can make it," she had said to him as she walked through the Woodward's chicken-yard, scattering grain for the hens, "and the only thing that can diminish its size is your decision to do so. And also, belief is a powerful influence—it's quite possible to talk yourself into an early grave, and climb in when the time comes." She had died three years later, at the age of twenty-eight.

Herewiss felt around inside himself, and looked for his soul. It was where it usually was, an amorphous silvery mass tucked down just a bit below his breastbone, snuggled up against the spine. The blue Fire was threaded all through it, a faint half-seen tracery like the lines of veins beneath the skin, glowing a pale blue-white. *Hold on,* he told the Flame affectionately, *hold on for a while longer. It won't be too long now. This should work.*

He reached out and teased loose a little strand of his soul-stuff; it stretched easily outward as he pulled at it. A faint trace of Flame came with it, twisting around its length, graining the strand with spiraling light like a unicorn's horn. Gently, for he didn't want to break the thread until he was ready, he eased it on outward and toward the dancing sparks of steel, into them, through them, and out again, and back in—winding the soulstuff through the structure, beckoning it in and around, luring it onward with promises of Power about to be achieved. The Flame followed after, hopeful. Herewiss tangled the bit of himself like a bright cord, weaving it through itself again and again, drawing it finer and finer, silver wire thinning out to silver web, and always followed by that faint blue flow of Fire. Finally the steeldust glitter could hardly be seen at all for the sorcerer's weave stranded through it.

Herewiss stood back a little, then cut the web's attachment to him with one sharp word.

It hurt; he had expected it to; but he had no time now to deal with the ache. The entangled soul would start undoing itself almost immediately if he didn't bind it. He spoke in his mind the word that would activate the binding sorcery, and it heard him and responded on the instant, the hard dark links of restrainment drawing in close around the shining bar, snicking in cold and tight like a sudden scabbard, prisoning the soulstuff within.

He stepped back to make sure that the sorcery would hold without his immediate supervision. It did. He poked at it once, experimentally; it resisted him.

Satisfied, he broke trance and opened his eyes.

He had to blink for a few moments; his eyes watered with the seeming brightness of the tower room. It was full of smith's furnishings; the middle of the room was taken up by the forge, a wide brick pit with a down-hanging bellows, and there was a pedal-powered grindstone in one corner. Anvils, ingots and scraps of metal were everywhere. A number of blanks of the Darthene steel were leaned up in a row against one wall, like so many barrel-staves.

The fire in the forge was out, and the tools were racked up on the walls. Halwerd, his son, was also sit-

28

ting on the floor, over against the other paneled wall beside the window; he had taken off his apron, and was doing an elaborate cat's-cradle with a piece of string. Herewiss never tired of the joys of having a smaller version of himself around, and spent a few minutes just watching the child. Halwerd sat there in his greasy green tunic, all dark curly hair and fierce concentration. He flipped his hands, and the cat's-cradle turned suddenly into a mess. "Dark!" he said.

"You're too young to be swearing," Herewiss said with affection.

"I'm nine," Halwerd said, as if that should have been enough. "Did it work?"

"Yes."

"It doesn't look any different." The boy gazed across the room, and Herewiss looked down at the piece of metal he held.

"No, it doesn't. Well, we'll see if it holds up tonight. It's full Moon, this is a good day for it. Though I could wait for the Maiden's Day Moon. What do you think?"

Halwerd considered gravely. "Do it tonight."

"All right."

Herewiss got up, wobbling a little from the backlash of the sorcery. "Oh my," he said. "I must be getting better at this, the backlash is hitting me faster than it used to."

"How many swords is this now?" Halwerd asked, starting the cat's-cradle over again.

"Twenty-three. No, twenty-four. Cheer up, Hal, maybe this'll be the last one." Herewiss tossed the sword-blank clanging onto the work table and looked around him as he stretched. He was a tall, slender man, lean and lithe and dark-haired, with a finely featured face and a mouth that smiled a great deal. His arms and shoulders were slightly overmuscled from much work at the forge; but the effect was not unpleasant. At first glance he gave an impression of spare, restrained power, the taut strength of youth.

But his deep blue eyes were beginning to look weary, and his face was gradually acquiring frown lines. "Be nice to turn this back into a bedroom," he said, "and get all this mess out of here, Dark eat it—"

"Grampa would say," Halwerd said, " 'you're not a good example. Watch your mouth.' "

"So he would. Listen, Hal—"

A pigeon landed on the windowsill with a clapping of wings. It strutted there, fluffing its gray-and-white feathers and looking confused. Herewiss looked at it, momentarily startled, and then unease began to trickle coldly down his back. It was one of the homing pigeons that he had given Freelorn for use in emergencies.

"Hold still, Hal." He walked smoothly around the forge to the window. In one quick motion he grabbed the pigeon before it had a chance to shy away. Stripping off the steel message-case, he threw the bird out the window, and fumbled at the little capsule with suddenly sweaty hands.

The stiff hinge cracked open, and the expected roll of parchment fell out on the floor. Herewiss picked it up, unrolling it, and the throbbing in his head quickened pace. The message said:

AM HOLED UP IN OLD KEEP THREE LEAGUES SOUTH OF MADEIL. A FEW HUNDRED STELDENE REGULARS AND ABOUT SEVEN HUNDRED CONSCRIPTS BESIEGING ME AND THE GROUP. I NEED A COMPETENT SORCERER TO COME GET ME OUT OF THIS RABBITHOLE. HAVE ENOUGH FOOD TO LAST US A FEW WEEKS, BUT MUCH LONGER THAN THAT AND IT WILL BE BOOT-CHEWING TIME. GET ME THE DARK OUT OF HERE AND I'LL BE YOUR BEST FRIEND. THE GODDESS SMILE ON YOU. FREELORN AS'T'RÄID ARLÉNI.

" 'High Lord of all Lords of Arlen', my — ! You know I *am* a bad example, Hal. Listen, did you see where your grandfather was?"

"He was down in the writing room a while ago," Halwerd said. "What happened?"

"Your Uncle Freelorn may be back for a visit in a month or so," Herewiss said, heading for the door, "but I have to go and get him first. Forget it, Hal, go get yourself some nunch."

"All right."

Herewiss loped down the long paneled stairway that curled around the inner wall of the tower, and hit the bottom of the stairs running. Down the south corridor he went at full speed, ignoring the surprised looks of household people and relatives, and ducked into the sixth room to his left. It was a bright place and warm, full of rich carving-work, typical of the Woodward. The fireplace was framed in the wings of carven sphinxes, and two-bodied dogs guarded the corners where the moldings met. Over one closet was carven in slightly frantic figures the history of the sixteenth Lord of the Brightwood, who had married a mermaid. The sunlight gleamed from the woodwork, and from the great brass-bound table which stood on eagle-claw feet in the middle of the room; but its surface was bare, and no one had been working there for some time.

I hope he didn't go out, Herewiss thought. *Damn!* He ran out of the room again, turned left and headed to the end of the south corridor. A stair led down from it to the central hall of the Woodward, where the Rooftree grew. He had no patience for the stairs, but hopped up onto the central banister, which had been polished smooth first by its craftsmen and then by the backsides of generations of the children of the Ward. At the bottom of the stairs he took a bare moment to nod courtesy to the Tree before he loped off across the tapestried hall, and out into the sunlight of the outer courtyard.

His father was there, kneeling in a newly dug flower bed and setting in seedlings. Hearn Halmer's-son was an average-looking man, a little on the lean side, dark-haired except for the places where he was going gray on the sides. He had the usual lazy, sleepy expression of the males of the Brightwood ruling line, and the usual blue eyes, and the large hands that could be so very delicate. Those hands had been mighty in war, so that Hearn had come through two battles with the Reavers and one border skirmish with only a cut or two. This had prompted some to suggest that he had pacted with the Shadow, and had brought his relieved family to refer to him as "Old Ironass." Now, though, he no longer rode to the wars, and it was often hard for visitors to the Woodward to reconcile the conquering Lord of the Brightwood with the quiet, gentle man who could usually be found training ivy up the Ward's outer wall.

"Father," Herewiss yelled, "he's doing it again!"

Hearn sat back on his heels in the loose dirt, brushing off his hands, and looked over at his son. "Who?"

"Here," said Herewiss, coming up and holding out the parchment, "read it!"

"My hands are dirty," Hearn said as Herewiss knelt down beside him. "Hold it for me."

"Dirty? It hardly matters if it gets dirty—" But Herewiss held it out, and his father rested hands quietly on knees and read it through. After a moment he snorted. "As't'räid Arléni, my ass!"

"That's what I said."

"Not in front of Hal, I hope."

"Father, please."

"So," Hearn said, "you're surprised?"

Herewiss laughed, a short rueful sound. "No, not really."

"And so you're going riding off to get him out of whatever he's gotten himself into."

"May I?"

"You're asking me?"

32

"You're the Lord."

Hearn chuckled and took a seedling out of the cup of water beside him. Herewiss noted with amusement that it was one of the ceremonial cups for Opening Night, the rubies flaring in the sunlight and making bright dots of reflection in the mud. "Could I stop you? Could the Queen of Darthen stop you? Could our Father the Eagle stop you if He showed up? Go on. But when you see the idiot, tell him from me that he'd better not sign himself as King of Arlen unless he's willing to do something about it."

"I had that in mind."

"You'd never say it, though, you're too damn kind. You tell him *I* said it. Will you be needing men?"

"I'm sorcerer enough to handle this myself, I think. And the less people involved, the better. If Cillmod hears that Brightwood people were involved, it could be excuse enough for him to break the Oath again and move in on Darthen."

Hearn planted the seed. "There speaks my wise son," he said.

"And besides—I don't want any Wood people getting killed because of this. And neither do you—but *you'd* never say it—because you're too damn kind."

Hearn laughed softly. "My wise son. But don't let it stop you from bringing him back here if he needs a place to stay. No one will hear about it from us."

Herewiss nodded and stood up.

"Take what you need," Hearn said. "Take Dapple, if you think he'd help. And Herewiss—"

Hearn turned back to his work, his strong hands moving the soil. "Be careful. I'm short of sons."

Herewiss stood there looking at his father's back for a moment, and then turned and headed back into the Woodward to start preparing for a journey.

The Brightwood is the oldest and most honored of the principalities of Darthen. It was the first of the new settlements established after the Worldwinning, by people who came down out of the eastern High-peaks and found the quiet woodlands to their liking after their long travels. It took them many years to free the Wood and its environs from the Fyrd that infested it, but while many other peoples were still living in caves in the mountains, the Brightwood folk were already building the Woodward in the great clearing at its center.

Though the Woodward is held by outsiders to be at the Wood's heart, the Brightwood people know that its real heart—or hearts, for there are several—lie elsewhere; in the Silent Precincts, secret, holy places where few people not born in the Wood or trained to the usages of the Power have ever walked. There, upon the Forest Altars hidden within the Precincts, the Goddess was first worshipped again as She used to be before the Catastrophe—invoked in Her three forms as Maiden and Mother and Wise Woman. There too Her Lovers are worshipped, those parts of Herself which rise and fall in Her favor, eternally replacing one another as Her consorts. Even the Lovers' Shadow is worshipped there, though with cautious and propitiatory rites enacted at the dark of the Moon. Other places of the worship of the Pentad there may be, but there are none older or more revered except the Morrowfane, which is the Heart of the World and so takes precedence.

Night with its stars spread over the Wood, and the pure silver moonlight made vague and doubtful patterns on the grass as it shone through the branches. Spring was well underway; the night was full of the smell of growing things, and the chill wind laced itself through the new leaves with a hissing sound.

In the center of the little clearing, before the slab of moon-white marble set into the ground, Herewiss knelt shivering. The indefinite blackwork filigree of moonshine and shadow shifted and blurred on his bare body, and gleamed dully from the sword he held before him. It was beaten flatter than it had been that morning, and had some pretense of an edge on it; but it was not yet finished. Herewiss had learned better than to waste time putting hilts and finishing on these swords before he tried them with this final testing.

The dappled horse tethered at the edge of the clearing stamped and snorted softly, indignant over having to be up at this ridiculous hour. But right now Herewiss had no sympathy for it, and he shut the sound out of his mind as he prayed desperately. It had to work. It *had* to. He had done a good day's spelling, a good piece of work, though he had paid dear for it, both in backlash and in the pain cutting away part of his *self* had cost him. But it might work. No, it *had* to. This was the Great Altar, the Altar of the Flame, the one most amenable to what he was doing, the one with the most bound-up power. And this sword felt better than any of the others he had tried; more *alive*. Maybe he had managed to fool the steel into thinking it lived. And if he had fooled it, then it would conduct the Power. His focus, his focus at last—

O Three, he said within himself, for no word may be spoken in those places, *Virgin and Mother and Mistress of Power, oh let this be the last time. Goddess, You're never cruel without a reason. You wouldn't give me the seed of Flame and then let it die unused. Let the Power of this place enter into me and stir the spark into Fire. And let that Fire flow down through this my sword as it would through a Rod, were I a woman. Oh, please, My Goddess, my Mother, my Bride,* please. *Let it work. In Your name, Who are our beginnings and our endings—*

He bowed his head, and then looked up again, shuddering with cold and anxiety, and also with weakness left over from that morning's sorcery. If only it would work. It would be marvelous to go riding off to Freelorn's rescue with a sword ablaze with the blue Fire. To strike the whole besieging army stiff and helpless with the Flame, and break the walls of the keep in the fullness of his Power, and bring Freelorn out of there.

To strike terror into the army just by being what he was—the first man to bear Flame since the days of Lion and Eagle! And the look in Freelorn's eyes. It would be so—

Herewiss sighed. *I never learn, do I. Let's see what happens.*

Delicately, carefully, he set the sword's point on the white stone of the altar, and took hold of the rough hilt with both hands. There was a change—a stirring— something in the air around him moved, waited expectantly; he could catch the feeling ever so faintly in his underhearing, that inner sensitivity that anyone experienced in sorcery develops. The Power of the place was alive, moving around him, surrounding him, watching. His own Power rose up in him, a cold restless burning all through his body, demanding to be let out.

He lifted the sword away from the stone, and held it straight up before him, point upward, watching moonlight and shadow tremble along the length of the blade with the trembling of his hands. And he reached down inside him, where the Flame was running hot now, molten, seething like silver in the crucible, and he channeled it up through his chest and down through his arms and out through his hands—

The sound was terrible, a thunderous silent shout of frustration and screaming anger as the blue Fire, the essence of life, smote against something that had never lived, had never even been fooled into thinking that it lived. *A silly idea,* Herewiss thought in the terribly attenuated moment between the awful unsound and the sword's destruction. *As if plain sorcery could ever mix successfully with the Flame. Stupid idea.*

And the sword blew apart, just that simply. Fragments and flying splinters shot up and out with frightening force, gleamed sporadically as they flew through light and shadow, ripping leaves off branches, burying themselves in the grass. One of them struck itself into

Herewiss' upper arm, and another into his leg just above the knee, though not too deeply. A third went by his ear like the whisper of death. He held in his cry of terror, remembering where he was, and dropped the shattered swordhilt in the grass.

He plucked the metal fragment out of his arm and threw it into the grass, grimacing. For a long while he knelt there, bent over, hugging himself as much against the bitter disappointment as against the cold. *I was so sure it would work this time. So sure . . .*

Finally he regained some of his composure, and finished picking the splinters out of himself, and turned to make farewell obeisance to the Altar. It seemed to crouch there against the ground, cold white stone, ignoring him. He forgot about the obeisance. He went straight over to Dapple and got dressed, and rode away from there.

It was several minutes before he passed the marker that indicated the end of the Silent Precincts. Just the other side of it he paused, looking up through the leaves at the starlit sky. "Dammit," he yelled at the top of his lungs, "what am I doing wrong? Why won't You tell me? *What am I doing wrong?*"

The stars looked down at him, cold-eyed and uncaring, and the wind laughed at him.

He kicked Dapple harder than necessary, and rode out of the Wood to Freelorn's rescue.

TWO

*If the cat who shares your house
will not speak to you, remember
first that cats, like the Goddess
their Mother, never speak unless
there is something worth saying,
and someone who needs to hear it.*
Darthene Homilies, book 3, 581

They were called the Middle Kingdoms because they
were in the middle of the world as men then knew it.
To the North was the great Sea, of which little was
known. Ships had gone out into it many times, seeking
for the Isles of the North mentioned in tale and ru-
mor, but if those Isles existed, no ship had come back
to tell about them. To the west, on the far western
border of Arlen, was a great and impassable range of
mountains. Legend said that the demons' country of
Hreth lay beyond them, but no one particularly cared
to brave the terrible snow-choked passes and find out.
Southward there were more mountains, the Highpeaks
or Southpeaks, depending on whether you were speaking Arlene or Darthene; no one had even ventured far
enough into them to find out if they ever ended,
though there were stories of the Five Meres hidden
among them, bound twelve months out of thirteen by
the relentless ice of the high South. Eastward, past the
river Stel, the eastern border of Steldin and Darthen
and civilized lands in general, the land stretched into
great empty desert wastes. Many had tried to cross
them; most came back defeated, and the rest never
came back at all. Those who did come back would occasionally speak of uncanny happenings, but most of

the time they flatly refused to talk about the Waste. The Dragons might have known more about what went on there, or in the lands over the mountains: but Dragons only talk to the human Marchwarders who are sometimes their companions, and the Marchwarders, when asked, would smile and shake their heads.

The Kingdoms were four: Arlen, Darthen, Steldin, and North Arlen. Through them were scattered various small independent cities and principalities. The Brightwood was one of these, though like most of the smaller autonomies it had joined itself to a larger Kingdom, Darthen, for purposes of trade and protection. Arlen and Darthen were the two oldest Kingdoms, and the greatest; between them they stretched straight across all the known lands, from the mountains to the Waste Unclaimed, slightly more than three hundred leagues. The border between them was defined by the river Arlid, which flows from the Highpeaks to the Sea, south to north, a hundred leagues or so. It was not a guarded border, for the two lands had been bound by oaths of peace and friendship for hundreds of years. That, however, might change shortly . . .

Herewiss rode along through the sparsely wooded, hilly country three days' journey south of the Brightwood, and thought about politics. It seemed that there was nothing in the world that could be depended upon. The Oath of Lion and Eagle had been sworn for the first time nearly twelve hundred years ago, and sworn again every time a King or Queen came to the throne in either country—until now. When Freelorn's father King Ferrant had died on the throne six years past, Freelorn had been in Darthen; but it might not have been possible for Freelorn to claim the kingship even if he had been in Prydon city when it happened. Ferrant had not yet held the ceremony of affirmation in which the White Stave was passed on to his son, and Freelorn's status was therefore in question. Power had been seized shortly thereafter by a group of the King's former counselors, backed by mercenary forces hired by the former Chancellor of the Exchequer; and this lord, a man named Cillmod, had declared Freelorn outlawed.

These occurrences, though personally outrageous to Herewiss, were not beyond belief; such things had happened before. But not six months ago, armed forces, both mercenaries and Arlene regulars, had moved into Darthen and taken land on the east side of the Arlid. Though the Oath had not been sworn again by the ruling junta, that did not make it any less binding on them. In all the years since its first swearing at the completion of the Great Road, neither country had ever attacked the other. Herewiss was nervous; he felt as if lightning were overdue to strike.

"Listen," his father had said to him, leaning on the doorpost of Herewiss' room three days before, "are you *sure* you don't want some people to take with you?"

"I'm sure." Herewiss had been packing; he was standing before his bookshelf, choosing the grimoires he would take with him. "Notice would be taken, there would be reprisals later. The situation would only get worse. And even with the biggest force we could muster, we wouldn't have a third enough people to crack a siege that size. Besides, the people need to be here, putting in crops." Herewiss took down a thick leather-bound book, filled with notes and spells of illusion.

"That's so . . . Have you got food?"

"Plenty." Herewiss dropped the book in his saddle-bag, along with another that already lay on the bed. The ornate carving of bed and paneling and windows was lost in evening dark, and only an occasional warm highlight showed in the light of the single oil lamp on the bedside table. "I cleaned out the pantry. I have enough trailfood to last me through four years of famine, and I ate a big dinner." He went over to a chest, lifted the lid and took out a white surcoat emblazoned

40

with the arms of the Brightwood: golden Phoenix rising from red flame, the oldest arms in the Kingdoms. "Should I take this, do you think?"

"Is there some formal occasion out in the wilds that you're planning to attend?"

"No. But if I need to exert political pull, it might come in handy."

"You could take my signet."

"What if I lost it? That's the second-oldest thing in the Wood, I'd never forgive myself if something happened to it. No, hang on to it. The surcoat should be enough—the device could be counterfeited, but the gold in the embroidery is real." He folded up the surcoat, stowed it in the saddlebag.

"Do you want some mail?"

"No. I'm going to travel light so I can move fast. Besides, why bother giving anyone the idea that I might be worth robbing? And I'm taking that damn turtle-shell of a leather corselet, and I have plenty of padding, and that nice light Masterforge knife you gave me last Opening Night. And the spear; and the cloak is good and thick— Anybody who gets past all that deserves to kill me, I think: and if they do, it'll prove that you and Mard were wasting your talents on me these sixteen years." Herewiss stood up straight from checking his bags. "Besides, I inherited your iron britches. Don't worry so much."

Hearn looked with concern at his son. Clothed in dark tunic and breeches and riding boots, cloaked in brown, Herewiss seemed one more shadow of the many in the room. The lamplight reflected from his eyes, and from the metal fittings of the empty scabbard hanging from his belt. "Son," Hearn said, "I'm not too worried about you. But the pattern that's been forming bothers me. I worry about Freelorn. Not so much the fact that he's been running around the Kingdoms like a crazy person for the past six years, staying at pettykings' courts until someone finds out where he is and tries to poison him. He's pretty alert about such things, usually. Or the business of his running around with his little swordtail and stealing for a living. He seems to steal from people who need it. But lately he's been coming to grief a bit too often, just missing getting caught—and you've been having to go and get him out of these scrapes. Now this thing; here he is, stuck in this old Keep with a thousand Steldenes waiting to starve him out—and *you're* going to go get him out of it. And alone. Herewiss, it's not really safe."

"I'll manage," Herewiss said. "What are you thinking, Father?"

"This. What happens when he gets into something that you can't get him out of?"

"By then I hope I'll have my Power . . ."

"But you don't have it yet, and if you get killed for Freelorn's sake, you never will. Son of mine—" and Herewiss' underhearing brought him a sudden wash of his father's sorrow, a feeling like eyes filling with tears—"I have long since reconciled myself to the fact that you're going to die young—by use of the Flame, or more slowly by all this sorcery. Yet I want you to be what you can. Here you are, the first male in an age and a half to have enough of the Fire to use—the first sign that the Kingdoms are getting back to the way things were before the Catastrophe. But you have to *live* to be what you can. At least for a little longer. And Freelorn is endangering you."

"Father," Herewiss said very softly, "what good is the Power to me if Lorn dies? He's the only thing I need as much as the Flame. Life would be empty without him, the Fire would mean nothing to me. There *are* priorities."

"Is your life one of them?"

Herewiss reached out, took his father's hands in his. "Da, listen. I won't follow Lorn into any of his famous last stands or impossible charges. I'll try not to let him get *into* them. I'd like to see him King again, yes—but I won't let him drag me into some crazy scheme that has a dead Dragon's chance against the

42

Dark of succeeding. However, I also won't let him get killed if there's any way I can help it—and if my life is the price of his continuing, well, there it is. I can't help how I feel."

Hearn sighed softly. "You're a lot like your brother," he said, "and just as hard to reason with. I gave you the oak as your tree at your birth, my son, and sometimes I think your head is made of it . . ."

"It was a good choice," Herewiss said, smiling faintly. "Lightning strikes oak trees more than any other kind. And I have to be crazy sometimes: I have a reputation to uphold. 'The only thing sure about the Lords' line of the Wood—' "

" '—is that there's nothing sure about them,' " his father finished, smiling too. "Fool."

"They told Earn our Father that He was a fool at Bluepeak, and look what happened to Him."

"I would sooner be father to a live son," Hearn said, "than to a dead legend."

"I'll be careful," said Herewiss.

"Have a safe journey, then. And good hunting."

So Herewiss had taken his leave of his other relatives and friends in the Woodward, and had said goodbye to the Rooftree, and then had stopped in the stable to choose a horse. He had originally been of a mind to take Darrafed, his little thoroughbred Arlene mare, a present from Freelorn—or perhaps Shag, his father's curly-coated bay warhorse. But as he had walked down the aisle between the stalls, Dapple had put his head out over his stall's half-door and looked at Herewiss as if he *knew* something. Herewiss was not one to ignore a sign when it presented itself.

The horse moved comfortably through the low hill country. As long as he kept to a steady southward course, Herewiss let Dapple have his head. The horse was a wise one. About a hundred years before, a Rodmistress had put her deathword on one of Dapple's ancestors and had decreed that the horses of that line would always have a talent for being in the right place at the right time. The talent had seemed to do their riders good as well. One horse, the third generation down, had carried an unsuspecting lady to the arms of the lover who had searched the Middle Kingdoms for her for twelve years. Another had led its thirteen-year-old mistress to the place where the royal Darthene sword, Fórlennh BrokenBlade, had been hidden during the Reavers' invasion of Darthis city. Having Dapple along, Herewiss reasoned, would make his father worry a little less—and might incidentally ease his way as he worked on getting Freelorn out of that keep.

For three days he had been riding through empty land. It was not bare—Spring had run crazy through the fields, as if drunk on rose wine, flinging wildflowers and garlands of new greenery about with inebriated extravagance. The hills were ablaze with suncandle and Goddess'-delight, tall yellow Lovers'-cup lilies and heartheal. Butterwort and red-and-blue never-say-die clambered up the gullies toward the hillcrests, and white mooneyes covered the ground almost everywhere that grass did not. But there were no people, no homesteads. For one thing, the land was poor for farming. For another, that part of the country was full of Fyrd.

The Fyrd had always been in the Kingdoms; they were said to be children of the Shadow, sent by Him to spread death and misery in the Goddess' despite, or even creations of the Dark itself, changed things which had been made from normal animals when the Dark still covered the world. Whatever the case, most of North Darthen was still full of the major Fyrd species—horwolves, nadders, keplian, lathfliers, maws, hetscold, and destreth. In Herewiss' time, the land around the Wood was free of them—kept that way by constant use of the Power and the cold-eyed accuracy of Brightwood archers. But outside the Wood's environs the Fyrd raided constantly, taking great numbers of livestock, and also men whenever they could get them.

Sheep were pastured here in the hill country, but all the shepherds came up together after the Maiden's Day feasts: both flocks and men stood a better chance in large numbers.

The hills were thinning out now and farms were beginning to appear. They became more frequent as Herewiss and Dapple descended into the lowlands, and one very large farm with stone markers indicated that Herewiss was close to the town he had been expecting to reach that evening. The farm was the holding of a prominent Darthene house, the Lords Arian. He could have stopped there and received excellent hospitality, being after all the next thing to a prince; but attention drawn to himself was the last thing he wanted at this point.

He rode on down from the hills, crossing a rude stone bridge over the Kearint, a minor tributary of the river Darst, and came to the forty-house town of Havering Slides just as dusk was falling. Most of the people who lived there were hands on the big Arian farm. Herewiss rode up to the gate in the wooden palisade around the town and identified himself. He was admitted without question.

The inn was as he had remembered it from earlier visits, a motley-looking place with a disjointed feeling to it; new buildings ran headlong into old ones, and afterthought second stories sagged on their supports over uneasy-looking bay windows. It seemed that some of the artisans who had done carving work in the Woodward had also passed this way. The gutterspouts were fashioned into panting hound-faces and singing frogs: crows stealing cheese in their wooden beaks leered down from the cupolas.

Herewiss rode up to the stable door and handed Dapple over to the boy in charge. As he strode toward the doorway of the inn, his saddlebags slung over his shoulder, he was greeted by the sudden and beautiful aroma of roast beef. After three days of nourishing but tasteless journey rations, the prospect of real food seemed almost an embarrassment of luxury. He paused at the door just long enough to admire the carving over it, a cross-grain bas-relief of a local Rodmistress casting the Shadow out of a possessed cow.

Herewiss pushed the door open and went in. It took his eyes a few minutes to get used to the dim interior of the place, even though there were oil lamps all around. He was standing in a fairly large common-room, crowded with tables and chairs and long trestled benches. The room was not too full yet, it still being fairly early in the evening. Several patrons sat about a table, dicing for coppers, and off in one corner a hulky farmer was devouring a huge steak pie in great mouthfuls.

It was the steak pie that particularly interested Herewiss. Bags in hand, he went to the kitchen door, which was carved with dancing poultry, and knocked.

The door opened, and the innkeeper looked out cordially. She was a tall slender woman, grayhaired but pretty, in a brown robe and a long stained apron. "Can I help you, sir?" she said, wiping her hands on a dirty gray towel.

"Madam," Herewiss said, bowing a little, "food and lodging for the night for myself and my horse would do nicely."

"Half an eagle," she said, looking at his clothes, which were in good repair.

"A quarter," he said, smiling at her with his best and most charming smile.

She smiled back at him "A quarter eagle and threepence," she said.

"Two."

The innkeeper smiled broadly. "Two it is. Your horse is inside?"

"He is, madam."

"Dinner, then?"

"Oh, *yes*," he said. The good smells coming out of her kitchen were making his stomach eager. "Some of what that gentleman is having, if there's another one—"

46

She nodded. "Anything to drink? We have wine, red and Brightwood white and Délann yellow, brown and black ale, and my husband made a fresh barrel of Knight's Downfall yesterday."

"Ale sounds good: the black. Which room should I take?"

"Up the stairs, turn right, third door to your left." She disappeared back into the kitchen's steam.

Herewiss hurried up the creaking stairs and found the room in question. It was predictably musty, and the floor groaned under him. The shutters screeched in protest when he levered them open to let the sunset in, but he was so glad to have a hot meal in the offing that the place looked as good as any king's castle to him. He dropped his bag in the corner, under the window, and changed into another clean dark tunic; then headed for the door. Halfway through the doorway, an afterthought struck him. He raised his hands to draw the appropriate gestures in the air, and since no one was near, spoke aloud the words of a very minor binding, erecting a lockshield around his bags. Then down the stairs he went.

He sat down at an empty table in a corner and spent a few moments admiring the window nearest him, which was a crazy amalgam of bottle-glass panes and stained vignettes. One of them, done in vivid shades of rose, cobalt and emerald, showed the ending of the old story about the man who fooled the Goddess into lifting her skirts by confronting Her with an illusion-river. There he lay under the trees at Harvest festival, inextricably stuck to and into an illusionary lover, while the Goddess and the harvesters stood around and laughed themselves weak. The man looked understandably mortified, and very chastened. He had been very lucky in playing his trick on the Maternal aspect of the Goddess—had She been manifesting as the Maiden at the time, She might not have been so kind. The Mother tends to be forgiving of Her children's pranks, but the Maiden is sometimes fatally jealous of Her modesty.

Someone blocked the light, and he looked up—a girl, maybe eighteen years old or so, with a droopy halo of frizzing black hair. She bent in front of Herewiss, putting his steak pie and ale on the old scarred table. Herewiss took brief notice of the view down her blouse, but he was more interested in the steak pie.

"Nice," he said. "A fork, please?"

"Hmm?" She in her turn was being very interested in Herewiss.

"A fork?"

"Oh. Yes, certainly—" She reached into her pocket and brought one out for him. Herewiss took it, wiped it off, and dove almost desperately into the pie.

"Ah, listen," she said, bending down again, and Herewiss began an intensive study of a piece of potato, "are you busy this evening?"

Herewiss did his best to look at her with profound sorrow. She really wasn't his type, and there was a mercenary look in her eye that sent him hurriedly to the excuse box in the back of his head. "If you're thinking what I think you are," he said, "I'm sorry, but I'm under vows of chastity."

"You don't look like you're in an Order," she said.

"Perpetual chastity," Herewiss said. "Or until the Eagle comes back. Sorry."

The girl stood up. "Well," she said, "if you change your mind, ask the lady in the kitchen where I am. I'm her daughter."

Herewiss nodded, and she went away into the kitchen. He sagged a little as the door closed behind her, and settled back against the wall.

That was a bit panicky of me, Herewiss thought as he began to eat. *I wonder what it is about her that bothers me so—*

He put the thought aside and concentrated on the hot-spiced food and the heavy ale. The common room began slowly to fill up as he ate; the local clientele was coming in from the fields and houses to enjoy each other's company. The big table nearest him was occupied by a noisy, cheerful group of farmers from the Arian landholdings, nine or ten brawny men and lithe ladies, all deeply tanned and smelling strongly of honest work. They called loudly for food and drink, and hailed Herewiss like a brother when they spotted him in his corner. He smiled back at them, and before long they were exchanging crude jokes and bad puns, and laughing like a lot of fools.

When the inn's cat strolled by, it was greeted politely by the farmers, and offered little pieces of meat or game. It declined all these graciously and in silence, and went on by, making its rounds. As it passed it looked hard at Herewiss, as if it recognized him. He nodded at it; the cat looked away as if unconcerned, and went on.

As the ale flowed and the evening flowered, the story-telling and singing began in earnest. Most of the stories were ones already known to everyone there, but no one seemed to care much about that—Kingdoms people have a love of stories, as long as the story wears a different face each time. Someone began with the old one about what Éalor the Prince of Darthen had done with the fireplace poker, which was later named Sársweng and had its haft encrusted with diamonds. Then someone else got up and told about something more recent, news only about a hundred and five years old, how the lady Fáran Fersca's daughter had gone out with her twelve ships to look for the Isles of the North, and how only one ship had come back after a year, and what had happened to it. This was told in an unusual fashion, sung to an antique rhyme-form by a little old lady with a surprisingly strong soprano. There was a great deal of stamping and cheering and applause when she finished; and several people, judging correctly that the lady was quite young inside, whatever her apparent age, propositioned her immediately. She said yes to one of the propositions, and she

49

and the gentleman went upstairs immediately to more applause.

In the commotion, the lute was passed around to the farmers' table and one of them started to sing the song about the Brindle Cat of Aes Arädh, how it carried away the chief bard of a Steldene king on its back because of an insulting song he had sung before the Four Hundred of Arlen, and what the bard saw in the Otherworld to which the Cat took him. Herewiss joined in on the choruses, and one of the ladies at the farmers' table noticed the quality of his voice and called to him, "You're next!" He shook his head, but when the man with the lute was finished, it was passed back to him. He looked at it with resignation, and then smiled a little at a sudden memory.

"All right," he said, pushed his chair back, and perched himself on the edge of the farmers' table, pausing a moment to tune one of the strings that had gone a quarter-tone flat. The room quieted down, and he strummed a chord and began to sing.

Of the many stories concerning the usage of the blue Fire, probably the most tragic is that of Queen Béaneth of Darthen and her lover Astrin. Astrin was taken by the Shadow's Hunting one Opening Night, and Béaneth went to her rescue. That rescue seemed a certain thing, for Béaneth was a Rodmistress, one of the great powers of her time. But the price demanded of her for Astrin's release was that Béaneth must mate with the Shadow, and take into herself whatever evil He would choose for her to bear. Béaneth, knowing that the evil to grow within her would warp her Power to its own use, lay down with the Shadow indeed, but killed herself at the climax of the act, thereby keeping her bargain and obtaining her loved's release.

Her little daughter Béorgan was five years old when all this happened. She made the decision early to avenge her mother, and determined that she would meet the Shadow on His own ground and destroy Him. She trained, and grew great in Power—and also in obsession—waiting and preparing for Nineteen-Years' Night, that night when it is both Opening Night and a full Moon. All the Kingdoms know how the story ends—how Béorgan went down to the Morrowfane on that night, being then twenty-four years of age, and opened the Morrowfane *Gate* beneath the waters of Lake Rilthor, and passed through into the Otherworlds. There she met the Shadow, and there she slew Him, on that one night of all nights when it is possible, when the Goddess' power conjoins with the returning Sun past midnight. Her triumph was short-lived, though, and so was she. She had never planned her life past that night, and in a short time wasted away and died. Even her victory was hollow, for however bright the Lover may be, still he casts the Shadow: seven years after He died, He was back again, leading the Hunting as always.

Freelorn had always loved the story, and some years back had composed a verse form of it, and a musical setting that Herewiss had liked. At the time, though, Freelorn's voice had been changing, and Herewiss had had to restrain himself from laughing as his loved sang that greatest of tragedies in a voice that cracked crazily every verse or so. He had even refrained from singing it himself for the longest while, for the sound of his pure, deep, already-changed tenor had made Freelorn twice as self-conscious as he usually was.

He sang the setting now, letting his voice go as he would have liked to all those years ago, pausing between verses to insert the last dialogue between Béaneth and Astrin, and later the farewell of Béorgan to her husband Ánmod, who later became King of both Arlen and Darthen because of her death. He forgot about the hot, smoky room, forgot about time and pain and the systematic destruction of swords, and just sang, feeling very young again for the first time in ever so long.

At the end of it he received tremendous applause, and he bowed shyly and handed the lute to someone else, going back to his table and his ale. There he sat for a few minutes, recovering. Someone began singing almost immediately, but the farmers started talking quietly among themselves. The contrast between the sung verses of terrible tragedy beyond the boundaries of the world and the homely talk of the farmers was abrupt, but pleasant; they had slow, musical voices, and Herewiss sat and dawdled with his ale, listening alternately to the words and the sound of them. One of the farmers started telling a long, drawn-out story of a loved of his who had gone traveling. "All the way to Dra'Mincarrath she went," he said in a drawl, "aye, all that way south, and then east again into the Waste she went, not knowing where she was going, on account of being lost. Right into the Waste Unclaimed, and north she turned after a little, on account of being lost again. And came in sight of that hold in the Waste, indeed, and—"

"Ssh!" said several of the other farmers, looking upset, and "She came out again," said one of them, seemingly the eldest. "Count her lucky; that place is bad to talk of, even here. Then where did she go? . . ."

Herewiss sat nursing his ale, a little curious at the sudden and vehement response. Hold in the Waste—? What could that be? No one lived out there—

His thought was broken by the underheard feeling that someone was looking at him with unkindly intent. He glanced up and saw the innkeeper's daughter. She was across the room, serving someone else, but he could feel her eyes on him. He looked down at his ale again quickly, not particularly wanting to see her bend over again.

There was a sudden motion to his right. He looked, and saw the cat, a big gray tabby with blue eyes, balancing itself on the table-edge after its leap. It lay down, tucking its forepaws beneath its chest so that it looked like a broody hen, and half-closed its eyes.

"Well, hello," Herewiss said, putting down his mug to scratch under the cat's chin. It squeezed its eyes shut altogether and stretched its neck out all the way, purring like a gray-furred thunderstorm.

Herewiss went back to the contemplation of his ale, rubbing under the cat's chin automatically for a few minutes. Then suddenly the cat opened up its round blue eyes. "Prince," it said in its soft raspy voice, "mind the innkeeper's daughter."

He laughed a little under his breath. "No one keeps a secret from a cat," he quoted. "May I ask what you're called?"

"M'ssssai," it said. "That is my inner Name, prince: the outer doesn't matter."

"I'll keep your secret," Herewiss said in ritual response, and then added, "but I have none to give you in return. I don't know it yet."

"Well enough. Time will come, and then you can come back and tell me."

"Forgive me," Herewiss said, "but how did you know who I am?"

"I've been in your saddlebag."

"It had a binding on it."

The cat smiled, and after a moment Herewiss smiled back at it. Cats, the legend said, had been created second after men, and had a Flame of their own, one which they had never lost.

"The very fact of a binding," M'ssssai said, "made me slightly suspicious. I could smell it from down here, and know you for its author. And the contents of the bags settled the matter. Only two men alive wear that surcoat, and you're too young to be one of them, so you must be the other."

"Granted."

"What are you doing with those grimoires in your bags?"

Herewiss made a face. "Isn't it said of my Line that there's no accounting for us? I'm a sorcerer. A part-time sorcerer, out seeing the world."

M'ssssai half-closed its eyes again. "Sorcerers usually stay at home unless they have something in hand. And you're more than just a sorcerer, prince. I know the smell of Flame."

"I have no focus," Herewiss said, very softly, "and no control. I can't use a Rod."

"The innkeeper's daughter," said the cat, "is a dabbler; she has just enough Flame to be able to smell it herself, though she has no focus either, and no control. But she's looking for a way to free her Power, and I dare say she's noticed at least part of what you are. If I were you, I'd keep the shields up around your bags tonight, or else sleep lightly. She's a brewer of semi-effective love potions, and she throws her curses crooked—she has a most undisciplined mind. Not to mention that she'd probably try to drain you—"

"A vampire?"

"In the bedsheets. But she's acquired a taste for it. I see too many people going out of here looking lost and drained in the morning."

"M'ssssai, I thank you." Herewiss scratched behind the cat's ears. "But why are you telling me all this?"

The cat smiled. "You have good hands."

M'ssssai stood up, stretched, arching its back, its tail straight up in the air. "Mind her, now," it said, and jumped down from the table, vanishing into the forest of trestles and benches.

Herewiss looked up cautiously. The innkeeper's daughter had just come down from upstairs, and was going through the kitchen door. He took his opportunity and eased out from behind the table, heading hurriedly for the protection of the shadows of the stairway. He took the stairs two at a time, sloshing ale in all directions, pausing at the top of the stairs to get his bearings; it was quite dark up there. Then he headed softly down the hall, trying to keep the floor from creaking under him.

His room door was ajar. He listened at it, but heard nothing. A swift cold draft was whispering through the crack. Gently he put his weight against the door; it opened with a low tired groan. There was no one inside.

He went in, still moving carefully, and bent down by the window to check his bags. The surcoat was ever so slightly mussed, unfolded just enough to clearly show the Phoenix charged on it; and the lockshield around the bags was parted cleanly in one place, an invisible incision right through the spell, big enough for a cat to put a paw through.

Herewiss laughed and got up. With flint and steel he lit the room's one candle, a stub of tallow in a smoky, cracked glass by the big four-poster bed. Even in the glass, the flame bent and bobbled wildly until Herewiss closed the shutters at the window. For a few seconds he regarded the wormholed old door.

"All right." he said softly. "Let her think I had a bit too much to drink." He crossed to the door and closed it without shooting the bolt, then flicked a word and a gesture back at the bags and dissolved the lockshield.

Herewiss pulled back the faded, patched coverlet and sat down on the bed. Immediately there was a sudden sharp feeling in the back of his head, a nagging feeling like a splinter, or the dull hurt of a burn. He got up again hurriedly, stripping the covers all the way back and feeling about the sheets. When he lifted up the pillow, there it was—a little muslin bag, with runes of the Nhàirëdi sorcerer's speech crudely stitched on it, and a brown stain that was probably blood.

Herewiss took his knife from the sheath at his belt and lifted the little bag on its blade, carrying it over to the table where the candle sat. It took him a little while to poke a large enough hole in it without touching it directly, but when he did, and shook out the contents, he nodded. Asafetida, crumbs of choke-pard and wyvernstooth; a leaf of moonwort, the black-veined kind picked in Moon's decline; and also a little lump of something soft—a bit of potato from his plate at dinner. He scowled. Elements of sleep-charm and love-charm, mixed together—with the moonwort to befuddle the mind and bind the sleeper to someone else's wishes.

What does she think I am? She must not know I'm a sorcerer or she wouldn't try something so ridiculously simple—'

Shaking his head, Herewiss laid the steel knife down on the little pile of herbs. "Ehrénië haladh séresh," he said, and spat on the blade. When he picked it up again, the moonwort had shriveled into a tight black ball, and the warning pain in the back of his head was gone.

He set the cloth bag afire with the candle flame, and carried it still burning to the window, opening the shutter and throwing the bag out along with the bits of herbs. Then he went back and stretched out on the bed, reaching for the mug. The ale was getting warm. He made a face, put the mug aside, and lay back against the headboard, crossing his arms and sighing. It was going to be a long wait.

At some time past one in the morning Herewiss was listening wearily to the sound of some patron of the inn wobbling about in the courtyard, singing (if that was the word) the old song about the King of Darthen's lover. The inn's good ale seemed to have completely removed any fears the drunk had ever had of high notes, and he was squeaking and warbling through the choruses in a falsetto fit to give any listener a headache. Herewiss had one.

The man had just gotten to the verse about the goats when Herewiss heard the door grunt a little, and saw it scrape inward a bit. He lay back quickly, peeking out from beneath lowered lids. There was another soft scraping sound, and in stepped the innkeeper's daughter, wrapped in a blanket against the cold. She looked long and hard at him, and it was all Herewiss could do to keep from grinning. After a few moments, satisfied that he was asleep, she smiled and crossed the room quietly to where his bags lay.

The one she peered into first was the one with the surcoat. Slowly and carefully she pulled it out and spread it wide to look at the device. There was no light in the room but the pale moonlight seeping in through one half-open shutter, and the dim glow of the torches down in the courtyard. It took her a while to make out the Phoenix in Flames, but when she did she bit her lip, then smiled again, and folded up the surcoat.

Deeper down in the bag she found the book bound in red leather, the unsealed one, and drew it out carefully. The innkeeper's daughter sat down on her heels and muttered something under her breath. A weak reddish light grew and glowed about her hands, clinging to the book's pages as she turned them. For a few minutes she went through the book, turning the leaves over in cautious silence. Then suddenly she stopped, and across the room Herewiss could hear her take in breath sharply. He watched her as she traced down one page with a finger, moving her lips slowly as she read.

That's a bad habit, Herewiss thought. *Let's see if I can't break you of it.*

The girl was holding the book closer to her eyes, and speaking softly. "Neskháired ól joméire kal stói, arvéya khad—"

Herewiss breathed out in irritation. *I might have known. Doesn't she know it's all illusion–spells? She can't know much about what real sorcery is, or what it does. And Goddess knows she would pick that one. She needs a lot more to be beautiful on the inside than she does on the outside. It's not going to work, of course. She's not making any passes, and she's set up no framework inside her head. Dark! I'll teach her to mess with things she doesn't understand—*

Herewiss cleared his mind and began to think of another incantation, on another page. He had long since

57

ceased to need to draw diagrams or make passes while conjuring. Constant practice had taught him to build viable spell-structures in his head, without external aids. He built one now, a fairly simple one that he had used many times to entertain Halwerd, an illusion-spell that required minimal energy and provided surprisingly sophisticated results. It went up quickly, in large chunks, taking form and bulking huge and restless—it was one of those sorceries that has to be used quickly before it goes stale. He completed the structure, checking once to make sure that it was complete, and thought the word that set it free to work.

The girl, intent on her reading, did not notice the air behind her thickening and growing dark. Something darker and more tenacious than smoke curled and roiled within a huge manshaped space in the air, until at last it stood complete behind her—a little tenuous at the edges, where its stuff wisped and drifted into the still air, but dark as starless midnight at its heart. The innkeeper's daughter finished reading the spell and raised one hand to feel at her face. In that moment the great dark shape put out a hand and brushed the back of her neck lightly.

She slapped absently at what she thought was an insect, and felt her hand go through something cold and damp. Her eyes went wide with startlement; she turned. She saw, and opened her mouth to scream. But Herewiss was ready. Since freeing the illusion, he had been readying another spell, and as she drew breath he said the word of control and struck her dumb and stiff. There she knelt, her mouth ridiculously open, head turned to look over her shoulder—probably a most uncomfortable position. Herewiss smiled, and got up out of the bed, praying that the backlash would hold off for a few minutes.

"Do you always go through your guests' bags at one in the morning?" he said, bending down to take the book away from her and toss it onto the bed. "And do all the rooms come equipped with that charming little addition under the pillow?"

She could not even move her eyes to follow him as he went to open the shutters wide. "Would you excuse us?" he said to the smoke-creature. There had always been controversy over whether illusion-creatures were alive and thinking in any sense of the words, but Herewiss, being both cautious and courteous by nature, treated his illusions as if they were both. "And while you're out there, please take that man down there and bed him down in the stable or something. If I hear that part about the goats again, I may turn him into one."

The dark shape waded slowly through the air, trailing streams of black smoke behind it, and climbed over the windowsill into the night. It drifted down silently into the courtyard.

"Would *you* like to be a goat?" Herewiss said, going back to look at the girl from behind, so that she could see him. "Or an owl might be better—you seem to like being up in the middle of the night."

He was bluffing outrageously, for no mere sorcery could do such things. She seemed not to know that, though. She stared at Herewiss wide-eyed, the terror frozen in her face. Outside, a voice broke off its singing. "Boy, izh really dark out here," it said, woozily surprised.

"Or maybe you'd like to bed down with my friend out there," Herewiss said, "since you do seem to be so eager, with that love-charm and all. I should tell you, though, he *is* a little cold—and you might have a baby afterwards, and I couldn't guarantee what it would look like."

He made a small adjustment in his mind and snapped his fingers, freeing her upper half but keeping her legs bound tight. She sagged and turned her face away from him quickly. "Tell me what you were after," Herewiss said.

"I—" She shuddered. "I don't want to share with *that*—"

"Then start talking."

She stared sullenly at the floor. "I smelled the Power," she said. "You have it. I want to know how. If a *man* can have it, then there has to be a way for me to bring *mine* out." She looked up, glared at him. "How did you do it?" she demanded bitterly. "Who did you pact with?"

"My my," Herewiss said. "You *are* a dabbler. Everyone has the Power, dear, didn't you know that? Men and women both, everyone born has the spark. But few have enough to do anything with. So very few. And Goddess knows there's more to it than just having enough Flame. What was the bag for, by the way?"

She scowled at the floor again, and would not answer him.

"A little draining to amuse yourself? I should tell you, the Bride doesn't look kindly on such things. Draining away your lovers' potency is likely to make you less of a woman, not more. And anyway, who taught you your Nhàired? Two of the words on the bag were misspelled, and there was too much asafetida. If you had left that there much longer, it would have started to recoil, and half the place would probably have tried to rape you. Try draining *that*."

Herewiss sighed. "You're not being very open with me," he said. "I'm in a quandary as to what to do with you. Maybe you really *do* want to be a goat." He went over to the bag on the floor and took out the other book, the one with the seals on it. Softly he said the word to undo the seals. The second word spoke the pages apart. He then went through the book slowly, looking for the right page.

The innkeeper's daughter was beginning to worry now. "Please," she said, "please, no—I'll do anything—"

She squirmed her torso at him, and Herewiss looked

up at the ceiling, shaking his head in mild amazement. "I'm not interested in that kind of anything," he said. "I might consider information, though. Tonight at dinner some people were talking, and someone mentioned a place called the hold in the Waste, and everyone else hushed them up. What is that? Why won't they talk about it?"

Fresh fear went across the girl's face like a shadow. "I don't know—"

His underhearing jabbed him hard under one rib, like the pain one gets from running too hard, and he knew she was lying. "Then I guess I'll have to turn you into a goat," he said, wondering how he was going to make the bluff good, and turned his attention to the page before him. "Fáslie anrástüw oi vëlien—"

"No, no, wait—" She looked around fearfully. "It's unlucky even to talk about it—"

"Being a goat isn't unlucky?"

"Uh—well. Out in the Waste Unclaimed, about forty miles or so into the desert, there's an Old Place— the oldest of the Old Places in all the world." She gulped. "It's full of the Old wreaking, and ghosts and monsters walk around there. Sometimes the desert around it—*changes* somehow, and becomes other places. I don't know how—"

"I know what you mean. Go on."

"They say that the rocks roll uphill, and water flows sideways along the hills there, or up the sides of valleys—and it rains scorpions and stones instead of water. Even the Dragons won't go near it; they say it's too dangerous. There are *doors* into Otherwheres—"

"*Doors?*" Herewiss echoed.

"That's all there is," the girl said. "It's not lucky to talk about it. It's a cursed place."

"No," Herewiss said, "just Old, I would imagine. We don't know enough about the Old people's wreaking to know their curses from their blessings. Forty miles into the desert. Near where?"

61

"North of Mincar," she said, "about four hundred miles north, on the far side of the Stel. But it's cursed—"

Herewiss stood there silently for a long few moments, holding the backlash away while reading the spell in the book, readying it. "That'll do, I think," he said. "But one thing only."

She looked at him in fear. "I don't trust any promises you might make about your future behavior," he said. "So I am going to give you a conscience of sorts."

He spoke the last word of the spell under his breath, and immediately the girl groaned and doubled over, clutching at her stomach. "The next time you sleep with a man or woman for whom you don't care, that will take you," he said. "Don't bother trying to rid yourself of it; if you meddle, you may find that particular avenue of pleasure permanently closed. And let me give you advice—don't play around with sorcery. It shortens the life."

He cut the air with one hand in a short quick motion, and the girl staggered to her feet and lurched without another word out the door.

Herewiss closed and sealed his book, fetched the other one from the bed, and put them back in his bag again. His head was aching violently, and his stomach churned, threatening to reject the steak pie.

Suddenly a dark shape loomed at the window. It was the smoke-creature, peering in curiously.

"Oh Dark, I forgot," Herewiss said. He gestured at the window, the same quick cutting motion. "Go free. Rr'hai! And thank you."

The creature bent a little with a passing night breeze, and dissipated silently.

"Ah, my head," Herewiss groaned as he headed back to bed. "Shortens the life indeed. I wish I _were_ dead."

He pulled the covers up around him again, and laid his throbbing head down on the lumpy pillow as tenderly as he could. The darkness was almost peaceful for a few moments—until the sound of a drunken countertenor began to float up from the stable, half a tone flat, singing of what the King of Darthen did with the shepherdess and her brother.

"Oh Goddess," Herewiss moaned, and buried his face in the pillow.

THREE

Opening Night is not so much a time of year as it is a state of mind. It can be invited, by no more difficult a measure than keeping one's eyes and heart open all the time. There are Rodmistresses who could not share in the Opening if they stood at the Heart of the World on Nineteen-Years' Night; and there are children, and the eager of heart, who can break the walls between the Worlds in broad day, and call the wonders through. Those who do not close their hearts to Possibility soon find their lives full of it.

Reflections in the Silent Precincts,
Leoth d'Elthed, ch. 7

The next day was gray and overcast, threatening rain. Herewiss left early, having been awakened by the impending light of dawn despite the fact that there was no sunrise to be seen. He didn't stop for breakfast, partly from a desire to hurry, and partly to avoid running into the innkeeper's daughter again. He felt a little guilty for laying as restrictive a spell on her as he had. But then again, she *had* been messing with his private property—and her actions had hardly been intended in benevolence—

"Aah, the Dark with it," he said to himself as the inn receded behind him. He was heading south again; Dapple was trotting along briskly and needing little encouragement to hurry.

Doors into Otherwheres. Such *doors* were legendary—they might open onto other times, like the Éorlhowe *Door* hidden in the mazes beneath the melted stones of the Howe in North Arlen; or other places, like the old King's *Door* in the Black Palace in Darthis; or other worlds entirely, as does the Morrowfane *Gate* beneath the waters of Lake Rilthor in southern Darthen. There were not many permanent *doors,* and they tended to be difficult of access and dangerous to use, because of time limits or unpredictable behavior. One of the Queens of Darthen acquired the sobriquet One-Hand when she crossed through the King's *Door* and it closed unexpectedly.

Out in the Waste? Well, it would be a good place to put them if there are time-gates. At least the Dragons would think so—they won't let anyone but March- warders near the Éorlhowe Door, and the human Marchwarders won't go near it themselves for fear of changing the past.

Herewiss sighed. He would have given almost any- thing to go through a time-*door,* or just look through one, to find out if things really happened as the histo- ries said they had. Or to see the great days of the past happen again—to see Earn and Héalhra take the Power upon Themselves at Bluepeak, to see the terri- ble Gnorn come tottering over the mountains and go up in a blaze of the blue Fire as the Lion and Eagle gave Themselves for the destruction of that last men- ace. Or to see the founding of the Brightwood, or of Prydon city, or Darthis. To watch the last stone being set into the paving of the Great Road, and watch the Oath of Lion and Eagle being sworn for the first time by Earn's and Héalhra's grandchildren. Maybe even to see what no man had seen, the Worldwinning, as the Dragons dropped out of the darkness and the Messen- ger in Her glory drove the Dark away—

I'm getting carried away with this, he told himself severely.

And you're enjoying it, another part of him an- swered him back. Well, why not? Dreaming was free. Consider this: how about going back to the day Free- lorn's father died, and finding out where old Hergótha had been hidden? That would certainly make Freelorn happy. True, Freelorn had Súthan now, and that was

65

not exactly a sword without lineage—the princes of Arlen had been carrying it since the time that Ánmod had used it to kill the Coldwyrm lairing in the fords of Arlid. But it was just that, a prince's sword, and Freelorn was King, if not in name, at least by right. Herewiss didn't need his underhearing to detect Freelorn's dissatisfaction with Súthan. He wanted Hergótha, which was the King's sword; he lusted after it the way some people lust after others' bodies and desire to possess them.

Hergótha, though, had gone missing after Ferrant's death—he had not been wearing it on the day his heart stopped, and it had never been found in the palace. Perhaps he had taken it with him past the *Door* into Starlight, and walked the shore of the final Sea with it slung over his back, the kingliest of the shadows that dwelt there. Or perhaps the Lion had taken it back into His keeping again, maybe to return it to the rightful wielder one day, if one of the Line ever came back to claim the throne. Herewiss doubted that Freelorn would have the patience.

To find Hergótha, bring it back to Freelorn—

This is ridiculous, Herewiss thought. *I don't know for sure that this place has time-doors in it—or any doors, for that matter—and if it it does, there's no guarantee that I'll be able to get through them. Or even make them serve my purpose.*

He sighed. It was still nice to think about. To look back in time. To see his mother. To see Herelaf—

Or to look forward in time, perhaps, and see how he would finally forge the sword that would work for him, then do it—

Yes. And if those *doors* looked out into other worlds, mightn't there be one world somewhere much like this one, except that both men and women had the Flame? Or maybe there would be a *door* into that long-past time before the Catastrophe, when everyone could use the Power—

Dapple stopped abruptly, and Herewiss looked up

in confusion. About a hundred yards away, at the foot of a little hill that rose suddenly from the grassland, stood a small building.

It was built of logs stood up on end and bound together. The roof was thatched, and there was one door, and a window on the side that faced him. It wasn't a house—there was no sign of a garden, or even a cow. A shrine, perhaps?

His curiosity nudged him, and he pulled on Dapple's reins and rode up to the place. He dismounted before the open doorway. "Hello—?" he called. No one answered.

There was a wooden plaque fastened next to the door, and though it was weathered, the runes were deeply scratched and easy to read. OF OUR LADY OF LIBERATIONS, it said. TAKE, USE, CLEAN, BLESS, AND GO SAFELY.

Herewiss stepped in and looked around. The inner walls were plastered, and there were scenes painted on them in a primitive and vigorous style, the colors bright, the figures stylized, stark and clean. In the middle of the room was a rough offering table. Dead leaves and bits of grass were scattered about on the table and floor. Something made an irritated twitter, and Herewiss looking up saw a sparrow's nest high in the corner, where the plaster had fallen away and left an opening to the outside.

He smiled at the appropriateness of the place, for there was one aspect of his personality sorely in need of liberation. The few minutes it would take to clean and reconsecrate the shrine wouldn't be wasted. Besides, if the Goddess were to come to his house when *he* wasn't there, and if it were full of leaves and such, *She* would certainly clean it up.

For a moment he grinned at the image of the Tripartite Lady busy in the Woodward with a broom. But the Goddess had never been known for standing on ceremony. On Her travels through the world She tended to leave home Her Cloak which is the night sky, and the Robe glorious as Moonlight, in favor of plainer and more utilitarian clothes. Even at that most sublime and beautiful of times, when She comes to share Herself in love—as She comes to every man and woman born—even then She rarely appears in any of the Forms or Manifestations attributed to Her by legend. At least once in a lifetime, a person will know the joy of being held in the Goddess' arms; for each it is different, but for all it is the same. Although She comes as just another person, with human quirks and wrinkles, sometimes She comes in the form of someone you know—perhaps even your own loved, by way of an affectionate joke. And She *never* comes when or where you expect Her. As the proverb says, "The Goddess is as likely to come in the window as through the door."

Herewiss found a broom in one corner, not much more than a mildewed bunch of birch twigs, and did his best to sweep up all the detritus on the floor. As he swept, he looked at the figures painted on the plaster. One wall depicted the Triad in its first form—Maiden, Mother and Wise Woman, Their hands joined to show that They were One: and then underneath that, the Maiden with Her hands full of stars, busy with creation. But Her back was turned to the other Two, illustrating the Error. Behind the Three of Them hung the symbol for the great Death, the downpointing Arrow, and only the Eldest of the Three saw it. Her hand was outstretched to Her younger self, but the Maiden paid no mind, and went on creating as if Her works would last forever.

The next panel was not so skillfully wrought as the first, or perhaps the painter had not liked the subject. In it the Maiden stood in Her sorrow, Her hands covering Her face, as She realized the nature of Her error—She had forgotten about Death, and had already spoken the Final Word that set the Universe on its way. There was no getting rid of Death now, and this whole Universe would have to run down and die itself before She could try again to make it perfect. The

Mother and the Wise Woman stood beside Her, trying to console Her: but for some things there is no consolation.

The following panel showed the Maiden's solution for Her own grief and guilt. She knew Her other selves in the manner of woman with woman, and became with child. Now She sat on the birthing-stool, and was no more Maiden, but Mother. The children She bore were twin sons, and She suckled Them one at each breast with a smile of maternal joy. The panel below showed the Twins grown already, beautiful young men, Her Lovers, and She stood between Them and They all three embraced one another. Then came the New Love, and the Lovers knew each other and found yet another joy. In the painting, Their mouths touched with almost ritual solemnity, even as Their strong arms strained about each other and They strove to be one.

But then the great Death entered in, casting the Shadow over the Lovers, filling Them with jealousy, each desiring to alone know the other Lover to the Mother's exclusion. The downpointing Arrow hung over the scene as the Goddess stretched out Her hands to Them, pleading with Them. But reason is no match for the Shadow, which can darken the mind of even a God; all either Lover could perceive was that His Mother still loved the other—it seemed a temptation to unfaithfulness. The Lovers' hands went about each other's throats, and They choked the lives out of each other. The Triad stood above Them in sorrow and together They lifted up the dead, and with Them entered into that Sea of which the Starlight is a faint intimation, therein to be renewed and reborn, to close the circle and make all things whole again.

The last panel, near the door, showed why the shrine had been built. There was a sorrowing mother with her four dead children in her arms, three little girls and a boy; and the inscription, MY CHILDREN. THE PLAGUE CAME IN THE NIGHT. HAVING

PRONOUNCED, SHE SETS FREE. MAY I MEET THEM ON THE SHORE.

Herewiss stopped there, leaning on the broom, saddened. He thought how it must have been for that poor mother, building this place with her own two hands, most likely, hard by that little hill which probably housed her children's bodies: painting those scenes, slowly and with care, and trying to find some sense in the deaths of her little ones. Probably there wasn't any; but at least she had left something beautiful behind in their memory, and it may have been having something to do that brought her at least partway through her grief.

He swept the last of the leaves out the door, picked a few that he had missed off the altar, and threw them out. The sparrow chittered faintly in its nest, and Herewiss looked at it with affection. Another mother, and her children, safe and comfortable. The nameless lady who built this place would probably be pleased.

He went out to where Dapple stood grazing, and rummaged around in the left-hand saddlebag until he found what he wanted, his lovers'-cup. Herelaf had made it for him, a long time ago. It was of white oak, simply carved and stained, with a border of leaves running around the outside just under the lip, and Herewiss' name scratched under the foot. He could remember watching Herelaf carve it. "When it's finished," his brother had said, "take good care of it and it'll last you a long time—"

It certainly had. Fourteen years. Herelaf had been dead for twelve of them.

Herewiss took a waterbag out of the pannier, and filled the cup with it. Carefully, so as not to spill any, he carried the old brown cup into the shrine, and set it on the altar.

"Mother of Days," he said softly, looking for the right words, "Mother of Stars—bless the lady who built this place, and her children, whether they're reborn or not—may she find love again, and may they too. Take

70

care of the people who pass here: keep the Fyrd off them, and the terrors of night: and save them from loneliness. And take care of Freelorn for me, until I get there, and afterwards too." He paused, swallowed the lump that was filling his throat. The hurt was twelve years gone, it was silly to be still crying about it. "And take care of Herelaf—let him come out of the Sea and find joy—"

He picked up the cup, drank quickly. It was harder to cry with his head tilted back and his eyes squeezed shut. By the time he had drained the cup, he was back in control again.

"—and help me find my Power when I get back home," he said. "In Your name, Who are our beginnings and our endings—"

He went out of there in a hurry. Dapple had stopped grazing, and was looking at him inquisitively. It had begun to rain. "Let's go," Herewiss said. "Freelorn is waiting." He undid his rolled-up cloak from the back of his saddle and swung it around him. The rain began in earnest then, pelting down hard. Herewiss made as if to mount, and to his utter surprise Dapple reared up and danced away from him, whickering.

"What??" he said. "What's the matter?"

The horse's eyes were calm, but when Herewiss reached for the reins, Dapple backed away again. "What, then?" said Herewiss. "Am I supposed to stay here?"

Dapple took a step backward and gazed at him.

"Dammit, when Dareth made your family smart, I wish she'd made you a little more verbal! All right, let's see what I can find—"

Herewiss pulled his cloak more tightly around him and slipped the hood over his head, then leaned up against the wall of the shrine and closed his eyes. He tried to put his underhearing out around him like a net. It was a fickle talent, one which often refused to manifest itself when it was needed, and for a moment or so he couldn't find it at all. He concentrated, and tried to listen—

—tried—

Warmth?

—he listened harder—

Very faint warmth. A banked fire. No, more like a fire being rained on, going out gradually. The first drops splattering into the flames, and the fire in panic, seeing its own destruction.

What in the world is that? Not a human reading, no one I ever read felt anything like this. It feels so dry, and I can hear the heat—

Fire in the rain. The fire in terror, the flames being beaten down, steam arising and panic mixing with it—

Somewhere over to the west—

—coming this way—

—fairly close, in fact—

Herewiss opened his eyes and looked westward. The rain was making it difficult to see clearly: it was coming down hard, a silver-white rushing wall, the typical spring cloudburst that seemed to beat the air right into the ground. If there was something out there, it would have to come a lot closer before he would be able to see it.

Fire, dwindling, dying out— Whatever it was, the source of the feeling *was* coming closer: the image had intruded on Herewiss' underhearing that time without his having to listen for it. There was something of a push behind it, like a yell for help.

Herewiss pulled his hood further down over his face and took a few steps into the rain, following the feeling. It wavered, grew a little stronger. Possibly it was sensing him too. Herewiss squished along for several minutes, shivering as the rain soaked through his cloak.

A shadow loomed suddenly behind the gray rain-curtain, and Herewiss slowed down a little. It was bigger than he was—

(—fire in the rain—)

He went closer to it.

A horse?

It staggered toward him. A horse indeed; but a miserable sickly-looking thing, wobbling along on spindly legs. Its mane and tail were plastered to it, its skin was scalloped deep between its ribs and drawn drumtight over the sunken belly. The horse's eyes bulged out in their sockets, staring horribly. It looked as if it had been starved and abused by a whole town full of people, one after another. It looked ready to die.

Herewiss reached out with his underhearing again, to make certain. He got the same feeling: a fire, going out, almost too tired and weak now to be afraid any more. Steam rising, flames dying—and indeed there was steam wavering about the horse's hide, as if it had been ridden hard on a cold day.

He went over to the poor stumbling thing, took its head and stopped it. It regarded him dully from glazed eyes, taking a long long moment to realize what he was. And a feeling stirred in his head. The horse was bespeaking him.

(Help . . .) it said. (Dry . . .)

It collapsed to its knees.

Herewiss was utterly amazed. No one had ever bespoken him but his mother, who had had the talent as a by-product of her Flame; they had used it so commonly between them while she was alive that some of his more remote relatives in the Ward used to accuse him of disliking her, since when together they rarely spoke aloud. But after her death he had hardly ever used the talent again. There were no others in the Wood who had it, not even Herelaf; and after numerous disagreements with the Wardresses of the Forest Altars, Herewiss had little to say to them, and no desire to share himself with them in the superficial union that accompanies bespeaking.

But a *horse*?

Then again, something in a horse's shape could very well have the bespeaking ability. Rodmistresses sometimes took beast-shapes. If that was the case, though, why the distress—and why that strange underheard reading like none he had ever experienced?

Dry, it had said. It wanted to get out of the wet? Well, the shrine was close enough, but in a moment the horse would likely fall right over, and Herewiss doubted he could drag it all the way back. Well, then—

He grabbed it by the nose, and it whuffled in protest. Had it been in any better shape, it would certainly have bitten him; but now as he pulled at it the horse moaned pitifully and struggled to its feet again. Herewiss pulled it, step by trembling step, back the way he had come. It was a long way.

(It hurts,) the creature said, bespeaking him piteously. (It *hurts!*)

(I know. Come on.)

This close to it, touching it, Herewiss' underhearing was coming much more fiercely alive. He could feel the creature's terror as if it was his own, and moreover he could feel its agony, for with every drop of rain that touched it the horse was seared as if by hot iron, a terrible cold fire, pain that ran and trickled like molten metal. Abruptly it collapsed before him, spindly knobby foal's legs folding in every direction as it fell; and then it screamed out loud and within, both at once, a terrible sound of pain and despair as it tried to flinch away from the wet ground to which it had fallen.

Herewiss stood there, shaken to the heart by the sound of its terror. *I can't carry it or drag it—I'll hurt myself—*

It screamed again, thrashing helplessly against the ground.

Oh, damn, damn, dammit to Darkness! Herewiss thought, and took a great breath of resolve. He bent down, put his arms around the barrel of its ribs just behind the forelegs, and began to pull. It was terribly heavy, but nowhere near as heavy as a real horse

74

would have been, even one as emaciated as this creature seemed to be. He could hear it wheezing with pain as he got its forequarters a little way clear of the wet grass and dragged it along. His own muscles began to protest after the first few seconds: a clenching cramping bar of pain riveted itself around his chest and upper back and began to squeeze. The muscles above his groin knotted with such violence that they threatened to tear. Herewiss wanted desperately to drop the horse, just for a moment's rest, but he was also deadly afraid of hearing that terrible lost scream again. He kept pulling, pulling, cast a look over his shoulder. The shrine was a dark shadow through the rain, not too far away. And another shadow was approaching with a sound of wet squishing footfalls. Dapple came up through the rain, looked at Herewiss, and then turned sideways to him, facing him with the saddlebag in which the rope was coiled.

"Thanks!" Herewiss said, reaching up with one arm to get the rope out. He uncoiled it, wound a bight around the strange horse's chest behind the legs, knotted it, and tied the other end to Dapple's saddlehorn. Dapple began backing steadily toward the shrine, and with Herewiss holding the horse partly clear of the ground, they got it to the door of the shrine quickly. There was a slight problem with getting the horse through the door—Herewiss had to drop the horse on the floor halfway in and go around to push its hind legs inside. When he had managed that, he undid the rope, coiled it, stowed it, and went back into the shrine. He dropped to his knees beside the horse's head, gasping for breath and rubbing at his outraged abdominal muscles.

"Well," he said. "Now what?"

The horse lay there with its sides still heaving, its breath rasping in and out, harsh with pain, as if it had been ridden to the point of foundering. Herewiss looked at it through the odd detachment that sometimes accompanies great exertion. In color the horse was a brilliant roan-red, and its stringy-wet mane and tail were pale enough to be golden when they were dry. Under the taut-drawn skin, it had a beautiful head, fine-boned like that of a racehorse.

But racehorses don't bespeak people, Herewiss thought. *And the way the rain was hurting it. Water . . . Could this be a fire elemental, then? People meet them so rarely, the stories say. But the reading I got from it—*

Herewiss closed his eyes and listened again. A feeling like fire, still, but not being rained on any more. Gathering strength, burning a little hotter, growing—

He bespoke it, making the thoughts as clear as he could. (What happened?)

(Don't shout,) it answered faintly.

(Sorry. What happened?)

Its thought was weak, but had an ironic tone. (I didn't know enough to come in out of the rain. Get out of me for a little, will you?)

Herewiss did, and pushed himself over to where he could lean against the wall. The horse was still steaming slightly. He reached out a hand to touch one of its legs, and then jerked it away again, sucking in breath between his teeth. His fingers were scalded.

A fire elemental. I'm in trouble.

The legends were fairly explicit about elementals of any kind being capricious, dangerous, tricky, difficult to constrain by most methods. Flame was said to be of help, but a lot of good that did *him*. Sorcery was almost useless. Some of the old stories that were part of the Woodward's small archive came to Herewiss' mind. His great-great-great-great-aunt Ferrigan was supposed to have had dealings with some of them, water and air elementals mostly, and she had lived through it; but who knew whether the stories were true, or whether the methods recommended in them were likely to be of any use?

Herewiss looked with apprehension at the horse. *I'm going to find out, I guess,* he thought. The creature's breathing was slowing, and it looked less emaciated than it had before. He shrugged his cloak back, and then realized that the air in the shrine was getting much warmer. And the roan seemed to be drying out as he watched. In fact, it was becoming better fleshed out—muscle seemed to be appearing, laying itself down on the bones. It lay there, growing sleek, growing whole—

(What are you called?) Herewiss asked.

It bespoke its Name to him, and Herewiss started back and reflexively shielded his eyes, though there was nothing really there to shield them from. The elemental showed him a terrible blazing ball of fire—the Sun close up, it seemed to be saying—and out of that blinding disc a sudden immense fountain of flame leaped up, streamed outward like a burning veil blown in a fierce wind. Then it bent back on itself with an awful arching grace, and fell or was drawn back into the vast sphere of flame below. That single pillar of fire would have been sufficient to burn away all the forests of the world in a moment; but the creature bespoke the concept casually, as a small everyday kind of thing, not a terribly special Name. And—he shuddered—it made free with its inner Name as if it had nothing to fear from *anything*. Oh, he *was* in trouble—

(Sunspark,) Herewiss said, after he regained his composure a little. (Would that be it?)

(That's fairly close.) It looked up at him from the floor. Its voice was sharp and bright, and currents of humor wafted around it as if the elemental balanced eternally on the edge of a joke. (What's your name?)

(I'm called Herewiss, Hearn's-son.)

(That's not your Name,) it said, both slightly amused and slightly scornful. (That's just a calling, a use-name. What is your *Name?*)

(You mean my inner Name?) Herewiss said, shocked and terrified.

The elemental caught his fear and was confused by

it, then perceived the qualifier and was confused further still. ("Inner"? How can a Name be "inner" or "outer?" You are what you are, and there is no concealing it. Don't you know what you are?)

(Not completely, no.)

More confusion. (They *told* me this was a strange place. I see that directly. How can you be alive, and thinking, and able to talk to me, and *not* know?)

(That's the way things are here,) he said. (By the way, if this is "here," where's "there"?)

It showed him, and he had to hold his head in his hands for fear it would burst open from the immensities it suddenly contained. "There," it seemed, was the totality of existence. Not the little world he had always known, bounded by mountains and the Sea; but his world and all the others that were, all of them at once, a frightful complexity of being and emptiness, and other conditions that he could not classify.

Herewiss knew that there were other planes of existence—everyone knew that—but he tended to think of them as being separated from the world of the Kingdoms by distance as well as by worldwalls, and accessible only by special *doors* such as the ones he was looking for. Sunspark, though, had more than an abstract conception. He had breached those walls under his own power, had made his own *doors* and walked among the worlds. Herewiss, seeing as if through Sunspark's mind, could actually perceive the way they were arranged. They all *overlapped* somehow, each of them coexisting in some impossible fashion with every other one, a myriad myriad of planes arranged on the apparent surface of a sphere that could not possibly be real, since all of its points were coterminous with all of the others. Still, all the countless places held distinct positions in relation to one another. Each of them was a thread in the pattern—a Pattern past his understanding, or anyone's, actually, though some few by much travel might get to know small parts of it, or might come to understand the spatial relationships on a limited scale. It could be traveled, but the order and position of the worlds within it changed constantly, from moment to moment. The important thing was to know what the Pattern was going to do next.

During the brief flickering moment when Herewiss tried to perceive the thought in its entirety, he knew with miserable certainty that he stood, or sat, right then, upon an uncountable number of locked *doors*. If he only had the key, he could step through and be anywhere, anywhen he could possibly imagine. Sunspark had the key. The hope and jealousy that ran through Herewiss in that one bare moment were terrible, but they didn't last long; they dwindled and fragmented as the thought did when Sunspark finally pulled away from the contact. Herewiss found himself left with a few pallid shreds of the original concept. *I'm not big enough of soul to hold so much at once, I guess*, he said to himself when he could think clearly again. *Well, time will come, I hope —*

(That's where you come from?) he said.

(Somewhere there. I've forgotten exactly where: I've been so many places. Does it matter?)

(No. Can you take other people into those—those places?)

(No. It's a skill that each must learn for himself.)

(Oh . . .) Herewiss sighed, shook his head. (Well. You're a fire elemental, aren't you?)

(I am fire, certainly,) it said.

(How did it happen that you got caught out in the rain?)

(I was eating,) it said, and Herewiss thought of the distant brushfire he had seen. (I was careless, perhaps—I knew the storm was coming, but I thought I could elude it just before it started to rain. However, the rain came very suddenly, and very hard, so that the shock weakened me—and then it wouldn't let up. I thought I would go mad or mindless—we do that when too much water touches us. It is a terrible thing.)

(It is that.)

(You saved me,) it said, almost reluctantly, and there was something in its tone that made Herewiss regard it with sudden suspicion. (I —) — and it cut itself off. Herewiss's underhearing caught a faint overtone of concealment, fear, artifice. (Thank you,) it finished, a little lamely.

The omission made it almost too plain. The old legends said that elementals and creatures from other planes respected nothing in the worlds but their own ethic. That ethic, called the Pact, stated that travelers-between-worlds *must* help one another when need arises, return favor for favor, lest the overwhelming strangenesses and dangers of the many worlds should wipe out the worldwall-breaching ability and all its practitioners forever. Sunspark was not sure whether Herewiss knew about the Pact, and it was trying to avoid the responsibility—

(Sunspark,) Herewiss said, doing his best to mask his slight uncertainty with a feeling of conviction. (You would have been left mad and in horrible pain if I hadn't helped you.)

It looked at him, no emotion showing in its eyes or its tone of thought. It moved its legs experimentally. (I think I could stand up now—)

(Sunspark. You owe me your well-being at this moment. Otherwise you would be out there still, in the rain.)

It shuddered all over, so that its nonchalance of thought did not quite convince him. (What of it?)

(A favor for a favor, Sunspark. Until the End.)

He held his breath, and held its eyes and mind with his, and waited to see whether the line that appeared again and again in Ferrigan's old tale would work.

Sunspark looked at him, its eyes distraught. Herewiss' underhearing caught its consternation and unease, its desire to be out of there, away from this horrid narrow little creature who knew of the Pact but didn't even know what its own self was—

(Sunspark,) Herewiss said again, this time putting a

crack of impatience and threat into the thought, an impression of his disgust at the elemental's trying to slip out of an obligation by concealment. (A favor for a favor.)

It closed its eyes. (What do you want?)

(*Sunspark!*)

It sighed inwardly. (Until the End,) it agreed. (What do you want of me?)

(Uhh—) Herewiss paused for a long moment. (I'm not really sure yet. Get up, if you think you can, and we'll discuss it.)

Sunspark struggled a little and then heaved itself all at once to its feet. It stood there for a moment swaying uncertainly, like a new foal. (That's better,) it said. (You know, I am likely to be a lot of trouble to you—)

Herewiss stood up too: it was distinctly unnerving to have something the size of a horse looking down on you and talking to you, especially when it wasn't really a horse. (You're trying to frighten me,) Herewiss said. (The stories *are* true, it seems. If you refuse to aid me, you're forsworn, outside the Pact, outside the help of any of the other peoples who walk the worlds. No traveler survives long under such conditions. You owe me a favor, a large one, and you will repay it.)

The elemental looked at him with grudging respect. (I will. You understand, though, why I did not—)

(Of course. You weren't sure whether I lay within the Pact or not, and who wants to be bound when it's not necessary? But I'm within it, by intention at least; and if that's not enough, there's ancestry.)

(Oh?) It understood him, but there was some slight confusion about some of the nuances he had applied to the thought, and Herewiss didn't know which ones.

(Yes. I am descended from Ferrigan Halmer's-daughter of the Brightwood Line: she walked between the worlds, or so our traditions say. My father is presently Lord of the Brightwood—)

Sunspark stared at Herewiss, and emitted a wave of

total shock and incredulity. (Your progenitor is still alive??)

(Uh—yes. My mother is dead, though—)

(Well, of course. Why two different concepts for your progenitors, though?)

(??) Herewiss said. He was becoming more than slightly confused. himself. (One of them is a man, and the other was a woman—)

There was a brief silence. (You are a hybrid? Well, such matings aren't unheard of in parts of the Pattern—)

(Uhh—no. "Man" and "woman" are different forms of the same creature.)

(Oh. Like larval and pupal?)

Herewiss was shaking his head in amazement. (Well, uh, not really—)

The elemental was bewildered, but still intrigued. (This is too hard for me,) it said finally. (I cannot understand how your "father" is still extant after union. But whatever—there are patterns within the Pattern, and no way to understand them all. No matter. Your "father" was a master of energies, you said—)

(I did? Well, yes, you could say that, though how you mean it and how *I* mean it is—)

(Later. What does his mastery have to do with you?)

(Well, among other things, when he dies, I'll inherit the Wood—)

(Well, of course. How can it be otherwise, but that progeny shall take their progenitors' energy unto them?)

(Uh—right.)

(I think I see. Are you seeking to bring your progenitor to his ending that you may have his energies?)

(!!!) Herewiss said, too puzzled to be angry. (No. I am traveling to find a friend who is being held against his will, and to release him.) Herewiss kept the thought as simple as possible, feeling that this was no time to go into the political ramifications.

He could feel Sunspark pondering the whole thought curiously, taking it apart. (Oh. This person is your mate?)

(!!) Herewiss said again. (Uh—my loved, yes.)

Sunspark looked with interest at the concept "loved." (Your mate. And you will unite and engender progeny? You seem a little young for it . . .)

(It, ah, it doesn't quite work that way. You see, we are both men . . .)

(Yes?) It waited politely for the explanation. Herewiss sagged against the wall, looking for the right words.

(Well—See, Sunspark, in this world, "progeny" are—well, there are many ways to achieve union, but there is only one way to have a child. The women bear the children, always; and though men may know men in, uh, union, and women may lie with women, a child only happens if a man lies with a woman. There have been times when babies were supposed to have happened when women lay together—but it's hard to say, because men have been sleeping with the women too.) Herewiss, to his utter surprise, was becoming embarrassed. Even Halwerd at four years of age had not been as completely confused about sex as Sunspark obviously was. (My loved and I are both males and cannot have "progeny" of our own.)

Sunspark digested this. (Yours is not a fruitful union? Yet you pursue it? Such behavior is not survival-oriented for a species.)

Herewiss laughed. (No, it isn't really. That is why the Goddess gave our kind the Responsibility. When we come of age—)

(Oh. You come into heat too? Well, there is *one* similarity, anyway.)

(Uh, not really, I think. But. When we come of age, or soon after, we *must* have union in such a manner as to reproduce ourselves at least once—one union for a man, two bearings for a woman. After that, union is our own business, and we may love whom we please.)

The roan stallion stood there and mused over this. Sunspark was fully recovered now, and it looked truly magnificent, like the mount of a King—its hide was a true deep crimson, bright as blood, and its mane and tail glittered like wrought gold even in the subdued light from the door.

(How very strange,) it said. (Union again and again, it seems, without consummation. And even without progeny!—So your "loved" is in durance?)

(Yes.)

(And you are going to free it?)

(Him. Yes, and then go back to my work.)

(This is *definitely* too much for me,) Sunspark said. (You will go to your mate—and *not* unite—and then go do something else?)

(Well, we may, uh, unite, but—yes.)

(What else could you possibly want to *do*?)

Herewiss sighed. (I have, mm, a certain kind of Fire within me—)

(Yes: that's why I was heading in this direction, and the rain felt less over here. But I could feel the fire, and I thought we might be related—though I didn't understand how you could not be distressed by the water. I see that we aren't relatives, though, except in a rather superficial manner.)

(That's for sure,) Herewiss said. (At any rate, I have this Fire—but not control of it. With the Flame, one must have a tool, a focus with which to dissociate it from one's self, or it won't work. I'm looking for such a focus. It would be a shame to die of old age and never have had use of the Flame at all . . .)

(Excuse me. "Die"?)

(!!!) Herewiss said, and Sunspark jumped a little from the suddenness of the thought. (Uh . . . cease to exist?)

(That is an impossible concept.)

(. . . pass on? Go through the *Door* into Starlight?)

(Oh, you mean leave your present form,) Sunspark

said. (I see. Why the time limit, though? Is it a game?)

Herewiss shook his head slowly, not knowing what to say. Sunspark sensed his bemusement, and fell silent.

(Where are you headed?) Herewiss asked.

(I have been roaming—like all the rest of my kind. I am condemned to restlessness. But you have bound me to you by the Pact, and I must pay back your favor in kind.)

Herewiss thought for a moment. (Well enough, then. If you'll keep company with me until you have opportunity to save my life, I'll consider the favor paid. With the things I'm going to be doing, it shouldn't be too long . . .)

(Done, and done,) Sunspark said. (Shall we match off energies to bind the agreement?)

(??)

(It is in the nature of my kind,) Sunspark said, (to match off energies whenever possible. The loser's energies are bound to the winner's, so that when the winners come to mate, their progeny are more powerful than the parents. I think you would probably consider it as something of a social exchange. Like—) it slipped a little further into his mind to find an analogue— (like clasping hands?)

(With a little knuckle-work,) Herewiss said, grinning. (I hear a certain air of permanence in the thought, Sunspark. Are you looking for a way to make an end of me accidentally, and so be free of our agreement?)

(Make an end? Oh, I see, force you to change form.) Sunspark chuckled softly, with innocent savagery. (I told you I was probably going to be trouble for you,) it said.

(Yes,) Herewiss said, laughing himself. (Trouble indeed. Sunspark, I am minded to try my strength with you. I would like to engage in a social exchange with you: I'd sooner have a friend than someone whom I could never trust, and that's what you'd most likely be without this—)

It looked askance at the concept "friend." (You want to *mate* with *me*?) it said incredulously. (How perverse. And how very interesting—)

There was a sudden smile in its voice that made Herewiss awfully wary. (I didn't say *that*,) he said. (Never mind it now, Spark, there seem to be differences in our ways of looking at things, and with a little luck we will have leisure to discuss them later— How are these matches usually handled?)

(Best two falls out of three.)

(So be it. I have certain limitations that you haven't, though, and I will ask that you take them into consideration so that the match will be a fair one.)

(Who ever said anything was fair?) said the elemental in surprise.

(True, but it behooves us to try to make it that way,) Herewiss said. (Will you agree not to burn me up, or otherwise kill me?)

("Kill"? Oh, form-change. My, you have a lot of ways to say it. What a shame, that is one of the best ways to win a fall. Why should I refrain?)

(I don't want to leave this form yet.)

(Is it that comely? You can always get another, can't you?)

(Not just like this one, certainly; the process isn't under my control at all. And besides, I would no longer be able to reach my loved if I left it.)

(That would be tragic,) Sunspark said, (but then, all union is tragic, when you come right down to it . . . Oh, very well. There is something here that I don't understand, and since you keep insisting, it must be important. I won't "kill" you. Shall we begin?)

(Right here??)

(Where better?) said Sunspark, and then the change came upon him, and Herewiss had no time to think about anything.

The creature that leaped at his throat had many of

the worst characteristics of Fyrd—a nadder's coily, scaled body walking on the ugly hairy legs of a bellwether, and the knife-sharp claws of a keplian at the ends of those legs. Herewiss wrestled wildly with it, trying to get some kind of decent hold, but there were too many legs, and the thing seemed to weigh as much as he did. The fact that he was braced against the wall helped him somewhat, but Sunspark had perceived that. There were legs pushing at his own, trying to knock him off balance.

Herewiss spread his legs wider, strove to feel the balance flowing through them, the upflowing power of the earth, as Mard, his weapons instructor, had taught him. After a few straining moments the power began to come. Sunspark, though, feeling the change in the tension of its opponent's muscles, shifted its attack toward Herewiss' head. Herewiss was confused, for the form Sunspark had taken seemed to have no real head, nothing which he in turn could attack—the top half ended in a blunt place where the serpent-like body came to an end, and talons erupted from it in a clutching rosette like some malignant flower. They grabbed and slashed at him, and it was all Herewiss could do to hold the thing at a distance.

For a long moment their respective positions did not change. Then Herewiss found a fraction more leverage than he'd thought he had, and slung the creature away from him, halfway across the room. The naddercreature cracked into the offering table and lay still for a moment.

(First fall,) said Sunspark. (Not bad. Are you ready?)

He sucked in a few deep breaths. (Come ahead—)

It flashed a bright, edged feeling like a sharpened smile at him, and changed again. A sudden hot wind began to fill the room as its physical form dwindled away, and Herewiss suddenly had a hunch that it would be wiser not to breathe for the rest of this bout. He sucked in one last gulp of air before Sunspark had time to finish the change—and then found himself being pressed brutally from all sides, his muscles being painfully squeezed, his eyes smashed back in their sockets, his joints being broken open, his skull being crushed by something that clothed him all around like a stormwind turned in on itself. Herewiss held onto his lungful of air, but then it too was pressed out of him, and white lights danced behind his closed eyes as the awful pressure began crushing him down into unconsciousness—

He slapped the ground to which he had fallen, hoping that Sunspark would understand the gesture. Immediately the pressure let up, and he lay there for a few seconds, at least until the lights went away. He felt as if he had been run over by a cart.

(That one was mine, I think,) came the quiet voice. (Shall we take the third?)

(Go ahead,) Herewiss said. He dragged himself to his feet, and braced himself once more against the wall.

The air swirled, coalesced, and Sunspark stood before him in the red roan form again. But it did not move, just looked at Herewiss.

—and then it was inside Herewiss' head, and Herewiss began to understand the elemental's statement that he was fire. The quiet, familiar confines of Herewiss' mind went up in a terrible conflagration. His brain and body burned inside, thoughts and emotions threatening to drown in heat and pain. But Herewiss held on, held part of himself away from the burning, concentrated on survival, on the help that this creature could be to him if he could bind it. He was not as afraid of fire as most people might be—fire was his companion at work, his old familiar friend. He bore the marks of his acquaintance with it all over his arms, pink places where blisters had been. This fire, a fire of the mind, was no different, really. He withstood the flames for a long few moments, making sure of his control. Then, (Two can play at this,) he said—

—and thought of water: storms of it, deluges of it, cold and free-running: the shaded place in the Wood where the Darst runs through, widening out into the pool he and Lorn used to swim in during the summers. The leap out from the green bank, and the splash, first too cold, then just right, cool clear liquid softness covering all the body, sliding, surrounding—

He heard Sunspark scream.

—the Sea, the northern Darthene coast in late summer, waves crashing and spray flying cold and salty, a blue infinity of water that could swallow an elemental without even noticing—

The contact broke. Herewiss stood there, sweating and trembling, and saw that Sunspark was doing the same. It looked at him, pleased and irritated both.

(You have nothing to fear from me,) it said. (I am bound to your will until you see fit to release me. I should have let the Pact-oath be the term of our agreement—)

(Maybe you should have,) Herewiss said, (but I for one have no need to keep you past the time of the original agreement.)

(You can afford to be generous,) Sunspark said grumpily. (I've never lost a match before. Shows you what comes of being fair.)

(Sometimes,) Herewiss agreed. (Come on, Sunspark, let's go; the rain's stopped.)

They walked out of the shrine. Above them the clouds were moving eastward before a brisk wind. (One thing I will require of you,) Sunspark said, (and that is that you keep water off me.)

(That's easily done; there are spells—)

Dapple was grazing again; as Herewiss approached him he looked up placidly, as if to ask what would happen now.

(Hmm. Sunspark, will you mind if I ride you?)

(It's a binding of energies, is it not? It seems appropriate.)

He transferred his gear to Sunspark's back, piece by

piece, and finally took the bridle off Dapple and rubbed the horse's nose. "It's a long way back home for you," he said, "but you can't help but find your way there. Though they might be confused to see you without me. Here—"

He put the bridle on Sunspark and then went to rummage in the saddlebag, finally finding the little steel message-capsule from Freelorn's pigeon, along with the scrap of parchment it had contained. Inkstick and brush were further down in the bag. Herewiss wet the brush from his mouth, scrabbled it against the inkstick, and paused for a moment. *Should I—? Oh, why the Dark not, he loves riddles!*

"From Herewiss Hearn's-son to his sire," he wrote. "Your son's making good on his hire:
He sends you your horse
 (and regards, Lord, of course)
and the news that the prince rides with Fire."

He stood there for a moment and read through it again to make sure of the scansion. Then he enclosed the note in the capsule and tied it around Dapple's neck with the cord from the saddlebag.

"Have a safe trip home," he said. "And thanks."

Dapple nuzzled him in the chest, turned, and trotted off.

Herewiss swung up into the saddle, intrigued to feel Sunspark's heat seeping up through it. (I hope the leather doesn't crack,) he said. (We're heading south. The place where Freelorn is stuck is about a five-days' ride from here—)

(For a horse,) Sunspark said with an inward smile. (We'll go faster; I'm curious to see this "loved" of yours. You'd better hold on tight.)

Several times that night and the next day, the country people of southern Darthen and northern Steldin pointed and wondered at the sudden meteor that blazed across their skies and did not strike the ground anywhere.

FOUR

"Are you a sorcerer?" said Ferrigan curiously.

"Dear me, no!" the Pooka said,
shocked. *"Who wants to be a sorcerer? You spend five days of a
week recovering from one day's
spelling: and if you die in the middle of a spell, it takes three months
before the headache goes away."*

"Tale of Ferrigan and the Pooka,"
from Tales of Northern Darthen,
ed. Hearn, ch. 8

The place was old enough to have been built in the
first wave of Darthen's colonization. It was hardly
more than a crude castle keep built of fieldstone. For
outworks it had nothing more than an earthen dike,
surrounded by a ditch that had once been full of
sharpened stakes. They were long since rotted away,
the place having been abandoned for some newer,
more defensible castle of hewn stone.

But the keep was still quite solid, thick-walled
enough so that an earthquake could hardly have
brought it down. There were no windows but arrow-
slits, the towertop was deeply crenellated, and the door
was of iron a foot thick, judging by the fact that it had
not rusted away in all the intervening years. Time had
been kind to the place. Its mortar had grown stronger
with age, and only here or there was any stone shattered by frost. It was a redoubt worthy of the name, and
it stood there at the center of the cuplike vale with
stolid rocky patience, frowning at the surrounding
hills, antique and indomitable.

Herewiss stood about two miles away, atop one of the long bare surrounding ridges, and frowned back at the keep. It was surrounded by a fairly large force, disposed around it for the siege in the usual Steldene fashion. The troops were about half a mile or so from the walls, separated into four large camps, each oriented to one of the compass points. Herewiss agreed with Freelorn's estimate; there were about a thousand of them, and maybe more.

"For five people!" he said aloud. "Steldin must be awfully nervous."

Sunspark stood beside him in the red roan form, idly switching flies with its long glittering tail. It looked at the besieging army with supreme disdain, and snorted softly. (It hardly matters. Give me half an hour and I will bring the fire down on them and leave not a one alive.)

(Sunspark, I don't want to kill, there's no need. Restraint is considered a virtue in these parts.)

The elemental snorted again, flicking its tail at a nonexistent fly and fetching Herewiss a stinging blow across the back.

(Behave yourself or I'll make it rain on you again.)

(That's no mastery, there are rainclouds coming in anyway: it'll be pouring after nightfall. You keep me dry, now!)

(I keep my promises. You'll be fine. Look, it's getting on toward sundown—I want you to take a message to Freelorn for me.)

(What, am I a pigeon?)

(Spark—)

(All right, all right.)

(Get in there any way you like, so long as it's unobtrusive. Say to Freelorn that I'm waiting for nightfall to make my move. Tell him that he should try not to be too bothered by what he sees—I'm going to try to go past the bounds of battle-sorcery he's seen in the past. Tell him how to find this spot—or better still, after I'm finished, go and meet them and bring them here.

There are times when Lorn needs a map to find his own head.)

(Shall I tell him that too?)

(No, I've told him enough times myself. When you finish with that, get back here. This place is wild enough so that there might be a few Fyrd wandering around. I don't want to get eaten while I'm trying to concentrate on my spelling.)

(Tell Freelorn this. And tell Freelorn that. There are six people in there, oh Master mine. What does he *look* like?)

Herewiss sighed a little. (Look for a small man, about a span short of my height, with longish dark hair and a long mustache, and a sense of humor like yours. Chances are the idiot will have on a surcoat with the White Lion on it—as if he hasn't attracted enough attention already. Is that enough for you?)

(If there are only five other people in there, then I think I can manage.)

(Then get going.)

Sunspark's horse-shape wavered and went molten, gathered itself together and swirled about with a blast of oven-heat, became a bright amorphous form that put out wings and rose against the sky, cooling and darkening. A moment later a red desert hawk spiraled up a thermal partly of its own making.

Herewiss sat down, making a face at the smell of scorched grass, and considered what he was going to do. It wasn't going to be easy to dispose of an army this large. There weren't too many of the Steldene regulars among the forces; most of them were conscript peasantry, ununiformed and hurriedly armed. That would be a help. But the regulars and their commanders would have seen real battle-sorcery before. They would be familiar with the tricks of the trade, and unafraid of illusion. Herewiss did have some advantages; he had a great deal of native power, and access to references and methods about which most sorcerers knew nothing. Also, the fact that there was no other army attacking them in concert with the illusions would confuse the Steldenes somewhat. By the time any of them realized what was happening and tried to mobilize a force to stop him, it would be too late. He hoped.

A thousand men. Herewiss shook his head. The King of Steldin must have been worried about the possibility of the Arlene countryside rising against his people when they brought Freelorn home—or the possibility of Freelorn getting away, and the Arlene mercenaries moving into Steldene lands in retaliation. If the Oath of Lion and Eagle wasn't protecting Darthen from Cillmod's incursions, the King of Steldin had good reason to worry.

Sighing, Herewiss looked at the thunderheads massing on the northern horizon. The storm would make a fine cover for their escape. He disliked the prospect of leaving over wet ground that would take their trail. But speed, and fear, and the direction in which he would lead his friends, would confound the pursuit. Now he had to concern himself with the sorceries he would need.

Herewiss spent at least half an hour leafing through the grimoires, memorizing pertinent passages and wishing he weren't so ethical. To frighten a thousand men into flight was more difficult than killing them. It would have been simplicity itself to turn Sunspark loose. The elemental's methods were swift and brutally efficient, and its conscience would be clean afterwards. To Sunspark death was nothing more than a change from one form to another; shapes donned and doffed without a thought. Or Herewiss himself could have laid warfetter on the lot of them, leaving the whole army deaf and blind and stripped of their other senses, fighting nothing but their own terror, and probably dying of it. But his conscience was not as accommodating as Sunspark's. The last time he had slain was one time too many, and even if that had not been the case, there was still sorcerer's backlash to consider. To lay warfetter on so many people was to open the way for a huge cumulative backlash to strike *him*, one which would certainly leave him either dead or insane.

So Herewiss chose illusions as his weaponry, picking those spells with the least combined aftereffects and the easiest access into a man's mind. He would have to alter the formulae to accommodate so many people, and the backlash would get him proportionately—he would be unconscious for a couple of days. As he went through the book, making his final choices in the fading light, Sunspark dropped out of the sky onto his shoulder.

(Loosen up a little with the talons, please,) Herewiss said. (Did you find him?)

The hawk snapped its beak with impatience. (Of course. He's waiting for you.)

(Was there a message?)

(Your friend greets you by me,) Sunspark said, (and says, "Get me the Dark out of here.")

(That's Lorn. Sunspark, I'm going to need a good while to get ready for this. You'll have to stand guard while I meditate. Also I'll need your services during the sorcery.)

(As you say.) Sunspark whirled and dissolved in heat again, reappearing in the red roan persona.

(You really do like that shape, don't you.)

The elemental curved its neck, looked around to admire its shining self. (Stallions are sacred to the Sun hereabouts, and the shape has a certain elegance, I must admit—)

(You're vain, firechild, vain,) said Herewiss, smiling. He walked off a little distance and unlaced his fly to relieve himself before the long sorcery; Sunspark followed, regarding the process with interest.

(You are *really* strange,) it said. (Why bother drinking water if you're just going to throw it away again? And what is this "vain" business? I'm *gorgeous*, you've said so. I don't understand why you can tell me that I'm beautiful, but I can't tell myself—)

(Spark, shut up, please.)

Sunspark strolled away a few paces and began cropping the grass in silence, leaving little scorched places where it had bitten through. Herewiss settled himself comfortably on the ground and began to compose himself for the evening's work.

Sorcery, like all the other arts, is primarily involved with the satisfaction of one's own needs. Though a sorcerer may mend a pot or raise a storm or set a King on his throne with someone else's benefit in mind, still he is first serving his own needs, his own joys or fears or sorrows. To work successful sorcery one must first know with great certainty what he wants, and why. Otherwise the dark secretive depths of his mind may take the unleased forces and use them for something rather different than what he thinks he wants.

In addition, sorcery is affected by how completely the sorcerer's needs are filled before he begins— whether he's hungry or tired, secure in his place in life, whether he is loved or has someone to love. It's easy for a hungry sorcerer to find food by his art, since the need fuels his skill. But it's much harder for that same starving sorcerer to, say, open death's *Door* and sojourn in the places past it. And only the mightiest of sorcerers could manage to conjure Powers or Potentialities if he hadn't eaten for a week, or felt that his life was in danger for some reason. Sorcery is ridiculously easy to sabotage. Beat your sorcerer, frighten him, deprive him of food, ruin his love life—destroy one of his fulfillments, and he'll be lucky to be able to dowse for water.

So Herewiss sat there in the grass, as the Sun went down and the thunderclouds rolled in, and he strove to shut out all external things and evaluate his inner self. A brief flicker of thought went across his mind like lightning, a white line of discomfort and irritation: *if I had the Flame, I wouldn't need to go through this rigmarole. Will alone is enough to fuel the blue Fire, you think a thing and it's done.* But he put the thought aside. Freelorn was waiting for him.

Herewiss sounded himself. He was well-fed, not thirsty or cold or tired. He was the Lord's son of the Brightwood, as usual, had a home and family and people that he could call his own. Love—there was his father, and Freelorn of course—the knowledge of their feelings for him was a warm steady support at the back of his mind.

Then after a moment he reached out and took hold of the thought he would have liked to banish, the lack of Flame, the lack of completion, and turned it full-face to study it. Oh, he was so empty in that one place inside of him. It should have been full of blue Fire and prowess and shouting joy. Instead it ached with emptiness, as parts of him sometimes did after love-making. It was a vast stony cavern that echoed coldly when he walked there. Nothing but a faint flicker illuminated it, a single tongue of blue, like a candle lit for a wish to find its way by.

Herewiss turned wholly inward, walked in the still, dry air of that place, listened to the sound of his passage as it bounced back from the walls, a distant, hollow step. He went toward the little blue fire, crouched down beside it where it sprang from a crack in the bare rough rock. Though there was no wind passing through the darkness, the Flame trembled, and Herewiss put his hands around it to shelter it. It was a sad little fire, afraid of dying before it was unleashed to burn through the rest of him, terrified of going out forever. Herewiss was surprised, and pierced with sorrow. He had never really pictured the Flame as anything but a possession of his, no more emotional than an arm or leg. Yet here it was, frightened of endings as he himself was, lonely in the dark.

He spent a little time there, trying to comfort it with his presence and the warmth of his hands. The Flame seemed to stand taller for the attention, and burned more brightly, its light shining through the translucence of his skin like a seedling star. Finally Herewiss stood up straight again and gazed down at the tiny tongue of cold fire. If it would die some day, then that was the Goddess' will. It was better to have treasured the wonder this long than never to have had it in him at all.

Herewiss turned his back on the Flame and went out of that dark place, looking for Freelorn's image inside him. Besides need, sorcery was also fueled by emotion: commitment lent it power and efficacy. He would summon up his emotion as a smith might beat out iron, slowly, with care and skill and calculated brutality. Then he would turn it loose, take it in hand like the weapon it was and scatter an army with it, use it to make his illusions real and full of fear.

He didn't have to walk far. The path to where Free-lorn dwelt was a wide one, one that Herewiss traveled often when his friend was gone. It was a bright place. A lot of it looked like the halls of Kynall castle in Prydon, where they had lived together for a while, all white marble and sunlit colonnades—very different from the dark, carven walls of the Woodward. Some of it looked like Freelorn's old room in the castle, cream-colored walls veined in green, Freelorn's old teak four-poster bed with the hack-marks in it from Súthan, armor and clothes scattered around in adolescent disorder. They had had good times there together, lounging around and tossing off horns full of red Archantid as they talked about the things that the future might hold.

But there was a lot of it that looked like the Bright-wood, too, and it was there that Herewiss finally found him. The image of a dead spring day was there, all sun on green leaves, and Freelorn newly arrived with his father King Ferrant on a visit of state. Herewiss, of course, was both within that memory and without it. From the outside he looked at Freelorn and marveled that he had ever really been that young.

Lorn didn't even have a mustache yet, and he looked laughably unfinished without it. And he was so little, so very small for his age.

Freelorn was as nervous as a new-manned hawk, trying to look in all directions at once. He hung onto the golden-hilted sword at his belt with one white-knuckled hand, and spurred his sorrel charger till it danced, meanwhile staring around him trying to see if any of the Wood people had clothes as grand as his, or such a sword, or such a father. From within the memory Herewiss, fourteen years old, looked with mixed disdain and jealousy at the newcomer. He was loud and flashy and arrogant, the way Herewiss had imagined a city princeling would probably be. He had disliked Freelorn immediately, and he saw himself frown and turn away from Hearn's side to stalk back into the Woodward, fuming quietly at this foreign invasion.

Then suddenly the scene changed, faded into darkness and stars seen through leaves and branches. The Moon sifted down through silvered limbs to pattern the smooth grass around one of the Forest Altars, and shone full and clear on the altarstone in the midst of the clearing. On the low slab of polished white marble Freelorn sat, huddled up with his head on his knees, shaking as if with cold. Beneath the trees at the edge of the clearing Herewiss stood very still, confused, wondering why the Prince was crying. At the same time he was resisting the urge to laugh; the idea of the Prince of Arlen *sitting* on one of the Forest Altars and weeping was ludicrous. But disturbing—it wasn't right for a prince to be seen crying, and Herewiss wanted him to stop. . . .

The scene shifted again, ever so slightly, and Herewiss was sitting next to his friend-to-be, trying to help, his arm around him; and Freelorn put his head against Herewiss and cried as if his world was ending. "No one likes me," Freelorn was saying, in choked little sobs, "and I don't, don't know *why*—"

They began to see through each other that night.

Herewiss had been playing cold and silent and mature, and Freelorn merry and uncaring and free; that night they began coming to the conclusion that there was at least one more person with whom the games and false faces were unnecessary. The next morning they looked at one another shyly, each studying the other's weak places as he himself knew he was being studied, and decided that they would not attack. They spent the next month teaching each other things, and savoring the one joy that comes of having someone to listen, and care. Their friendship became a settled thing.

Herewiss gave the scene a nudge of adjustment. They were in rr'Virendir, the King's Archive in Prydon castle, sitting with their backs against one of the huge shelves filled with rune rolls and musty tomes. It was dark and cool, and the air was laced with the dry dusty smell of a great old library. The summer sun burned down outside, and the Archive was one of the few comfortable places to be. The assistant Keeper was snoring softly in his little office down at one end of the long room; Freelorn, who due to a hereditary title was the Keeper of the Archive, was hunched up against the very last row of shelves with Herewiss.

"I don't want to learn all this stuff," he was saying. "I'll *never* learn it all. I'm a slow reader anyway, it would take me the rest of my life."

"Lorn, you've got to." Herewiss was fifteen now, and feeling terribly broadened by his travels; this was his first trip to Prydon, and the first time he had ever been more than ten miles from the Wood.

"I don't need it!" Freelorn said, scowling at a pile of parchments that lay on the ground next to him. "Look at all this stuff. Half of it is so rotten away I can hardly read it, and the rest of it is in some obscure dialect so full of thee's and thou's that I can't make sense of it."

"Lorn," Herewiss said with infinite patience, "that one on top is a rede that has been copied over more times than either of us knows, because no one knows

100

what it means, and it's tied to the history of your Line somehow. It's Lion's business, Lorn. That makes it *your* business. This whole place is your business. That's why you're its Keeper."

"Dammit, Dusty, I love my family's history. Descent from the Lion is something to be proud of. But I don't want to sit around reading when I could be out doing great things!"

"What did you have in mind?"

"Are you making fun of me?"

"No."

Freelorn made an irritated face. "I don't *know* what kind of great things. But they're there, waiting for me to get to them, I know it! I want to see the Kingdoms. I want to take ship for the Isles of the North, and talk to Dragons. I want to climb in the Highpeaks and see what the lands beyond the mountains look like. I want to go into Hreth and kill Fyrd. I want to find out what the Hildimarrin countries are like, I want to—oh, Dark, *everything!* And you know what I get to do?"

"You get to stay home and be prince for a while. Listen, Lorn, it's not that long ago you were in the Wood with me. That's not traveling? Almost two hundred leagues away? What about the mare's nest we saw on the way back? That's not adventure? You wanted the nightmare, maybe? She would have had you for breakfast. We saw three wind demons and a unicorn, and heard the Shadow's Hunting go overhead, and you want more? Goddess, Lorn, what's it take to make you happy?"

"Danger. Intrigue. Hopeless quests. Last stands. Heroism! Courage against all odds! Valor in defeat!"

"You remember when we used to play Lion and Eagle?"

"Yes, but—Dusty, what's that got to do with this?"

"How many times did we stage Bluepeak out behind the Ward?"

"Every day for a month at least, but—"

"Did you notice something interesting? We always got up again afterwards. Earn and Héalhra didn't."

"Yes, They did. They come back once every five hundred years—"

"—and the last two times no one recognized Them for years, because They didn't come back as Lion and Eagle. That's not important here, though. Lorn, I'm not—oh, Dark." Herewiss reached over and took Freelorn's hand, slowly, shyly.

"My father," he went on, looking at his boots, "keeps saying, 'A king is made for fame and not for long life.' Which is all right as long as it's some other king—but Lorn, it's going to be *you* some day, and I'm not sure I want to see you die. No matter how damn heroic your last stand is." He closed his eyes. "I'm probably going to go the same way; Brightwood people *never* die in bed. They vanish, or get eaten by Fyrd, or turned into rocks, or something weird like that. All the old ballads make my ancestors sound just wonderful, but they have to be divorcing the emotion from the reality in places. *I* don't want to find out how it feels to vanish."

Freelorn nodded. "I don't really want to end up bleeding somewhere either—but on the other hand, it'd be neat to be a robber baron, putting down the oppressor and giving money to the common people. Or to be a wandering sorcerer, doing good deeds and slipping away unnoticed—"

Herewiss sighed, and a wild impulse compounded of both daring and humor rose up in him. "All right," he said. "Hopeless quests are what you want? Valiant absurdity? Something that the Goddess would approve of?"

"What the Dark are you talking about?"

"Lorn, *I'm* on a quest."

"Say *what*?"

Herewiss grinned at the sudden confusion in Freelorn's face. He considered and discarded several possible ways of explaining things, and finally simply held out his hands. Usually he had to close his eyes when he made the little tongue of external Flame that was all he could manage. But he strained twice as hard as usual this time for the sake of keeping his eyes open. He didn't want to miss the look on Freelorn's face.

It was an amazing thing. It was so amazing that Herewiss broke out laughing like a fool, and lost his concentration and the Flame both a moment later. He laughed so hard that he had to hold his stomach against the pain, and all the while Freelorn stared at him in utter amazement.

Finally Herewiss calmed down a little, caught his breath, wiped his eyes.

"You have it," Freelorn said softly. "You have it."

"It looks that way."

"You have it! *Dusty!!*"

"That's me."

"MY GODDESS, YOU HAVE IT!!!"

"Sssh, you'll wake up Berlic."

"But you have it!" Freelorn whispered.

"Yeah."

And then Freelorn looked at Herewiss, and the joy in his eyes dimmed and flickered low.

"But a focus—"

"I tried. Can't use a Rod."

There was a long long silence.

"Lorn," Herewiss said. "This is my secret. And yours, now. My mother taught me a lot of sorcery when I was younger, but there was always something else I could feel in the background that I knew wasn't anything to do with that. I didn't know what it was until last year—I made Flame accidentally in the middle of a scrying-spell. I thought it might have been a fluke, but it's not, it's there, and it's getting stronger. If I can channel it, I can use it. And the Goddess only knows what I'm going to use for a focus. Will this do for a hopeless quest?"

Freelorn was silent for a little while.

Then he looked at Herewiss again.

103

"I am the Keeper of the Archive," he said, solemnly, as if he were summoning Powers to hear him. "There must be something in here that would help you. I'm going to start looking. And when I find it—"

Herewiss smiled a little. "When you find it," he said.

They hugged each other, stirring up dust.

The memories were making Herewiss feel warm inside. The analytical parts of him approved: he was heading in the right direction. The warmth was building, washing through him—

He shifted the scene again, and it was night out in the eastern Darthene wastelands, a hundred miles or so from the Arlene border. They were on their way to Prydon again after a trip to the Wood, and the day's riding had left them exhausted—Freelorn was anxious to get home, and they had spared neither themselves nor the horses. It was cold, for Opening Night was approaching, and they lay close to their little fire and shivered. The stars were beginning to fall thickly, as they do at Midwinter when the Goddess is angriest, when She remembers Her own thoughtlessness at the Creation, and flings stars burning across the night in defiance of the great Death. Herewiss lay on his back gazing up at the sky, watching the distant firebrands trace their silent paths out of the heart of the Sword, which constellation stands high on winter nights. Freelorn lay curled up in a tight bundle next to him, facing west.

"Dusty—"

Herewiss turned his head to him.

"Let's share."

Within the memory, Herewiss, now sixteen, went both warm with surprise and pleasure, and cold with fear. It was a thought that had occurred to him more than once. But he had always pushed it to the back of his head for one reason or another. Freelorn was

104

younger than he was inside, and easily frightened. He wouldn't want to scare Lorn, ever—

—yet no one in the world knew him as well as Lorn did, no one else cared as much about all the little things in Herewiss' life and how he felt about them: he could share things with Lorn that he would never dare say to anyone else, and never be afraid of the consequences. And Lorn mattered so much to him. His loved. Yes. And he was beautiful outside, too, small and strong and fine to look at—

I paid off the Responsibility long ago. I can love whom I please—

"You want to?" he said aloud.

"Yeah."

Herewiss felt at the knot of fear inside him, wondering what to do about it. If Lorn wanted to—

But—

"I had to think about it for a while before I could say it," Freelorn said quietly, from inside the blankets. "If you don't want to, it's all right."

"No, it's not that—"

Freelorn chuckled a little, so adult a sound coming out of him that it startled Herewiss. He identified it as one of Ferrant's laughs, which Freelorn had borrowed. "I should have asked," Freelorn said. "Your first time?"

"No! —I mean, yes. With a man."

They were quiet for a little. Freelorn turned over on his back and looked up at the sky, watching a particularly bright star blaze out of the Sword and clear across the night to the Moonsteed before it went out. "There's not much difference," he said, "except that, instead of being different, we're alike. Some things are easier—some are harder—"

The voice was still suspiciously adult, and Herewiss looked at Freelorn for a moment and then smiled. "Your first time too, huh?"

Freelorn's face went shocked, then irritated, and finally sheepish-smiling. "Yeah."

Herewiss laughed softly to himself, and reached out to hug Freelorn to him. "You twit!" he said, laughing into Freelorn's blankets until the tears came.

They held each other for a long time, and then drew closer. Outside the memory, Herewiss looked on with quiet amusement, and with reverence, feeling as if he was watching an enactment of some old legend being staged by well-meaning amateurs. In a way, of course, he was: the Goddess' Lovers always discover each other after being initiated by Her—one of the things which makes for the tragedy of Opening Night, when the Lovers, male or female as the avatar dictates, destroy one another in Their rivalry. But this was an enactment of the birth of that new relationship, and the freshness and innocence of it easily compensated for whatever ineptitude there may have been as well.

"Oops—"

"Huh? Did it hurt?"

"Yeah, a little."

"Well, let's try this instead—"

"Ohhh . . ."

"Hmmm?"

"No, no, don't stop. It feels so good."

Silence, and further joinings: warm hands, warm mouths, growing comfort, trust flowing. The slow climb on smooth wings, easing into the upper reaches, then gliding into the updraft, soaring, daring, higher, higher—

—sudden and not to be denied, the brilliance that is not light, the dissolution of barriers that cannot possibly break—

—a brief silence.

"Oh, Dark, I'm sorry. I hurried you."

"Oh, no, no, don't be. It was—it was—oh, my. . . ."

"I saw your face." A warm arm reaches around to pillow Herewiss' head; gentle fingers stroke his jawline, his lips, his closed eyes. "You looked—so happy. I was glad I could make you feel that way."

"I felt . . . so *cherished*."

"It was something I always wished somebody would . . . do for me . . ."

"You mean you *haven't*. . . ."

"No."

"Oh, my dear loved.—Can I call you that?"

"Why not? It's *true*—oh, Dusty—!"

"Lorn, you're crying—? Are you all right, did I say something wrong—"

"No, no,—it's just—nobody ever called me their loved before—and it's—I always wanted—I'm *happy*—!"

"Oh, Lorn. Come here. No, come on, if we're going to share ourselves with each other, that means the tears too. My loved, my Lorn, it's all right, you're happy—"

"But, but my face gets—gets funny when I cry—"

"So does mine. Who cares? You're beautiful. I love you, Lorn—"

"Oh, Goddess, Dusty, I love you too. I was just scared—I didn't see how someone as gorgeous as you could ever want to share with me—"

"Me? Gorgeous? Oh, Lorn—"

"But you are, you are, don't you see it? And inside, too." A chuckle through passing tears. "It's almost unfair that anyone should be so beautiful as you are inside. But it makes me so *happy*— Am I making sense?"

"Yes. Oh, Lorn, I want you to feel what I felt, I want to give you the *joy*—you deserve it so much . . . and it makes me so happy to make *you* happy. . . ."

"Mmmmmm."

A long, slow smile in the darkness. "Oh, you're beautiful when you smile like that."

". . . 'Cause what you're doing is beautiful. Mmmmmmm. . . ."

—and again the slow dance, stately circlings on wings of light—

—and much later, the long drift down.

Silence, and falling stars.

Outside the memory, Herewiss wept.

Inside the memory, Freelorn held Herewiss, and Herewiss held Freelorn, and their hearts slowed.

"Again?"

"I don't know if I could. . . ."

A chuckle. "Neither do I."

Another silence.

"Hey, maybe we should get married some day."

"Are you thinking of us, or of marriage alliances?"

"It could be good both ways. Hasn't been an alliance between our two Houses since the days of Béorgan."

"And you know how *that* turned out. I don't to be history, Lorn, I just want to be *me*."

"Yeah."

"So think about us, then, and leave politics out of it."

"Can we?"

Herewiss thought about it. "At least until our fathers leave us their lands. I'm tired, Lorn."

"Yeah. We've got a long ride tomorrow."

"Yeah."

They held each other against the cold, and fell asleep.

Herewiss dwelt on the scene for a little while, and then reluctantly changed it again. Another night, another place out in the cold. The battlefield where they fought the Reaver incursion, far to the south of the Wood. The night after the battle, and Herewiss wounded in the shoulder with the blow that he took for the King's daughter of Darthen. Later on that blow had gotten him awarded the Whitemantle. But at this point Herewiss lay huddled on the ground, wrapped in his own tattered campaigning cloak, innocent of honors. He was cold and tired, and in pain from the wound. The hurt of it kept pulling him in and out of sleep every time he moved. During one hazy time of almost-sleep, a figure came softly toward him in the dark, and Herewiss didn't move, didn't particularly care who it was—

"Dusty?"

He tried to get up, and Freelorn was down beside him, helping him. "Quiet, quiet—do you know how long I've been looking for you?" His voice was frightened.

"No."

"I couldn't find you. I thought you were—"

"I'm not, obviously. I heard you were all right and so I asked these people to bandage me up and let me sleep. They did. Very nice folks—"

"That's interesting," Freelorn hissed. "Because you're behind the lines. Do you mind coming with me before they find out who we are and carve the blood-eagle on us? Lucky for you you have that ridiculous southern accent—"

"Behind the lines?"

"The *Reaver* lines! It's obvious you're being saved for something besides dying in battle. If you haven't managed it by now—Oh, Dusty, come *on*!!"

"I lost a lot of blood. I think I need a horse. Oh, poor old Socks, he got killed right out from under me—"

"Blackmane is here, I brought him. Come on, for Goddess' sake—"

The next while was a nightmare, an interminable period of jouncing and wincing and almost falling out of the saddle. The wound reopened, and Herewiss bit his moans back with great difficulty. Blackmane was stepping softly; he seemed to have something tied around his feet. Herewiss later found out that they had been pieces of Freelorn's best clothes—his Lion surcoat, the one embroidered in silver and satin, that he had loved so well. But in the midst of the hurt and the fresh bleeding, as they passed through the enemy lines and slipped past guards, Herewiss heard himself thinking, like a chant to put distance between one and one's pain, *He really must care about me. He really must—*

The slow wave of love that Herewiss had been

109

building was coming to a crest. He let it grow, let it build power. He would need it. Holding himself still in the twilight inside him, he reached out a tendril of thought to Sunspark.

(What?) it said. Its voice seemed distant, and he could perceive no more of the elemental than a vague sensation of warmth.

(Warn away anything that approaches. Don't hurt it, just keep it away.)

(It would be easier to kill.)

Herewiss prevented himself from being angered. He couldn't afford it at this stage of the sorcery. (It would disturb the influences I'm working with. Take care of me, Spark. If I have to drop what I'm doing suddenly, the backlash may catch you as well.)

(Whatever.)

He returned fully to the awareness of his inner self, and watched with approval as the anger grew. He encouraged it. *This is my friend: my loved: a part of me; this is who they want to take and kill! Will it happen? Will it?* Will it?

The answer was building itself like a thunderhead, piling threateningly high. He turned his attention away from the building storm of emotion and started to work on the sorcery proper. This was going to be more difficult, in a way; it was like building a house of cards in a high wind. It was, indeed, building a house of words to confine a storm of wrath until he needed it. The spells had to be built, word by cautious word, each word placed delicately on edge against another, stressed and counterstressed, pronunciations clean and careful, intentions plain. The words were sharp as knives, and could cut deeper than any sword if they were dropped or broken. A word here, and another one there: this one placed with care atop two others, taking care always to keep the whole structure in mind—too much attention to one part could collapse others. Here a jagged word like cutting crystal, faceted, many-syllabled, with a history to it—don't pause too long to admire the glitter of it, the others will resent the partiality and turn on you. There a word fragile as a butterfly's wing; indeed, the word has lineal ties with the Steldene word for butterfly— but don't think of that now, this winged word has teeth too. Put it down, give it a touch of adjustment. There. Now the next—

Herewiss was doing what only a very few sorcerers of his time, or any other, could do: building a spell without reference to the actual words written in the grimoire. It requires a good memory, and great courage. The mind has a way of shaping words to its liking, and that can be fatal to a sorcery and the one who works it. But keeping himself conscious enough to actually read the words from his books would have meant a diversion of needed power, and Herewiss was worried enough to forego the safer method. He was making no passes, drawing no diagrams to help him: those measures would have cost him energy too. The greatest sorceries are always those done without recourse to anything but the words themselves, and the effect they have on the minds of the user and the hearer. But Herewiss didn't think about that. It would have scared him too much.

He built with the words, making a structure both like and unlike the towering concentration of love and anger within him. The structure had to be big enough to let the emotions flow freely, strong enough to contain them—but it also had to be small enough not to scrape the barriers of Herewiss' self and damage him, and light enough for him to break if the sorcery got out of hand. The balance was perilous to maintain, and once or twice he almost lost it as a word shifted under another's weight. Another one turned on the word next to it—they were too much alike—and savaged it before Herewiss could remove the offender and put another, less violent, but also less effective, in its place. He had to make up for the loss of power elsewhere, at the top of the structure. He wasn't sure

111

whether it would stand up to the strain or not, and the whole crystalline framework swayed uncertainly for a moment, chiming like frozen bells in the wind, like icy branches brittle and metallic—

It held, and he surveyed it for a moment to be sure that nothing was left out. Satisfied, he took a long moment's rest.

(Sunspark?)

(?)

(Almost ready.)

(It's getting ready to rain.)

(In here, too. Hang on.)

He composed himself and examined the structure one last time. It was ready; all it was missing was the tide of emotion that had to be imprisoned inside of it, and the last three words that were the keys, the starting-words. He had them ready to hand, and the emotion had built to the point that it rolled like a red-golden haze all about the insides of his self, looking for an outlet. He began to direct it into the structure. It was hard work; it wanted to expand, to dissipate, as is the way of most emotion. But he forced it in, packed it tighter. It billowed and churned within the caging words, blood-color, sun-color, alive with frustration. He took two of the words of control in his hands. One of them was simple, smooth and opaque, though of a shape that could not exist in the outer world without help. He tucked it into the structure at an appropriate point, and then placed the other near it, a yellow word with a confused etymology and a lot of legs.

The third one was in his hands, ready; the gold-and-red storm seethed, rumbling to be let out. Now all that remained was for him to become conscious enough to direct the course of the sorcery, while remaining unconscious enough to set it working. Herewiss shifted about in his mind, found the proper balance point. Then with one hand he took the last word and shoved it into the structure. With the other he grabbed hold of his outer self and pulled his mind behind his eyes again. He looked out.

The Othersight, the perception of the hidden aspects of things, is a side effect of most large sorceries, a hallucination, an effect of the intense concentration involved. But no two people who experience the Othersight report the same kind of perceptions. Herewiss thought that having looked as deeply into one's self as one must to make a great sorcery work, perhaps the outside world can't help but present itself as it really is. Perhaps the stresses involved in the great sorceries manage to open the *Door* past Death just a crack, that *Door* which it takes Flame to open completely—and what the sorcerer really sees are the appearances of things in the Next Domain, the Mirror of Completion which the Goddess made to console Herself for the Error—the impossible place where everything seems to be as it *should* be.

Whatever the reasons, Herewiss looked out of himself and saw things transfigured. The old keep was made of the bones of the earth, and a sort of life throbbed in it still, a deep gray light like the glow behind closed eyelids on a cloudy day. All around it the men and women of the Steldene army shone, a myriad of colors from boredom to fear—mostly weighted toward the blues and greens, smoky shades of people who wished themselves somewhere else. Many of them also showed the furry outlines of those who are willing to let others do their thinking for them. *Well, army types, after all*, Herewiss thought. *Now for it.*

Behind him, in the back of his mind, the pressure was becoming alarming. He let it build just a little longer, the red haze beating within the glittering framework like a second heart, throbbing, pulsing—

Go free! he thought, and the sorcery flowed away and outward from him, sliding down the hill. He could see it now with the Othersight, instead of just sensing it as a construct inside him. Though it flowed like water, it still bore the marks of his structuring, faint traceries of words and phrases gleaming through it like stars through stormswept clouds. The sorcery rolled down and away, expanding, slipping slowly and silently over the besieging forces, over the hold and the surrounding land. Finally it slowed, finding the boundaries that Herewiss had set for it in the spell. It stopped and waited, moving restlessly. To Herewiss' eyes the whole valley was filled like a cauldron with slowly boiling mist, and the men and the hold shone faintly through it.

All right, he thought. *First, boundaries that they can see—*

In a wide ring around the keep, the air began to darken. Within a short time a wall of cloud half a league in diameter surrounded the hold and the Steldene forces, a threatening roiling cloud that walled away the last of the sunset, leaving the field illuminated only by the lurid choked light at the bases of the thunderheads. Herewiss looked down at the cloudwall, watched it pulse and curl in time with his heartbeat.

A little tighter, he thought. The ring drew inward until it was about a mile across. The men and women within it looked around them and became very uneasy. Herewiss could see the drab greens and blues start to shade down through murky violet as they knew the cloud for something unnatural. There were dark-bright flickers as swords were unsheathed, the brutalized metal living ever so slightly where hands touched it and charged it with disquiet.

Good. Now just a few minutes more—

The last of the sunset light faded from the storm-clouds. Now there were no stars, and no Moon, not even a horizon any more. Fear built in the camps below Herewiss until all the swirling mist was churning dusk-purple in his sight, and people were moving about in increasing agitation.

Good. Now for the real work.

He put forth his will, and shapes began to issue from the wall of cloud. They were vague at first, but as his control and concentration sharpened, so did they, gaining detail and the appearance of reality.

He started small. Fyrd began to slip out of the dark mist, moving down on the besiegers with slow malice. Great gray-white horwolves snarling softly in their throats, nadders coiling sinuously down toward the hold, spitting venom and shriveling the grass as they went. There were dark keplian, almost horse-shaped, but clawed and fanged like beasts of prey; destreth dragging scaled bodies along the ground, lathfliers beating heavily along on webbed wings and cawing like huge, misshapen battle-crows. Herewiss made sure that his creations were evenly distributed around the army. In a flicker of black humor he added a few beasts that had lurked in his bedroom shadows when he was young, turning them loose to creep down toward the campfires on all those many-jointed legs of theirs.

The temper of the army was shading swiftly darker, the deep purple turning into the black of panic in places. There were still spots, though, where the commanders stood and knew that this was illusion-sorcery. They showed pale against the darkness of their fellows, suspicious green or nervous murky-blue as they tried to rally their people.

They're holding too well. Fyrd are too real, maybe. Legends, then—

A gigantic ravaged figure came tottering through the cloud, a look of ugly rage fixed on his face. It was the Scorning Lover, of whom Arath's old poem sings. Attracted by his beauty and brilliance, the Goddess had come to him and offered what She always offers, Her self, until the Rival comes to take the Lover's place. But this young man had had a calculating streak, and as price for sharing himself had asked eternal youth and eternal life. The Bride tried to warn him that not even She could completely defeat Death in this universe, and told him he was foolish to try. He would not listen, and She gave him the gifts he asked and left him, for the Goddess cannot love one who loves life more than Her. And indeed as the centuries passed, the Lover did not die—nor did he grow, frozen as he was in the throes of an eternal adolescence. Time and time again he tried to kill himself, but to no avail; immortality is just that. And after all that time, all thought and hope had died in him, leaving him a demon, a terror of waste places, killing all who fell into his hands while bitterly envying their deaths. He stumbled toward the army now, raging with pain from the thousand self-inflicted wounds that can never heal, and never kill him, his clawing hands clutched full of gobbets of his own immortal flesh—

The forces on the eastern side, from which he approached, gave way hurriedly, consolidating with those to the north and south.

Herewiss smiled with grim satisfaction, and out of the cloud to the north summoned the seeming of the Coldwyrm of Arlid-ford, which doomed Béorgan had killed with the help of her husband Ánmod, Freelorn's ancestor. The thing crawled down the slope, an ugly unwinged caricature of the pure hot beauty of a Dragon. The Wyrm was scaled and plated, but in a sick fishbelly blue-white rather than any Dracon green or gold or red. A smell of cold corruption blew from it, like fetid marshes in the winter, and the ground froze with its stinking slime-ice where it crawled. The Wyrm's pale blue tongue flickered out, tasting the fear in the air, and the cold black chasms of its eyes dwelt on the huddling troops before it with malice and hungry pleasure.

The commanders were trying hard not to believe in what they saw. But the campfires were too faint to show whether any of the stalking shapes had shadows or not. The army was collecting into a frightened mass of men and women at the southeast side of the keep.

Just a little more pressure, Herewiss thought, *and they'll be ready for Sunspark. Something that'll be sure to panic them all . . . Dark, I could—it's almost*

116

blasphemy, and no battle-sorcerer in his right mind would ever try it. That fact alone might do it. And, anyway, it is for Freelorn's sake, and I don't think his Father would mind the use of His seeming—

Herewiss hesitated. *It's for love,* he decided. *I just hope Lorn's watching.*

From the south, as might have been expected, pacing slowly out of the cloud, came a great form that cast its own silver-white light about it. It was a Lion, one of the white Arlene breed, longer of mane and tail than the tan Darthene lions which run in prides. But this Lion was twenty times the size of any ordinary one; it towered as tall as the keep. And its eyes held what no earthly lion's ever had—intelligence, frightening power, towering wrath. It was Héalhra Whitemane, in the shape that He took upon Himself at Bluepeak, where the Fyrd were broken and scattered; the Father of the Arlene kings, and one of the two males ever to have use of the Power. Herewiss halted his other creations where they stood, banished the Fyrd altogether, and poured all his power into making this one illusion as real as it had been in his boyhood dreams. Earn Silverwing should have been there too, the White Eagle companioning the Lion as They had always been together in life. But Herewiss doubted he could handle it and do Them both justice. He poured himself out, and the Lion approached in His majesty, His growl rumbling softly in the air like the thunder waiting in the clouds above. He drew to a halt no more than three or four spearcasts from the tightly clustered army, and looked down at them, towering over them—shining, silver-white, His eyes grim and golden—

In the Othersight the army was a black blot of leashed panic, terror with nowhere to run. Now, while they could not move to prevent the damage—

Herewiss gave the sorcery an extra boost, a push of power to keep it alive while he turned his attention away from it. Then he turned to Sunspark, looking at it with the Othersight—

—and was amazed. Sunspark burned beside him, almost intolerable even to his changed and heightened vision—burned as flaming-white as the pain at the bottom of a new wound. Its outline was that of a stallion still, but confined within that outline was the straining heart of a star, an inexpressible conflagration of consuming fires. Now Herewiss began for the first time to understand what an elemental *was*. This was one note of the song the Goddess sang at the beginning, when She was young and did not know about the great Death. One pure unbearable note of the song, a note to break the brain open through the ears and the burnt eyes. A chained potency looking for a place to happen, a spark of the Sun indeed, whose only purpose was to burn itself out, recklessly, gloriously. One more falling star, one more firebrand flung against the night by the Creatress in Her defiance.

Herewiss slipped warily into Sunspark's mind, confining himself to the narrow dark bridge that represented his control over it, a sword's-width of safety arching over unfathomed fires. (Sunspark. Go, take their tents, their wagons, everything, and burn them. I don't want us being followed.)

(And the men?) Its inward voice was no longer a thing of concepts, but of currents of heat and tangles of light.

(Don't kill!!)

It resisted him, testing, defying his control, and in his heart Herewiss shuddered. He had not really understood what a terror he had chosen to bind. Its fires ravened around him, barely constrained by its given word. Nothing more than its sense of honor kept him from being consumed, but at the same time it was not above trying to frighten him into releasing it. And it did not understand his scruples at all. (What is death?) it sang, its upleaping fires dancing and weaving through the timbre of its thought. (Why do you fear? They would come back. So would you. The dance goes on forever, and the fire—)

(Maybe for you. But they have no such assurances, and as for me, you know my reasons. Go do what I told you.)

It laughed at him, mocking his uncertainty, and the flames of its self wreathed up around Herewiss, licking, testing, prying at the cracks in his mind. It was without malice, he realized; it was only trying to make him understand, trying to make him one with it, though that oneness would destroy him. He held his barriers steadfastly, though in some deep part of him there was a touch of longing to be part of that fire, lost in it, burning in nonambivalent brilliance for one bare second before he was no more. The greater part of him, though, respected death too much, and refused the urge.

(Go,) he said again, and withdrew himself. Sunspark gathered itself up, leaped, streamed across the sky like a meteor, a trail of fire crackling behind it and lighting the lowering clouds as if with a sudden disastrous dawn. The men before the Keep, frozen in their silent regard of the Lion, saw Sunspark coming and knew it for something perhaps more real than they were. The few minds still bright with disbelief bent awry and went dark as if blown out by a cold wind. Herewiss, though shaken, turned his thought back to his sorcery, and as Sunspark swept down among the tents of the soldiers, the Lion roared, a sound that seemed to shake the earth clear back to where Herewiss sat.

It was too much. The army broke, scattering this way and that in wild disorder, screaming. Sunspark flicked from place to place in the first camp, the one on the eastern side, leaving explosions of white fire behind it. The flames spread with unnatural speed, leaping from tent to wagon as if of their own volition. Herewiss opened a door in the encircling cloud, parting it to the northward, and people began to flee through it. Sunspark saw this and hurried the process. It dove into the southern camp like a meteor and ignited it all at once into a terrible pillar of flame, driving the stampeding army around the west side of the keep and toward the opening in the cloudwall. They fled, officers and men together, with their screaming horses. Sunspark came behind them, though not too closely, spitting gledes and rockets of fire with joyous abandon.

Herewiss sighed and dissolved his remaining illusions, the Lion last of all. The great white head turned to regard him solemnly for a moment. Herewiss gazed back at it, seeing his own weary satisfaction mirrored in the golden eyes, himself looking at himself through his sorcery; then he withdrew his power from it with a sad smile. The image went out like a blown candle, but Herewiss imagined that those eyes lingered on him for a moment even after they were gone . . .

He shook his head to clear it. The backlash was getting him already.

(Sunspark?)

(?) It paused and looked back at him, a tiny intense core of light far down in the field.

(Are they all out?)

(Nearly.)

(Good. Look, the keep door is opening—it's all fire there, go and part it for Lorn and his people and bring them through.)

(As you say.)

Slowly, hesitantly, six faintly glowing figures rode out of the keep and paused before the flaming eastern camp. The bright blaze that was Sunspark joined them there, and they all headed toward the fire, which ebbed suddenly.

The Othersight departed without warning, in the space of a breath. The sorcery dwindled and died away, the wall of cloud evaporated, emotion dissipating before the wind of relief. Herewiss sagged, feeling incredibly empty and drained. The fragile spell-structure swayed and fell and shattered inside him, the bright crystalline fragments littering the floor of his mind, sharp splinters of light hurting the backs of his eyes. Backlash. He put his hands behind him and braced himself against the ground, fighting it. There was one more thing he had to do.

The pain in his head was like hammers on anvils—he laughed at the thought, and found that it hurt to laugh, so he stopped—but he held himself awake and aware by main force, waiting. It was hard. After a while there were hands on him, helping him up. Herewiss opened his eyes and knew the face that bent over him, even in a night of impending storm and no stars.

"Lorn," he whispered, reaching out, clinging to him.

"Herewiss. Oh Goddess. Are you all right?" The voice was terrified.

"Yes. No. Get me up, Lorn, I have something to do. When I finish, tie me on Sunspark here—"

"Fine. Up, then, do it, you've got to rest."

"You're telling me. Where's Sunspark?"

"The horse, he means. Dritt, give me a hand. Segnbora, help us—"

"Right." A new voice. Female. *Where did she come from? Never mind.* Strong hands stood him up, guided him to Sunspark.

He put out his hands, braced himself against the stallion's shoulder. "N'stai llan astrev—," he began, spilling out the simple water-deflecting spell as fast as he could, for the darkness was reaching up to take him—

He finished it, and sagged back into the supporting arms. "East," he said, but his voice didn't seem to be working properly, and he had to push the words out again harder, "straight east—"

Darkness deeper than the stormy night enfolded him, and as he drowned beneath the black sea roaring in his ears, he felt the rain begin.

FIVE

Silence is the door between Love and Fear: and on Fear's side, there is no latch.

Gnomics, 33

Sunset was glowing behind his back when Herewiss woke up. He opened his eyes on a wide barren vista of earth and scattered brush, streaked with crimson light and long shadows. He stretched, and found that he ached all over. It wasn't all backlash; some of it was the pain of having been tied in the saddle and taken a great distance at speed.

"Good evening," someone said to him.

He didn't recognize the voice, a deep, gentle one. Then as he turned his head, the memories snapped back into place. The new person, the woman. This must be her.

Looking up at her, Herewiss' first impression was of large, deep-set hazel eyes that lingered on him in leisurely appraisal, and didn't shift away when he returned the glance. And hands: long, strong-fingered hands, prominently veined, incongruously attached to little fragile bird-boned wrists and too-slender arms. She was very slim and long-limbed, wearing with faint unease a body that didn't seem to have finished adolescence yet. But her muscles looked taut and hard from assiduous training. She sat crosslegged on the ground by Herewiss' head, those strong hands resting quietly on her knees, seemingly relaxed. But his underhearing, hypersensitive from the large sorcery he had worked, gave him an immediate feeling of impatience, an impression that beneath the imposed external calm seethed something that *had* to be done and *couldn't*. Her dark hair was cut just above the shoulders; Herewiss looked at it and smiled. *She wants to make sure they know she's a woman,* he thought, *but she doesn't have the patience for braids . . .*

"Good evening to you," he said, propping himself up on one elbow and then frowning—he had forgotten how sore he was. "I'm sorry I missed your name when we were on the way out—"

"You were hardly in a condition to remember it if you'd heard it," she said, reaching out to touch hands with him. "Segnbora, Welcaen's-daughter."

"Herewiss, Hearn's-son," he said, touching her hand, and then flinching. No matter how fordone he might be, there was no mistaking the feel of Flame. And she was full of it, spilling over with it. It had sparked between their hands, faint blue like dry-lightning, as if trying to fill the empty place in him. Something very like envy whirled through Herewiss' mind, to be replaced immediately by confusion. With power like *that*, what was she doing *here*?

She was rubbing her hands together thoughtfully, and still looking at him, her curiosity more open. But at the same time she read the look in his eyes, and her expression was rueful. "You felt right," she said softly. "The funny thing is, I think I did too . . ."

For a few moments more they regarded each other. Then Segnbora dropped her eyes, reaching down with one hand to play with the peace-strings of her sword, sheathed on the ground beside her.

"That was some sorcery you worked," she said, and looked up again. Her face was all admiration, masking whatever else was in her mind. "You were out for two days."

"Where are we now?"

"About fifteen miles from the border with the

123

Waste. We only have to cross the Stel. Freelorn will be glad you're awake. He was worried about you."

"Don't know why," Herewiss said, and sat himself up with a little effort. "He knows I always take the backlash hard."

"I'm sure. But he never saw anything like *that* display before. Some of the effects were—"

"Unexpected."

"Yes. Especially that business with the fire."

"Where is he?" Herewiss said hurriedly.

"Out hunting. They left me here to watch you. This is safe country, too empty for Fyrd, I think. They'll be lucky to find anything. Dritt is here too."

He looked around and located Dritt sitting atop a boulder, a big stocky silhouette against the sunset. He was munching something, and Herewiss became immediately aware of the emptiness of his stomach.

Segnbora was rummaging in a pouch. "Here," she said, handing him an undistinguished-looking lump of something crumbly.

"Waybread?"

"Yes."

It looked terrible, like a lump of pale dirt with rocks in it. He bit into it, and almost broke a tooth.

"Goddess above," he said, after managing to get the first bite down, "this is *awful*."

"And what waybread isn't?"

"Worse than most, I mean."

"It's also more sustaining than most."

"I think I'd rather eat sagebrush."

"You may, if they don't find anything out there. Eat up."

She took a piece too, and they sat for a few minutes in silence, passing Segnbora's waterskin back and forth at intervals.

"The fire," Segnbora said suddenly. "And your messengers—the hawk, that ball of flame that met us when we came out—those really interested me. Those were no illusions—those were *real*."

He studied her uneasily, not responding, trying to understand what she was up to. She was looking thoughtfully over his shoulder at something fairly close by. Herewiss put his mind out behind him and felt around. Sunspark was some yards behind him with the other horses, once again a vague blunt warmth wrapped in the stallion-form, grazing unconcernedly.

(?) it said.

(Our friend here—) Herewiss indicated Segnbora.

(So?)

(I think she sees you for what you are.)

Sunspark waved its tail, making a feeling like a shrug. (Well, you *did* say I'm worth looking at. How are you feeling, by the way?)

(Better, thank you.)

(Thank me for what? I didn't have anything to do with it. How do you do that, anyhow?)

(Do what?)

(Get out of yourself like that. Leave the body and go elsewhere. That's quite a trick.)

(I wasn't really—well, I guess—oh, later.) Herewiss returned his attention to Segnbora. She continued to gaze past him for a moment. Remotely he could sense Sunspark lifting its head, returning her look.

(Another relative,) it said. (This world seems to be full of my second cousins.)

"An elemental?" Segnbora said, turning her eyes back to Herewiss.

"Yes. Why?"

"You have no sword." She gestured at his empty scabbard.

"I *beg* your pardon?" Herewiss said, shocked.

"I'm sorry—I didn't mean to change the subject. But I'd been meaning to ask you about that."

Herewiss felt outrage beginning to grow in him, and a voice spoke up in his memory, the scornful voice of some Darthene regular way back during the war. ("Spears and arrows are a *boy's* weapon! Afraid to get up close to a Reaver? . . . A man isn't a boar to be

125

hunted with a lance. A man takes on another man blade to blade . . . Earn's blood must be running thin in the Wood . . .")

Oh, Dark, I thought I got over this a long time ago! Herewiss took a deep breath and pushed the anger down. "It may be none of your business," he told Segnbora, as gently as he could.

"Then why are you so obvious about it? You wouldn't be wearing that around if you didn't want to attract attention to it. Freelorn's people think it's something to do with a family feud or some such, and they won't mention it for fear you'll take offense. But there's something else there—"

"Freelorn knows. And he doesn't speak of it either," Herewiss said, trying to frighten her away from the subject with a sudden knife-edge of anger in his voice.

"Maybe someone should," she said, so very softly that he sat back in confusion. "I saw how he looks at that scabbard. He looks at it, but he doesn't look at it—as if it was a maimed limb. He hurts so much for you. I didn't know why—but now— It's a matter of Flame, isn't it?"

"Listen," Herewiss said, "why should I discuss it with you? We've barely met."

Segnbora smiled at him, that dry, rueful smile again. "Fair enough," she said. "Let me tell you about me, a little, and you'll understand. I come of fey stock from a long way back—several generations of Rodmistresses and sorcerers. The female line has descent from Gereth Dragonheart, who was Marchwarder with M'athwinn d'Dháriss when the Dragons were fighting for the Éorlhowe—a terribly eminent family. And I'm something of an embarrassment to them."

She chuckled softly. "We usually come into our Power early, if it's there. They took me to be tested when I was three years old, and they weren't disappointed. The Flame that was in me shattered all the rods and rings and broke the blocks that they gave me to hold, and the testers got really excited. They said to my mother and father, 'This one is a great power, or will be when she grows up—you should have her trained by the best people you can find. Anything less would be a terrible waste.' So they did. And I studied with Harandh, and Saris Elerik's-daughter, and the people at the Nhàirëdi Institute in Darthis, and I did a year with Eilen—"

"That old prune?"

"You know her. Yes. And others too numerous to mention. I hardly spent more than a year or two in the same place."

"It's not very good policy to change teachers so often," Herewiss said. "I wouldn't think there would be time to build up a good relationship—"

"You're right, it's not, and there wasn't," Segnbora said. "There was this little problem, you see. I had too much Flame. I kept breaking the Rods they gave me to work with: they would just blow right up, boom, like that—" She waved her arms in the air. "—any time I tried to channel through them. And all my teachers said, 'It's all right, you'll grow out of it, it's just adolescent surge.' Or, 'Well, it's puberty, it'll be all right after your breasts grow.'" She chuckled. "Well, they grew all right, but that wasn't the problem. I began wondering after a while why each teacher kept referring me to another one, supposedly more experienced or more advanced—once or twice I made so bold as to ask, and got long lectures on why I should let older and wiser heads decide what was best for me. Or else I got these short shamefaced speeches on how I needed more theory, but everything would be all right eventually."

Herewiss made a face.

"That's how I felt," Segnbora said. "Well, what could I do? I gave it a chance, stuffed myself with more theory than most Rodmistresses would ever have use for. It was better than facing the truth, I suppose. And eventually I got to be eighteen, and they took me to the Forest Altars in the Brightwood, and I spent a year there in really advanced study—or so they called it— You know the Altars?"

"I live in the Brightwood," Herewiss said dryly. *And a lot of good it did me!* "Go on."

"Yes. Well, when I turned nineteen, and Maiden's Day came around, they took me into the Silent Precincts, and I swore the Oath and they brought out the Rod they had made for me. They were really proud of it, it came from Earn's Blackstave in the Grove of the Eagle, it'd been cut in the full of the Moon with the silver knife and left on the Flame Altar for a month. And they gave it to me and I channeled Flame through it—"

"—and you broke it."

"Splinters everywhere, the Chief Wardress ducked and turned around and took one right in the rear. Oh, such embarrassment you haven't seen anywhere. The Wardress claimed I did it on purpose—she and I had had a few minor disagreements on matters of theory—"

"Kerim is a disagreement looking for a place to happen."

"Yes," Segnbora said tiredly, "indeed she is. Well. They went down the whole Dark-be-damned list of trees, and I broke oak Rods and ash and willow and blackthorn and rowan and you name it. Finally the Wardresses who were there shrugged and said they'd never seen anything like it, but they couldn't help me. So here I am, so full of Power that sometimes it crawls out my skin at night and changes the ground where I lie—but I can't *control* so much of it as to heal a cut finger, or bring a drop of rain." She sighed. "A whole life wasted in the pursuit of the one art I can't master."

Herewiss sat there and felt an odd twisted kind of pleasure. *So I'm not the only one like this! Well, well—* But then he pushed it aside, ashamed of it.

"Precisely," Segnbora said, her voice tight, and Herewiss blushed fiercely. "Oh," she said, and smiled again, "they really push you at Nhàirëdi: my underhearing got awfully good."

"I'm sorry—"

"Don't be. I must confess the same thought crossed my mind when I realized what your problem was. I'm sorry, too."

Herewiss sighed. "You're a long way from the Forest Altars."

She shrugged. "How long can a person keep trying? I spent three more years in the Precincts, fasting and praying and trying to beat my body into submission—I thought I could tame the Power that way." She snorted. "It was a silly idea. I ended up half-wrecked, with the Fire almost dead in me from the abuse. I had to let it rest for a long time before it would come back. Then after a while I said, 'What the Dark!' and just went off to travel. The Power's going to wither up in me soon enough, but there's no reason to be bored while it does. I made Freelorn's acquaintance in Madeil; and traveling in company is more interesting than being alone. Especially with him." She chuckled.

"But you still have a lot going for you," Herewiss said, though the empty place in him realized how such a statement might feel to her. "You studied at Nhàirëdi: you certainly got enough sorcery from them to make yourself a living by it—"

Segnbora shrugged again. "True. But I have better things to do with my life than spell broken cartwheels back together or divine for welldiggers or mix potions to make men potent. Or thought I had. I spent all those years cultivating the wreaking ability—and then nothing came up. I was going to reach inside minds and really understand motivations—not just make do with the little blurred glimpses you get from underhearing, all content and no context. I was going to untwist the hurt places in people, and heal wounds with something better than herbs and waiting. To really *hear* what goes on in the world around, to talk to thunderstorms and soar in a bird's body and run down with some river to the Sea. I was going to move the forces of the world, to command the elements, and *be* them when I chose. To give life, to give Power back to the Mother. To sing the songs that the Stars sing, and hear them sing back. And they told me I'd do all that, and I believed them. And it was all for nothing."

She looked out into nothing as she spoke, and her voice drifted remotely through the descending dusk as if she were telling a bedtime story to a drowsy child. From the quiet set of her face, it might have been a story laid in some past age, all the loves and strivings in it long since resolved. But the pain in her eyes was here-and-now, and Herewiss' underhearing caught the sound of a child, awake and alone in the darkness, crying softly.

He sat there and knew the sound too well; he'd heard it in himself, in the middles of more nights than he cared to count. "If you had it, you know," he said, trying to find a crumb of comfort for her, "you'd probably just die early."

He had tried to make a joke of it, an acknowledgment of shared pain. But she turned to him, and looked at him, and his heart sank. "Who cares if you die early," she said very quietly, "as long as you've *lived*."

He dropped his eyes and nodded.

They sat and gazed at the sunset for a little while.

"I'm sorry," Segnbora said eventually, pulling her knees up to her chest and wrapping her arms around them. "The problem is much with me these days: it's dying, you see. But it must be worse for you. At least for me there's hope—"

"There's hope," Herewiss said harshly, "just fewer people to believe in me. A lot fewer."

"That's what I meant," she said, and to his surprise, he believed her. "That jolt you gave me when we touched—you certainly have enough to use. If you live in the Brightwood, you must have tried the Altars too—"

"Yes."

"And?"

"They turned me away."

"They did *what*?"

"I couldn't use a Rod."

"Well, of *course* you couldn't! It's a woman's symbol, your undermind would interfere with it. What were they thinking of?" She was all indignation now, and Herewiss, feeling it was genuine, warmed to her a little. "You're a *man*, what did they expect? And just because you couldn't use a Rod, they gave up on you?"

"Yes."

Segnbora frowned at Herewiss, and he leaned back a little, stricken by the angry intensity of the expression. "There are few enough women since the Catastrophe who have the Power," she said, "less than a tenth of us—and no men at all— Do they think there are enough people running around using Flame that they can afford to throw one away? A *male*, no less." She shook her head. "They must have been crazy."

"I thought so at the time."

"What did they say?"

Herewiss shrugged. "I asked for help in finding something else to use as a focus. I thought that, since the sword is very symbolic of the Power for me, that I might use one as focus. They said it was hopeless, that the Power was a thing of flesh and blood and the lightning that runs along the nerves, and that it could never flow through anything that hadn't been alive, like wood. Well, I said, how about a sword made of wood or ivory? Oh, no, they said to me, the sword in concept and design is an instrument of death, and unalterably opposed to the principles of the Power. They just wouldn't help me at all. I guess I didn't fit their image of how a male with the Power would act, when one finally showed up. So I left, and went my own ways to study."

He stretched a little, making an irritated face. "Well, for whichever of the reasons they gave me, they've been right so far. I tried using various sorceries to condition the metal of a sword to the conduction of Flame—that was silly, the Power and mundane sorceries are two entirely different disciplines. But I tried it. I tried swords of wood, and ivory, and horn, and bone, but those didn't work. I finally started forging my own swords and using my blood at various stages—melding it with the metal, tempering the sword with it, writing runes on the blade with it."

"Nothing, though."

"Well, not quite. Once, the business with the runes, that began to feel as if it would work—almost. Not quite, though. There was a stirring—something was starting to happen—but the sword still felt wrong. Most of them do. It could be they're right about the dichotomy between swords and life."

"Maybe you need to know your Name," Segnbora said.

Herewiss went stiff for a moment, feeling threatened by the subject. The matter of Names wasn't usually mentioned in casual conversation, and certainly not between two people who had just met. But Segnbora's tone was noncommittal, and her expression reserved: she shifted her eyes away as he looked at her. Herewiss relaxed a little.

"Maybe," he said, looking away himself, his fingers playing idly with the empty scabbard. "But I don't know how to find it. I mean, I'm not all that sure who I'm supposed to *be*. I have ideas—but it's like water in a sieve. I pour myself into them, into this role, or that identity, and they won't hold me. I'm a passable sorcerer—"

"A little more than passable."

"Yes, well—but that's not what I want to be. Sorcery is an imposition on the environment, a forcing, a rape. The Power is a meshing, a cooperation, like love. You don't *make* rain: you *ask* it to, and usually it will, if you ask it nicely. You know that. I have no desire to be just a very talented rapist, when I have the potential to be a lover, even a clumsy one. So . . . I'm all right as a warrior, but I don't have a sword; and I don't want to kill anyone anyway. I'm a good scholar, I know six dead Darthene dialects and four Arlene ones, I can read runes a thousand years old. But there's more to life than sitting around translating rotting manuscripts. I'm not much of a prince—"

Segnbora's eyebrows went up. "My Goddess. You're *that* Hearn's son? I didn't make the connection—that's a fairly common name up north."

Herewiss bowed slightly from the waist, smiling. "The same."

"And I thought *my* family was impressive. I'm sorry; please go on."

"Well, there's not much to say about it, really. I don't know—I'm so many people, and no one of them is all of *me*—"

Segnbora nodded. "I know the problem."

"There was a while when I was giving the problem a lot of thought: I said to myself, 'Well, maybe the Power will follow if the Name is there.' So I tried all the ways I could think of to find out. Fasting—yes, you know how that is—and a lot of time spent in meditation. Too much. Once I sat down and turned everything inward, *everything*, and what happened was that I got stuck inside and couldn't find my way out again. I rattled around in the dark and struck out at the walls, but they seemed to be mirrored—and I found myself thinking that if I hit the walls, I would hurt the inside of *me*—and there were voices in the dark, some of them seemed to belong to my parents, or to people I knew: some of them were kind, but some were ugly and twisted—I didn't get out by myself. It just wore off three days later, and I woke up stiff and sore and hungrier than I had been when I started, if that's possible. I won't go that way again. I might never get out."

Segnbora stretched her arms over her head and let them drop to encircle her knees again. "I heard it said

133

once," she said, so softly that Herewiss had to strain to hear her, "—oh, a long time back—that to find your Name, you have to turn the mind and heart, not inward, but outward rather: that you have to live outward, paying no attention to the voices in the dark— or, rather, accepting them for what they are, but taking their advice only when it pleases you, and not allowing yourself to be driven by them. Looking always forward and outward, not back and in."

"Nice," Herewiss said. "I understand *that* not at all. How can you get to know yourself by looking *out*? Who other than yourself can tell you what you are, or what you're going to be?"

"I don't know. I haven't found my Name, either. Maybe I never will."

They sat there in depressed but companionable silence for a while. Then Herewiss looked up and grinned at Segnbora. "Well," he said. "Maybe I can't command wind and wave, but I *can* do this much—"

He cupped his hands before him, and beside him Segnbora leaned close to watch. Herewiss closed his eyes, reached down inside him, found the flicker of Flame within him, breathed softly on the little light, encouraged it, cherished it, and then willed—

It flowed there in his outstretched hands, a tiny wavering bloom of fire that grew and bent in the wind of his will: as vividly blue as a little child's eyes, with a hot white core like a newsprung star, but gently warm in his hands—

It went out, and he folded his hands together and strove to thank the Power in him, rather than cursing at it for being so feeble. He looked at Segnbora. "Can you?"

She smiled at him. "Watch," she said, and reached out before her as if to support something that Herewiss could not see, hanging in the air. It came before he was ready for it, sudden, brilliant, so bluely brilliant that it outraged his eyes and left dancing violet afterimages; a lightning flash, a starflower, a little sun, hanging in the air between her hands. For a moment there was an odd blue day in the desert, and everything had two shadows, sharp short black ones laid over long dull streaks of red-purple light and darkness. Then the light went out, and Segnbora let her hands fall. "As you see," she said, "I can't maintain it; there's too much intensity. Maybe I can find work as a lighthouse beacon."

Herewiss looked up at Dritt, who still sat on his rock, unconcerned, eating. He had spared them no more than a curious glance. "Do you do this often?" Herewiss said.

"Every now and then, in dark places. They've seen it before, they think it's an illusion. None of them but Freelorn would know the real wreaking from sorcery if it walked up and bit them. And Freelorn has never said anything about it.—Oh, here he comes now—"

They stood up, and Herewiss wobbled for a moment as a wave of dizziness washed over him. He made a mental note to be careful of the backlash for the next couple days. Four forms on horseback were approaching slowly, and the horse in the lead had a young desert deer slung over its withers.

Herewiss stood there, his hands on his hips, and watched the figure in the saddle of the lead horse. Their eyes met while the riders were still a ways off, and Herewiss watched the smile spread over Freelorn's face, and felt his own grow to match it. The horse ambled along toward the camp, and Freelorn made no attempt to hurry it. An old memory spoke up in Freelorn's voice. "I hate long goodbyes," it said, looking over a cup of wine drained some years before, "but I love long hellos. . . ."

(Are you going to do it now?) Sunspark asked, with interest.

(Do what?)

(Unite.)

(Ah, hells, Spark! Don't ask questions like that. It's not polite.)

(Not what?)

(Oh, Mother of everything. . . . No, Spark, we're *not* going to unite right now. Hush up.)

The group drew rein and dismounted, and Herewiss glanced at them only briefly. They all looked about the same as they had when he had last seen them. Lang, a great golden bear of a man, slid down out of his saddle like a sack of meal, grinned and winked at Herewiss, and went off to start a fire in the lee of the boulder. Tall, skinny, cold-eyed Moris with his beaky nose swung down from his horse, nodded to Herewiss and spoke a word of greeting: but his eyes were mostly for big Dritt, still up on the rock, and for him Moris' eyes warmed as he climbed to sit beside him. Harald, a short, round, sparse-bearded man, staggered past with the deer over his shoulder; he waved a hand at Herewiss and hurried past him, puffing.

And then Freelorn eased himself out of the saddle. Segnbora went quietly off to help Lang with the fire. Herewiss went slowly and calmly to meet his friend—

—and was hugging him hard before he knew what happened, his face crunched down against Freelorn's shoulder, and much to his own surprise, tears burning hot and sudden in his eyes as Freelorn hugged him back. *Five-in-Heaven, did I really miss him that much? I guess I did. . . .*

(Goodness!) someone commented in the background. (Where are the progeny?)

(Sunspark, *what* within the walls of the world are you talking about?) Herewiss said in laughing irritation as he prolonged the hug.

(That wasn't union? I thought you had changed your mind and decided to go ahead. You give off discharges like that just for *greeting* each other? Isn't that wasteful?)

(Oh, Sunspark, later.)

Herewiss and Freelorn held each other away a little, and Freelorn was laughing, and sniffling a little too.

"Goddess Mother of us all, look at you!" he said. "You're bigger than you were. You *cheat*, dammit!"

"No, I don't. Lorn, your mustache is longer, you look like a Steldene."

"That was the idea, for a while. Look at the *arms* on you! That's what it is. What the Shadow have you been doing?"

"I'm a swordsmith," Herewiss said. "I hammer a lot. If you want to look like this, you can, but it'll take you a year or so. That's how long I've been at it. Lorn, you twit, what's the use of trying to look like a Steldene if you're going to wear *that* around?" He nodded at Freelorn's black surcoat, charged with the Arlene arms, the white Lion passant guardant uplifting His great silver blade.

"Who's going to see it out here?"

"That's not the point. You were wearing it in Madeil, weren't you?"

"No—my other one got stolen out of my saddlebag. Let me tell you what happened—"

"I can imagine. For such an accomplished thief, you get stolen from awfully easily. How many times have I—oh, never mind, come on, sit down and tell me. Tell me everything. We haven't talked since—Goddess!—since not last Opening Night, but the one before. When you came to the Wood."

"Yeah." They sat down by a chair-sized boulder and put their backs to it. Herewiss slid an arm around Freelorn's shoulders. "Let's see, let's see—" Freelorn chewed his mustache a bit. "After we left the Wood, we went west a ways—stayed in the empty country east of Darthis until spring came. And then south. We made a big wide detour around Darthis, didn't even cross the Darst until Peaksend or so—"

"That is quite a detour. Any trouble?"

"No. That was the interesting thing, though. One Darthene patrol stopped us and I was *sure* they knew who I really was. I lied splendidly about everything, though, and they let us go. You wouldn't know anything about that, would you?"

Herewiss laughed softly. "Oddly enough, I would. My father has been exchanging letters with Eftgan recently, and the Queen is not happy with Cillmod and the cabal in Arlen. Not at all. She told Hearn in one letter that she considers the real Arlene government to be in exile. Right now she doesn't dare openly support or recognize you: she's so new to the Throne, and she hasn't got the power balances among the Four Hundred completely worked out yet. But because of the Oath of Lion and Eagle she feels obligated to do *something* for you. Those guards may or may not have known who you were—but if they did, they had orders to let you pass unhindered. You're safe in Darthen, so long as you don't make yourself so visible that they have no choice but to notice you."

"What about public opinion?"

"I think that may have influenced her a little. Most of Darthen is in outrage over Cillmod having the gall to break Oath. Especially the country around Hadremark, where a lot of people went homeless after the burning, and all the crops were ruined. But Eftgan's hands are tied. She can't really move against Arlen, or she'd be breaking Oath herself. She's strengthened the garrisons on the Arlid border, but there are ways to sneak past those. She even went so far as to ask the human Marchwarders in Darthen to talk to the Dragons, ask *their* help—but the answer is pretty likely to be the same as usual. The Dragons won't get involved."

"Granted."

"So in a way, you're her best hope. The story running in Darthen seems to be that you're alive and traveling around to raise force so that you can get Arlen back. The people seem to approve. They want the Lion's Child back on the Throne again, much for their own welfare as for yours."

Freelorn nodded. " 'Darthen's House and Arlen's Hall,' " he recited,

> " 'share their feast and share their fall—
> Fórlennh's and Hergótha's blade
> are of the same metal made,
> and the Oath they sealed shall bind
> both their dest'nies intertwined—' "

" 'Till the end of countries, when
Lion and Eagle come again,' " Herewiss finished. "You always did like that one."

"I recite it nightly," Freelorn said with a somewhat sour expression, "and hope that both our countries live through this interregnum."

"They'll manage, I think. But after you went south, what?"

"We went a little more to the west, nearly to the Arlene border—" Freelorn went on, telling of a close encounter with a large group of bandits, but Herewiss wasn't really listening with all of him. He nodded and "mm-hmm"ed in the appropriate places, but most of his mind was too full of the sight and nearness of Freelorn—the compactness of him, the quick brilliant eyes and fiery temperament, the bright sharp voice, the ability to care about a whole country as warmly as he could about one man—

Herewiss' memory flicked suddenly back to one of those long golden afternoons in Prydon castle. He had been stretched out on Freelorn's bed, staring absently at the ceiling, and Freelorn sat by the window, picking at the strings of his lute and trying to get control of his newly changed voice. He was singing the Oath poem with a kind of quiet exultation, looking forward to the time when he would be King and help to keep it true: and the soft promising melody wound upward through the warm air. Herewiss, relaxed and drifting easily toward sleep, was wound in a daydream of his own—of a future day brightly lit by the blue sun of his own released Flame. Then suddenly he was startled awake again by a shudder of foreboding, a cold touch of prescience trailing down his spine. A brief flicker-vision of *this* moment, lit by a fading sunset instead of the brilliance of midafternoon. The same poem, but not sung: the same Freelorn, but not King: the same Herewiss, but not—

"—and left them in our dust—What's the matter? Getting cold?"

"No, Lorn, it was just a shudder. The Goddess spoke my Name, most likely."

"Yeah. So, anyway, we left the southeast and came back this way. Stopped at Madeil, and that's where my surcoat got stolen."

"Your good one, I suppose."

"Yeah. I don't seem to have much luck with them, do I? They've probably sold it for the silver by now. But word of whose it was got out, and evidently the Steldenes have been feeling the weight of Cillmod's threats, since they sent all those people after us. I didn't believe it. I said to myself, when they came piling up outside that old keep, I said, 'Time to call in help.' Which I did. Goddess, what a display that was."

"Thank you."

"Are you all right? I mean, that messenger, and the fireball, and the Lion—oh, the Lion! That was beautiful. Beautiful. Just the way He always looks to me . ."

"Oh. You see Him regularly?"

"Shut up! You know what I mean. But are you all right?"

"Just a touch wobbly—it'll pass in a couple of days. I never did anything on that scale before. In fact, I didn't know I had it in me. I guess I found out . . ."

Freelorn laughed softly. "I dare say. But listen: what have you been doing?"

Herewiss shrugged, trying to think of some way to put a cheerful face on a year's worth of broken swords, wasted time, and pain. He couldn't, and anyway, Freelorn would have caught him at it.

"Forging swords," he said. "I got tired of breaking old ones. At one point Hearn offered me Fánderë—he thought that since the legend says that Earn forged it, it might be a little more amenable to the Power—but I just couldn't. That sword is older than the first Woodward, and I knew I would destroy it. It was just as dead to the touch as all the others. So finally I apprenticed myself to old Darg the blacksmith. You remember Darg—"

"I certainly do. The old one-eyed gent with the lovely daughter. I think you had ulterior motives."

Herewiss laughed. "Not really. Though I could tell you that Méren and I came of age at the same time, and since we had always been best friends, we decided to relieve one another of the Responsibility as soon as we could. She had twins—they'll be coming to the Ward for fostering soon, since Mother left no love-children behind her. Goddess, I miss them—they're nine now: though Halwerd always reminds me that he's a quarter-hour older than Holmaern. He helps me with the forging sometimes, working the bellows. I put a forge together up in the north tower, and he watches me working the metal, and asks a thousand questions about tensile strength and temper and edge. He has a blacksmith's heart, that one, and he's going to have to be Lord of the Brightwood after me. I don't think he really approves."

"The business with swords made of griffin-bone and ivory and such—I take it that didn't work."

"No. What use is a sword made of ivory? It seems that it *has* to be a working sword. Yet a real sword is an instrument of death—and to make it carry life—"

"You'll find a way."

"I wish I had your faith in me."

Freelorn stretched a little, discomfort and concern flickering across his face. "Well, whatever—you'll keep trying. Where are you going now? Back home?"

"I'm heading east."

"From *here*?"

"From here."

"But Herewiss—listen, it was a brilliant idea to head this far east—even if they'd had their supplies intact, they wouldn't follow us this close to the Waste. But another fifteen miles or so will take you right up to the Stel—"

"I don't intend to stop there, Lorn. On the way down here I came by some interesting information—" Briefly he told of his encounter with the innkeeper's daughter, and what she had told him. Freelorn nodded.

"There's an Old place like that down by Bluepeak in Arlen, just under the mountains," he said, "though it must not be as haunted, or whatever—the Dragons took it as a Marchward some years ago, and there are human Marchwarders there too. This place, though— if the Dragons won't go near it, I don't like the idea of your going there. What do you want it for, anyway?"

"There are supposed to be *doors*, Lorn. It could be that I could use one of them to go across into a Middle Kingdom where males have Flame, and train there. Or if there's no *door* that goes there already, I might be able to *make* one of them do it—"

"How?" Freelorn said, all skepticism. "Worldgates are supposed to be a Flame-related manifestation, since they're partly alive, aren't they? I mean, you need wreaking to open them. When Béaneth went to Rilthor, even though it was Opening Night and a full Moon, she still needed Fire for the Morrowfane *Door*. And there's that story about the Hilarwit, and Raela Way-opener, and it's always Flame—"

Herewiss listened patiently. He had had this argument with himself more than once. "So?"

"So! I don't think you can do it like that! You need control of Flame, and you haven't got it—"

"You could be right."

"And—what?"

"What you're saying is true, Lorn, as far as we know. According to the old stories, which usually have truth in them. But each instance is different. And if you're going to quote examples, well, what about Béorgan? Despite her expertise and her power and all the information she had access to, she still couldn't have had all the facts. Why else would she have bothered trying to kill the Lover's Shadow, when He was just going to come back?"

"She was driven," Freelorn said, "by her desire for vengeance. It blinded her."

"Maybe. That's not the point. The *point* is that I have to try. There's no telling till I do. It may be that those *doors* are set to turn to the use of whatever mind or power comes along. And it may not. But it's a place of the Old wreaking, which was always Flame-based, and damned if I'm not going to try tapping it."

"Herewiss, you're not seeing what you're getting into—"

"Lorn, are you scared for me?"

Freelorn, who had been warming to the prospect of a good argument, opened his mouth, shut it, and scowled at Herewiss, a dark stabbing look from beneath his bushy eyebrows. "Yes, dammit," he said at last.

"Then why don't you just *say* so."

Freelorn made a face. "All right. But I spent a lot of time in the Archive, and I know more about Flame and its uses from my reading than most Rodmistresses do—"

"Reading about it and having it are two different things. No, Lorn, don't start another mad. Do you think I don't appreciate all the research you did? But theory and practice are different, and I'm not a usual case. And look at us: half an hour together, after almost a year apart, and already we're fighting."

"Tension. I'm still nervous from two nights ago."

"Fear. You're afraid for me."

"*Yes!* You want to go poking around in some bloody pile of stones in the middle of nowhere and nothing, a place that was there since before the Dragons came, for

Goddess' sake!—and which *they* won't go near because it's too dangerous. Damn right I'm afraid! How would you feel if our positions were reversed?"

Herewiss gave the thought its due, and did his best to put himself in Freelorn's place for a moment. "Scared, I guess."

"Petrified."

"And how would *you* feel if our positions were reversed?"

Freelorn sighed and let his hunched-up shoulders sag. "Scared too, I suppose."

"Yeah. But I have to go."

Freelorn nodded. "You have gotten a little too big to sit on." The sudden bittersweet memory looked at Herewiss across the span of years: the day after Herelaf died, and Herewiss drowning in a brine-bitter sea of pain and self-hatred, wanting desperately to kill himself. Trying and trying to do it, first with the sword that had killed Herelaf, then with anything that came to hand—knives, open windows. Freelorn, filled to overflowing with exasperation, fear for Herewiss, and his own pain, finally knocked Herewiss down and sat on him until the tears broke loose in both of them and they wept to exhaustion, clutching at each other.

"I have," Herewiss said, setting the memory aside with a sigh.

"Well, then, I'm coming with."

"Of course," Herewiss said.

Freelorn's eyebrows went up. "You sneaky bastard—"

Herewiss grinned. "It was a good way to make sure you realized what you were getting into before you said yes."

Freelorn grinned back. "I'm still coming with you."

"And the rest?"

"They're with me. We couldn't stop them from coming along. This is better—much better than you going alone."

"Yes, it is."

(And what am I, then?) Sunspark said indignantly.

144

(An elemental, Spark. But people need people.)

(I don't understand that. If you say so . . .) It went back to its grazing.

"And besides," Herewiss added, "I can use someone else who's well read in matters of Flame and such—you may see things about the place that I wouldn't."

"I don't want to see any 'things.' "

"Lorn, please."

"Did you talk to Segnbora?"

"Yes. Very interesting person. She should be of great help to us too. How did she happen to join up with you? She didn't mention."

"Oh, it was in Madeil. It was how I found out that my surcoat had gone missing. We were in this inn, drinking quietly and minding our own business, when in come a bunch of King's guardsmen looking for me! Well, the lot of us got out of there, with the guards chasing us in five different directions. I went down a dead end, though, and the one who'd followed me cornered me there. I was pretty hard pressed, he was a lot bigger than I was, and just a little faster. And all of a sudden this shadow with a sword in its hand just melts out of the alley wall and *ffft!* the guy sprouts a hand's length of sword under the breastbone. It was her; she'd followed me from the inn. There she stands, and she bows a little. 'King's son of Arlen,' she says, 'well met, but if we don't hurry out of here you're going to be neck-deep in dungeon, with King Dariw's torturer dancing on your head.' It seemed a good point."

"I could see where it would, yes."

"So off we went, back to the inn again. Up she went, cool as you please, got our things from our rooms. The innkeeper sees her, and he says, 'Madam, if you please, where are you going with those?' and Segnbora smiles at him and says, 'Sir, if you want every skin of wine or tun of ale in your place to get the rot, ask on. Otherwise—' and out the door she goes, gets the horses from the stables and rides off. We met her a few streets away and got out of there in a hurry."

Herewiss chuckled. "I wonder why she did it."

"I asked her. Evidently she's related to one of the Forty Noble Houses, and she said something about '*They* may not hold by the Oath, but *I* do, by Goddess—' I believe her."

"I think you can."

Freelorn smiled a little. "Well, this venture will be safer with all of us along. Damn, I hope you're right about the *doors!* Suppose there was one into an Arlen where I'm King—"

"You'd be there already. And how would you feel if you *were* King, and another Freelorn popped out of nowhere to contest your claim to the Throne?"

"I'd—uhh."

"—kill the bastard? Very good. Better stay here and do what you can with *this* world."

Freelorn looked at Herewiss and smiled again, but this time his eyes were grave.

"Come on," he said, "let's see how dinner is doing."

Stars shone on them again; this time the warm constellations of Spring, Dolphin and Maiden and Flamesteed and Stave. The Lion stood near the zenith, the red star of its heart glittering softly through the still air.

They held one another close, and closer yet, and found to their delight that nothing seemed to have changed between them.

(Well?) someone said out of the darkness.

(Well what?) Herewiss answered. (No, let me guess. "Where are the progeny," right?)

(Mmp, yes.)

(Spark, I thought I explained it to you. It doesn't work that way. We're both males. And even if we weren't. . . .)

Herewiss caught the clear image of Sunspark looking outward into otherness, toward the unimaginable heart of the Pattern, as a man might roll his eyes up

146

and ask the Goddess' help. (I know. Later,) it said, and withdrew.

Herewiss sighed, and smiled, and held Freelorn closer.

After a while, a quiet chuckle in the darkness.

"Hmm?"

"Lorn, you remember that first time we shared at your place?"

"That was a long time ago."

"It seems that way."

"—and my father yelled up the stairs, 'What are you doooooooing?' "

"—and you yelled back, 'We're *fuck*innnnnnnnnng!' "

"—and it was quiet for so long—"

"—and then he started laughing—"

"He didn't stop for days."

"Yeah."

A silence.

"You know, he really loved you. He always wanted another son. He always used to say that now he had one."

Silence.

"Lorn—one way or another, I'm going to see you on your throne."

"Get your Power first."

"Yeah. But then we get your Throne back for you. I think I owe him that."

"Your Power first. He was concerned about that."

"Yes . . . he would have been. Well, we'll see."

A pause. A desert owl floated silently overhead and away, like a wandering ghost.

"Dusty?"

Herewiss started a little. No one had called him by that name since Herelaf's death.

"What?"

"After I'm King—what will you do?"

"I haven't the faintest idea."

"Really?"

"I haven't thought about it much. I don't let myself.—Heal the sick, I guess, talk to Dragons—make it rain when it's dry—travel around—walk the Otherworlds—"

There was a sinking silence under the blankets: suddenly disappointment and fear flavored the air like smoke. "??" Herewiss said, confused by the perception. His underhearing sometimes manifested itself at odd moments, but never without reason.

"Dusty—don't forget me."

"Forget you? Forget you! How do I forget my loved? Lorn, put it out of your mind. How could I forget you? If only fr—"

Herewiss cut himself off, shocked, hearing the thought complete itself inside his head. "—*from all the trouble you've caused me—*"

"From what?"

My Goddess. How can I think such a thing? What's the matter *with me!!* "—from the fact that you're the best lay in four kingdoms and nine principalities—"

He put all his conviction into the words; certainly the statement was true as far as he was concerned. He heard Freelorn pause, weigh the words, their timing, the emotion behind them, to see if they were real or faked. Then Freelorn made a small sound in his throat, a brief quiet sigh of acceptance. "You're not bad yourself," he said.

"Again?"

"Why not? The night is young."

"And so are we."

148

SIX

Whatever may be said of the Goddess, this much is certain; She enjoys a good joke. For proof of this, examine yourself or any other member of the human race closely—and then laugh along with Her.

Deeds of the Heroes, 18, vi

"I thought you said it was just another fifteen miles."

"Well, I thought it was . . ."

"Maybe the river changed its banks."

"The Stel? Unlikely. Maybe I got us lost."

"Likely."

The seven of them rode along through country that was becoming increasingly inhospitable. The gently rolling scrub country of northern Steldin had given way to near-desert terrain. It was afternoon, and hot. A steady, maddening east wind blew dust into their eyes, and into their horses' eyes, down their collars and up their sleeves, into their boots and even their undertunics. Even the most casual movement would sand some part of the body raw.

Herewiss sighed. For the past two hours or so Freelorn had been straining his eyes toward the horizon, swearing at himself for having lost the river. He had been abusing himself so skillfully that Herewiss, in exasperation, had joined in and helped him for a few minutes. Now he was regretting it.

"Lorn, Lorn, the Dark with it," he said. "You *can't* lose the Stel. If you just go east far enough, you're bound to run into it."

"It is possible," Freelorn said tightly, "to lose just about anything."

"Including your mind, if you work at it hard enough. Lorn, relax. Worse things could happen."

"Oh?"

"Certainly. A cohort of Fyrd could find us. Or the Dark Hunt. Or the Goddess could sneeze and forget to keep the world in place, and we'd all go out like candles. Don't be so grim, Lorn. It'll work out all right."

Freelorn's poor Blackmane, half-blind with the dust, sneezed mightily and them bumped sideways into Sunspark. Herewiss' mount didn't respond, but Blackmane danced away with a whicker of scorched surprise, nearly throwing Freelorn out of the saddle. He regained his balance and looked suspiciously at the stallion.

"None of our horses care much for that one of yours," he said. "What happened to Darrafed?"

"She's home."

"Dapple?"

"He was with me part-way. I sent him back."

"Is that safe?"

Herewiss laughed. "Safe? Dapple? He'll probably rescue a princess on the way home."

"Where did this one come from, then?"

"I don't know," Herewiss said, which was certainly the truth. "I found him."

"I know that look," Freelorn said. "You've got a secret."

Herewiss said nothing, and tried to keep from smiling.

"I know that look too. 'You will find out in the proper time,'" Freelorn said in a squeaky imitation of some earlier Herewiss' voice. "Well, whatever . . . Are those trees?"

Herewiss squinted. "No. Those are rocks."

"Are you sure?"

"Yes."

"Wonderful. Where the Dark is the river!!!"

"It'll be along. Lorn, you didn't tell me. What were you doing in Madeil?"

"Oh . . . I was meeting a man who was supposed to know a way into the Royal Treasury at Osta. He had been there as a guard some years back, but he moved to Steldin when my father died and everything was going crazy."

"Did you meet him?"

"Oh, yes. That was what we had been at the tavern for. It was about half an hour after he left that the guards came in."

"Why were you still there?"

Freelorn looked guilty. "Well . . . it had been so long since any of us had a chance to get really drunk."

"So you did it there in the middle of a city, with all those people around who you didn't know? Lorn, you know you get talky when you're drunk . . . what if you'd spilled something?"

Freelorn said nothing for a second, said it so forcefully that Herewiss went after the unspoken thought with his underhearing to try to catch it. . . . *talk about being drunk*, it said in a wash of anger, . . . *what about Herelaf?* And then it was smashed down by a hammer of Freelorn's guilt. *How can I think things like that? . . . wasn't his fault . . .*

Herewiss winced away. *Even Lorn*, he thought. And then, *Goddess, did I do that? If this is the kind of thing I'd be doing with the Power, maybe I'm better without it.*

"I'm sorry," he said aloud. "Lorn, really."

"No—you're right, I guess. But we did find out about the way into the Treasury—there's a passage in off the river that no one knows about."

"What about the guards who are there?"

"There aren't many left who know about it—all the lower-level people have been replaced by mercenaries, and many of the higher levels left in a hurry when Cillmod had me outlawed. They could see the way

151

things were going to be going. At present that entrance isn't being guarded."

"What sort of things do they have there?"

"No treasure, no jewelry—just plain old money. My contact said that there are usually about fourteen thousand talents of silver there at any one time."

"What are you thinking of?"

"My Goddess, you have to ask?"

"No . . . not really. Lorn, do you think you have any chance to pull this off?"

Freelorn hesitated for a long moment. "Maybe."

Caution?! Herewiss thought. *He's being* cautious? *I'm in trouble.*

"Are you *sure* those are rocks?"

"Yes. Lorn, how many people do you think you're going to need to get into the place?"

"Oh . . . my own group will be enough."

Ten would be better. Herewiss thought glumly, *and twenty better still. More realistic, surely.* "Don't do it," he said out loud.

"Why not? It's the perfect chance to get enough money to finance the revolution—"

"Your father should be an example to you," Herewiss said tiredly, "that no one supports a dead King."

"A what?"

Herewiss sighed. "I'd like to see your plans before you go ahead and do it," he said. "Maybe I'll come with and help you. But Lorn!—I don't believe that five people are going to be enough."

"Six.—Those *are* trees, dammit!"

"Six," Herewiss said softly, watching Freelorn kick Blackmane into a gallop.

(Is he always so optimistic?) Sunspark asked.

(Usually more so.)

(Will not this additional foray keep you from getting back to the work you have to do?)

(Yes, it will—)

Herewiss thought about it for a moment. *The timing,* he thought, *until now I had always thought it was*

coincidental. But the timing is just a little too close—
oh, Dark. What can I do?

(What?)

(I was thinking to myself. Catch up with him, will you, Spark?)

(Certainly. He was right, by the way—those are trees—)

(How can you tell? I can't see them too well with the dust, I admit, but—)

(I can feel the water. I hope there's a bridge there; I'm not going to take a ford in what they would consider the normal fashion.)

(So jump it, Spark. They're already sure that you're not quite natural: a spectacular leap won't give much away at this point.)

They drew even with Freelorn again. "Rocks indeed!" he shouted over the noise of the horses' hooves. "Your eyes are going bad."

"Too much reading, probably."

"Yeah. Look—there's a house, I think—"

"Where?"

"A little to the left. See it?"

"Uh—I think so. The dust makes it hard. Who would live out here, Lorn? There's not a town or village for miles in any direction, and this is practically the Waste!"

"Maybe whoever lives there wants some peace and quiet."

"Quiet, maybe. Peace? With the Waste full of Fyrd?"

"Well, maybe it isn't, really. How would anyone know? If there's nothing much living in the Waste, there can't be many Fyrd, either. Even Fyrd have to live on something."

"It makes sense. There *are* so many stories—Lorn, that's an awfully big house. It looks more like an inn to me."

The rest of Freelorn's people gradually closed with the two of them. "What's the hurry?" yelled Dritt.

153

Freelorn pointed ahead. "Hot food tonight, I think—"

They slowed down somewhat as they approached the river. It was running high in its banks, for the thaw was still in progress in the Highpeaks to the south. Trees lined the watercourse for almost as far as they could see, from south to north. These were not the gnarled little scrub-trees of the desert country, but huge old oaks and maples and silver birches. Though they leaned backward a little on the western bank, their growth shaped by the relentless east wind out of the Waste, they still gave an impression of striving hungrily for the water. Branches bright with flowers reached across the water to tangle with others just becoming green. Somewhere in the foliage a songbird, having recovered from the sudden advent of all these people, was trying out a few experimental notes.

"It *is* an inn," Freelorn said. "There's the sign— though I can't make out what's on it. Let's go."

"Lorn," Herewiss said, "how has your money been holding up?"

"I am so broke," Freelorn said cheerfully, "that—"

"Never mind, I have a little. Lorn, you're *always* broke, it seems."

"Makes life more interesting."

Usually for other people, Herewiss thought. *Oh Dark! I'm cranky today.*

"—and besides, if I spend it as fast as I get it, then no one can steal it from me."

"That's a point."

Herewiss frowned with concentration as he did the math in his head. *Prices will probably be higher out here—say, three-quarters of an eagle or so—and there's seven of us . . . so that's . . . uhh . . . damn, I hate fractions! . . . well, it can't be more than seven. Wonderful, all I have is five. Maybe the innkeeper'll let us do dishes . . .*

The inn was a tidy-looking place of fieldstone and mortar, with three sleeping wings jutting off in various directions from the large main building. A few of the many windows of diamond-paned glass stood open, as did the door of the stable, which was set off from the inn proper. A neat path of white stone led down from the dooryard of the inn, past the innsign, a neatly painted board that said FERRY TAVERN, and down to the riverbank, where it met a little fishing pier. Just to the right of the pier was the ferry, a wooden platform attached to ropes and pulleys so that it could be pulled across from one side of the river to the other whether anyone was on it or not.

The place was marvelously pleasant after the long ride through the dry empty country. They dismounted and led their horses into the dooryard, savoring the shade and the cool fragrance of the air. The inn was surrounded by huge apple-trees, all in flower: the only exception was the great tree that shaded the dooryard proper, a wide-crowned blackstave with its long trembling olive-and-silver leaves. Its flowers had already fallen, and carpeted the grass and gravel like an unseasonable snowfall.

"Goddess, what a lovely place," Freelorn said.

"I just hope we can afford it. Well, go knock on the door and find out—"

"You have the money, *you* do it."

"This is *your* bunch of people, Lorn—"

The door opened, and a lady walked out, and stood on the slate doorstep, drying her hands on her apron. "Good day to you!" she said, smiling. "Can I help you?"

They all stood there for a second or so, just appreciating her, before any of them began considering answers to the question. She was quite tall, a little taller even than Herewiss. The plain wide-sleeved shirt and breeches and boots she wore beneath the white apron did nothing to conceal her splendidly proportioned figure. She was radiantly beautiful, with the delicate translucent complexion of a country girl and eyes as green as grass. What lines her face had seemed all from smiling, but her eyes spoke of gravity and formidable intelligence, and her bearing of quiet strength and power. She wore her coiled and braided hair like a dark crown.

"Ahem!" Freelorn said. "Uh, yes, maybe you can. We're interested in staying the night—"

"Just interested?" she asked, raising an eyebrow. "You're not sure?—Is it a money problem?"

"Well, lady, not really," Herewiss began, still gazing at her with open admiration. *Oh my,* he was thinking, *I never gave much thought to having more than one loved at a time—but I might start thinking about it now. She's like a tree, she just radiates strength—but she's got flowers, too—*

She looked back at him, a measuring glance, a look of calm assessment, and then smiled again. It was like day breaking. "It's been a long time since anyone was here," she said. "Let's take it out in trade. If you're agreeable, let one of you share with me tonight, and we'll call it even. You're leaving tomorrow, I take it—"

They nodded assent.

"Then it's settled. Go on in, make yourselves comfortable. Two tubrooms on the ground floor if anyone wants a bath—I'll help with the water after I've taken care of your horses. Dinner's two hours before sunset.— Go on, then!" she said, laughing, stepping down from the doorstep and shooing them like chickens. Bemused, Freelorn and his people started going inside.

Herewiss turned to lead Sunspark toward the stable. "No, no," said the lady innkeeper, coming up beside him and reaching across Herewiss to take the reins.

"Uh, he's a little—I'd better—" Herewiss started to say, watching in horror as Sunspark suddenly lifted a hoof to stomp on the lady's foot.

"It's quite all right," the lady said, and hit Sunspark a sharp blow on the nose with her left fist. The elemental danced back a step or so, its eyes wide with surprise.

The lady smiled brightly at Herewiss. "I love horses," she said, and led Sunspark away.

(Be nice!) Herewiss said.

(I think I'd better,) Sunspark replied, still surprised.

Herewiss followed the others inside and found them standing in a tight group in the middle of the cool dark common-room, all talking at once. "All right, *all right*!!" Freelorn yelled over the din. "There is no *way* to arbitrate this; we'll have to choose up for the chance."

"How about a fast game of Blade-on-the-Table? Dritt said.

"The *Dark* it would be fast—it would need six elimination hands, and I want my bath *now*. Besides, you cheat at cards. It'll—"

"I do *not*!"

"—have to be lots. Look, there's kindling over there, and some twigs: we'll draw sticks for it."

"Fine," Moris said darkly, "and who holds the sticks?"

"I'm the only one I trust not to gimmick the draw, so—"

This observation was greeted with hoots of skepticism. "What about me, Lorn?" Herewiss said. Freelorn looked at him with an expression close to dismay.

"You're right," he said. "Go ahead, give them to him—he's got an honest streak."

Herewiss received the twigs and spent a few moments snapping them to equal lengths, all but one, which he broke off shorter. He turned back to the others. "Here."

Freelorn chose first, and made an irritated face; his was long. "The river I didn't mind losing so much," he said, "but this—aagh!"

Dritt chose next and came up long also, as did Moris and Lang after him. Then Segnbora chose.

"Dammit-to-Darkness," Freelorn said, with immense chagrin. "Well, give her our best."

Segnbora smiled, tossed the short stick over her shoulder for luck, picked up her saddlebags from the floor, and headed up the stairs to find herself a room. "See you at dinner," she said.

"That could have been *me*," said Harald softly. "If I'd just gone ahead of her . . ." He followed Segnbora up the stairs.

Moris and Dritt went away, muttering, to raid the kitchen.

Lang kicked a chair irritably and went outside.

"I wish it had been me," Freelorn said quietly.

"You're not alone." Herewiss put an arm around him, hugging him. "But, Lorn—how long has it been since we had a bath together?"

Freelorn regarded Herewiss out of the corner of his eye. "Years," he said, smiling mischievously. "Though of course you remember what happened the last time—"

"Gee, I'm not sure, it was so *long* ago—"

"C'mon," Freelorn said, "let's go refresh your memory."

Everyone who had good clothes to wear, or at least clean ones, wore them to dinner that night. They sat around the big oaken table down in the common-room and admired one another openly in the candlelight. Herewiss wore the Phoenix surcoat, and Freelorn beside him wore a plain black one, still grumbling softly over the loss of his good Lion surcoat with the silver on it. Lang and Harald wore plain dark shirts with the White Eagle badge over the heart, for they had been Queen's men at the Court in Darthis before taking up with Freelorn. Dritt wore a white peasant's shirt bright with embroidery around the sleeves and collar, a farmer's festival wear: while Moris beside him looked dark and noble in the deep brown surcoat of the North Arlene Principality. Segnbora, down at the end of the table, was wearing a long black robe belted at the waist and emblazoned on one breast with a lion and upraised sword—the differenced arms of a cadet branch of one of the Forty Noble Houses of Darthen.

The food did justice to the festive dress. Dinner was cold eggs deviled with pepper and marigold leaves, roast goose in a sour sauce of lemons and sorrel, potatoes roasted in butter, and winter apples in thickened cream. Moris made a lot of noise about the eggs and the goose, claiming that the powerful spices and sours of Steldene cooking gave him heartburn; but this did not seem to affect the speed with which he ate. There also seemed to be an endless supply of wine, which the company did not let go to waste.

Once the food was served, the lady innkeeper took off her apron, sat down at the head of the table, and ate with them. In some ways she seemed a rather private person; she still had not told them her name. This was common enough practice in the Kingdoms, and her guests respected her privacy. But when she spoke at all it became obvious that she was a brilliant conversationalist, possessed of a dry witty humor that Herewiss found himself admiring even as he envied it. She seemed more interested in hearing her guests talk, though, and she was eager for news of the rest of the Kingdoms. One by one they gave her all the news they could remember: how the new Queen was doing in Darthen, the border problem with Cillmod, the great convocation of Dragons and Marchwarders at the Éorlhowe in North Arlen, the postponement of the Opening Night feast in Britfell fields. The lady put in a delicate question here or there, applying gentle leverage to the conversation, and it came around eventually to where the company had been, and why.

At this point Herewiss roused himself from a woozy and pleasurable contemplation of the wine—real Brightwood white, of three years before, from the vineyards on the north side of the wood—and started paying attention to Freelorn. Lorn had been quiet for much of the meal, especially during the discussion of Cillmod's depredations in Darthen: but as the wine had warmed in him, and even now while Herewiss listened, he dropped a word *here,* or a reference *there,* that couldn't help but make it plain to a discerning listener just who he was supposed to be. *Goddess!* Herewiss thought in a kind of still horror, *how skillfully he undermines himself. He hasn't said his name once, but she* has *to know who he is—and I doubt he's even aware of what he's doing. If I confronted him with it, he probably wouldn't understand me. Dammit-to-Darkness, he's got to watch the wine—is this what he did in Madeil? No wonder they went after him—*

Herewiss looked up at the lady and found her looking past Freelorn at him, an expression of faint discomfort on her face. Perhaps she understood something of what was happening, for she began easing the conversation gracefully away from Freelorn and was soon gossiping lightly with Segnbora about one of her relatives in Darthen.

Freelorn once again became interested in the wine, and Herewiss sighed and did the same. A little current of unease, though, still stirred on the surface of his thoughts. *Where is she getting this stuff?* he wondered. *It's a long way south from the Wood, through dangerous country. And I've never heard mention of this place—which is odd—*

There was motion at the end of the table; the lady has risen. "It's been a pleasure having you," she said. "I could go on like this all night—but I have an assignation." She smiled, and Segnbora smiled back at her, and most of Freelorn's people chuckled. "If one or two of you will help me with the dishes—maybe you two," and she indicated Dritt and Moris, "since you obviously liked the looks of my kitchen earlier—"

Everyone got up and started to help clear the table— all but Herewiss, who hated doing dishes or tablework of any kind. Out of guilt, or some other emotion perhaps, he did remove one object from the table—the carafe full of Brightwood white. He went up the stairs with it, into the deepening darkness of the second story, feeling happily wicked—and also feeling sure that someone saw him, and was smiling at his back.

Herewiss' room had a little hearth built of rounded river-stones and mortar. It also had something totally unexpected, a real treasure—two fat overstuffed chairs. Both of them were old and worn; they had been up-holstered in red velvet once, but the velvet was worn pale and smooth from much use, and was unraveling itself in places. Herewiss didn't care; they were both as good as kings' thrones to him. He had pulled one of them up close to the fire and was sitting there in happy half-drunken comfort, toasting his stocking feet. The red grimoire was open in his lap, but the light of the two candles on the table beside him wasn't really enough to read by, and he had stopped trying.

A steady presence of light at the far corner of his vision drew his attention. He looked up, and gazing across the bare fields saw the full Moon rising over the jagged stony hills to the east. It looked at him, the dark shadows on the silver face peering over the hill-crests at him like half-lidded eyes, calm and incurious.

He stared back for a moment, and then slumped in the old chair and reached out for the wine cup.

There was a soft knock at the door.

So comfortable was Herewiss that he didn't bother to get up, much less reach for his knife. "Come in," he said. The door edged open, and there was the lady innkeeper, cloaked in black against the night chill.

At sight of her Herewiss started to get up, but she waved him back into his seat. "No, stay put," she said. Pulling the other chair over by the hearthside, she sat down, pushing aside her cloak and facing the fire squarely.

Herewiss let himself just look at her for a moment. Beauty, maybe, was the wrong word for the aura that hung about her, though she certainly was beautiful. Even as she sat there at her ease, she radiated a feeling of power, of assurance in herself. More than that—a feeling of certainty, of inevitability; as if she knew exactly what she was for in the world. It lent her an air of regality, as might be expected of someone who seemed to rule herself so completely. A queenly woman, enthroned on a worn velvet chair that leaked its stuffing from various wounds and rents. Herewiss smiled at his own fancy.

"Would you like some wine?" he said.

"Yes, please."

He reached for another cup and poured for her. As he handed her the cup their hands brushed, ever so briefly. A shock ran up Herewiss' arm, a start of surprise that ran like lightning up his arm and shoulder to strike against his breastbone. It was the shock that a sensitive feels on touching a body that houses a powerful personality, and Herewiss wasn't really surprised by it. But it was *very* strong—

And he was tired, and probably over-sensitive. He lifted his cup and saluted the lady.

"You keep a fine cellar," he said. "To you."

"To you, my guest," she said, and pledged him, and drank. He drank too, and watched her over the rim of the cup. The fire lit soft lights in her hair; unbound, it was longer than he had expected, flowing down dark and shimmering past her waist. Some of it lay in her lap, night-dark against the white linen of her shift and the green cord that belted it.

"This is lovely stuff," Herewiss said. "How are you getting it all the way down here from the Brightwood?"

The lady smiled. "I have my sources," she said.

She lowered her cup and held it in her lap, staring into the fire. The wine was working strongly in Herewiss now, so that his mind wandered a little and he looked out the window. The Moon was all risen above the peaks now, and the two dark eyes were joined by a mouth making an "o" of astonishment. He wondered what the Moon saw that shocked her so.

"Herewiss," the lady said, and he turned back to look at her. The expression she wore was odd. Her face was sober, maybe a little sad, but her eyes were bright and testing, as if there was an answer she wanted from him.

"Lady?"

"Herewiss," she said, "how many swords have you broken now?"

Alarm ran through him, but it was dulled; by the wine, and by the look on her face—not threatening, not even curious, but only weary. It looked like Freelorn's face when he asked the same question, and the voice sounded like Freelorn's voice. Tired, pitying, maybe a bit impatient.

"Fifty-four," he said, "about thirty or thirty-five of my own forging. I broke the last one the day I left the Wood."

"And the Forest Altars were no help to you."

"None. I've also spoken with Rodmistresses who don't hold with the ways of the Forest Orders or the Wardresses of the Precincts, but there was nothing *they* could do for me either. But, lady, how do you know about this? No one knew except for my father, and Lorn—"

He looked at her in sudden horror. Had Lorn been so indiscreet as to mention the blue Fire—

She shook her head at him, smiling, and was silent. For a while she gazed into the fire, and then said, "And how old are you now?"

"Twenty-eight," he said, shortly, like an unhappy child.

The lady rubbed her nose and leaned back in her chair until her pose almost matched Herewiss'. "You feel your time growing short, I take it."

"Even if I had control of the Power right now," Herewiss said, "it would be starting to wane. I'd have, oh, ten years to use it if I didn't overextend myself. Which I would," he added, smiling a little at himself. "Oh, I would."

"How so?" She was looking at him again, a little intrigued, a little bemused.

Herewiss drained his cup and stared into the fire. "Really! If I came into my Power, there I'd be, the first male since Earn and Héalhra to bear Flame. That is, if the first use didn't kill me. Think of the fame! Think of the fortune!" He laughed a little. "And think of the wreaking," he said, more gently, his face softening, "think of the storms I could still, the lives I could save, the roads I could walk. The roads . . ."

He poured himself another cup of wine. "The roads in the sky, and past it," he said. "The roads the Dragons know. The ways between the Stars. Ten years would be too high an estimate. Better make it seven, or five. I'd burn myself out like a levinbolt." He drank deeply, and set the cup down again. "But what a way to go."

The lady watched him, her head propped on her hand, considering.

"What price would you be willing to pay for your Power?" she asked.

The question sounded rhetorical, and Herewiss, dreamy with wine and warmth, treated it as such. "Price? The Moon on a silver platter. A necklace of stars, or one of the Steeds of the Day—"

"No, I meant really."

"Really. Well, right now I'm paying all my waking hours, just about; or I was, before I had to get Freelorn out of the badger-hole he got himself stuck in. What more do I have to give?"

He looked at her, and was surprised to see her face serious again. Something else he noticed; there was an oddness about the inside of her cloak . . . He had thought it as black within as without, but it wasn't. As he strained his eyes in the firelight, there seemed to be some kind of light in its folds, some kind of motion, but faint, faint— He blinked, and didn't see it, and dismissed the notion; and then on his next look he saw it again. A faint light, glittering—

No, no—it must have been the wine. He rejected the image.

The lady's eyes were intent on him, and he noticed how very green they were, a warm green like sunlit summer fields. "Herewiss," she said, her voice going very low, "your Name, would you give *that* for your Power?"

Of all the strange things he had heard so far, *that* startled him badly, and the wine went out in him as if someone had poured water on the small fire it had lit. "Lady, I don't know my Name," he said, and wondered suddenly what he had gotten himself into, wondered what kind of woman kept an inn out here on the borders of human habitation, all alone—

He looked again at the cloak, with eyes grown wary. It was no different. In the black black depths of it something shone, tiny points of an intense silvery light, infinite in number as if the cloak had been strewn with jeweldust, or the faint innumerable stars of Héalhra's Road. Stars—?

She looked at him, earnest, sincere; but the testing look was also in her eyes, the look that awaited an answer, and the right one. A look that dared him to dare.

"If you knew it," she said, "would you pay that price for your Power?"

"My Name?" he said slowly. Certainly there was no higher price that he could pay. His inner Name, his own hard-won knowledge of himself, of all the things he could be—

But he didn't know it. And even if he had, the thought of giving his inner Name to another person was frightening. It was to give your whole self, totally, unreservedly; a surrender of life, breath and soul into other hands. To tell a friend your Name, that was one thing. Friends usually had a fairly good idea of what you were to begin with, and the fact that they didn't use it against you was earnest of their trustworthiness. But to *sell* your Name to a stranger—to *pay* it, as a price for something—the thought was awful. Once a person had your Name, they could do anything to you—bind you to their will, take that Name from you and leave you an empty thing, a shell in which blood flowed and breath moved, but no life was. Or bind you into some terrible place that was not of this world. Or, horrible thought, into another body that wasn't yours; man or beast or Fyrd or demon, it wouldn't much matter. Madness would follow shortly. The possibilities for the misuse of a Name were as extensive as the ingenuity of malice.

But—

—to have the Power.

To have that blue Fire flower full and bright through some kind of focus, *any* kind. To heal, and build, and travel about the Kingdoms being *needed*. To talk to the storm, and understand the thoughts of Dragons, and feel with the growing earth, and run down with the rivers to the Sea. To walk the roads between the Stars. To be trusted by all, and worthy of that trust. To be *whole*.

Even as he sat and thought, Herewiss could feel the Power down inside him; feeble, stunted, struggling in the empty cavern of his self like a pale tired bird of fire. It fluttered and beat itself vainly against the cage-bars of his ribs every time his heart beat. Soon it wouldn't even be able to do that; it would drop to the center of him and lie there dead, poor pallid unborn otherlife. Whenever he looked into himself after that, he would see nothing but death and ashes and endings. And then soon enough he would probably make an end of himself as well—

"If I knew it," he said, and his voice sounded strange and thick to him, fear and hope fighting in it, "I would. I would pay it. But it's useless."

He looked at the lady innkeeper and was faintly pleased to see satisfaction in her eyes. "Well then," she said, pushing herself a little straighter in the chair, "I think I have a commodity that would interest you."

"What?" Herewiss was more interested in her cloak.

"Soulflight."

He stared at her, amazed, and forgot about the cloak. "How—where did you get it?"

"I have my sources," she said, with a tiny twist of smile. She was watching him intently, studying his reactions, and for the moment Herewiss didn't care whether she was seeing what she wanted to or not.

"Are you a seeress?" he asked.

She shrugged at him. "In a way. But I don't use the drug. It fell into my hands, and I've been looking for someone to whom I might dispose of it."

For a bare second Herewiss' mind reeled and soared, dreaming of what he could do with a dose of Soulflight drug. Walk the past and the future, pass through men's minds and understand their innermost thoughts, walk between worlds, command the powers and potentialities and speak to the dead—

But it was a dream, and though dreams are free, real things have their price. "How much do you have?"

"A little bottle, about half a pint."

Herewiss laughed at her. "I would have to sell you the Brightwood whole and entire with all its people for that much Soulflight," he said. "I'm only the Lord's son, not the Queen of Darthen, lady."

"I'm not asking for money," she said.

"What then? How many times do I have to sleep with you?"

She broke out laughing, and after a moment he joined her. "Now *that*," she said, "is a gallant idea, but unless you have the talisman of the Prince who shared himself with the thousand virgins, I doubt you could manage it. Not to mention that *I'd* be furrowed like the fields in March, and I wouldn't be able to walk for a month. How would I run the place?"

Herewiss, smiling, looked again at her cloak. The fire had died down somewhat, and he could see the stars more clearly—countless brilliantly blazing fires, burning silver-cold. He also perceived more clearly that there was a tremendous depth to the cloak, endless reaches of cool darkness going back away from him forever, though the cloak plainly ended at the back of the chair where the lady leaned on it.

He looked at her, dark hair, green eyes like the shadowed places about the Forest Altars, wearing the night sky for her cloak. He knew now with certainty who she was; and awe stirred in him, and joy as well.

"What's the price, lady?" he said, opening himself to the surges building inside him.

"I'll give you the drug," she said, "if you will swear to me that, when you find out your inner Name, you'll tell it to me."

Herewiss considered the woman stretched out in the old tattered chair. "Why do you want to know it?"

She eased herself a little downward, looking into the fire again, and smiled. After a little silence she said, "I guess you could call me a patroness of sorts. Wouldn't it be to my everlasting glory to have helped bring the first male in all these empty years into his Power? And as all good deeds come back to the doer eventually, sooner or later, I'd reap reward for it."

Herewiss laughed softly. "That's not all you're thinking of."

"No, it's not, I suppose," said the innkeeper. "Look, Herewiss; power, in all its forms, is a strange thing. Most of the power that exists is bound up, trapped, and though it tries to be free, usually it can't manage it by itself. The world is full of potential Power of all kinds, yes?"

He nodded.

"But at the same time, loss of power, the death of things, is a process that not even the Goddess can stop. Eventually even the worlds will die."

"So they say."

Her face was profoundly sorrowful, her eyes shadowed as if with guilt. "The death is inevitable. But we have one power, all men and beasts and creatures of other planes. We can slow down the Death, we can die hard, and help all the worlds die hard. To that purpose it behooves us to let loose all the power we can. To live with vigor, to love powerfully and without caring whether we're loved back, to let loose building and teaching and healing and all the arts that try to slow down the great Death. Especially joy, just joy itself. A joy flares bright and goes out like the stars that fall, but the little flare it makes slows down the great Death ever so slightly. That's a triumph, that it can be slowed down at all, and by such a simple thing."

"And you want to let me loose."

"Don't you want to be loose?"

"Of course! But, lady, forgive me, I still don't understand. What's in it for you?"

The lady smiled ruefully, as if she had been caught in an omission, but still admired Herewiss for catching her. "If I were the Goddess," she said, "and I am, for all of us are, whether we admit it to ourselves or not— if I were she, I would look at you as She looks at all men, who are all Her lovers at one time or another. And I would say to Myself, 'If I raise up that Power, free the Fire in him, then when the time comes at last that we share ourselves with one another, in life or after it, I will draw that strength of his into Me, and the Worlds and I will be the greater for it.' And certainly it would be a great thing to know the Name of the first male to come into his Power, lending power in turn to me, so that *I* would be so much the greater for it . . ."

Herewiss sat and looked for a moment at the remote white fires of the stars within the cloak. They seemed to gaze back at him, unblinking, uncompromising, as relentlessly themselves as the lady seemed to be.

"How do I know that you won't use my Name against me if I ever do find it out?" he said.

The lady smiled at him gently. "It's simple enough

to guard against, Herewiss," she said. "You have only to use the drug to find out Mine."

The look of incalculable power and utter vulnerability that dwelt in her eyes in that moment struck straight through him, inflicting both amazement and pain upon him. Tears started suddenly to his eyes, and he blinked them back with great difficulty. Full of sorrow, he reached out and took her hand.

"None of us have any protection against that last Death, have we," he said.

"None of us," said the innkeeper. "Not even She. Her pain is greatest; She must survive it, and watch all Her creation die."

Herewiss held her hand in his, and shared the pain, and at last managed to smile through it.

"If I find my Name, I will tell you," he said. "I swear that by the Altars, and by Earn my Father, and by my breath and life, I'll pay the price."

She smiled at him. "That's good," she said. "I'll give you the drug to take with you tomorrow morning."

A silence rested between them for a few minutes; they rested within it.

"And if I should in my travels come across *your* Name," Herewiss said, "well, it'll be my secret."

"I never doubted it," she said, still smiling. "Thank you."

For a while more they sat in silence, and both of them gazed into the fire, relaxed. Finally the lady stretched a bit, arching her back against the chair. The shimmer of starlight moved with her as she did so, endless silent volumes of stars shifting with her slight motion. She looked over at Herewiss with an expression that was speculative, and a little shy. He looked back at her, almost stealing the glance, feeling terribly young and adventurous, and nervous too.

"Let's pretend," he said, very softly, "that you're the Goddess—"

"—and you're My Lover—?"

"Why not?"

"Why not indeed? After all, You are—"

"—and You are—"

—and for a long time, They were.

Something awoke Herewiss in the middle night. He turned softly over on his side, reaching out an arm, and found only a warm place on the bed where She had been. Slowly and a little sadly he moved his face to where Hers had lain on the pillow, and breathed in the faint fragrance he found there. It was sweet and musky, woman-scent with a little sharpness to it; a subtle note of green things growing in some patterned place of running waters, sun-dappled beneath birdsong. He closed his eyes and savored the moment through his loneliness; felt the warmth beneath the covers, heard the soft pop of a cooling ember, breathed out a long tired sigh of surrender to the sweet exhaustion of having filled another with himself. And despite the empty place beneath his arm, that She in turn had filled so completely with Herself, still he smiled, and loved Her. With all the men and women in the world to love, both living and yet unborn, She could hardly spend much time in one place, or seem to.

He got up, then, moving slowly and carefully with half-closed eyes so as not to break the pleasant half-sleep, half-waking state he was experiencing. Herewiss wrapped a sheet around himself, went out of the room and padded ghost-silent down the hall to listen at the next door down. Nothing. He pushed the door gently open, went in, closed it behind him. Lorn was snoring faintly beneath the covers.

Herewiss eased into the bed behind Freelorn, snuggled up against his back, slipped an arm around his chest; Freelorn roused slightly, just enough to hug Herewiss' arm to him, and then started snoring again.

Herewiss closed his eyes and sank very quickly into sleep, dreaming of the shadowed places in the Bright-

171

wood, and of serene eyes that watch eternally through the leaves.

When Herewiss came down to breakfast, Freelorn was there before him, putting away eggs and hot sugared apples and guzzling hot minted honey-water as if he had been up for hours. This was moderately unusual, since Freelorn almost never ate breakfast at all. More unusual, though, was the fact that he was up early, and looked cheerful—he was usually a late riser, and grumpy until lunchtime.

Herewiss sat down next to him, and Freelorn grunted by way of saying hello. "Nice day," he said a few seconds later, around a mouthful of food.

"It is that." Herewiss looked up to see Dritt and Moris come in together. Dritt was humming through his beard, though still out of tune, and Moris, usually so noisy in the mornings, went into the kitchen silently, with a look on his face that made Herewiss think of a cat with more cream in his bowl than he could possibly finish.

Herewiss reached over to steal Freelorn's mug, and a gulp's worth of honey-water. "Is she making more?"

Freelorn nodded. "Be out in a minute, she said."

Segnbora came down the stairs, pulled out the chair next to Herewiss, and sat down with a thump. She looked a little tired, but she smiled so radiantly at Herewiss that he decided not to ask her how it had been.

"Did you give her our best?" Freelorn asked, cleaning his plate.

"It was mutual, I think."

Freelorn chuckled. "I dare say. Where are Lang and Harald?"

"They'll be down—they were washing up a few minutes ago."

"Good. We should get an early start—if we're going to find this place of yours, I want to hurry up about it. And I would much rather see it in daylight."

"Lorn, I doubt it's any worse at night."

"*Everything* is worse at night. With one exception."

"Is that all you ever think about?"

"Well, there *is* something else, actually. But it's easier to make love than it is to make kings."

Lang came thumping down the stairs and sat down across from Segnbora. "How was it?"

"Oh *please!* It was fine."

"This hold," Lang said, "will we be seeing it tomorrow?"

"If the directions I got are right."

(They are,) Sunspark said from the stable. (Tomorrow easily. I can feel the place from here.)

"Before nightfall?"

"I think so."

"Good."

"I wish you people wouldn't worry so much," Herewiss said. "It's not haunted, as far as I can tell."

"—which can't be far. Nobody will go near the place! Morning, Harald."

"Morning." Harald sat down across from Herewiss. "How was she, then?"

Segnbora sighed at the ceiling. "She was *fine*. Twice more and I can stop repeating myself . . ."

"Can you blame us for being curious? I mean, a lady like that—" But as Lang said it, the smile on his face caught Herewiss' eye. A little reflective, that smile, and a little reminiscent, almost wistful . . .

The kitchen door swung open, and Dritt and Moris and the innkeeper came out laden with trays; more eggs, more steaming honeywater and hot apples, with a huge bowl of wheat porridge and a pile of steamed crabs from the river. They put the things down, and as the grabbing and passing commenced, Herewiss looked over the heads of Freelorn's people to catch the lady's eye.

She was back in her workday garb, the plain homespun shirt and breeches, the boots, the worn gray apron; her hair was braided again into a crown of coiled plaits. Though she was no less beautiful, she seemed to have doffed her power, and Herewiss began to wonder whether much of their night encounter mightn't have been a dream provoked by good wine. But she returned his glance, and smiled, winking at him and patting one of her pockets, which bulged conspicuously. Then back she went into the kitchen.

Herewiss reached for a mug of honeywater, and a plate to put eggs on.

"How was it?" Dritt said to Segnbora.

Segnbora smiled grimly, and put a fried egg down his shirt.

When it was time to go, they gathered outside the door that faced the ferry, and the lady innkeeper brought out their horses. First Lang's and Dritt's, then Harald's and Moris', and then Segnbora's and Freelorn's. Herewiss watched as the lady spoke a word or two in Segnbora's ear, and when Segnbora smiled back at her, shyly, with affection, Herewiss felt something odd run through him. A pang, a small pain under the breastbone. He laughed at himself, a breath of ruefulness and amusement. *Why am I feeling this way? Am I so selfish that I can't stand the thought of someone else sharing Her the same night I did? What silliness. After last night, I'm full in places I didn't even know were empty. Such joy—to know that the Goddess Who made the world and everything in it is holding you and telling you that She loves you, all of you, even the parts that need changing—I should rejoice with Segnbora, for from the look on her face this morning, she has known the joy too. . . .*

The lady brought out Sunspark last of all. To judge by the arch of his neck and the light grace of his walk, he was in remarkably good temper. When Herewiss took the reins, the lady bent her head close to his.

"It's in the saddlebag," she said. "Remember me."

"I will."

"I'll remember *you*. You understand me—somewhat

174

better than most." And she smiled at him; a little reflective, that smile, a little reminiscent, almost wistful. . . .

Herewiss swung up onto Sunspark's back; the others were already ahorse, awaiting him.

"Good luck to you all," said the innkeeper, "and whatever your business is in the Waste, I hope you come back safe."

They bade her farewell in a ragged but enthusiastic chorus, and rode off to the ferry. There was not much talk among them until they crossed the river; though Sunspark bespoke Herewiss smugly as they waited for the second group to make the crossing.

(The lady is likely to lose her guests' horses, the way she keeps her stable,) it said.

(Oh?)

(She left my stall open. Did you know there are wild horses hereabouts?)

(It wouldn't surprise me.)

(And what horses! Look.)

Herewiss closed his eyes and slipped a little way into Sunspark's mind. It was twilight there, and the plain to the west was softly limned and shadowed by the rising Moon. And standing atop a rise like a statue of ivory and silver, motionless but for the wind in the white mane and the softly glimmering tail, there was a horse. A mare.

(How beautiful,) Herewiss said. (So?)

(It was an interesting evening.)

(I thought you didn't understand that kind of union,) Herewiss said.

(The body has its own instincts, it would seem,) Sunspark answered, with a slow inward smile. (It will be interesting to try on a human body and see what happens. . . .)

Herewiss withdrew, with just a faint touch of unease. He wasn't sure he wanted to be involved in the experiment that Sunspark was proposing.

(But there was something more to it all than that,)

Sunspark went on, sounding pleased and puzzled both at once. (When first I saw . . . her . . . I thought she was of my own kind, for she was fire as well. And I the emergency of progeny. Yet . . . there was union, which ends in glory, in the dissolution of selves and the emergency of progeny. Yet . . . there was union and a glory even surpassing that of which I have been told. And I am still one. . . .)

(What happened to the mare?)

(Oh, she lived,) Sunspark said with a flick of its golden tail.

(By your standards or by mine?)

(Yours. Even had things not gone as they did, I would have been far too interested to have consumed her.)

(I'm glad to hear it. . . .)

Herewiss opened his eyes to watch Segnbora, Dritt and Freelorn approach, pulling on the ferry-rope. Dritt was facing back toward the opposite bank, looking at the lone figure that stood and watched them. Experimentally, Herewiss reached out with his under-hearing. He caught a faint wash of sorrow from Dritt, overlaid and made bearable by an odd sheen of bright memory. Then the perception was gone.

Something was strange. When the group was assembled again and once more riding eastward into the rocky flats, Herewiss rode up to Freelorn's side and beckoned him apart.

"A personal question, Lorn,—" he said softly.

"Yes, I did."

"Did *what*?"

"Sleep with her last night." He said it a little guiltily, shooting a glance at Segnbora out of the corner of his eye. "Before she did, I guess. And let me tell you, she was—"

"Please, Lorn."

"Listen, I didn't—I mean—"

"Lorn, how long has it been since something like

that mattered with us? You love me. I know that. I have no fears."

"Yes, well . . ."

"Besides," Herewiss said, grinning wickedly, "so did I."

Freelorn laughed. "She gets around, doesn't she?"

"It looks that way."

"Just out of curiosity—what time was it when you—"

"About Moonrise—yes, I remember the Moon coming up. I had a lot of wine, but that much is—Lorn, what's wrong?"

Freelorn was shaking his head and frowning. "Couldn't have been."

"Couldn't have been *what*?"

"Moonrise. Because she was with *me* at Moonrise."

Herewiss sat there and felt it again—that odd hot thrill of excitement, of anticipation. But different, somehow sharper in the daylight than it had been in the twilight.

"Segnbora," he called.

She reined Steelsheen back and joined them. "What, then?"

"This is a little personal, granted—"

"And I didn't save any eggs. Oh, well."

"No, no. I was just wondering. What time was it when you and the lady were together?"

"Now it's funny you should mention that—"

"Oh?"

"—because I just overheard Dritt discussing that same subject with Harald. And he was saying that the lady had visited *him* about the time the Moon came up, and I was . . . thinking . . ."

She looked at them for a long few seconds, and Freelorn blushed suddenly and became very interested in Blackmane's withers. Herewiss watched Segnbora. She stared for a few seconds at the reins she held, and then looked over at him again.

"It *was* the Bride, then."

He nodded.

When she spoke again, the sound of her voice startled Herewiss. Her words went gentle with awe, and Herewiss had heard women take the Oath to the Queen of Silence with less reverence, less love. "You didn't ask," she said, "and I will tell you. No sharing I have ever known was like last night. Oh, give as you will, there's only so much that can be shared in one evening, or one day, before the body gives out, gets sore, gets tired. There's always some one place left uncherished, some corner of the heart not touched, or not enough—and you shrug and say, 'Oh, well, next time.' And next time that one place may be caressed to satisfaction, but others are missed. You make your peace with it, eventually, and give all you can so that your own ignored places feel warmer for the giving. But last night—oh, last night. All, all of me, all the depths, the corners, the little fantasies I never dared to—the sheer delight, to open up and know that there's no harm in the sharing anywhere, only *love*—" She turned her face away; Herewiss could feel her filling up with tears. "To have Her slide into bed behind me," Segnbora said quietly, "and put Her arms around me, and hold my breasts in Her warm hands, and then slip down a little and kiss the lonely place between my shoulderblades that always wanted a kiss, and never got one. And without asking. . . ."

She smiled, and let the tears fall.

Freelorn looked up at Herewiss again, and he was smiling too. "It was like that," he said. "Funny, though, I wasn't expecting it so soon."

"She never comes to share Herself when you expect Her," Herewiss said. "That's half the joy right there."

Freelorn nodded.

"How She must love us," Herewiss said. "To share with us *all*, to give us so very much—I can't understand it. Just for my own part, even. What incredible thing have I done, or will I do, to earn—to deserve such, such blessing, so much love. . . ."

"You're reason enough," Freelorn said, very quietly.

"And, besides, She cherishes what's returned. What could we possibly give the Mother that She couldn't make better Herself, except love? She could *make* us love Her—but it wouldn't be the same."

Herewiss reached out and took Freelorn's hand. "I was thinking mostly in terms of you, Lorn."

Freelorn chuckled, squeezed Herewiss' hand hard. "And anyway," he added after a moment, "She can afford to be generous. They say that most of the time She drives a hard bargain."

Herewiss looked down at his front saddlebag, and at the slight bulge in it.

"That's what I hear," he said.

SEVEN

Memory is a mirror—but even the clearest mirror reverses right to left.

Gnomics, 418

When frogs fell all around them out of the clear hot sky, smacking into the dust and sand with understandable grunts and squeaks, the party was surprised, but not too much so. When it hailed real stones, instead of ice, they covered their heads with helms or shields and made small jokes about the quality of the weather in this part of the Waste. When, while climbing a rise, they noticed that the rocks dislodged by their horses' hooves were rolling up the hill after them, they shrugged and kept on riding. Stranger things were likely to happen.

"There it is," Herewiss said. He pointed through the blown dust-clouds at a low gray shape on the horizon.

"Are you sure it's there?" Freelorn said. "Look how it wobbles."

"That's heat, and this damn dust. We'll be there in an hour or so, I would say."

Sunspark snorted. (Nothing so involved,) it told Herewiss. (It's just the fabric of existence warping. A ripple in the Pattern.)

The idea made the hair stand up all over Herewiss. (Oh,) he said, beginning to worry.

(It's not hard to do. You want to see?)

(Uh, no! Not right now, I mean. . . .)

180

(I know. Later.) It chuckled.

"What are those?" Lang muttered, shielding his eyes. "Towers?"

"Hard to tell from here. We'll see when we get closer."

They cantered on across the desert. Herewiss was in high good spirits, expectant as a little boy at Opening Night waiting for the fireworks to start. To some extent it was infectious. Most of Freelorn's people were joking and straining their eyes ahead in anticipation. Segnbora was rigidly upright in the saddle, her sword loose in its sheath. Sunspark was occasionally forgetting to keep its hooves touching the ground. But Freelorn was frowning, resolutely refusing to get excited.

"Well," he said, "we haven't been eaten alive yet. But I reserve judgment until we leave."

"We? Lorn, if the place is safe, I'm staying."

"Not for long, surely."

"For as long as I have to."

"You don't mean you're planning to *live* there for any length of time!"

"Uh huh."

"You," Freelorn said with frank irritation, "are a crazy person."

"You know us Brightwood people," Herewiss said, "the only sure thing about us—"

"—is that you're all nuts," Freelorn said, refusing to finish the quote. "Let's see what the place is like before you make up your mind."

"Who's that?" Harald yelled. His eyesight was better than anyone else's, and for a moment they all squinted through the dust at the faint figure ahead of them.

"No horse," Segnbora said. "No tent, *nothing*—"

"No one lives out here!" Moris said.

"Not for long, anyway, without a horse or a water supply," Herewiss said. "Let's see who it is—could be they need help—"

They rode closer. The figure stood there with its arms folded, watching them approach. It didn't move.

(He's not there.)

Sunspark's thought was so sudden and shaken that Herewiss gulped involuntarily. (??)

(He's not *there*. Or—he appears to be, but he's not an illusion; he's *real*. And yet he's not—)

(Make sense, Spark! Is this something you've encountered before?)

(No. It's as if he were not wholly present, somehow—his thoughts are bent on us, but his body isn't *here* enough for his soul to be—)

(Where's his soul, then?)

(Ahead—)

"He looks familiar," Moris said, rising up in the stirrups to stare ahead.

"Yeah—" Freelorn squinted. "Damn this dust anyway—"

They approached the waiting man, came close enough to see his face—

Freelorn's mouth fell open. Herewiss was struck still as stone, and Sunspark danced backward a few paces in amazement. Segnbora spoke softly in Nhàired, drawing a sign in the air.

Dritt sat on his horse, his eyes wide, and looked at himself; the same elaborately tooled boots, the same dark tunic and light breeches, the same long silver-hilted sword, the same sandy hair—

Dritt stood there in the dust and looked at himself. He put out a hand to one side, as if to steady himself against something. "Sweet Goddess," he said, just loudly enough for them to hear, "oh *no!*"

And he turned away, and was gone—

—with a soft sharp sound like hands clapped together, and a swirl of stirred-up dust—

Dritt swayed a bit in the saddle, and Moris was beside him in a moment, putting a hand on his arm. "Take it easy," he said, "*you're* here, and that's what matters. No telling what kind of a sending that was—"

"That was *me*," Dritt said with conviction. "Not a

sending. Not a premonition, or an illusion, or anything like that. *Me.* I could feel it."

Freelorn turned to Herewiss, almost in triumph. "*There.* You want to live in a place where things like *that* happen?"

"Lorn, we're not even there yet."

"I know. I *know.*"

They sat on their horses in a tight little group before the place, and stared at it.

It was built all of shining gray stone that looked like granite, sparkling with deeply buried highlights. The outer wall, perfectly square and at least forty feet high, completely surrounded the inner buildings, an assortment of keeps and towers, some leaning at crazy angles as if half-toppled by an earthquake. Some were seemingly unfinished, having great gaps in them. Some were shorn off oddly at the top, as if the stone had been sliced by giant knives. Nowhere were seams or jointures apparent at all; the place seemed to have been carved from single immense blocks of stone. And though there were windows in the inner buildings, there was no opening in the outer wall anywhere. It towered up before them, slick and unscaleable as glass.

"Well," Freelorn said with scarcely disguised satisfaction, "*now* what?"

Herewiss made an irritated face, but Sunspark laughed privately, unconcerned. (I think,) the elemental said, (it is time to disabuse them of the idea that I am a horse.)

(What? You're going to jump it?)

(No, nothing like that. Just inside the wall I can sense a courtyard. I will take part of the wall away.)

(Can you *do* that?)

(It'd be silly to suggest it if I couldn't,) Sunspark said, amused. (Get off and take everyone back a good ways, a quarter of a mile or so. I'm going to have to exert myself a little, but the stretch will do me good.)

Herewiss dismounted. "Lorn," he said, "let me up

behind you, will you? We're going to have to back off a little."

"Uh, look," Freelorn said, sounding a little alarmed, "I don't want you to strain yourself—"

"Let's go."

Herewiss put his foot in Blackmane's stirrup and swung up behind Freelorn. He was aware of Segnbora regarding him with a small and secret smile; he winked at her. "Back the way we came," he said to Freelorn, "a quarter mile or so."

"But your horse—!!"

"Sunspark is going to take part of the wall away," Herewiss said. "We'd better back off."

"*Sunspark* is—"

With Freelorn in the lead, shaking his head, the group rode back into the desert. After a while Herewiss stopped them.

"Far enough," he said. "Now then." (Are you ready, Spark?)

(Yes.)

(Will it be all right for us to look?)

(Mmm—yes, I'll damp the light a little. You'll probably feel the heat, though.)

"It's going to be hot," Herewiss said, "and bright. Be warned."

(Go ahead,) he told Sunspark.

For a few seconds there was nothing, only the sight of the high towers peering over the wall, and the small red-brown horse-shape standing before the stone. Then Sunspark reared.

—Searing brightness like a sunseed fallen to earth and exploding into flower! A hard stabbing brilliance like a knife through the eyes! And a crack of thunder like being hit in the face, followed by a wave of stinging hot wind—

By the time they got their horses back under control again, the light and the heat were gone. There was only the little red horse-shape, standing before a huge gap in the wall.

Freelorn turned to look over his shoulder at Herewiss. "You were *riding* that?"

Herewiss smiled at him. "Let's go see what the inside of the place looks like." They rode back to the wall, and dismounted, looking at it in wonder. About a hundred feet of the wall's four-hundred-foot length was gone. The edges of the sudden opening were perfectly smooth, though slightly duller than the slick polished stone of the wall's outer surfaces; the seared stone was crackling as it cooled.

Sunspark walked over to Herewiss, its eyes glittering with pleasure. (That was fun.)

(The stone, Spark, where did it go?)

(I consumed it. Anything'll burn if you heat it enough. It made a nice meal.)

(But stone—?)

Sunspark smiled at Herewiss in its mind. (I have to eat *sometimes*.)

(Sunspark, I beat you two falls out of three—)

(You wouldn't let me burn you,) Sunspark said. (Otherwise there would never have been a second fall.)

(I think we'd better go in.) Aloud he said, "Lorn?"

"Yeah, what?" Freelorn was gazing in through the opening at the courtyard. It was paved in the same shining gray stone, and at the other side of it was a low, oblong structure like a great hall.

"Let's have a look."

"You first," Freelorn said.

"All right, me first—"

Herewiss walked cautiously through the opening. Immediately it was much quieter: the sound of the wind seemed muted and far away. There was no dust on the pavement at all, and like the walls it stretched without a seam or crack from one side of the courtyard to the other. Sunspark's hooves clattered loudly on it as it followed him in.

Freelorn and his people came close behind Herewiss. No one spoke. Though the place was quieter than the surrounding desert, that was not what was oppressing them. The sheer stone walls and the crazily tilted towers rising above the central hall seemed to be *ignoring* them somehow—as if nothing human beings could do there would ever make a difference, as if the suddenly breached wall were a matter of no consequence at all. The place had an aura about it as of impassiveness and unconcern—as if it were alive itself, in some kind of way, and did not recognize *them* as living things.

"This paving," Lang said softly, "it isn't level."

"Yes is it," Harald said, almost whispering. "You can see that it is—"

"It doesn't feel that way."

"No, it doesn't," Herewiss said, very loudly. "And why are we whispering?"

A ripple of nervous laughter went through the group.

"There's something about this place," Segnbora said. "Some of these towers, the—the perspective of them seems wrong somehow. They're *off*. That one over the big square building, it should look closer than the other one behind it, tilting off to the left— but it *doesn't*."

"Let's see what the inside is like." Herewiss headed toward the opening in the building before them, wide and dark.

They left the horses hobbled in the courtyard and followed him in. It wasn't as dark inside as they had expected. They stood at one side of a great square room, with a huge opening in the stone of the ceiling, like a skylight; it was positioned directly over what appeared to be a fire-pit raised some feet above the floor on a platform. Around the walls of the hall were doors opening onto vaguely-lit passageways. Through one of these they could see a flight of stairs leading upward. The stairs were uneven, one broad one being staggered with two steep narrow ones as far up as they could see.

"Well," Herewiss said, "if this is the dining hall, I wonder what the bedrooms are like? Let's look."

The group went slowly across the hall, clustered together. "I keep expecting something to jump out of one of those doors," Freelorn said, as they started up the stairs.

"Well, I doubt it would be one of the original inhabitants," Herewiss answered. "The lack of furniture makes me think they moved out permanently—unless they have very severe tastes in their decorating."

At the top of the stairs they paused for a moment. There was nothing to be seen but a long, long corridor full of open doorways into dark empty rooms. One door, the fourth or fifth one down on the left, must have opened to a room with a window; sunlight poured out through it and onto the opposite wall.

"We could look at the view," Herewiss said, and started down the hall. He looked into the first door he passed—

—and halted in mid-step. Freelorn bumped into him, and Lang into Freelorn, and Segnbora into Lang, and they all looked—

There was no room behind the door. The stone of the doorsill was there, hard and solid under their hands as they reached out to reassure themselves of it: but through the opening cut in the glittering gray they saw a mighty mountain promontory rearing upward from a sea the color of blood. Pink foam crashed upward from the breaking waves and fell on the rose and opal beaches; the wind, blowing in from the sea, stirred trees with leaves the color of wine, showing the leaves' flesh-colored undersides. The mountain was forested in deep purples and mauves; a cloud of morning mist lay about its shoulders.

Herewiss reached out, very very slowly, and put his hand through the doorway. After a moment he withdrew it, rubbing his fingers together.

"It's cooler there," he said, "and damp. Lorn, this is it. *Doors into Otherwheres—*"

They moved on slowly to the next *door*.

It showed them sand, endless reaches of it; butter-colored sand, carved by relentless winds into rippled dunes with crests like knives, stretching from one horizon to the other in perfect straight lines. A corrugated desert, showing not one sign of life, not the tiniest plant or creature. The sky was such a deep pure blue-violet as one sometimes sees in the depths of a lake at evening.

"If you cut our sky with a knife," Segnbora whispered, "it would bleed that color."

"Come on—"

The next *doorway* opened on a hallway of gray stone, crowded with seven people who looked through a *doorway* at a hallway of gray stone, crowded with seven people who looked through a *doorway* at a hall-way—

"Dear Goddess!!" Freelorn said, and spun to look behind him. There was nothing there but another *doorway,* this one showing a volcano erupting with terrible, silent violence against a night sky. A flying rock fell close to the *door* as he watched. He flinched back and Herewiss reached out to steady him.

"It's all right. Let's go on."

"What if that had come through?"

"I don't know if it can—though it does seem likely. Look at the sun coming out of this one—"

They gathered before the next *door*. "Suns, you mean," Dritt said. They looked down on a placid sea-shore. Out over the dark water, one small red sun was going down in a fury of crimson clouds: another one, larger and fiercely blue, shone higher in the sky.

"Two suns." Moris' voice, usually loud and abrasive, was hushed. "Two *suns!* What kind of place *is* that?"

"Goddess only knows. Look at this one—"

The group relaxed a little, broke slightly apart as each person went looking through a separate *doorway,* each looking for a wonder of his or her own.

"—*blue* trees?"

"What the Dark is *this*??"

"Look, it's *our* country. Moris, isn't that the Éorl-howe? And the North Arléne peninsula—"

"This one is under water—look, there goes a fish!"

"I didn't know the Goddess *made* birds that big."

"It's snowing here, I can't see a thing."

Herewiss was standing before a *doorway* that showed nothing—nothing at all, a vague blurry darkness. Not the darkness of night, but an absence, an absence of anything at all. He looked at it, and his heart was beating fast. An unused *door*? Maybe—

Freelorn came to him from further up the hall, took Herewiss' arm and began to pull him along. "What? What?" Herewiss said, but Lorn wouldn't answer him. He pulled Herewiss in front of one *door*. "Look," he said.

The *door* showed them a view from a high place, looking down into a landscape afire with a sunset the color of new love. Below and before them stretched a fantastic growth of crystalline forms, islanded between two rivers; jutting upward against the extravagant sky like prisms of quartz or amethyst or polished amber, but scored and carved and patterned, dappled with sunset light. They grew in all sizes and shapes, a forest of gigantic gems, spears of opal and dark jade and towers of obsidian. They caught the light of day's end and reflected it back from a thousand different planes and angles, golden, red, orange, pink, smoky twilight blue; a barbaric and magnificent display of a god's crown jewels, the diadem of Day set down between the crimson rivers as the Sun retired. One spire reached higher than all the others around it, a masterwork of crystal set in gray stone and topped with a spearing crown of silver steel. On the crown's peak a single ruby flared, pulsing like a Dragon's eye, and rays of light struck up from the circlet like pale swords against the deepening blue. In the silences of the upper sky, a crescent Moon smiled at the evening star that flowered beside it.

Beside Herewiss, Freelorn moved softly, as if afraid

189

to break a dream. "What is it?" he whispered. "Is it real?"

"Somewhere it is."

"Is it really what it looks like, a city? How did they build it? Or did it grow? And is that glass? How did they make it that way—?"

Herewiss shook his head, and out of the corner of his eye he caught sight of Segnbora moving slowly and silently toward the *door,* like one entranced. He reached out and caught her by the arm, and she pulled at him a little, wanting to be let go.

"No," he said. "Segnbora—look at the view. The *door* opens out onto somewhere very high. There may be ground under it, but there may not be. You could step out onto nothing. And it would be a short flight for someone who doesn't have wings."

She stared out the *doorway* with longing, the colors of the softening sunset catching in her eyes. "It might be worth it," she said.

"Come on—"

The next *doorway* was dark, but not as the one Herewiss had seen. In the endless depths of its darkness, stars were suspended: not the remote cold stars of night in the desert, but great flaming swarms of them, hot and beautiful, cast carelessly across the boundless black reaches of eternity. And close, so close you could surely put your hand out and pluck one like an apple. They spun outward from a blazing common core, burning like the sudden fiery realization of joy—

Freelorn took a step toward the *doorway.* "This is the *Door,*" he said, very softly, *"the Door—"*

Alarm stirred in Herewiss, drowning his appreciation of the beauty in sudden concern for Freelorn. "Not the last *Door,* not the *Door* into Starlight, no," he said. "You can't see that until you're dead, Lorn, or have the Flame—and you're in neither condition—"

"But my father—"

"That's not where he is." Herewiss took Freelorn by his shoulders, as much from compassion as from fear that he might cast himself through. "Your father is by that Sea of which the Starlight is a faint intimation. And though they're lovely, those are just stars. Not the final Sea."

Freelorn turned away, but Herewiss was troubled: there had been no feeling of release, of giving up the vision, no feeling of Freelorn accepting what *was*. "Lorn—"

"Let me be." Freelorn walked away from him, walked down the stairs, oblivious to the wondering comments of his people as they peered through one *door* or another.

Herewiss stared after him, worrying. He was distracted after a moment by a touch on his arm: Segnbora looked up at him. There was concern in her eyes. "Are we staying the night?" she asked.

"I think so."

She turned to look through the starry *door,* and sighed. "That's been much on his mind lately," she said.

"It's *always* on his mind," Herewiss said sadly. "As you'll find when you've known him as long as I have."

Segnbora nodded and went off to look through another *door.*

Damn, Herewiss thought. *There's going to be crying tonight. . . .*

That night they camped in the great hall around the firepit. There was no need to gather firewood, for Sunspark decided to inhabit the deep-set hearth, and it burned there the night long. Freelorn and his people made much of it, and Sunspark flamed in unlikely shapes and colors for quite a while, showing off. But Herewiss was vaguely uneasy about something, and found himself bothered by the occasional perception of bright eyes in the fire, watching him with an odd considering look.

(You're quiet tonight,) Herewiss commented.

The fire twisted and wreathed in an impressive and

ornamental shrug. (You're going to do it again,) Sunspark said, (and there still won't be any progeny. How many times do you have to do it?)

Herewiss sighed.

(Well, I'm sorry,) Sunspark said, (but you people are weird. I wish I could find my way home and tell my relatives about you, but they'd think I was making it up.)

Herewiss smiled. (Even if we were making a baby,) he said, (it would still take quite a while. . . .)

(With all that expenditure of energy, there should be immediate results!)

(Not really.)

(For such a shortlived race,) Sunspark said, (you're awfully patient.)

(There's more to it than progeny,) Herewiss said.

(Oh? What?)

Herewiss took a long breath.

(Later,) Sunspark said, with affection, and set about tying its upleaping fires into knots.

Everyone ate hugely that night, and went to bed early. Dritt went off to investigate one or another of the *doors* before he slept.

After being gone for not more than a few minutes he came down the stairs again, looking slightly dazed.

Freelorn and Herewiss were sitting with their backs to the firepit, working at a skin of Brightwood that Freelorn had liberated from the Ferry Tavern; the lovers'-cup was halfway through its fifth refill, and both of them looked up at Dritt with slightly addled concern as he went by.

"It was me," he said. "May I?" He gestured at the cup.

"Sure," Freelorn said.

Dritt reached down and took a long, long drink. "This morning," he said, "that was me, just now. I went upstairs, and it was daytime in one of the *doors,* and there were people coming—the first people that any *door* showed—and I got a little excited and walked through it to have a look."

"What was it like," Herewiss said, "going through?"

"Like nothing. Like going through a door." Dritt put the cup down. "Thanks. So I waited there for a while—and of course, it was us. Of course. It shook me a little at the time, and I stepped back, and then I couldn't see me any more—"

"Which of you couldn't see you?"

"Hell," Dritt said, a little bemused, "I'm not feeling terribly picky about the details right now. I'm going to bed."

"G'night."

"Yeah, good night . . ."

Dritt wandered away toward Moris' bedroll, and Herewiss picked up the cup and finished it. "How much more of this is there?" he said.

"There's another skin."

"Lorn, you amaze me. What else did you take out of there that wasn't nailed down?"

"No, no, I was a good boy. Only took the wine. I knew you'd like it, and I don't think the lady minded."

"No," Herewiss said. He chuckled then. "Lorn, this has been some month for me . . ."

"How?"

"Just the strange things happening—and then seeing you again. It's good to have you close." He put an arm around Lorn, hugged him tight.

"Yeah, it's good to be with you too . . . Listen, what are you going to do now?"

"Stay here."

Freelorn was quiet for a long moment.

"Lorn, I have to. I need this place. You saw the *doors*, you know what they can do. I have to try to find one that'll do what I want it to." Herewiss put out his hand to the lovers'-cup and played with it a little, turning it around and around. *Please,* he was thinking. *Please, Lorn, don't start this*—not now—

193

"I wish you wouldn't stay," Freelorn said.

Herewiss didn't answer.

"If you cared," Freelorn said. "If you did care, about how I feel, the way you say you do, you wouldn't worry me by staying here. This place isn't natural—"

"Neither am I, Lorn." *Damn, I know that phrasing. He's going to cry. And then I'll start crying. And he'll get anything out of me he wants to, just like he always does—*

"But you'll be all alone here—"

"Sunspark will be here. You saw what it did to the outer wall. I don't have much to be afraid of with a watchdog like *that*."

"Herewiss. Listen to me." Freelorn looked at him, earnestly, his face full of pain and hard-held restraint and the need to make Herewiss understand. Herewiss' insides went *wrench* at the sound of the tears rising in Freelorn's voice. "This place—there's too much *power* here for other forces not to have taken notice of it. What is it you told me once, that as soon as you came into your Power, or started to, that would be the time to watch out, because new Powers are always noticed? And as soon as they come into being, the old Powers come to challenge them, to test them and see where they fit into the overall pattern?"

"Yes, but—"

"—and here's this place, there must be *incredible* power bottled up in it to make it do the things it does. And you'll sit here, merrily forging swords, and getting stronger and stronger, and Sunspark staying with you, a Power in its own right certainly—you think you won't attract notice? *Doors* open both ways, you know. Things can come in those *doors* as well as go out: if you needed proof, Dritt just gave it to you. Suppose something comes in while your back is turned?"

"Lorn—" *Listen to him fighting the tears. Oh, Goddess, how can I refuse him? I don't want to hurt him but* I have to stay here—

194

"—listen, you could stay here a few days, a week, two maybe; we'd stay with you. And then you could come with us when we raid the treasury at Osta, and get the money we need to hire mercenaries—"

"Lorn, that whole Osta thing is crazy. I don't want you messing with it. Besides, mercenaries may not be the way to handle this. I would prefer to pull it off without shedding blood."

"You're awfully careful with other people's blood," Freelorn said, a touch of anger beginning to creep into his voice now. "And not enough with your own. Is that it? You figure that since Herelaf died by your sword, you should too? Something out of Goddess knows where should come up on you while you're busy working on the one sword that will redeem you, and kill you then? Atonement? Blood shed for blood shed? There is a certain poetic justice to it—"

"Lorn, stop it." *He's goading me on purpose, now. He must be so very afraid. But I never thought he would hurt me like this— Is he so afraid that he can't give in a little, let me have my own way? The danger isn't that great—*

"If you die under conditions like that," Freelorn said, his anger growing, "your death will mean *nothing*. Herelaf would shake his head at you, and he'd say, 'Dad was right, your head *is* made of wood, just like everything else in this place—'"

I won't yell at him. I won't. He's my loved—"Lorn, I never thought that you—"

"—but you're determined to die before you forge that sword and reach your Power, because success would mean giving up your guilt—and you haven't really worked on anything else since Herelaf died. It's sharper than any sword, by now. You stick it into yourself every chance you get, and bleed a little more of your life and your power away, so that every time there's a little less of you left to pursue the search, a little less chance that you'll succeed. Now, though, you're getting close to success, and so you have to risk your life even more wildly by messing with places like this alone—"

"Lorn, *shut up!* Who brought me this journey, anyway? I would likely never have *heard* about this place if I hadn't been coming to get you out of that damn keep. And if the way you carried on at the Tavern is any indication, you're a fine one to be talking about how to get yourself in trouble; it's plain enough to see how they caught on to who you were in Madeil! And as for nursing guilts, how about you? Maybe it is easier to make love than to make Kings, but it's also easier to talk about being a King than it is to *be* one! You've never forgiven yourself for being out of the country when your father died, instead of by his side to do the whole heroic last-stand thing that you always wanted; and you were too damn guilty about it to go back and try to take his throne, because you didn't think you deserved it! Idiot! Or coward! Which? You could have gone back and tried to make a stand, tried to take the Stave—the people and the Four Hundred would have supported you; you're the Lion's Child. But no, you chose government-in-exile, mooching off poor Bort until he died. At least you had the sense to get out of Darthen until Eftgan's reign was settled, and she remembers the favor; she likes you as much as Bort did, it would seem. Lucky for you—otherwise it'd have been all over with you by now. Lately you couldn't lie your way out of an open field—"

"Dammit, Herewiss—!"

He almost never calls me by name. Sweet Goddess, *he's mad. But so am I—* "—shut up, Lorn! And don't come mouthing to me about deathguilt, because yours has nothing on mine, and even if it did, it's fairly obvious that you wouldn't be handling it any better. At least I'm trying to deal with mine—"

Freelorn's mouth worked, and nothing came out. Herewiss stopped, his satisfaction at Freelorn's anger suddenly draining out of him. *This is a thing I never knew about us,* he thought in shock. *We resent each*

*other. My Goddess. Can love and resentment like this
live in the same person at the same time and not kill
each other?*

"What are you going to do?" Freelorn said, his voice
tight.

"I'm going to stay here." Herewiss made his voice
noncommittal, unemotional. He was trembling.

"Then I'm going to Osta. And I'll see you when I
see you. Good night." Freelorn got up and went to the
corner where his bedroll was laid out; he wrapped
himself up in his cloak and lay down with his face to
the wall and his back to Herewiss.

Oh, Dark, Herewiss thought, *we've had fights before . . .* But he couldn't stop shaking, and something
inside him told him that this had been no normal
fight. (Died by your sword,) Freelorn's voice said,
again and again, echoing like the cold howls of the
Shadow's Hunting through midwinter skies. And, *He
never said anything like that to me before.* Never—

He sat there a long time, unmoving, staring at Freelorn's turned back, or at the lovers'-cup, half-full of
wine, sitting on the floor beside him. Sunspark burned
low at his back, watching in silence.

(Spark—) he said.

(Do you do that often?) it said very softly.

(Uh—no. Not really.)

(It is a considerable discharge of energies.)

(It—uh—is that.)

(Such random discharges,) the elemental said,
(usually preclude the possibility of union—)

(Yes,) Herewiss said. (They do.)

(He is—no longer your mate?)

The elemental's thought made it plain that such an
occurrence was quite nearly the end of the world; and
Herewiss, beginning to sink downward into his pain,
was inclined to agree. (I don't know,) he said, (oh, I
don't—No, I really don't know . . .)

He got up, went over to where Freelorn lay, reached
down and touched him. "Lorn—"

Nothing. He might as well have touched the gray stone of the hold and asked it for an answer.

He lay down, wrapping himself up in his cloak too and stretching out beside Freelorn. But he did not need his underhearing to perceive the wall of hostility that lay between them like a—like a sword thrown in the middle of the bedroll. There was a stranger on the other side of the wall, a stranger who wanted fiercely to be left alone, who would strike out if bothered—

It was like trying to lie still on hot coals. Herewiss got up and went away, back to the firepit. Bright eyes looked out of the shifting flames at him.

(??)

(He doesn't want to talk to me. Maybe he will in the morning. Sleep heals a great many ills, including unfinished quarrels, sometimes—)

(I wouldn't know. I don't sleep.)

(Tonight, I doubt I will either.) Herewiss sighed. (I'm going outside for a bit, Spark.)

It flickered acquiescence at him and cuddled down into the coals, pulling a sheet of fire over itself.

Herewiss paused, looking over his shoulder at Freelorn. His loved lay still unmoving, but Herewiss could feel the space around him prickling with anger and frustration.

Oh, hell, he told himself. *Let be. You know how Lorn is. He does a two-day sulk and then everything's all right again.*

But we never fought like this—

He walked to the front doorway of the hold and looked out. The gray walls of the courtyard were walls of shadow now, hardly to be seen at all except where their tops occluded the sky. Herewiss leaned against the doorsill, sighed again, folded his arms and gazed up at the stars. His brain was jangling like windchimes in a storm of fears and fragmented thoughts; it took him a long few moments to calm down and greet the blazing desert stars, the Mother's sky, as it deserved to be greeted. It took him a few minutes more to realize that the constellations with which he was familiar were nowhere to be seen.

Uhh—wait a moment—!

Very quietly, so as not to disturb Lorn or anyone else who might have been trying to sleep, Herewiss stepped across the courtyard, past the dozing horses, to the doorway which Sunspark had opened. As he passed through it, the sound of the solano, the relentless spring wind of the Waste, reasserted itself; somewhere to his left he heard the squeaks and chirrups of a colony of bounce-mice going about their nightly business. He looked up at the cold-burning sky. Dragon, Spearman, Maiden, Crown, all the constellations of spring shone unperturbed high in the clear air.

How about that, Herewiss thought. He went back into the courtyard, and looked up. Within the walls, the sky glittered again with alien stars, strange eyes looking down on him from a nameless night.

This is the place, all right, he thought as he headed back toward the hall. He sighed again. Part of him was indulging itself in a delicious shivering excitement at the prospect of where he was. The rest of him was weighed down with the aching feeling of the angry, untouchable presence on the other side of the bedroll. He slowed down. *I don't really want to go back in there—*

—oh, Goddess, yes, I do—

—but—

He stopped still in his indecision, and as he listened to the odd silence that prevailed within the walls, he heard something more. Someone was outside, playing a lute. The individual notes stitched through the quiet like needles through dark velvet, bright, precise: but the pattern they were embroidering was random. There was a pause, as Herewiss listened; and then a chord strung itself in silvery lines across the still air, and another after it, gently mournful, though in a major key. When a voice joined the chords, singing in a light contralto, Herewiss was able to localize the sounds better. Whoever it was was somewhere to the left, around the corner of the building.

The tone of the singing, though he could not make out words, had touched Herewiss at the heart of his mood—night-ridden, melancholy. He went quietly over to the corner of the hall, leaned against the warm gray stone, peered around. Segnbora was there; sitting on the smooth paving with her back against the wall, her cloak folded behind her to lean on, a wineskin by her side. Her head was tilted back against the stone, relaxed, and the lute rested easily on her lap. If she noticed Herewiss, she gave no sign of it, but kept on serenading night and stars like a lover beneath some dark window.

> "—and she fared on up that awful trail
> and little of it made:
> She stood laughing on the peak-snows
> with the new Moon in her hair—"

Herewiss listened with interest. *With her deep voice, who'd suspect she had a high register? Needs a little work on her vibrato, but otherwise she sounds lovely—*

"Thank you!" said the deep voice, with laughter. The strumming continued as Segnbora looked over at him and smiled. "You going to stand there all night, or will you sit down and have a little wine?"

"Um," Herewiss said, as he went over to sit against the wall beside her. "I may have had more than I should already."

She raised an eyebrow at him, at the same time squeezing the lute's neck and wringing a tortured dissonant chord from it. "That bad, huh?"

"You underheard what went on in there?"

She shook her head. "These walls are good insulators. But once you came outside, it felt like someone was trying to beat a dent out of a big pot with a sledgehammer. Noisy."

"Sorry," Herewiss said.

"For what? A lot of it was the walls, anyway: they make even a fourth-level ideation echo as if it were being shouted in a cave." She stroked the lute again, and it purred in minor sevenths. "I take it he doesn't approve of your staying here."

"No."

"I can't say that I would, either, if I were in his place—but you have to stay. There's too much possibility here—"

Herewiss looked at her. (You *would* understand,) he said, bespeaking her.

(I'd better. Please, prince, the mindtouch—let's not and say we did. With these walls all around, the echo is really bad.)

"That's why you came outside?"

She nodded. "Partly. Every time someone subvocalized, my head felt like a gong being struck."

"I didn't feel much of anything. You have sensitivity problems?"

Segnbora chuckled. "Normally—if that's the word for it—I hear everything from fourth level up. Sometimes, if I'm drunk enough, or tired enough, I'll only pick up subvocals. But *this* place—" She sighed in exasperation, shook her head. "Or maybe it's because of my period. Though usually I don't have that problem with the hormonal surge. But I was getting tired of hearing people's bladders yelling to be emptied, and stomachs complaining that they weren't full enough, and neural leakage rattling like gravel in a cup. All multiplied by five. . . ."

"I used to wish I had that kind of sensitivity—"

"Don't. Unless you also wish to be able to turn it off. I can't. And it's awful. I'm tired of hearing Dritt's conscience chastising him about his weight problem, and Moris wondering if Dritt really loves him when he's so skinny, and Harald's arthritis crunching in his knee, and Lorn wanting Hergótha every night when he cleans Súthan. . . . Just tired." She closed her eyes,

201

rubbed the bridge of her nose as if a headache was coming on.

"I'm sorry," she said then, lifting her head. "I hear good things, too: I don't mean to whine." She reached down for the wineskin.

—*But even the good things make me feel so lonely*, Herewiss underheard her finish the thought. He closed his eyes in pain.

Segnbora looked at him quickly; her eyes were worried, and then in a tick of time they went regretful. "I leak, too," she said sadly. "I should have mentioned. Wine?"

"What kind?"

"Blood wine."

"Which region?" Herewiss asked, interested. The grapes were only grown along the North Arlene coast, where a combination of capricious climate and daily beatings of the vines produced an odd wrinkled grape, and eventually a sweet red liqueur with a hint of salty aftertaste—hence the name.

"Peridëu. My family has a connection with the vintners—one of my great-aunts cured their vines of white rot, oh, years back. They keep sending us the stuff every year or so."

"I might have a sip of that."

Segnbora passed Herewiss the wineskin, and he drank a couple of swallows' worth and restoppered it. "I didn't know you were a lutenist," he said.

"I'm not, usually." She smiled in the dark, leaned her head back against the stone, looking up. "But it's a good excuse. No one goes outside *just* to look at the stars, you know. So I take the lute with me sometimes."

Herewiss chuckled, jerked a thumb at the sky. "You noticed."

"How not? But what do you think I'd do, come running in yelling, 'Hey, look, everybody, the stars are all wrong'? Lorn would love *that*." She laughed too. "I was going to tell you before we left, in case you hadn't seen it already." She touched the lute strings again, tickling them into a brief bright spill of notes like laughter, a half-scale in the Hakrinian mode. Herewiss settled back against the wall, and looked at the sky once more, regarding the bright eyes of the elsewhere-night as they regarded him. "So what else aren't you," he said, "besides a lutenist?"

The scale modulated into the chords Herewiss had heard while peeking around the corner. "I'm not a poet," Segnbora said, "and not a singer, and not a dancer, and not a loremistress. . . ." She laughed softly. "Better not to be too many things at once: it scares people. Besides, in the case of the dancing, better they shouldn't see. I love to dance, but I'm afraid I'll look funny—so I don't, unless I'm *very* drunk . . . and then in the morning, I don't remember it anyway. . . ."

She keeps laughing, Herewiss thought. *As if she has to convince herself it's funny. But it's not working. . . .* Aloud he said, "So how's your dancing when you're drunk?"

"No one else remembers," she said. "They're all drunk too."

"Then it doesn't matter, does it?"

"No, I guess it doesn't." She smiled at him, a more relaxed look, almost a benediction. "You *do* understand."

"I'd better," he said, and they laughed together. "I'm about singing the way you are about dancing. Goddess knows why—they tell me I have a good voice—but I'm just shy. . . . What was that you were singing before? I didn't recognize it."

"Huh? Oh. 'Efmaer's Ride.' It's south Darthene, came north with my mother's side of the family. We were related to her, remotely." Again the chords, soft and sad for all that they were in a major key.

"Wasn't she the Queen who disappeared?"

"Well, according to the song, she didn't just disap-

203

pear. You know the stories about Sai Ebássren in the mountains, south of Barachael?"

"Sounds familiar. Maybe it has another name I know it by—"

"In Darthen they call it Méni Auärdhem."

"Glasscastle, yes. The place in the sky that appears every so often—"

"Not very often, really. There are Moon phases and lighting conditions involved, it's very complicated. But anyway, Efmaer's loved killed himself, and since suicides go to Glasscastle, Efmaer went to get her Name back from him. She took the sword Shadow with her—"

"How much of this is true?"

Segnbora shrugged. "It was a long time ago. But we know that Shadow existed, and the Queen went missing. It's a nice song, anyway—"

"Does it have a happy ending?"

"It depends," Segnbora said. "See, here's the last verse—" The lute whispered the sorrowing chords, and Segnbora's voice was hardly louder.

> "She stood laughing on the peak-snows
> with the new Moon in her hair,
> and she smiled and set her foot upon
> the Bridge that isn't There:
> She took the road right gladly
> to the Castle in the sky,
> and Darthen's sorrel steed came back,
> but the Queen stayed there for aye. . . ."

"So," she said, modulating out of the last chord into a minor arpeggio, "who knows? No one came back to tell whether Efmaer found what she was looking for, or whether she was happy. . . ."

"Glasscastle is where you go when you're tired of trying, isn't it? I remember hearing something like that." Herewiss sighed.

Segnbora looked at him sharply. "Don't you dare even think of it," she said. The anger in her voice caught Herewiss by surprise, and Segnbora too, after a moment. More gently she said, "You'll get where you're going, prince. They'll be singing about you for centuries."

"The question is, will they be happy songs? . . . And besides, even when you're in the middle of a song, you don't always feel like singing. *I* don't right now. . . ."

She reached out a hand and touched his where they lay folded in his lap. "He'll come through it," she said. "He's in love with you, that's all."

"Then why can't he see why I need to be here?!" Herewiss said, surprised again by anger, this time his own. More softly he added, "He knows how much the Fire means to me—"

"He's in love with *you*," Segnbora said again, almost too softly to be heard.

Herewiss held very still. Not even the lute broke the silence.

"Yes," he said. "I see what you mean."

"If I were you," Segnbora said, "I'd get some sleep."

Herewiss nodded, stood up, stretched. "Thanks for the wine," he said.

He headed back toward the courtyard and the hall. Her voice stopped him.

"Brother—" she said. Herewiss turned to look back at her. She was a shadowy shape, dark against the dark wall, surprisingly bright where starlight touched her— swordhilt, belt buckle, finger-ring, cloak-clasp, and the half-seen eyes. In the stillness he felt the air go suddenly thick and sharp with power, mostly hers, partly his. She *was* having a surge, hormonal or not, and it had touched his own Fire, roused it—

—his precognition came alive, as it had once or twice before. The image was blurred and vague, and out of context, strange-feeling. Darkness, and cold, and somewhere a bright light, but bound up, concealed—

She's hiding, something in him told him suddenly. *But why? From what?*

The feeling ebbed, drained away, leaving the air

205

just air again, and Segnbora was just a young woman sitting against a wall, not a numinous shadow-wrapt figure gazing at him through darkness and silence. She looked back and shuddered all over. Herewiss wondered what she had seen.

"It doesn't matter," she said. "I didn't see anything clearly. That wasn't what I was going to say. Prince, you *will* do it. I'll help any way I can."

She cares a little, he thought in quiet surprise. *More than a little.*

Well, she would.

He bowed to her, the deep bow of greeting or farewell from one veteran of the Silent Precincts to another. "Sister," he said; and there was nothing else to say. He went around the corner and back inside.

Nothing had changed. Lorn's people were all asleep, and Lorn was still rolled up in his cloak, in a tight angry-looking ball. He was snoring.

Herewiss stopped by the firepit, sank down wearily into his chair. The flames flurried momentarily higher, and Sunspark was looking at him again.

(So how is the night?)

(Strange,) Herewiss said, (but then that could be expected.) He sat there for a little while and avoided looking in Freelorn's direction.

(I'm never going to get to sleep by myself,) he said eventually. (Maybe I should take something—)

He stopped short.

(The Soulflight drug—)

(?)

(The innkeeper at the Ferry Tavern gave it to me. If I took a little, I could probably drop right off into pleasant dreams—though with the smaller doses you sometimes don't remember what happens to you—)

(You could probably use some pleasant dreams tonight,) Sunspark said.

Herewiss went and got the little bottle out of his saddlebag, then sat down by the firepit again and regarded it. He unstoppered it and put his nose to the opening. There was a faint sweet odor, like honey. He stuck his finger in, took a little and licked it off.

The taste was extremely bitter; he choked a little as he put the stopper back in the bottle and set it aside. *Well,* he thought, *let's see what happens—*

He leaned back and closed his eyes, and waited.

—an easy, drifting passage into—
. CRASH!!
—and he looked around him, terribly shaken. All was still, nothing was wrong anywhere that he could see. It had been one of those falling-dreams that slams one suddenly into the wall between sleep and waking, and out the other side.

False alarm. One more time—

—drifting easily downward into empty lightless places, filled with uncaring as if with smoke: spiraling down, sailing on wings feathered with fear, and now suddenly the—
WHAT??! NO!!
Cold dusk, a gray evening, no sunset pouring crimson-gold through treetops and touching the Woodward with fire: torches quarreling weakly with the evening mist: and silence, deadly silence. No children running and playing, though even on chill evenings they would be out this late, resisting their mothers' attempts to get them back inside. Little sound, little movement. Walk quietly up to the great carven door, pass silently through it. Greet the Rooftree with reserve, and go by; up the stairway, left at the top of the stairs and down through the east gallery, but softly, softly. Someone is dying. Turn right into the north corridor, one of the more richly carven ones, and keep going. There on the walls is carved the story of Ferrigan, your ancestress, and the panels show her rebuilding the Woodward after its burning, with the help of creatures not wholly human. You always loved her story, that of a person who mastered her own pow-

ers and went her own way, disappearing into the Silent Precincts one day, never to be seen again. Herelaf liked that one too. But very shortly now Herelaf will be past liking anything at all, at least in *this* life. Walk softly, and go on in: last room on the right, the corner room, the room that is the heir's by tradition.

There is the bed, there is Herelaf, the sword out of him, now; your father standing there, not looking at either of you, not daring to. For fear that he will see one of you die, and the other of you live. Oh, he loves you well enough: that much is certain; but right now Hearn is finding it hard to love you at all, who were so stupid as to play with swords while drunk. Herelaf is lying very still, looking very pale. How strange. He was always the darkest one in the family; you used to tease him about it sometimes, saying that there must be Steldene blood in him somewhere; and he would grin and say, "Mother never told us half of what she did while she was out Rodmistressing. You can sleep with some strange sorts in that business. Maybe something rubbed off." That was the way he always was: big, gentle, inoffensive, easygoing; no one had a bad word for him, not a single person anywhere, most especially not the many people he called loved. There were enough of them in the Wood, men and women both, and people used to marvel that he never took one loved with an eye to marriage. "I like to spread myself around," he would always say. "So far there's nobody that special that I'd want to give all of me to just them. But maybe . . ."

Forget *that*. He's going to die tonight, and all the chances close down forever. You did that to him. Yes you did. Don't try to deny it.

DAMMIT LET ME OUT OF HERE!!!

Hearn stands there, looking like he wishes he were anywhere else than this—facing down the Shadow Himself, *anywhere* but here. But he cannot desert either of you: he knows that you both need him now, both of you need him there desperately, and Hearn was always brave. Maybe not prudent; certainly if he were prudent he would go out of here. But brave.

Herelaf lies there, drained dry, waiting for the Mother to come for him. She can't be far; his body has a castoff look about it already—or maybe it is his closeness to the *Door* that is apparent, and the light from that Sea of which the Starlight is a faint intimation is shining through him, as if he were a *doorway* himself. The gray light makes everything in the room look unreal, except Herelaf—and he will be unreal soon enough.

You go over to him, kneel sidewise by the bed, take his hands in yours. They are chill, and this shakes you more terribly than anything else; his hands were always warm, even in wintertime when you always went clammy and stiff with the cold. Herelaf, now, with those big warm hands of his—big even for a Brightwood man—getting cold; getting dead. You did it. Oh yes.

NOT THIS AGAIN!! PLEASE, NO!!

Oh yes. "Dusty," he says, his beautiful soft deep voice gone all cracked and dry and shallow with pain. "Little brother mine. It wasn't your fault."

The words go into your head, but they make no particular sense. At least they didn't then. They do now, and it hurts at least twice as much, because you know it *was* your fault. Then, though, you bury your face in those cold hands, punishing yourself with the terror of what is going to happen. The Mother is kind, but inexorable; when She comes, there's no turning Her back. And you know She's coming.

"Dusty, are you listening to me? Look at me." He turns your face up to him, and you try to look away, but it's no good; even dying those hands have all their strength.

You look at him: dark curly hair like yours, big around the shoulders like you got to be eventually; the droopy sleepy eyes, the smile that never comes off. Even dying, there's a ghost of it apparent, a slight curling-at-the-corners smile. He loves you. That's the worst part of it all, really.

"Don't do anything stupid," he says. "I expect you to stay right here and get things straight. You're going to be the heir now. You have a lot to learn. Don't run out on Dad."

And you nod, the pain becoming even worse as you realize that this is a lie. There is *nothing* that will keep you here after Herelaf dies, not pleas nor threats nor even Hearn's need. You have a worse one; punishment of the deathguilt, and getting it attended to as quickly as possible, before the deed starts to rot and smell up the Wood. You know you'll try to go after Herelaf, to achieve whatever justice is meted out on that last Shore to those who murder their brothers.

Lying to your brother on his deathbed. You *are* worthless.

He flicks a tired, tired glance at the bandage around his middle, and at the stain spreading on it. "Wasn't your fault," he says wearily. How that voice used to sing in the evenings; now it can barely speak. Herelaf looks up at something, Someone on the other side of the bed. He smiles faintly. "Mother," he says.

And then is still.

And you get up, and wander away.

Into the gray places where nothing matters.

Here's a window. That's as good as anything else.

Someone is stopping you. It's Freelorn.

Damn him anyway.

You pull yourself gradually out of his grip and wander off into the gray places again. Where nothing matters.

You emerge occasionally to try to make an end of yourself. They stop you. You wander off into the gray again.

Nothing matters.

Nothing.

It's all gray.

*THANK GOODNESS THAT'S OVER. HOW DO
I GET OUT OF THIS?*

Gray mist, cold. There are voices, remote, speaking
words in other languages; other wanderers lost in the
gray country. You ignore them.

And someone singing. Freelorn? Yes. The voice is
changing, and cracks ludicrously every other verse.

> " 'On the Lion's Day,
> when the Moon was high,
> then the Queen went to the Fane
> for her loved to die;
>
> " 'On that Night of dread,
> opened up the deeps,
> and she knew the Shadow there,
> and in Rilthor forever she sleeps;
>
> " 'And her daughter wept,
> vengeance in her heart,
> and swore herself as vow
> to take her mother's part,
> bating love and breath
> till the Shadow's death:
>
> " 'And she laid Him dead,
> and herself she died,
> never dreaming all the while
> that in His death, He lied . . .' "

You shake your head sadly. Freelorn's song, to be
sure, redolent as usual of last stands and heroism past
the confines of time and expectation. But all Béorgan's heroism couldn't change the fact that the
Shadow was stronger than she, immortal, more permanent than death. What use is anything, anyhow—all
hearts chill, and all loves die, and maybe the time has
come for yours too—there in the mist, beckoning, waits
the dark shape with the heart of iron and the eyes of

ice, and all you have to do is despair; He'll do the rest—

Oh, Mother. No.

You summon your strength, and go away from there quickly, before the cold eyes see you and mark you for their own. Here, now, the mist is thick, and a little warmer. Faintly you can sense a body passing by, not far away—

> "—nor any day in dawning,
> nor any night in eve:
> and all the empty silences—"

—a quiet voice, unfamiliar, singing a fragment of something to itself. It passes through the gray and is gone again. Follow it, if you can: it might show you the way out—

Suddenly in the grayness a tall form appears before you, vague through the fog. You press closer to it to ask for directions. Even if it can't tell you the way out, company would be welcome.

It's company, all right.

It's you.

Now you know how Dritt felt this morning. This is the you that you have seen in clear pools and mirrors; but changed. He's about three inches taller than you are, more regal of carriage. He moves with easy unthinking grace, whereas you just kind of bump along. He doesn't have those ten extraneous pounds on the front of his belly, where you have them; his eyes are bluer; his muscles are lithe under the smooth skin. He doesn't have any of your moles, and his face is unlined where your frown has long since indented itself; he doesn't have the little scar just above the right eye where Herelaf hit you with the fireplace poker when you were three and he was five. His face is serene, wise, joyous. You look at him with awe, reach out to him—and your hand goes through him. He's a dream-Herewiss. You might have suspected as much. *I never looked* that *good,* you think.

212

He doesn't really see you; he is interacting with someone else who isn't there. Someone who is dreaming about you. Well, if you follow him, you may get back to the real world again.

He moves away through the mist, and you go along with him, feeling a little unnerved to be in the company of such perfection—even if he *is* you.

Eventually the fog begins to clear a little, and you find yourself back in the hold again. Your body is sitting over by the firepit. You glance at it and look away quickly. Two of you at once is a bit much, and three, especially when the third has all the imperfections, is almost more than you can bear. The dream-Herewiss is conversing with a dream-Freelorn over in the corner. Their eyes are warm as they look at one another, and their faces smile as they speak words of love. Freelorn is curled up in his usual ball again, snoring noisily. You might have known it was his dream of you—he never *could* see those little imperfections of yours, even when you pointed them out. Goddess love him.

You're tired, and sad, and you want to call it a night, so you ease yourself back over toward yourself and melt down into the body, pulling it up and around you like the familiar covers of your own bed—

He woke up with a terrible taste in his mouth, and a raging headache. Sunspark was nearby, in a state of agitation such as he had never perceived in it before.

(Where were you? Your body was here, but I couldn't find your *self*—I thought you'd done that "dying" thing you keep talking about—)

(I'm all right,) Herewiss lied, rubbing at his aching eyes. (Where's Lorn?)

Sunspark vanished without answering.

Freelorn was gone.

Freelorn's people were all in such a state of embarrassment that Herewiss found it difficult to be in the same room with them, and he went away into other parts of the hold, wandering around, until he heard their horses' hooves clatter out of the courtyard into the Waste. When he came downstairs, though, he found one of them still there. Segnbora was puttering around the hall, checking Herewiss' supplies to make sure he had enough of everything.

"He just left," she said from the other side of the hall, not stopping what she was doing. "Very early this morning, he got dressed, saddled Blackmane, and rode out. I don't think he even stopped to pee. His trail will be easy enough to follow."

Herewiss nodded.

Segnbora stood up, hands on hips, surveying the supplies. "That should do it. I should go after them, now; he'll miss me, and get mad—"

"I wouldn't want that to happen," Herewiss said.

Segnbora looked at him with deep compassion. "He'll get over it."

"I hope so."

She went out to the courtyard and spent a few silent minutes saddling Steelsheen. Herewiss followed her outside listlessly. When she was ready, she gave the saddle a final tug of adjustment, then went very quickly to Herewiss; she took his hands in hers, and squeezed them, and standing way up on tiptoe kissed him once lightly on the mouth. "I'll give it to him for you," she said. "He'll be all right; we'll take care of him. Good luck, Herewiss. And your Power to you—"

Then she was up in the saddle and away, pelting off after the others, leaving nothing behind but a small cloud of dust and a brief taste of warmth.

Herewiss watched her go, then turned back. The hold swallowed him like a mouth.

EIGHT

*It is perhaps one of life's more interesting
ironies that, of the many who beseech the Goddess to send them love, so few will accept it
when it comes, because it has come in what
they consider the wrong shape, or the wrong
size, or at the wrong time. Against our prej-
udices, even the Goddess strives in vain.*

Hamartics, s'Berenh, ch. 6

(Sunspark?)

   (?)

(What do you make of this?)

   (Just a moment.)

Herewiss sat crosslegged before one of the *doors,*
making notes with a stylus on a tablet of wax.
Through the *door* was visible an unbroken vista of
golden-green hills, reaching away into unguessable dis-
tances and met at the mist-veiled horizon by a violet
sky. The brilliant sun that hung over the landscape
etched Herewiss' shadow sharply behind him, and
struck gray glitters from the wall against which he
leaned.

Sunspark padded over to him in the shape of a
golden North Arlene hunting cat, the kind kept to
course wild pig and the smaller Fyrd varieties on the
moor. It peered through the *door,* its tail twitching.

(Grass. So?)

(That's not the point. I've been by this *door* five
times today, and that sun hasn't moved.)

(It could be a slow one. You remember that one yesterday that went by so fast, three or four times an
hour. There's no reason this one couldn't be slow.)

(Yes, but there's something else wrong. That grass is

215

bent as if there's wind blowing, but none of it *moves*.)

(That might just be the way it grows. There are a lot of strange things in the worlds, Herewiss—) It stepped closer to the *door*. (Then again— Look high in the *doorway*. Is there something in the sky there?) It craned its neck. (By the top of the left post.)

Herewiss squinted. (Hard to tell, with the sun so close—no, wait a moment. Does that have wings?)

(I think so. And it's just hanging there, frozen.) Sunspark shrugged. (That could be your answer. This *door* may be frozen on one moment—or if it's not, it's moving that moment so slowly that we can't perceive it.)

Herewiss put down the tablet of wax in its wooden frame, and stretched. (Well, that's something new. What was that one you were looking at?)

(Nothing but empty sea, with four suns, all small and red. They were clustered close together, not spaced apart as most of them have been when they're multiple.)

(So—) Herewiss picked up the tablet again. (That's the nineteenth one with more than one sun, and the eighty-ninth one with water. More than half of them have shown seas or lakes or rivers. Who knows—the Morrowfane itself might be through one of these *doors*. No people in that one?)

(None that I could see. Perhaps they live below the surface—)

(Could be. Well, people have been much in the minority so far. Maybe whoever built this place was more interested in other places than other people.)

(What you would call people, anyway.) Sunspark chuckled a little inside. (Would you call *me* "people"?)

Herewiss looked at it. The cat-face was inscrutable, but his underhearing gave him a sudden impression of hopefulness, almost wistfulness. (I think so,) he said. (You're good company, whatever.)

(Yes, well. "Company" is something that I have not

had much practice being. There is usually no need for it—)

(Among your kind, maybe. We need it a lot.)

(It is the way your folk were built. It seems strange, to want another's company before it comes time for renewal, for the final union.)

(It has its advantages.)

(In the binding of energies, yes—)

(More than that. There's more than binding. *Sharing.*)

(I have trouble with that word. Giving away energy willingly, is it?)

(Yes.)

(It seems mad.)

(Sometimes, yes. But you usually get it back.)

(Such a gamble.)

(Yes,) Herewiss said, (it is that.)

(What happens when you don't get it back?)

(Then you've lost energy, obviously. It hurts a little.)

(It should hurt *more* than a little. Your own substance is riven from you; part of your *self*—)

(Depends how much of yourself you give away. Most of the time, it's nothing fatal.)

(Well, how could it be?)

(It happens, among our kind. People have given too much, and died of it; but mostly because they convinced themselves that they were going to. In the end it's their own decision.)

(Mad, completely mad. The contract-conflict is safer, I think.)

(Probably. But it doesn't pay off the way sharing does when it turns out right.)

(I don't understand.)

(It's the dare. The gamble, taking the chance. When sharing comes back, it's—an elevation. It makes you want to do it again—)

(—and if it fails the next time, you'll feel worse. A madness.) It shrugged. (Well, there are patterns

217

within the Pattern, and no way to understand them all. How many *doors* have we counted now?)

Herewiss looked at the tablet. (A hundred and fifty-six. Five of the lower halls and half this upper hall. Then there's that east gallery, and the hallways leading from it—)

Sunspark's tone of thought was uneasy. (You know, there is no way that all these rooms could possibly be contained within this structure as we beheld it from outside. There's no room, it's just too small.)

(Yes, I know—but they're all here. What about that row of rooms between the great hall downstairs and the back wall? They couldn't have been there, either. Of course it was all right; after a few days they *weren't*. Four *doors* went missing from this hall alone earlier this week, but here they are again—)

(The next one along was one of the ones that vanished. Let's see what it looks like now.)

Herewiss got up, and they walked together down to the next *doorway*. It showed them night-time in a valley embraced by high hills; behind the hills was a golden glow like the onset of some immense moonrise. The valley floor was patterned with brilliant lights of all colors, laid out in an orderly fashion like a grid-work. Down from the gemmed heights wound a river of white fire, pouring itself blazing down the hillsides into the softly hazed splendor of the valley's floor. There were no stars.

(Now *those* may be people,) Sunspark said after a moment, (but not my kind, or yours, I dare say. What do you say to a white light?)

(I don't know. What do you say to a horse, or a pillar of fire?) Herewiss grinned a little, and made a note on his tablet. (This next one was gone too. Let's look—)

They moved a few steps farther down the hall, and stopped. The *door* showed them nothing. Nothing at all.

(Sweet Goddess, it came back,) Herewiss said. (I

was wondering what this one might be, and I had a thought—it could be a *door* that was never set to show anything before the builders left. An unused blank. It appears and disappears like all the other *doors* in the place, but it doesn't show anything.)

(I don't know.) Sunspark looked at the *door* dubiously. (It gives me a funny feeling—)

(Well, let's see.)

Herewiss blanked everything out, slowed his breathing, and strained his underhearing toward the *door, past* the *door*—

—strained—

(Nothing,) he said, and opened his eyes again. (Can't get into it like I can some of the others. Spark, would you do a favor and get my grimoire for me? The one with the sealed pages.)

(You're going to try to open this *now*?)

(Is there a better time? I had a good night's sleep. I ate a big breakfast. Let's try.)

Sunspark went molten and flowed down the hall like a hot wind. A few minutes later he returned, a young red-haired man with hot bright eyes and a tunic the color of fire, carrying the book. Herewiss reached out and took it, unsealed the pages and began riffling through them.

(Damn,) he said after a moment. (Nothing is going to—well, no, maybe this unbinding—no, that's too concrete, it's for regular doors. This one—no— Dammit.)

He paused a moment, then started running through the pages again. (This one. Yes. It's a very generalized unbinding, and if I change it here—and here—)

(I thought Freelorn said that it took Flame to open a *door*.)

(Yes, he did, and he was probably right, dammit, since *doors* are more or less alive. But this is an unbinding for inanimate objects, and if I make a few changes in the formula, it might work. I have to try something.)

(Will you need me?)

(Just to stand guard.) Herewiss sat down cross-legged against the wall again, breathed deeply and started to compose his mind. It took him a while: his excitement was interfering with his concentration. Finally he achieved the proper state, and turned his eyes downward to read from the grimoire.

"M'herië nai náridh veg baminédrian á phröi," he began, concentrating on building an infrastructure of openness and nonrestriction, a house made out of holes. The words were slippery and the concepts kept trying to become concrete instead of abstract, but Herewiss kept at it, weaving a cage turned inside out, its bars made of winds that sighed and died as he emplaced them. It was both more delicate a sorcery and more dangerous a one than that which he had worked outside of Madeil. There the formulae had been fairly straightforward, and the changes introduced had been quantitative ones rather than the major qualitative shifts he was employing here. But he persevered, and took the last piece away from the sorcery, an act that should have started it functioning.

It sat there and stared at him, and did nothing.

He looked it over, what there "was" of it. It should have worked: it was "complete," as far as such a word could be applied to such a not-structure. *Maybe I didn't push it against the* door *hard enough,* he thought. *Well—*

He gave it a mighty shove inside his head. It lunged at him and hit him in the back of the inside of his mind, giving him an immediate headache.

Dammit-to-Darkness, what did I—did I put a spin on it somehow? The shift could have done that, I guess. Well, then.

He pulled at it, and immediately it slid toward the *doorway* and partway through it. The sorcery came to a halt, then, and sat there twitching. Nothing came out of the *door.*

Maybe if I wait a moment, he thought.

220

He waited. The sorcery stopped twitching and fell into a sullen stillness.

Herewiss lost his temper. (Dark!) he swore, and lashed out at the sorcery, backhanding it across the broad part of the nonstructure instead of dissassembling it piece by piece, slowly, as he should have. It fell apart, nothingness collapsing into a higher state of nonexistence—

Something came out the *door*.

He opened his eyes, and just enough of the Othersight was functioning to give him a horrible dual vision of what was happening. The *door* itself was still dark to his normal sight; but the Othersight showed him something more tenebrous, more frightening, a hideous murky knotted emptiness, the whole purpose of which was containment and repression. It was a prison. And the prisoner was coming through the *door* right then; a huge awful bulk that could be possibly be fitting through that *door*, but was: a botched-looking thing, a horrible haphazard combination of bloated bulk and waving, snatching claws, with an uncolored knobby hide that the filtered afternoon light was refusing to touch. Herewiss caught a brief frozen glimpse of teeth like knives in a place that should not have been a mouth, but was; then the Othersight confused itself with his vision again, and he was perceiving the thing as it was, the embodiment of unsatisfied hungers, a thing that would eat a soul any chance it got, and the attached body as an hors d'oeuvre. He underheard a feeling like the taste at the back of the throat after vomiting, a taste like rust and acid.

Through the confusion of perceptions, one thought made itself coldly clear: *Well, this is it. I tried, and I did wrong, and now I'm going to pay the price.* The sorcery had already backlashed, leaving him wobbly and weak, and he watched helplessly as the thing leaned out of the *door* over him and examined him, assessing the edibility of his *self* as an epicure looks over a dinner presented him—

Something grabbed him. Herewiss commended his soul to the Goddess, hoping that it would manage to get to Her in the first place, before he realized that Sunspark had him and was running.

(Where—) he said weakly.

(*Anywhere,* but out of *here!* I have seen those things before, and there is no containing them—)

(But it *was* contained. Spark, what is it?)

(The name I heard applied to it was "hralcin." If you desire to stay in this body, we had better get you away from here quickly. They eat *selves*—)

(Your kind too?)

(No one knows. None of my people have ever had a confrontation with one of the things, as far as I know, and I would rather not be the first.)

Herewiss realized that Sunspark was still in the human form, running with him down the stairs and into the main hall. Behind them there was a great noise of roaring and crashing.

(Do you think it could kill *you?*)

(I don't know. I don't think so. But I have heard of those things taking souls, and the souls never came back, not that anyone ever heard of in the places where I've traveled. They say that one or two of those can depopulate a whole world, one soul at a time. We could go through one of the *doors* until it goes elsewhere—)

(Sunspark, put me down.)

(*What??*)

(Let me go.)

Sunspark put Herewiss down on the floor of the main hall and turned into a pillar of white fire, towering from floor to ceiling. Herewiss wobbled to his feet.

(I don't know how I managed to call it—)

(You said that the spell you were using was originally for inanimate objects?)

(Yes, but—)

(There's your answer. The thing is not alive. Why

do you think it eats souls? When it has gotten enough of them, it gains life—)

(We've got to get it back in there.)

(You are a madman,) Sunspark said. (There is no containing the things within anything short of a worldwall.)

(But it *was* contained! If it was in there, and bound, it can be gotten in there again, and *re*bound—)

(Whoever put it in there knew more about it than we do, certainly. This much *I* know, they don't like light much. I can keep it away from us, I think. But it's only a matter of time until it leaves this place and gets out among your poor fellow men—and then there will be trouble.)

(It mustn't happen. They don't like light?)

(No.)

(Maybe we can drive it back in through that *doorway*. Then I could bind it back in again—)

(But it takes you forever!) Sunspark's flames were trembling: the crashing was coming down the stairs. (And the thing would make a quick meal of you. It's got your scent, and once these things smell soul they pursue it until they catch it—)

Herewiss was sucking in great gulps of air, desperately fighting off the backlash. (I can decoy it back into the *doorway*. It'll follow me. Then I'll come out again, and you will hold it in with your fires until I can weave the necessary spell—)

Sunspark looked at Herewiss, a long moment's regard flavored with unease and amazement. (I can hold it off from *you*—)

(Sunspark, Sunspark, if that thing can empty whole worlds of people, what will it do to the Kingdoms? Come on. We'll let it into the hall, and I'll duck back up behind it, and you drive it up behind me. Then up, and through the *door*, and you can hold it in—)

(Very well.)

The hralcin came careening down the stairs, all horrible misjointed limbs and claws reaching out toward

Herewiss as it staggered from the stairwell and across the floor. (I can direct the fire and the light pretty carefully,) Sunspark said, (but try to keep out from in front of me, or else well ahead. I am going to let go.)

(Right.)

Herewiss stumbled off to Sunspark's right, and the hralcin immediately changed direction a little to follow him. At that moment Sunspark went up in a terrible blaze of light and heat, so brilliant that it no longer manifested the appearance of flames at all—it was a fierce eye-hurting tower of whiteness, like a column carven of lightning. The hralcin screeched, put up several of its claws to shield what might have been eyes, a circlet of irregular glittering protuberances set in the rounded top of its pear-shaped body. Herewiss dodged around it and scrambled up the stairs, slipping and falling on the slime the thing had left.

At the top of the stairs he paused for just a moment, feeling sick, and things went red and black in front of him as his body tried to faint; but he wouldn't let it. The stench in the hall was terrible, as if the hralcin carried around the rotting corpses of its victims as well as their souls. He went staggering down past *doorway* after *doorway*, and finally found the right one. It was still black, and he quailed at the thought of going in there, maybe being imprisoned there himself, never finding the way out again, and the hralcin coming in after him—

He heard it screaming up the stairs after him. He thought, *Lorn, dammit!*

He went in.

Immediately the darkness shut down around him, as if he had crawled back into a womb. There was no smell, no sound, nothing to see: he reached out and could feel nothing at all around him. He turned, looked for the *doorway*. It was still there, though hard to see through the murkiness of this other place, and it wavered as if seen through a heat haze.

There was something wrong with his chest. He was

breathing, but it was as if there was nothing really there to fill his lungs.

He inched back to the *doorway*, put his head out to breathe. The hralcin was coming down the hall, back-lit brilliantly by the pursuing Sunspark. It saw Herewiss, screamed, and came faster. Herewiss took a long, long breath, like a swimmer preparing for a plunge. *It could be your last,* he thought miserably, and ducked back into darkness.

Silence, and the *doorway* was vague before him again. He had a sudden thought. Herewiss edged around to the side of the *doorway*, until he was seeing it only as a very thin wedge of light, and then as a line, like that of a normal door open just a crack. He put his hand gingerly into the place *behind* the *door*, where the hallway would have been in the real world.

Nothing, just more darkness.

He slipped around and hid in it, his pulse thundering in his ears, the only thing to be heard.

There was a rippling, a stirring. Right in front of him, hardly a foot from Herewiss' nose, the hralcin seemed to bloom out from a flat, irregularly-shaped plane into complete and rounded existence. He started back, then watched it blunder further into the darkness; Sunspark's light washed through the *door* after it and limned it clearly. Even muted and blurred by the darkness of this other place, Sunspark's brilliance was still blinding. Herewiss could imagine what the heat must be like. But if it let up for so much as a second, the hralcin would only come out again—

Herewiss ducked out from behind the *doorway*, his lungs screaming for air, and threw himself through, diving and rolling. Behind him he could feel the vibrations of the hralcin's scream through the water-dark space, cut off sharply as he passed through the *doorway* and crashed to the ground. His face and hands were seared by Sunspark's fires. He dragged himself behind the elemental, and the burning less-ened a little, though the air in the hall was still like an oven: the stone was reflecting back much of the heat of its flames.

(Are you all right?)

(Not really. But we have to finish this—)

A claw waved out through the *doorway*, and Sunspark blazed up more fiercely yet. The reflected heat stung Herewiss' burned face terribly, but the claw and the limb to which it was attached were withdrawn.

(It is building up a tolerance,) Sunspark said. (Hurry up.)

Herewiss found the grimoire half-hidden under a great glob of slime. He grabbed the book, fumbled at the pages. (I am, I am—)

Another claw came out the *door*. Sunspark spat a tongue of flame at it, and the claw disappeared. The smell in the hallway became much worse.

Bindings, inanimate—great bindings—they'd better *be!* Herewiss threatened himself into a semblance of calm, started building the necessary structure around and against the *doorway*. Luckily it was a very simple and straightforward one, requiring more power than delicacy, and his need was fueling his power more than adequately. "—é n'srádië!" he finished, sealing it, standing away from the structure in his mind. (All right, Spark, let's see if it holds.)

Sunspark dimmed down its fires, and the hralcin slammed against the binding thrown over the *door* as if against a stone wall. The binding held, though Herewiss trembled with the reflected shock.

The hralcin hit the wall again. It still held.

And again.

And again.

The wall held.

Herewiss sagged back against the hot stone, regardless of getting burnt. Sunspark was in the man-shape again, helping him. (My room,) Herewiss said, the backlash hitting him with redoubled force. (I think I need a nap—)

Before Sunspark had gotten him halfway down the stairs, he was having one.

He woke up in his bed in the tower workroom, a makeshift affair of cushions and blankets that Sunspark had filched for him from one place or another. It was dark; the room was lit only by the two big candles on the worktable. Herewiss looked up and out the window, seeing early evening stars.

(Well. About time.)

He turned his head to the center of the room. Sunspark was there, enfleshed in the form of a tall slender woman with dark eyes and hair the color of a brilliant sunset, long and red-golden. She sat in a big old padded chair, looking at him with slightly unnerving concern. She was gowned all in wine-red, and her sleeves were rolled up.

(How long has it been?) Herewiss said, propping himself up on one elbow.

(A night and a day.)

(The hralcin—)

(The binding is holding very nicely.) Sunspark got up, went to Herewiss and laid her hand against his forehead: it burned him slightly, but he bore it. (Better,) she said. (Last night there was little difference between the feel of your skin and mine; but the fever is down now. How are the burns?)

(They sting a little. The skin is tight, but I'll live, I think.) Herewiss looked around him: there was a big bowl on the floor with a sponge in it, and the dark liquid inside it smelled like burn potion.

(Were you *using* that on me?)

(Yes. The recipe was in your grimoire, and you had most of the herbs in your supplies—)

(But the water, Spark. I thought you couldn't touch it—)

(A minor inconvenience, in quantities that small—I shielded my hand with a cloth, anyway. It makes a feeling like a headache, nothing so terrible. Can you get up and eat?)

My Goddess—it's, she's worried *about me, she* cares *—what a wonder!* (Spark, thank you— I could eat a Dragon raw.)

(No need, really. I could cook it for you.)

Herewiss sat up straight and stretched. He was stiff from the burns, but not too much so, and the backlash had diminished to the point where he only felt very tired.

(Oh. You brought a new chair?)

(From the little town up north where I've been getting the food. They've started to leave things out for me at night; some of them leave doors and windows open.) She chuckled and got up, going out of the room and down the hall to another room where supplies were kept. (I guess the news got around when their neighbors started finding pantries empty of food and full of raw gold.)

(I would imagine.) Herewiss was surprised at Sunspark's initiative on his behalf.

(And not far from here there's a subsurface cavern full of raw gems of all kinds, though mostly rubies. I took the chair and left them a ruby about the size of a melon. Soon the streets will be filling with furniture.)

Sunspark came back in with a few slices of hot venison on a trencher of bread. Under her arm was a skin of Brightwood white, the last of Freelorn's liberated supply.

(Don't carry it like that—you'll warm it up!)

(Oh. Sorry.) She laid the skin on the table with the food, and Herewiss stared at it a little morosely as Sunspark went rummaging through his bags to find the lovers'-cup. (I wonder where he is,) thought Herewiss. (Probably stuck in some damn dungeon in Osta, trying to figure out a way to bribe the guards to send me a message . . .)

Sunspark looked at Herewiss as she set the cup on the table and poured the wine. She said nothing.

(I wish he were here,) Herewiss said.

Sunspark shook the skin to get the last few drops out, stoppered it, and put it away. (You would probably quarrel again,) she said.

(How would you know?) Herewiss said, stirred slightly out of his tiredness by anger. (You're rather new at this sort of thing to be so understanding of it, don't you think?)

(Some aspects of it,) Sunspark answered without rancor. (But some are much like the ways of my own people. There are still more likenesses between our kinds than there are differences, I think.)

(So what are you basing your feeling on, that we would quarrel again?)

Sunspark sat down among the cushions, hesitated a little. (He's seeking to bind your energies, that one is,) she said.

(As I bound yours? Ridiculous. He's my loved.)

(But that *is* a binding. *Your* loved, you said. It's not the same kind of binding as there is between us, true. But you have—commitments, you have set ways in which you treat one another—)

Herewiss remembered the terrible alienness of the last night with Freelorn, the feeling of having a stranger in the bed—all the more terrible because the stranger had been his loved not half an hour before. (The way he treated me is nothing I ever saw before.)

(Well enough. But when one form of binding doesn't work, an entity tries another—)

Dully, Herewiss began to eat. The food was tasteless. (And he was doing that?)

(It could be. Your strength is considerable, though. It comes as no surprise that he went away so angry. I think he'll try again, but not the way he did last time—)

(It seems so useless. I need my Power—I thought he understood that—)

(The little one, the shieldmaid,) Sunspark said, (*she* understands. I think he might envy that a little.)

Herewiss considered it.

(That seems all she does, though; understand,) said Sunspark. (Which may cause problems—But enough. Eat!)

He ate, and began to feel a little less tired and light-headed—but he could feel the depression beginning to creep up on him. Maybe—maybe there was something he could do. There was, after all, the Soulflight drug—

(Sunspark,) he said, (the bottle of drug, would you get it for me?)

She regarded him with an odd startled look. (Will you hazard it again? I'm not sure this place is good for its use. There are influences here that may have contaminated your use of it the last time—)

(The last time was bad because the argument was fresh, Spark,) Herewiss said. (I could use a little something to cheer me up, to relax me—)

(*Relax* you?? Herewiss, you are fresh from a bout of sorcery; you slept for a night and a day! You know how debilitating the drug is! It'll be the end of you if you abuse it!)

(What are you worrying about?) Herewiss said. (I'd come back.)

Sunspark looked at him, her face still, though Herewiss could feel the roil of emotions that she did not yet know how to make into the proper expressions. She turned and went out of the room very quickly.

A pang of guilt smote him immediately. *That was mean of me,* he though. *But it* is *funny that it should be so concerned*—

He stopped in mid-chew. All the little kindnesses that he had been accepting from Sunspark; all the small gentle gestures: the chair, the food it brought back from the villages on the edge of the Waste, the swordblanks it had been fetching all the way from Darthis— But he had been judging it by human standards. No elemental would act like that normally. He compared the Sunspark of his first acquaintance, rough, uncaring, fierce of demeanor, testing him with

230

thoughtless ferocity, with this one—calm, considerate, a tamed power waiting on him at table. A fire elemental, handling *water* for his sake. And now concerned about his death, where before it had not even believed in it. The feelings he had underheard when it went out of the room: fear? Pain?

Maybe love?

Oh, no, he thought again. *It couldn't possibly have understood about love, and I did try so hard to teach it. And now it knows. And it wants to try it out, the same way it tried to unite with me before—but this time on my terms—*

He put down what was left of the bread, and stared across the table at the lover's-cup. *It needs, now. I have taught it loneliness, which it never knew before. And now I'm going to have to teach it pain, because I can't be what it needs, but I will go get what I need—*

The cup sat there, full of wine and promise. It was the Goddess' cup, the cup poured for Her at each meal to remind those who ate that all set before them was, one way or another, the product of Her love—as were the people with whom they ate. When the meal was done, if there were lovers there, the youngest of them would drain the cup together in Her name. If one was alone, one said the Blessing for the Sundered and drank it in their own name and the name of their lover, wherever that one might be. Herewiss remembered how it had used to be in the lonely days when he was young. He had been rather ugly, and when he drank the cup and called on the Loved Who Will Be to await his coming, he secretly despaired of its ever happening, of ever finding another part of himself. Now, in these later days, at least he had a name to speak; but most of the time he seemed to be drinking the cup alone, and for the past month or so the ceremony, once a reassurance and a joy, had become bitter to him.

Here, though, was a possibility. To take the Soulflight drug, and step out of the body, and go in search

231

of Freelorn; to meet him outside the flesh, so that they could admire anew each other's inner beauties, without the bitter base emotions clouding their eyes. To look upon one another transfigured, and share one another in the boundless lands beyond the *Door*, united in an ecstasy of freedom, of joy and omniscience and incalculable power—

Sunspark came back in with the bottle. Her eyes were shadowed and she would not look at Herewiss directly; her eyes lingered on the lovers'-cup as she came to stand by the table. Herewiss reached out and took the bottle from her.

(Thank you,) he said.

Her eyes flicked about uncomfortably. Herewiss reached out, took her warm hand, looked up and caught those eyes and held them. Deep brown-amber eyes, shot with sparks of fire, looked fearfully back at him.

(Sunspark,) he said, (don't worry, I'll be all right. *Please* don't worry.)

She squeezed his hand back, but the fear in her eyes was no less. She turned and left.

Herewiss reached for the lovers'-cup, unstoppered the bottle and poured the drug into it, just a little more than he had used the last time. He mixed the wine to dissolve the drug, and drank.

Then he sat back, his eyes closed, and waited.

It was like falling asleep this time. But not falling; rising, rather, a floating feeling, as if he and the chair both were borne upward. After a time this ceased, and the silence rang in his ears like a song. He opened his eyes, and raised his hand.

It came out of itself, slipping free; his own large hand, but changed—both more sensitive to what it touched, and more sensitive somehow to its own *handness*. Just curling it and flexing the fingers outward again was an exquisite feeling. The shell of flesh from which it had emerged was so inadequate-looking, so stiff and cold and pitiful a thing. Herewiss stood up and came free of himself effortlessly. He did not give his body a second look; he scorned it, and thought himself elsewhere.

Immediately he was away, and the instantaneous transition itself sent a ripple of pure pleasure through him like the first anticipation of the act of love, the deep glad movement at the center of one's self. He was standing in air, as if on some high mountain, and below him was spread all the world known to men, from the Waste in the east to the mountains in the west. More than that, he could sense the lives of the people who lived in those lands, all the lives in the Kingdoms, mens' lives and animals' and Dragons' and other creatures', spun about and through each other, threaded into a vast and intricate tapestry of movement and being. It was very like the Pattern that he had glimpsed in Sunspark's mind. Once this vastness would have frightened and confused him, as the Pattern had. Now, though, something had happened to his mind. He could see it, see *all* of it, comprehend it, predict the motions of men and the intimate doings of their hearts; perceive the deepest motives, the best-hidden dreams and loves, and see how they moved the people who owned them, or thought that they owned them—

He hung there in the starlit stillness for a long time, using his power, letting his mind range free, tasting thoughts and emotions from a great distance. As he used the ability, it sharpened, deepened, and soon the hardest, coldest minds were yielding up their secrets to him. He walked the hot bright hearts of Dragons and knew what they thought, and why. He found their secrets, and learned the Draconid Name, which only the Dweller-at-the-Howe knows, and passes on to the new DragonChief when she takes office. Where he sensed resistance, he bent his thoughts against it, and passed through into knowledge. The ability widened until he was hearing the thoughts of mountains and rivers, until he knew what the trees say to one another in their slow silent tongue, and what Day says to Night when they pass at the border of twilight. And still he listened, and listened, caught up in the intricacies and vastnesses of his own power, drunk with it—

There was a new note. A note at the bottom of things, a deep bass note that somehow wound itself into the fabric of everything that was, and Herewiss perceived it first with interest, and then with growing horror. By the time he realized what it was that he heard, it was too late. His power was total; as he pushed it, it grew; he had grown into hearing the note, and he could not now grow out of it.

It was the deepest bass note in all the worlds; the sound of the Universe running down.

He heard it everywhere. It twined through the structure of the tiniest blade of grass and dwelt in the hearts of stars; the empty places far above the earth were full of it; the core of the world sang it slowly and softly to itself, the Sea whispered it with every wave, the wind sighed with it and fell silent. Men shook with it as they were pushed out of the womb, and breathed it out as they died. Its long slow rumbling shook mountains into dust. The bright remote satellites of stars fell into their parent suns, and the suns devoured them, and then died themselves, dwindling into nothing, and darknesses *deeper* than nothing. From these wells of notness the bass note sang loudly as the voice of the earthquake; they were great devouring abysses, wombs of unbirth teeming with potential lost forever. Herewiss reeled, tried to flee. It was no use. He strode among the suns and through glowing clouds that were like violet and golden veils cast across the face of the darkness; he moved like a god through great spiraled treasuries of flaming stars, and knew the thoughts of the inhabitants thereof, from the greatest to the smallest; but the bass note followed him everywhere. It was wound through all the songs, the darkness at the bottom of every light.

He fled back in terror to the silver-blue mote of

light that held the Kingdoms, and descending into it, walked the bottoms of the seas, and the rivers of fire beneath the mountains; but the note was there. He passed through the minds of men and Dragons again, and there it dwelt too, though in a more subtle fashion. There was a defense against the death, and that defense was love; it was effective, though only on a small scale, and only temporarily. But unknowing, men flung love away from them with insane regularity, trying to defeat the Death with strength instead. Herewiss moved from place to place, seeking desperately some place or mind free of the Death, but there were none. Despairing, he judged humankind and found them fools and madmen. In their crazy pride they chose to ignore the fact that Death is the ultimate swallower of all strengths, and that only the ephemeral vulnerability of love can hope to combat it at all—

And then he realized what he had been perceiving, and stopped in the middle of a flowering meadow somewhere in Darthen. The place blazed up in the night with a brilliance of green fire, the warm growth of spring, but like all else the fire had the seeds of death in it. Herewiss stood there, and mourned, understanding at last.

This is how the Goddess sees it, he thought. *Everywhere She looks, She sees the Error. Against the fall of Night, only Love will suffice—and even that, even Her love, which was enough to create the worlds, is not enough to keep them from being destroyed—only to slow the Death down. She loves them—and Her children throw it away. Oh, Mother . . .*

He shook his head. *I'm forgetting myself. It was for love's sake that I came this journey. Where is Freelorn?*

The thought was enough. Herewiss was there, standing by some little creek in eastern Darthen, looking at Freelorn—

—and at Segnbora, with whom Lorn was moving softly under the blankets.

Herewiss wanted to leave on the instant, but by the time he had conceived of the idea, it was too late: he had already perceived the situation in its entirety with his heightened sight. The bitter shock and loneliness that washed over him could not obscure it. Here was Freelorn, sleeping with Segnbora: well, that was not entirely unexpected, or terribly unusual. Herewiss had gathered some time back that Segnbora often slept with one or another of the men, for her own pleasure, or theirs. But he looked at the two of them, and saw their thoughts and motivations from top to bottom. Segnbora's were pleasant enough, at least on the top levels. Under the long slow swells of her passion, he could feel pity, compassion, gentleness, a desire to console, to reach out and touch and straighten a hurt and angry mind, to support until the status quo should reassert itself; the desire to give Freelorn back to Herewiss in a few months, tuned, as it were—made gentle again, gotten over his anger, grown into some kind of realization of his own problems and what he did to himself to cause some of them. A present, a thank-you to Herewiss for trust given and received. Under that, though, the motives were darker. Control. She looked at Herewiss and Freelorn and envied them: she had no lover of her own, had tried once or twice, but her own fears had stifled the loves; she could not give, and did not understand why; she thought she trusted, but dared not open the deepest places. Love which has no roots in the depths, often dies when commitment runs shallow; such had been the case with her. She saw the trust between Freelorn and Herewiss, and coveted it, and tried to take a little of it for herself by intruding into the relationship ever so slightly. Leaving behind her a message, something to remember her by: *I may be incomplete, but there is something I did that you could not.* And below that, more primitive levels, where her passions raged in fire and ice, old angers, old fears, cruelly bound up past her present ability or desire to undo them.

And then Freelorn—in love, suddenly, with Segn-bora. Sharing, opening himself to her, letting himself give her his best. And a level down, sealed away from his own perception, anger, bitter anger at Herewiss, for being something other than what he was supposed to be. For daring to defy Freelorn's control, for daring to break the old patterns. And also anger at Segn-bora—for daring to understand what he could not about Herewiss, for daring to put the needs of the Power above anything else, for supporting Herewiss against him. For dividing them, for coming between them. For being a threat. Freelorn would use her then; would assert the only control over the situation that was available to him. He would take Segnbora and use her; and when her fears (which he had sensed) made her begin to back away from him, he would be safe again. He would be hurt, and she would be hurt, but *he* would be blameless. And later on, when Herewiss came home, he would see what seemed to have happened, and would forgive Freelorn, and everything would once more be the way it had always been. . . .

All this Herewiss saw and sensed, as he stood over them, watching the movements under the blankets, hearing the words of love spoken. He could not ward away what he had heard, or forget it. He had grown into the hearing, and now he could not grow out of it. He perceived Freelorn and Segnbora in all their tangled intricacy, knew the woven lights and darks of their selves; and backed away a little, afraid.

He understood them both, in terrible completeness, but he could not forgive them.

I have been cheated. Cheated. Something has been stolen from me. I never wanted to see this, no one should see this, not this way. Something's gone. Something's stolen. Something of mine—

Some nights after Herelaf had died, all that while ago, Herewiss had gone out into the Wood and had walked aimlessly through the cold night for a long, long time. After a while it had occurred to him that he

237

was looking for something—something that had been taken from him, unfairly, while his back had been turned. His innocence? Or else he had been looking for somewhere to get rid of this new thing that had taken possession of him; his guilt. But Herelaf was gone, taken, stolen, his brother whom he loved. And instead of the love, only the deathguilt remained, as if some thieving night-creature had taken away the love between them and left this in its place. A shiny hollow glittery guilt, one that reflected chill accusing lights back at him when he examined it. For a long time he had let it stay there, feeling that it was better to have *something* in that echoing empty place, than nothing at all. But now he looked at the cold cheap gleam of it and began to be revolted. . . .

But I was cheated. How can I love him now, knowing this? And it was the drug that did it! And You, Goddess! My love, my caring, You stole them from me—

A pause. A long one. And a slow dawning realization. My *love?* Mine? *The way he thinks I belong to* him, *with no thought for* my *wishes in the matter? Goddess, I'm no better than* he *is! And Herelaf, then—* Another pause. His fear rose suddenly up in him.

I could look, now. I have known whole worlds at once tonight, held all their thoughts at once. I could certainly know what makes me *work.*

With the very idea, he knew, just a little. There were two of him. Three. Nine. He multiplied suddenly, shattering in his inward vision into countless bright prisms, a frightening flurry of mixed motivations and swirling personality-pieces, dancing before his terrified observer-self like a snowfall set afire. They were all bits of him, and they were all hotly alive, and they were all arguing with each other. An impossible and confusing miasma of joys and fears and angers, they strove among themselves for dominance of him, the *him* that walked the world and acted as one being. He had never dreamed that there were so many of him, or that they were so at odds. Imposing control upon them seemed a ridiculous impossibility. And there were currents sweeping through the jeweled snow, winds of anger or hopelessness or pain, so that all his myriad selves were taken and moved by them— or did those selves *make* the winds to carry them where they wanted to go, and Herewiss with them, whether he wanted to go or not?

The one of him observing was horrified. *How much of what happens to me do I* make *happen? Oh Goddess, I don't want to see any more!*

There was a sudden consolidation. There were fewer of him now, but they sang together at him in tearing harmonies of challenge and promised pain. *No? You could know yourself. You could dare—*

No!

You could. More voices joining in the chorus, all his own, distracting discords blending with the purer notes of cold reason. *And if you don't dare, you'll never find out the truth about the world. Who sees clearly through a cracked glass?*

NO!!

Coward.

He wanted to weep, and found that he could not. *Maybe I'll dare later,* he said.

Maybe, came the reply, some of the voices pacified, some skeptical. And then one high clear voice, still his own, but with a cutting edge that went through him like a sword. *"Maybe" means never,* it sang in a minor key, *and you know it. With "maybe" you pronounce your own doom, and that of a thousand lives tangled with your own. A life of "almost" is its own reward.*

And then the masses dwindled away, and there was one of him again. He had never felt so lonely in his life.

First Herelaf gone.

Now Freelorn, abandoning him for the moment, intending to pick him up again later when he was more amenable, more willing to be what Freelorn wanted him to be. *I'm not a loved to him. I'm a tool. I'm a symbol for something else. I'm something to* use—

He wandered away slowly. He had come looking for joy. He had found only misery. *Cheated*—

Eventually he found himself back in the gray place again, isolated in the cold gray fog and glad to be that way. There he stayed for a while, sitting on the damp hard ground, letting his sorrows have free run through him, mourning his losses, sunk in his wounded self.

Unfortunately, he couldn't make it last. His own wry sense of humor began to betray him—there was no holding it in abeyance for long. *Well*, he thought, *I was a God for a little while, and that was nice—and then I died a little from something my loved did to me: that's the way the pattern usually runs, isn't it? So now I should go be reborn, so that the circle can be closed, and all things start again. It's such a nuisance*—

He laughed softly to himself, and the act destroyed the cold place around him, leaving him hanging free again amid the myriad brilliances of the Stars. *They look like my mind did,* he thought, his heart slowly opening out to them, rejoicing in them—celebrating the stately passage of their bright-burning companies, the way they opened shining arms to the wide darkness, blown swirling in slow grandeur by winds he could not sense. *But how calm, how serene. Is this what the Goddess' mind looks like, then?*

He hung there for so short a time, it seemed. He had perceived all these families of stars at once, and all the lives upon their worlds, and the knowledge had been as nothing. Now he turned his mind outward and found something that he could not comprehend, though he could feel the currents of it stirring around him—the vast breath of a Life greater than all life, to which all that lived would eventually return. He strove to understand, pushing his mind outward again, and found to his bewildered joy that, no matter how hard he pushed, the Sharer of that greatest Life was always far ahead of him. Herewiss finally gave himself up to the joy, his heart taking him into regions where cold thought could not.

Much later he came back to some knowledge of himself, and sighed, feeling diminished, but not alone. *It's good to know,* he thought, *that there's always something bigger than you are . . .*

He hesitated a moment longer, waist-deep in the stars, like a swimmer wondering whether to come out of a warm sea. *Oh, well,* he thought after a moment, *Sunspark was right—I was awfully tired. I shouldn't stay out much longer; I could die of it. But I could take a* little *more time. I'll walk home.*

He reached a little sideways, found the world he was looking for, and stepped into it, passing out of the starstrewn night into a place of endless soft golden mists. Other people also moved through the fog, but they were only faintly-perceived shadows going by. He could have conversed with them, but chose not to; he preferred them as silent company on the walk home, reassuring but unintrusive.

After a while the gray stone of the hold appeared through the haze. This surprised Herewiss a little, for he had expected to be able to find it only by feel—the place affected the worlds into which it reached, making a clearly perceptible bending in the stuff of space, something like the swirl-funnel that forms in stirred water. But the hold itself was manifesting here, and not merely the combined effect of its many *doors.*

It bulked clearer through the mist as Herewiss approached it. The stone was more silvery than gray, and it glittered and flashed softly with buried highlights, though there was nothing in the even golden mist to make it do so. And somehow the many odd angles and curves of its structure did not look as wrong here as they did in the "real" world. There was a logic to them, a unity of construction and purpose that he had occasionally sensed, but never really seen. Even the hole left when Sunspark had destroyed the outer wall somehow entered the logic of the design and made sense; it was as if it had been a planned addition, which had been predicted and taken into account during the building of the place. And indeed, now that he concentrated on it, Herewiss could perceive changes that were to come later: a tower missing here, a wing added there, a whole section slated to unfold within the heart of the building, protruding partly into an adjoining world. All planned, all accounted for. The hold sang with inevitability like a great piece of music, and Herewiss stood there for a while and admired it for the work of art it was.

Finally he sighed a little, and walked through the gate and across the hall, heading for the stairs that would take him back up to the work-tower and his waiting body. He looked through the doorways as he passed them, and was slightly amused to find that they showed only empty rooms, with windows looking out into the nighttime Waste. Of course, some of the rooms that could not have such views on the desert had them anyway, despite the fact that they should have looked down into the center court of the hold. Herewiss laughed softly; the place had a sense of humor that he appreciated. He trailed his hand along the wall as he went up the stairs, saying an affectionate hello, and the warm stone pushed back against his hand like a cat.

And here was the tower room at last, his tools and materials somewhat vague and hard to see on this plane, and his body sitting phantomlike in the chair, seemingly asleep—

—and standing close by it, as if guarding it—

—sweet Goddess, what was *that*?

To categorize it, to describe it, was to do it a disservice—that much he realized even as he tried to do so. Comparisons were unfair to it. It shook and burned with uniqueness, a hymn of piercing singularity; it was a poem wrought of glass and fire and the sudden taste of blood, an impossibility trying to become possible. Something that had never been, trying to *be*. Birth and death both happening at once in the middle of an existence, the pain and loneliness of both assaulting something that had invited them both willingly, though both were outside its experience—

(Sunspark?)

It turned and faced him. The comparison Herewiss had been trying to make suddenly made itself. He had perceived Freelorn and Segnbora in their totality, and himself partially, and had been amazed by the complexities he had found. Now he perceived Sunspark in its totality, for the first time. The experience at Madeil had been pallid and misleading compared to this.

Sunspark was a oneness. Not a tangle of warring motivations, not divided against itself. But *one*. A single, driving, driven force, an eternal constant, a *being*, an IS! And a tightly encapsulated one, it had been, wound around and through itself, dwelling within itself completely, needing none other. Of *course* its kind had no need for love or companionship in any form. They were *themselves*, gloriously self-contained, solitary as stars. When they finally grew tired of themselves—to the extent that the great Death could affect them—they found another in the same state and conjoined, united in an ecstasy of renewal, were lost in it forever and both reborn as new identities, a mix of parts of the two that formed them.

But Sunspark—

Sunspark had become unique.

Sunspark was changing. Daring to change. *Trying* to change.

It had managed to conceive of something totally outside of its needs. It had come to understand love, and it was daring to experience it, flying with doomed valor into the face of something that could only cause it infinite pain. But daring it nonetheless, for the sake of the dare, for the possibility of learning something new, of becoming something it had never been or known. Reaching out into the darkness outside of itself, as Herewiss had turned himself outward and sought to grow into the Universe. None of its kind had ever dared so. It knew as much, and trembled with fear even as it bent over Herewiss' stiff body and feared for *him,* loved *him.* It broke the laws that the Universe had set up for its kind: and it knew what it did, and it feared—*but it loved*—

Sunspark faced Herewiss, and perceived him. It feared him; feared that he would inflict pain upon it—pain, that amazing newness, all the more terrible for Sunspark's inexperience with it. The elemental's complete horror of pain rippled through its changing fires, plain to see.

Yet it welcomed him—

—and reached out to him—

and *dared to love him*—

Herewiss stood there, torn, daunted, amazed, yet exalted by its courage—

(Sunspark—)

(Herewiss,) it said, and its use of his name was wound about with fire and gentleness both. (Thy body—it weakens.)

His emotions were burning through him now like fire themselves. (I was so lonely,) he said, (and I never knew—never understood that you were like this—the *bravery*—Sunspark, I'm *sorry!*)

It grew, its fires swelling, towering with love, terror, pain— (O my loved, don't be—don't be—just get back quickly before you die!)

The courage. The sheer daring. He was swept up, carried past his fear and through to the other side—

—*he loved too*—

(For this little while,) Herewiss said, exultant, euphoric—loving— (it can wait.)

He reached out. (Shall I dare less than you?) said Herewiss.

Sunspark came to him.

(—*embracing the heart of a star, and being embraced by it: part of that fire, lost in it, burning in*

244

non-ambivalent brilliance forever and forever: being and not-being, victory, surrender, death and birth lying in one another's arms at last, after long estrangement: the loneliness filled: the insatiable fires satisfied—)

In the morning, Sunspark learned how to cry, and Herewiss remembered how again.

NINE

*"Now indeed may it be seen," said Earn, "that our
life's days are ended." "That were ill seen," Héalhra
made answer. "Wherefore," said Earn, "seeing that
we shall meet again by the Shore of that Sea of
which the Starlight is a faint intimation?" "'S
truth," said Héalhra, "my loved; yet though our
Mother waiteth on that Shore, still here would I
remain with thee. For life and breath are sweet.
And also, She loveth not well those who let Life and
Love, Her gifts, slip away through a grip made loose
by resignation. Dearly She bought those gifts for
us, and dearly shall the children of Night purchase
them from me in turn. Well the Goddess loveth the
driver of a hard bargain."*

Battle of Bluepeak, tr. Erard, ch. 16

Herewiss woke up hounded by small urgent voices in
the back of his brain, voices that told him to hurry,
that gave him just time enough to relieve himself before steering him back in to work, that pushed him so
that he found himself at the anvil before he was even
fully awake. The day began with a sleep-blurred image of his hands holding the tongs, and the tongs resting on the anvil with nothing held between them, and
Herewiss standing there, staring with fuzzy expectant
confusion at the pores and dents in the anvil's metal.
What am I doing here? he thought, and reached for a
swordblank, and called for Sunspark to come dwell in
the firepit.

The morning fell away in chunks and half-glimpsed
pieces, casualties of the insistent rhythms of hammering. Each stroke rang a second away, and every second
was just like every other. There was the swing of the
hammer, the bunching of muscles, the jolt and clang

of the metal ringing and rebounding away from itself,
the sword jumping away from the anvil and the hammer from the sword, again and again and again, the
old familiar beat renewing itself with the dogged per-
sistence of some hard heart. *Again* and *again* and *again*.
A brief pause here when the pressure of his bladder
became too much; another moment stolen there when
the rawness in his throat made him stop to drink; and
always the impatient voice of his fear rustling softly
just under his proper hearing, like rats in the walls of
his self. Herewiss was slightly aware of Sunspark
watching him from the forge, of bright eyes in the fire,
looking at him with concern. But he dared not let
himself respond to the look; to do so would have been
to waste precious time. He let the hammering take
him and use him for its own purposes. It was rather
pleasant to not think at all, just to be arms at the end
of a hammer—

(Herewiss.)

He dared not stop. He kept on hammering.

(Herewiss. You asked me to let you know about
that binding at intervals.)

(Mmph.) *Again* and *again* and—

(It's holding rather nicely—under the circumstances,
that is. But you're going to have to try to control your
fear a little better. When you discharge so strongly, the
binding weakens.)

(I'll remember.)

(But Herewiss—how can you expect to control yourself properly with as little sleep as you've been getting?
An hour there, two there—)

(Spark,) he said, pacing his thoughts between the
hammer-blows. (My loved. I haven't *time*. Something
is happening. The Fire's going out. I have to hurry—)

(Your fear is killing it,) the elemental said softly. (I
couldn't have understood that before. Now I know.
Freelorn has gone off to Osta without you, and there's
been no word all this month and more. You fear for
him. I hear the terror singing while you sleep; it runs

247

from you like blood. And you feel that you should be with him, though if you were, you couldn't be working—)

(Some things are even more important than Flame.)

Sunspark was silent for a moment. (And the hralcin,) it said, (the matter of its unbinding that troubles you so. That fear is killing your Power too. I hear the sound of it every now and then: "if I *had* the Fire," you think, "what kinds of things would I be letting loose by my carelessness?" You are working against yourself, my loved—)

(Sometimes, Sunspark, you hear too much for your own good.) The thought was a slap of anger, and Sunspark shrank away, out of Herewiss' mind entirely, dwindling down to a few uncertain tongues of fire shivering among the coals. Herewiss sighed then, ashamed of himself, looking at the elemental in the firepit and realizing that it was the first thing he had really *seen* all day.

(Spark,) he said as gently as he could. (Love, I'm sorry. Oh, come out of there.) He put the hammer down on the anvil, atop the blank he had just finished.

(You are angry at me.) Its voice was subdued and fearful.

(It passed. Spark, you have to learn that around these parts it's possible for two partners in a union to be angry with one another without the union being destroyed. Come out of there—)

It put up a few cautious tongues of fire and then flowed over the edge, a bright firefall that pooled and rose upward to envelop him. Silently the elemental wrapped its warmth around and through Herewiss, filling all his cold empty places with its glowing self. They were joined for a few minutes, and Herewiss looking inward saw all his fears flare into incandescence. He could see the shapes of them clearly now, and while the union persisted they were not fears any more. He saw them as Sunspark perceived them, as energies bound into strange fanciful shapes that meant little against the larger scale of things. The sensation was pleasant, and Herewiss stood there for a long while, eyes closed, letting himself be cared about and reassured.

(You matter, Spark,) he said softly. (You matter very much.)

It pulsed warm within him, a deep silent flare of fulfillment.

(But I have to work . . .)

It unwrapped itself, slowly, regretfully. (Let us work that sword to red heat again, so you can quench it, and I'll go watch the binding.)

(That sounds fine. Back in the pit then . . .) Herewiss tried to chuckle, but the sound came out wrong. All the places that Sunspark had filled and warmed so thoroughly with itself were bleak and cold again, and his fears were back, all the more shadowy for having been so bright.

He laid the blade of the sixty-third sword in the forge and turned away, wishing that Sunspark would melt it accidentally.

The grindstone was useful for times when Herewiss didn't want to think. The noise of it rasped on his nerves, and the vibration rattled far down his spine so that any session with it left him in a state of profound and unfocused irritation. For this reason he usually didn't use it, preferring to blow the sword up before putting a good edge on it. Today, however, anything that would shut out thoughts of the hralcin was welcome.

He sat there behind the stone, pumping away at the pedals until his legs threatened to cramp (which diversion he would also have welcomed). The irritation fed on itself, making him pump faster and press the sword harder against the turning stone, until sparks fountained from it, and again and again it grew too hot to handle. By the end of a couple of hours, the sword had an edge on it that was much better than it needed, and in some places had gone to wire and would have to be stropped.

(Herewiss?)

(Mm?) He was working at it with the horsehide strop now, holding the sword between his knees as he worked and taking a certain cranky pride in the quality of his work. The blade would need some finishing work with oil and smoothing stone, but the edges had already acquired that particular silvery sheen that swordsmiths strive for, the mark of a blade that will cut air and leave it in pieces.

(We have company.)

(!!) He looked up from his work. (Who?)

(From the feel of them, Freelorn and his people. They are in high good spirits. No one else would be feeling that way out *here*, if the Waste is as ill-omened as you say.)

Herewiss frowned, and then smiled. (He has a talent for showing up when I have a piece of work in hand . . .)

(But then you're always working, loved. How could it be otherwise?)

(Hmp. True, I guess . . .) And Herewiss went cold with fear. (But, Spark, that binding . . . !)

The elemental shrugged. (I'm watching it. So far none of the parameters you described to me has changed. The hralcin hasn't bothered testing it in a while.)

(That could be good—and then again—)

(Well, whatever. Probably it will be all right if you don't get in another fight with Freelorn. The extra stress of having more people around might wear it a little, but you can reinforce now and again.)

(Yes . . .)

(So keep things subdued. I for my part will do the same. There's a stand of brush to the north of here that could use a fire, and I could use a meal. Maybe I'll be away for the night; that might decrease the stresses.)

(It's a thought. How close are they, Spark?)

(Some miles. You have time to finish that, at least.)

(All right. Watch that door . . .)

(Oh,) Sunspark said dryly, (if anything comes out of it, you'll know shortly . . .)

Herewiss thought of slime and the smell of burning, and stropped harder.

The polished outer walls of the hold had a walkway recessed into the top surface, sort of a double noncrenellated battlement, accessible by a long flight of those oddly staggered steps which led up from the inner courtyard. Herewiss leaned on the outer battlement and watched Freelorn and his people approaching. Sunspark, beside him, wavered and shimmered palely in the sunlight like heat-shimmer above a pavement in summer.

(Look at all those mules. I wonder who he stole them from?)

Sunspark made a don't-know-don't-care feeling. (There's something,) it said, (something that I couldn't catch while they were further away—can you hear it?)

Herewiss reached out with his underhearing. Because of his fatigue it wasn't working well. All he got was a faint confused impression of a number of emotional systems going about their business, and a fainter one of two specific systems somewhat at odds with themselves.

(Slight unease,) he said to Sunspark. (I'm a bit off today, and I don't usually do too well anyhow unless I'm at close range. They're half a mile away.)

Sunspark shrugged. (Freelorn,) it said, (and Segnbora, I think.)

Herewiss nodded slowly. (It didn't take long for

251

what I saw to start happening, alas. This isn't good, Spark, both of them are going to be spilling over with negatives, and the binding will suffer—)

(Work on Freelorn, then,) Sunspark said. (You would anyway—)

Herewiss caught a sudden pang of jealousy, a flurry of angry, swift-moving brilliances like swords flashing in sunlight. Sunspark was trying to conceal it, and Herewiss laughed softly.

(I bet you'd like to burn him.)

The elemental flinched away in chagrin. (I would,) it admitted.

(I think I would've been a little suspicious if you hadn't wanted to. We all do as our natures dictate, Spark. I know it's hard for you to understand how I can love you both; but believe me, I can, and I love neither of you the less for loving the other more—)

(I'm not sure I understand this.) Sunspark sounded ashamed.

(Trust me, Spark. I will not give you up for him.)

(Neither will you give him up for me—)

(That's right, little one. Firechild, trust me. You haven't done wrong yet by doing so. Nor have I,) he added with a gentle smile, (in trusting you. By rights and the Pact you could have parted company with me after you saved me from the hralcin.)

(It would seem,) Sunspark said, smiling back, (that there are some things more important than even the Pact. Do what needs to be done, loved. I'll be within call till this evening.)

It vanished. Herewiss looked over the wall at Freelorn, alone at the head of the approaching line, and went down the stairs to meet him.

At the bottom of the stairs Herewiss paused, slightly irritated by the sight of the dust lying thick all over the courtyard's polished gray paving. He was usually a tidy sort, but lately there had been too much to do— swords to be forged, *doors* to be looked through. And then the hralcin had come. He thought of cleaning the courtyard now, but he was too tired to want to do it by sorcery, and he didn't have a broom.

He walked across the court to where there appeared to be a solid wall, facing west. It was only a little illusion, rooted in where the wall would have liked to be, where it had been before Sunspark disposed of it. The illusion was a sop to his own insecurities. It made him nervous to live alone, or nearly alone, in a hold that had a great gaping hole in it. Herewiss looked up at the wall, reached out with his arms, and spoke the word that severed the connection between was-once and seems-to-be-now. The wall went away.

Freelorn and his people were very close, and Herewiss leaned against the wall and waited for them. *They're all there; thank You, Goddess. I couldn't cope with one of Lorn's guilts right now, if one of them had been hurt or killed. Or my own, now that I think of it . . .*

Blackmane whickered a greeting at Herewiss as Freelorn dismounted. *No Lion coat? Interesting!* Herewiss thought as Freelorn hurried over to him, his eyes anxious. Freelorn reached out hesitantly, took Herewiss' hands in his and gripped them hard. They stood that way for a long moment, each of them searching the other with his eyes, almost in fear.

"Well," Freelorn said, glancing at the ground and pushing the dust around with one booted toe, "I'm back . . ."

Herewiss reached out and drew Freelorn close, and hugged and kissed him hard.

For a few minutes they just hung on to one another, sniffling slightly. "I, uh," Freelorn said, his voice muffled by talking into Herewiss' tunic, "I was—oh, Dark, loved, you know how I am when I can't get my way."

"It's not as if I wasn't being a little stubborn myself. Or a little snide—Lorn, I'm sorry."

"Me too." Freelorn gave Herewiss a great bone-cruncher of a hug and then held him away, peering at him with concern. "Are you all right? You look as if somebody smote you a good one in the head. And look at your eyes, you have circles under them."

"Smote me—" Herewiss laughed. "I feel like it. It's been a busy week. Come on in, I'll tell you about it later." He looked at Freelorn, noticing something that hadn't been there before, a look of tiredness and discomfort and depression. "Are *you* all right?" he asked.

The expression on Freelorn's face went back and forth between relief and loathing. "Later," he said. "It's been a lively month."

Freelorn's people were leading their horses into the courtyard, and as Herewiss glanced toward them he saw Segnbora passing through the gate. Her expression was hard to make out clearly, for the late Sun was behind her; but she looked pained, and puzzled as well. Herewiss looked back at Freelorn, took him gently by the arm and began to walk back into the hold with him.

"Lorn, where did all those mules come from?"

"Osta."

"You *did* go ahead, then—"

"Yes indeed."

They passed into the coolness of the hold. "And you made it out all right."

"It's just as I told you, no one knew about the secret way in from the river. We didn't even have to kill any of the guards.—By the way, we brought a plains deer in with us. Didn't see any reason why we should use up your supplies."

"You always were a considerate guest. Lorn, what are all the mules for?"

"I was getting to that. They're for the money."

Herewiss led Freelorn into the great lower hall, and they sat down beside the firepit in chairs that Sunspark had brought in from the village to the north. "*Six mules?* How much did you get?"

Freelorn made a smug, pleased face. "Eight thousand talents of silver."

"Eight thou— You mean you went into the Royal

Treasury and *stole* all that money and got *away* again?"

"I didn't steal it," Freelorn said with mock-righteousness. "It's *my* money."

"My Goddess, maybe I should listen to you more," Herewiss said, reaching down for a brown earthenware bottle and the lovers'-cup. "Lorn, you should've killed the guards. It'd be kinder than what Cillmod's probably doing to them." He broke the seal on the bottle-stopper, opened the jug and poured.

"Maybe. But I have the money now. We can have a revolution."

"Just like that," Herewiss said with a laugh, and drank from the cup. "May we be one, my loved." He passed it on to Freelorn.

"As is She." Freelorn drank, and his eyes widened. "Lion's Name, this tastes like Narchaerid."

"It is."

"South slope, too. Mother of Everything, it's like so much red velvet. What year?"

Herewiss held up the jug to look at the bottom. "'92, it says."

"Dark, what am I worrying about the year for? How are you getting that out here?"

Herewiss flicked an amused glance at the firepit. An ordinary fire appeared to be blazing there, but the pattern of the flames had repeated twice since they'd been there. "I have my sources," he said.

"Well, whatever. How long can a revolution take, anyway? You should hear the kind of things going on in Arlen. The people are getting sick of Cillmod. It was a bad year at harvest, there were omens and portents: sheep miscarrying and two-headed calves being born, and fruit dying on the trees before it was ripe—" Freelorn drank deeply, and though his voice was excited with the prospect of kingship, his eyes over the rim of the cup were troubled. "In a lot of the little villages we passed through, everyone was hungry a lot of the time. It's bad, back home . . ."

"The reason is obvious," Herewiss said.

"Well, of course! Cillmod isn't stupid enough to go into Lionhall, and he hasn't been performing the priestly functions. I wish to Dark he'd try; it'd be interesting to see what he looks like after being hit by lightning."

Herewiss shook his head. "I doubt it would be anything so blatant; Lion's Justice is usually fairly subtle when it strikes. Look at old Beor the Sot who tried to conduct the Summer Affirmation with a lady who didn't want him. He got thrown by his horse."

"Mmph! The thing is, this is the time to go back and set things straight. The Arlenes are restless, they want a King again—"

"They *don't* want a war, I'm sure," Herewiss said. "And even so, you would need men, and most of the mercenaries in the Kingdoms are either working for Cillmod, or tied up with that miserable Reaver uprising down Geraithe way. Goddess only knows how long that's going to go on."

"Darthen might help us after it's settled, though—"

"I doubt it. Eftgan's armies have been taking heavy losses: she'll need time to recoup. And even then she might not want to move against Arlen. Cillmod is still leaning hard on the border territories."

"Dammit, doesn't anyone have any respect for the Oath any more? Cillmod breaks it—Eftgan won't uphold it—"

"The Oath has always been conditional on the welfare of the people of both countries," Herewiss said regretfully. He looked at Freelorn hard, assessing the restlessness, and the pain around the eyes.

Freelorn sank back into his chair, slightly subdued by the look. "I just want to be King," he said. "That's all."

Herewiss reached out, took Freelorn's hand and held it. "I missed you," he said. "And I'm sorry we fought. And sorrier that I didn't give you the benefit of the doubt when you said you could pull it off. I was wrong."

Freelorn looked at Herewiss, smiled. "It's all right," he said, and handed Herewiss the lovers'-cup. "We're one, loved."

"So may it be." Herewiss drank off the cup in three or four swift draughts and looked at it with satisfaction. "Let's get drunk," he said, "and I'll tell you my news after dinner."

"You mean I'm going to have to be drunk to believe it?"

Herewiss chuckled and poured more wine.

A long while later Herewiss and Freelorn and all his following sat around the firepit, in various states of repletion. The stripped-down carcass of the desert deer was still on the spit. The fire in the pit had died down to a soft glow of embers, with only an occasional tongue of flame showing. Most of Freelorn's people were half-dozing in their chairs, except for Segnbora, who had pled time-of-moon pains and retired early. Herewiss and Freelorn sat together, a little apart from the others, cups in hand.

"A hundred and eighty-four *doors*," Herewiss was saying wearily. "Permanent ones, that is. I gave up trying to count the ones that are here one day and gone the next: and a lot of them move around, whole new wings of the building appear and disappear. There are more *doors* at night than during the day-time, and more than half the *doors* at any one time show water; but outside of that . . ." He trailed off.

"And none of them was what you were looking for."

"I can't make them change," Herewiss said. "And the closest I've come is something that doesn't bear dis-cussing."

"No?"

Herewiss considered the wine in the lovers'-cup, breathed in, breathed out, a long moment of decision. "No," he said. "If there's a somewhere that men have

Flame, I wish them joy of it and good weather, 'cause *I'm* never going to get there. Not at this rate."

"No luck with the swords?"

"I break them," Herewiss said, fumbling around for the wine-jug and refilling the cup. "I should start a business. HEREWISS S'HEARN. SWORDS BROKEN. NO JOB TOO LARGE OR TOO SMALL."

Freelorn gazed at him sadly, and Herewiss shook his head and took another drink. "Lorn," he said softly. "what happened while you were gone?"

"Huh?"

"With Segnbora."

"That's one of the problems with having a sorcerer for a loved," Freelorn said in a resigned voice. "Let me have some of that."

"No . . . Lorn, the way you looked when you came in, and the way she looked at you . . . I'm not blind."

Freelorn drank some wine, held the cup in his lap. He looked suddenly very tired. "We—were in comfort with each other—it was nice. I fell a little in love with her, I guess. I needed to talk, especially after I left here so mad—though this had been going on to some extent while we were escaping from Madeil, before we got trapped. She was always there to listen, and what I thought seemed to *matter* to her, really did. So we—got close—but I began to notice that she never told me anything *back*, not that it says anywhere that you have to, but she never seemed to tell anything about herself. She would listen, but never give—or never really *share*."

He drank again. "Well, when I got lonely, I asked her to sleep with me, and she said yes. I guess I thought it might have been different there. But it wasn't. She still couldn't share." His voice grew lower, and the pain of the words scraped it raw. "She was good—she was *very* good—the way she was very good at listening. But she still couldn't, didn't share. Not that she wasn't responsive, or warm, but there was no—"

He gestured with the cup, looking for the right words. Finally he held the cup out to Herewiss to be refilled, and took a long moment's refuge in the wine. "She couldn't—I don't know. She couldn't let go. Couldn't trust me. I wanted so much for her to . . . but she didn't dare . . ."

Herewiss sat there and let the silence grow again. *And now he uses the pain to punish himself for what he knows to be his part in it,* he thought. "Was it your fault, Lorn? You sound guilty somehow."

"No . . . I don't know." Freelorn drank again. "I think maybe I slept with her because I missed you. Instead of you, as it were. Does that make sense?"

"It does. Though, Lorn, don't sell her short; there are enough good things about her that I'm sure she's worth sleeping with on her own. . . ."

They sat there in silence for a few moments. Freelorn looked around at the polished gray walls, dim in the faint firelight.

"I wish there was something I could do for you," he said mournfully.

"Lorn, you're my loved, you're my friend. I can live without the Power, but not without friends. And I may have to get used to living without the Power pretty soon—it doesn't have long to run in me without focus."

"What we need," Freelorn said solemnly, "is a miracle."

Herewiss began to laugh, the kind of laughter that is a breath away from tears.

"No, I mean it," said Freelorn. "I'm the King's son of Arlen, descended in right line from Héalhra Whitemane, and by the Goddess if there's anyone who has a right to ask the Lion for a miracle, it's *me*."

Herewiss laughed until he was weak and his sides hurt, though some small corner of his mind was surprised that he could laugh so hard over something so painful and serious.

"Me," Freelorn was saying, "I'll do it. I will." He

finished his cup of wine, and held it out to Herewiss again.

"Haven't you had enough?" Herewiss said as soon as he gained control of his laughter.

"I'm talking about miracles," Freelorn said with infinite weariness, "and all you're interested in is how drunk I am."

Herewiss poured again for Freelorn. "You throw up and I'll make you scrub the floor."

"Throw up! This stuff is like mother's milk," Freelorn said, spacing the words with exaggerated care. "Thanks." He smiled, a small gentle smile strangely at odds with his inebriation. "Come to bed with me tonight?"

"In a while. I have some things to take care of first. Wait for me?"

"I'm not going anywhere. Except," and Freelorn wobbled to his feet, "to sleep."

"Later, then."

Freelorn made his way around the firepit, nudging his people one by one. "Come on," he said, "everybody get up and go to bed . . ."

Herewiss got carefully to his feet and crossed the hall to the uneven stairs. As he went up them he noticed two *doors* that hadn't been there earlier in the day. He paused only long enough to note that one of them looked out on some green place with a river running through it, and the other on a waste of cold water beneath a bleak gray sky.

Coming up to the tower room, he dissolved the appearance of solid wall that camouflaged its *doorway*, passed through, and sealed it behind him. Sunspark was waiting for him on the furs and cushions in the corner, stretched out, lush and warmly beautiful in the silvery moonlight from the open window. Light from the two great candlesticks on Herewiss' work table caught in her red hair and touched it with coppery sparks and glitters.

(You were a long time coming,) she said.

(It's been a while since Freelorn was here. We had a lot to talk about.)

(I would imagine.) The sudden flicker of jealousy again, like bared swords in the moonlight; but not as strong as the last time.

(Spark, relax,) Herewiss said. He went to the window and looked out. The Moon was gibbous, waxing toward the full, and from the walls of the hold to the horizon, the desert shone silver and black. The midnight stars struggled feebly with the moonlight, cold and pale and mocking, faint as the Flame within him.

(I didn't mean it,) Sunspark said. (Ah, Herewiss, it's hard to do, this loving—)

(You meant it,) he said. (And, yes, this loving *is* hard. There is nothing harder, which is probably the way it should be, for there's also nothing more precious, I think. Spark, please, don't be afraid of me: I love you well as you are.) He leaned on the windowsill, wondering whether the wine was the source of the strange feeling inside him—a feeling like something trying to happen.

(Something's bothering you—) Sunspark got up and came to him, slipped warm arms around him from behind.

(No more than usual. Maybe I should go away for a little while, though, walk around in the world a little, get away from all these damn *doors* for a while—)

He stroked one of Sunspark's arms absently. (Maybe. Sunspark, I'm sorry, I'm just not in the mood tonight.)

(Oh? How's this, then? You liked it before.) The elemental shimmered momentarily, and when the wavering died down he stood there, a lithe young man, arms still around Herewiss.

(No, loved,) Herewiss chuckled, turning around and hugging him back, (that's not what I meant. I have some things to do, a feeling I want to follow up. That's all.)

(Well enough, then. I'm going to tend to that brush. Whatever this is about, though—be careful!)

(I will.)

Sunspark dissolved into flame, then went out altogether.

Herewiss stood at the window long enough to notice the faint radiance spring into life on the horizon. He turned away, then, went to a chest on one side of the room, opened it and rummaged around. He found the bottle of Soulflight, went over to the pile of cushions by the window, and sat down wearily.

He could feel time fast flowing over him, taking little pieces of him with it as a stream whirls flotsam resistlessly down its current. There was no more time. He was being worn away steadily by the days, and raggedly by his fears—Sunspark had been quite right about that. The image of the hralcin, ravening silently at the dark *door*, wanting him with an implacable hunger, moved again in the back of his mind. The sight of Freelorn and the sound of his voice hadn't driven the memory away—merely startled it into stillness, like the bright fierce glance of a hawk. Now the vague dark shape stirred, restless, and looked at him with deadly patience—

He cursed his overactive imagination, wishing that the hralcin would just go away and leave him alone. *But no achievement is without price,* he reminded himself, *most especially the dark ones*—

Herewiss looked at the little stone bottle, wondering if it was going to be worth it. After he came down in the morning, things would be no different. The hralcin would still be behind the *door*, hungering for him, and the Power would be no more his than it was now.

But Soulflight was good for walking the future as well as the past. He could go forward, look down the course of his life from its end and see if there was some way to forge the sword he needed. Or a way to stop the hralcin, to kill it—

No, no. When you use Soulflight to look forward, it

shows you options, chances, pathways—there's no way to tell which is actually going to happen. And even with the drug there are usually gaps in the pathways, variables that can't be predicted—

He rolled the bottle slowly between his hands. *And as far as the hralcin goes, I doubt that I could avail myself of any art that I might learn. I'm so tired, I couldn't turn the sky dark at nightfall. And by the time I'm strong enough to try something useful, that thing will probably come back and break the binding down. No, that's no good.*

Herewiss gripped the bottle hard. *No matter how I approach this mess, the answer keeps coming up the same—I'm not going to live out the week. Well, so be it. I plowed this crooked furrow and now I must sow in it. But by the Goddess, if I'm going to die, I'll die knowing my Name!*

He took the lovers'-cup, filled it with the last half-cup or so of the Narchaerid, and poured a dollop of the drug into it from the little bottle. It fell slowly, in a clear ribboning stream like honey, and he watched the bubbles in it as he poured. *I'll have to look at my Name before this night is over. But first I'll make my peace with myself, with Lorn—share myself with him completely past the Door, let him understand what's been happening, why I'm doing what I am. Maybe the understanding will help him handle my loss. Oh, Mother, I wish I didn't have to die, I wish I'd let that door alone, it's going to hurt Lorn so much when I'm gone—* He rubbed his eyes briefly. *Enough of that. I have to leave him in love and with joy, otherwise it'll be worse for him. And the others deserve my best, too. Their dreams will take them past the Door, I'll meet them there—and then go on. No shying away from the truth this time. Ups, better stop here—*and he pulled the bottle away, twirled it free of a last drop that clung to the lip. He stoppered the bottle and set it aside carefully. *I do want to come back.*

He swirled the cup to mix the drug with the wine,

and drank it right down, a long draft that made him choke a little. There was a burning at the back of his throat, but it passed. Herewiss reached over for another jug of wine—not Narchaerid, but a *vin ordinaire* from up north—poured a cupful, and sat down to wait for the drug to work.

He watched the moonlight move ever so slightly across the floor, and the silence of the desert night sank deeply into him. For a moment his eyes rested on this morning's sword, which lay up against the wall a few feet away. Nothing more than a long dead piece of steel, carven with no runes, untreated, untried in any way. He tried for a moment to think of something new to do with it, but could see nothing in his mind but the depressing sight of a fine sword, beaten out of strong tempered steel, shattering itself to splinters at the touch of the Power.

The image made him cringe, unwanted harbinger of reality that it was. The fragrance of the wine crept up his nose, fruity and sweet, and glad of the distraction he drank again.

As he did, a moth came flickering in the window. It fluttered around in confusion, bouncing and wobbling around the square of moonlight on the floor, until it saw one of the candlesticks. It flew straight toward the flame with directness that surprised Herewiss, circled it twice, three times, and dove headlong into the flame. There was a fizzing sound. The candle burned low for a moment, then sprang up again.

Herewiss sat there and felt the drug begin to work. He laughed, but the sound didn't seem to be coming from his own throat, though he could hear it plainly enough. The detachment extended itself to his thoughts as well. Part of him was sad for the moth, but the rest was uninvolved, though alert and observant. *A small thing, a small thing*, it seemed to be singing to itself, though in a minor key.

The disorientation came quickly. There was a spinning, a confusion, everything was subtly wrong, and

264

Herewiss struggled to his feet, or tried to. He had a bad time of it, his muscles didn't work, he seemed tied down to something. Then, with an abrupt slight rending sensation, he found himself no longer tied to anything. He rose up. He stretched, and though there was no feeling of moving muscles, his mind slipped outward and filled his form. He was himself, totally.

Herewiss looked down at his body, where it lay among the pillows. There was no sickening feeling of entrapment, this time, nor was there the limitless rapture he had felt with the second use of the drug, a feeling of being free of a decrepit prison. He looked down now and felt pride, and an odd kind of tenderness. Unfulfilled and incomplete he might be in many ways, but he had a fine body; slim and long and graceful, with the muscles corded hard in it from the strain of his disciplines and the forging of swords. It lay there, eyes closed, one arm outstretched toward the wine cup. It looked relaxed and innocent, and beautiful in an angular kind of way. *I always knew that a person's personality imprints itself on the body he wears,* he thought, *but I never thought to look at myself in that light—or if I did, I refused to believe what I saw. I am beautiful, Lorn and Sunspark have been right when they've told me so. How curious it is that I never felt that way when I've been awake and in it. Must be a matter of viewpoint . . .*

He turned away and looked around him. The walls of the room glowed softly with a subdued rose-golden radiance. It seemed that his guesses were right, that some kind of life did sleep in the stone. The sword lay up against the wall near him, a long dark oblong blot against the light. Herewiss held up his hands before him. In shape they were the same as always, but there was a difference about them, a subtle transparency, and below that the muted glow of suppressed Flame. The moonlight had an added piquancy to it, a feeling like the cold taste of bitten metal, and Herewiss marveled as he breathed it in.

He looked down at the wine cup. The wine left within it was a white blaze of light, an expression of all the sunlight and moonlight that had become part of the grapes. Faintly he could hear the cries of ecstatic agony uttered by the vines as their burden was ripped from them, and he felt at a distance the silver touch of rain. He caught the languorous thoughts of one of the young girls who had helped to press out the vintage, and he felt how it had been for her, the night before, under the pomegranate trees with her lover. All that experience was too much for Herewiss to leave untasted. He knelt down by the shell of himself, took up the essence of the cup and drank off the joy and sorrow and time within it at one draft. The tangled, vivid selfhoods of bees and vintners and young girls flowed down his throat like cinnamon fire, and left an aftertaste like a summer dawn. *I will never call a wine "ordinary" again,* he thought. *Never—*

Herewiss looked over his shoulder at the candle, and got up and went to it, amused and curious. The candle flame was an intricate web of bright energies, an entangled tracery of heat and light, in constant motion. Wobbling in earnest circles around and around it was the moth, a soft golden flicker, like a little flame itself. Apparently it had not noticed that it had died. Herewiss put out his hands and caught it carefully. It fluttered within his caging fingers, leaving here and there a wing-scale like pale gold-dust, and finally sat on one of his fingers and looked up at him with confused dark eyes.

He carried it to the window and opened his hands, offering it to the night. The moth sat bewildered for a moment or so. Then it caught sight of the flood of silver light pouring in the window, and fluttered out of Herewiss' hands, bobbling upward into the night, straight for the transfigured Moon.

He smiled up at the moth, wishing it well, and looked out at the night and the stars. They blazed, blue and brilliant, as if seen through one of the *doors* down the hall. The world seemed to be hanging breathless in the midst of a clustered cloud of them. Their light was not cold, now, nor were they mocking him. They were singing, a song almost too high for him to hear, like the song of the bat. The song had words, but the multitude of voices drowned out the meaning in a million blended assonances. Herewiss contented himself with a few minutes of standing there in that inexpressible glory of sound and light, taking it all in, hoping that he would remember it tomorrow, through the headache.

Lorn is waiting for me, he thought at last, *and so are my other guests, all of them, past the* Door. *I perhaps slighted them a little earlier: let me make up for that now. Downstairs—*

He exerted himself, and was there, standing in the midst of the silent main hall. Nearly all the people were asleep now, curled in dark silent bundles or stretched out beneath their cloaks. Dritt and Moris were still awake, unmoving, caring about each other in the darkness. Herewiss could feel the texture of their waking throughts moving softly between them, as they rested in the twilit borderland between love and sleep. Herewiss smiled at them. Later, he thought, he might ask to share himself with them.

He looked around, identifying Freelorn's people one by one. Most of them were dreaming, in some cases quite vividly, so that faint images of their minds' wanderings were apparent. Segnbora lay curled in one corner, dreaming more loudly than the rest; her dream towered against the ceiling, some huge gossamer creature under a firefly sun. Herewiss was intrigued, and went to where she lay.

He knelt beside her, studying her for a moment before he would enter the dream. A clear sight like that of the last drug experience was on him again, but this time it was a more intimate and kindly vision, informed with compassion, very unlike the coldly clinical evaluation of the last time. Segnbora's hand lay out on her cloak, and he looked at it and shook his head sadly. Under the frail casing of the skin, such a violence and potency of untapped Power raged that it should have burned her out from within. But he also saw the barrier that sealed it away from her use, a wall of old frozen fears that all the inner fires couldn't melt. And the rules forbade him to tell her what to do about it. He sighed, and entered in.

There was the smell of salt spray, and black pockmarked rocks worn smooth by the sea, and a hot white midsummer sun, and Segnbora sat atop a boulder festooned with clambering strands of kelp. A sea-ouzel was building a nest in a cranny of the boulder, and Segnbora was watching it intently. So was the Dragon that towered over her, a huge one, at its full growth but still young—no more than six or seven hundred years old. They watched the bird fly down to the surf line to pick up pieces of dead seaweed. Another ouzel appeared, carrying something in its beak that was not seaweed. Segnbora clucked to it, and with a whirring of wings the bird went up to where she sat. It alighted on her outstretched hand, dropping the object in her palm. Herewiss, standing next to the Dragon, looked at the thing. It was a gem, like a diamond but more golden, finely cut into a sparkling oval.

"It'll take a while to hatch," Segnbora said to the ouzel. "Do what you can, though." The bird picked up the jewel and flew down to the nest with it.

"But it's a stone!" Herewiss objected.

"Strange things won't happen," Segnbora said, "unless you give them a chance."

"I'm trying," Herewiss said.

"Yes, I see that. You're past the *Door*. The drug?"

"Yes."

"Oh well," Segnbora said, "a short life, but a merry one."

The Dragon bent its great head down toward Herewiss, regarding him. He bowed low, feeling that this creature was worthy of his respect. It was apparently

one of the Oldest Line of Dragons, the children of Da-
hiric Worldfinder, to judge by its green-golden scales
and golden spines. It spoke to him, but the words were
strange and he could not understand them. There was
warning in its voice.

"What?" Herewiss said.

"You don't speak Dracon?" asked Segnbora.

"I could never find anyone to teach me."

"She says that something is trying to happen, and
you should beware of it."

"That's what I thought," Herewiss said. "But to beware of it? . . . I don't understand."

"Neither does she. She says to look to your sword."

"But I don't have a . . . well, I suppose I do . . ."

"I don't think much more will fit in there," Segnbora said to the first ouzel, which had come back with
a piece of kelp nearly twice its size. It was trying val-
iantly to stuff it in the crevice, and failing. Herewiss
felt suddenly that there was no more to be found or
shared in this dream. He bowed again to the Dragon,
and waved to Segnbora, and came forth.

Herewiss stood up, wondering a little, and went over
to where Freelorn lay, curled up in a ball as usual. He
spent a moment or two just looking at his loved. Sleep
was the only time when Lorn lost his eternal look of
calculation, and Herewiss loved to watch him sleeping,
even when he snored.

Herewiss sat down beside him, the sweet sorrow of
the moment passing through him like the pain of im-
minent tears. This could very well be the last time in
this life—and if the hralcin got him, as seemed likely,
in any life at all. *Mother,* he said softly, *I give You
this night, as You gave me one of Yours. Whatever else
happened or didn't happen in this life, Lorn loved
me—loves me; and that's as great a blessing as the Fire
would be, and possibly more than I deserve. Take this
night, Mother, and remember me. You understood
me—a little better than most . . .*

He reached out to touch Freelorn's cheek, brushed

it gently. *I'm going to try to give you all the parts of me I never dared to,* he said. *I hope I can give you all the joy you deserve.*

Herewiss entered in.

There were clouds of haze, lit by a light as indefinite as dawn on a cloudy day, and vague soft sounds wove through them. He found Freelorn moving quietly through the mists, looking for something. Herewiss fell in beside him, and they paced together through the haze.

"Where are we, Lorn?"

"A long time ago," Freelorn said softly, "I used to come here alone. I was really young, and I would come talk to the Lion and ask Him for help with my lessons. I mean, I didn't know that you're not supposed to ask God for help with things like that. So I just asked. And it always seemed that I got help. Maybe I can get some now."

The mist was clearing a little. All around them was a stately hall with walls of plain white marble. Tall deep windows were cut into those walls, and lamps burned golden in the fists of iron arms that struck outward from the walls at intervals. There was no furniture in the hall of any kind.

At the end of the room was a flight of steps, three of them, and atop the steps a huge pedestal, and on the pedestal a statue of a mighty white Lion couchant, regal and beautiful. Herewiss knew where they were. This was Lionhall in the royal palace in Prydon; the holiest place in Arlen, where none but the Kings and their children might walk without mishap befalling them. Though Herewiss had never seen it before, in Freelorn's dream the place was part of his longed-for home, one which he had never thought to see again. And the Lion was not merely another aspect of the Goddess' Lover, but the founder of Freelorn's ancient line, and so family. Herewiss and Freelorn walked to the steps together, and stopped there, and felt welcomed.

"Lord," Freelorn said, "I promised I would come back, and here I am. Where is my father?"

It was a little strange to see them facing each other; Freelorn, small and uncertain, but with a great dignity about him, and the Lion, terrible and venerable, but with a serene joy in His eyes. "He's gone on," the Lion said gravely. "He's one of Mine now."

"But where is he? I can't find his sword, and it's supposed to be mine, and I must have it. I can't be King without his sword."

"He's gone on," the Lion said, and He smiled on them out of his golden eyes. "You must go after him if you want Hergótha."

"I'll do that," Freelorn said. "Uh, Lord—"

"Ask on."

"You are my Father, and the head of our Line?"

"You are My child," the Lion said, bending His head in assent. "Make no doubt of it."

"Lord, I need a miracle."

The Lion stretched, a long comfortable cat-gesture, and the terrible steel-silver talons winked on His paws for a second's space. "I don't do miracles much any more, son. You're as much the Lion as I am. *You* do it."

"It's not for me, Héalhra my Father; it's for Herewiss here."

Herewiss looked up, meeting the gaze of the golden eyes and feeling a tremor of recognition, remembering how his illusion had looked at him even after it was gone from the field at Madeil. "Son of Mine," the Lion said then, shifting his eyes back to Freelorn, "his Father the Eagle and I managed Our own miracles for the most part. I have faith in you, and in him."

Freelorn nodded.

"Go down to the Arlid, then," the Lion said, "and follow it till it comes to the Sea. Your father is in the place to which his desire has taken him, but to get there you'll have to go down to the shore first. Your friend will go with you."

They bowed down, together, and were suddenly out by the river Arlid, which flowed through the palace grounds. It was night, and the water flowed silverly by under a westering Moon.

"The Sea is a long way off," Herewiss said. Even as he said it, he perceived something wrong with him. He was being swept away with this dream, losing control. *Too much drug!* something in him cried, thrilling with horror. But the fearful voice was faint, and though it cried again, *Down by the Sea is the land of the dead!* still he walked with Freelorn by the river-bank, through the green reeds, toward the seashore.

"It's not that far," Freelorn said. "Only a hundred miles or so."

"It's a long way to walk," Herewiss insisted.

"So we'll let the water take us. Come on."

Together they stepped down through the sedges on the bank and onto the surface of the water. The Arlid was a placid river, smooth-flowing, and bore their weight without complaint. Its current hurried them past little clusters of houses, and moss-grown docks, and flocks of grazing sheep, at a speed which would normally have surprised them but which they both now accepted unquestioningly. Once or twice they walked a little, to help things along, but mostly they stood in silence and let the river flow.

"You really think your father has the sword?" Herewiss said.

"He has to." Freelorn's voice was fierce. "They never found it after he died. He must have taken Hergótha with him."

Herewiss looked at Freelorn and was sad for him, driven as he was even while dreaming. "It takes more than a sword to make a King," he said, and then was shocked at the words that had fallen out of his mouth.

Freelorn looked back at him, and his eyes were sad too. "That's usually true," he said, "but it's going to take at least Hergótha to make a king out of me, I'm afraid. I'm not enough myself yet to do it alone."

272

For a while neither of them spoke. The river was branching out now, the marshes of the Arlid delta reaching out northward before them, toward the Sea. Freelorn and Herewiss picked their way from stream to stream as along a winding path, stepping carefully so as not to upset the fish.

"I've never been this way before," Herewiss said, very quietly. He felt afraid.

"Maybe it's time," Freelorn said. "I was here once, when I was very young. Don't be scared. I won't leave you alone."

The river bottom was getting shallower, and sandier. The stream that bore them turned a bend, past a little spinney of stunted willow trees, and suddenly there it was, the Shore.

Herewiss looked out past the beach and was so torn between terror and awe that he could hardly think. Under the dark sky the Sea stretched away forever, and it was a sea of light, not water. It was as liquidly dazzling as the noon Sun seen through some clear mountain cataract. But there was no Sun, no Moon, no stars even; only the long vista of pure brilliant light, brighter than any other light that ever was. Herewiss began to understand how the Starlight could only be a faint intimation of this last Sea, for stars are mortal, and bound with the laws and ties of materiality. This was a place that eternity itself would not touch, and grass matter had no part in it.

The waves of white fire came curling in, their troughs as bright as their crests, and broke in foaming radiance on the silver beach, and were drawn in sheets of light back into the Sea. But all silently. There was no sound of combers crashing and tumbling, no hiss of exhausted waves climbing far up the sand: nothing at all. Along the shore there walked or stood many vague forms, shadows passing by in as deep a silence as the waves. Herewiss was very afraid. The fear held his chest in its hand and squeezed, so that the breath couldn't come in. He thought suddenly of the choking darkness behind the *door* in the hold, where the hralcin waited and hungered for him, and the fear squeezed harder. But Freelorn stepped from the water, and held out his hand, and Herewiss took that hand and went with him.

They went down the shore together, slowly, looking at each of the shadows they passed, but recognizing none. There were men and women of every age, and many young children walking around or playing quietly in the sand. There were couples, some of them young lovers, and some of them old, and some couples where one person ravaged by time walked with one hardly touched by it, but walked all the same with interlaced arms and gentle looks. Freelorn would stop every now and then and question one or another of the people they passed. They always answered quietly, with grave, kindly words, but also with an air of preoccupation.

Herewiss was not paying attention to either questions or answers. His fear was too much with him. All he perceived with any clarity was the rise and fall of the quiet voices, which arose from the silence and slipped back to become part of it again when the speakers were finished. He began to feel that if he spoke again, the words and the thoughts behind them would be lost forever in that silence, a part of himself gone irretrievably. But no one asked him to speak, and Freelorn led him down the sand as if he had a sure idea of which way they were headed.

"Are we going the right way?" Herewiss said finally, watching carefully to see if the thought behind the question became lost.

"I think so. This place will come around on itself, if we give it enough time."

They walked, and their feet made no sound on the sand. If time passed at all, Herewiss could not feel it flowing over him. They passed more people than he had ever seen or known, some of them looking out over the gently moving brilliance of the Sea, or standing rapt in contemplation of the sand, or of something less obvious. When somone turned to watch them pass, it was with a look of mild, unhurried wonder, a wonder which soon slipped away again. The fear was beginning to ebb out of Herewiss, little by little, when suddenly he saw someone making straight for them across the strand, not quickly, but with purpose.

He could hear his heart begin hammering in his ears again. "Your father?" he said.

Freelorn shook his head. "My father was a bigger man. Is."

Herewiss stopped, still holding Freelorn's hand. He knew that shadowed form, knew the way it walked, the loose, easy stride. "Oh Goddess," he whispered into the eternal silence. "Goddess *no*."

Freelorn looked at him with compassion, and said nothing.

Herewiss stood there, frozen in the extremity of terror. The world was about to end in ice and bitterness, an he would welcome it. He deserved no better. He waited for it to happen.

And out of the darkness and fixity to which he thought he had completely surrendered himself, a voice spoke; his own voice, not angry or defiant, but matter-of-fact and calm, speaking a truth: *If this is the worst thing in the world about to happen, we won't just stand here and wait. We'll go meet it.*

He stepped foward, pulling Freelorn with him, and the strain of taking the first step shook him straight through, like a convulsion. His bones, his flesh rebelled. But he kept going. The shadowy form approached them steadily, and they walked to meet it. Fear battered at Herewiss like a stormwind. He wanted to flee, to hide, anything, but he pushed himself into the teeth of the wind, into the face of his fear. He had been struggling against it, walking into it head down. Now he raised his head, and opened his eyes again. The wind smote tears into his eyes, and he looked up at his brother.

He was as he had been the day he died. Tall and

dark-haired, like most of the Brightwood line, with the droopy eyes that ran in Herewiss' family, he came and stood before them. His eyes smiled, and his face smiled, and the blood welled softly from the place where Herewiss' sword had struck him through, an eternity ago.

"Hello, Herelaf," Freelorn said.

Herewiss let go of Freelorn's hand and sank down to his knees in the sand, trembling with terror and grief. He hid his face in his hands, and began to weep. All the things he had wanted to say to his brother after he died, all the apologies, all the guilt, everything that he had decided to say when they met after his own death, now froze in his throat. And the worst of it was that he felt quite willing to let the tears take him. Anything was better than trying to deal with the person who stood before him.

But there were hands on his hands, and they pulled gently downward until Herewiss had no choice but to squeeze his eyes shut and turn his head away. "Dusty," his brother's voice said, "don't you have *anything* to say to me?"

The old name, so rarely used, so much missed, pierced Herewiss with more pain than he had thought possible to stand without dying—but then, how could he die on these shores? He sobbed and coughed and caught his breath, and finally dared to look up again into his brother's face. There was no anger there, no hatred, not even any sorrow. Herelaf was glad to see him.

"Why are you so surprised that I'm here?" his brother said. "You know how the drug works. I'm as likely to turn up in your realm as you are in mine. And if you walk here, you're more than likely to run into me."

"I—" Herewiss choked, cleared his throat. "I suppose I knew it. But I was so sure that I wouldn't, wouldn't lose control—"

"—and run into me. Yes, I can imagine." Herelaf

276

held Herewiss' hands in his, and the touch was warm. "I'm glad you came."

"But—but I killed you—!" The words were too much for him, despite all the thousand times he had whispered and moaned and cried them into the darkness in the past. He crumpled back into tears. Freelorn was crouched down beside him, holding him again, and his brother's hands touched his face to wipe the tears away.

"Herewiss." The voice was still young, but there was power in it, and Herewiss was startled out of his weeping. "You didn't kill me. We were drunk, and messing with swords in a dark room, and you made one of those grand gestures with your sword, and I lost my balance and fell on it, and I died. You didn't kill me."

"But I should have been more careful—I shouldn't have encouraged you—"

"Herewiss, I started it."

"But—"

"Dusty, I *started* it. Listen, little brother mine, did I ever tell you a lie? Ever? Doesn't it strike you a little funny that I'd start trying to lie to you *here*, where there can be neither lying nor deception?"

Herewiss scrubbed at his eyes and looked up again. "You're still bleeding," he said.

"So are you, kid, and that's why. This is a peaceful place, there's healing to be had here before we go on. But the thoughts of the living have power over those who've gone on, just as the dead have some influence over the lives and ways of the living."

"But you're not really dead!" Herewiss cried. "You live, you're here—"

"I'm here. But alive? Not the same way you are. I finished what I had to do."

"But it was so senseless—you were young, and strong, and in line for the Lordship—" The tears broke through again. Herelaf shook his head.

"Little brother," he said, and he held Herewiss' hands hard, "I was all of that. And we loved each other greatly, and I loved my life, and when I first got here I raged and screamed and tried to get back into the poor broken body. But knowledge comes with silence here, and soon I found that it wasn't senseless. What sense there is to it may seem evil to us, but that's because it's past our understanding."

"I wish I could believe that—"

"Herewiss, I *know* this. I did what I was there to do while I was there, and then I came here, and when it's time, I'll go on to something else. That's the way things are."

"But—I don't understand. What did you *do?*"

Herelaf smiled at him. "That, like the matter of Names, is between me and the Mother. Besides, I may not be finished yet."

"I—oh, what the Dark! Herelaf, I wish I could stay here with you—I failed so miserably with the Flame—"

Herelaf laughed, and the mingled pain and joy that the sound struck into Herewiss was amazing to feel. "Goddess, Dusty, what a crazy idea. You don't even know what you're *for* yet, and already you want to abandon the battlefield! Idiot. So tell me. If you can tell me, you might be able to stay."

"I never really gave it much thought—"

"A lot of people don't. *I* certainly never did."

Herewiss frowned in irritation. "I," he said, "am the first man in a thousand years to have enough of the Flame to use, and know it."

"That's what you are, or what you have been—not what you're *for*. You just have to go back and find out the answer. Allow yourself to be what you can, and that will point you toward what you're *for* like a compass needle seeking north."

"But—"

"Shut up. You always were a great one for butting around, looking for holes in what you didn't want to hear. That hasn't changed, at least. Listen to me, Dusty. I'm only a ghost. No, look at me—" Herewiss had turned his face away, but Herelaf took both his brother's hands in one of his, while with the other he took Herewiss' face and turned it to him. "I'm only a ghost, Dusty. I can't hurt you any more, unless you make me. Since I fell onto your sword, you haven't been able to use one, not even to fight with—I guess because of me, or what you think you did to me. But the time's coming when you're going to need a sword. And you won't feel right with one, it won't do you any good, it'll turn in your hand unless you acquit yourself of my 'murder.' *You have things to do.* Better things than sitting around sorrowing for me. And I have better things to do than walk this shore and bleed."

Herewiss knelt there on the sand, and felt Freelorn's arms around him, and his brother's eyes upon him, and he shook. He didn't know what to think, or what to say.

"I'm not angry, Dusty," Herelaf said softly. "There's no anger here after one comes to understand things. I was set free at the appropriate time. How could I be angry about that? But we're in bondage, both of us, and you can free us both. Turn me loose. Turn yourself loose. *You didn't kill me.*"

"I—" Herewiss looked at his brother, and at the truth in his eyes, and for the first time began to feel something strange and cold curling in his gut. It was doubt, doubt of the crenellated certainties he had walled into his mind, and the doubt twined upward, curling around his heart and squeezing it hard. "I—"

PAIN. Sudden, terrible, and Herewiss foundering in darkness, the shore and the Sea's light and Freelorn and his brother's gentle voice all gone at once, lost, no light, no sound, only an awful tearing pain through his head and his heart and the place where his soul usually slept. Tearing, gnawing, and then just aching, and still the darkness, but there was a floor under him now—at least he thought there was, yes, his hands were against it, that was a pillow, and ohh his head hurt, spun and throbbed—and dear Goddess, what was that noise?

A howling. A sick ugly howling like an ax being sharpened too long, and mixed with it other sounds, human voices crying out in terror, the sound of scrabbling claws and—

Herewiss tried to stand up. The binding spell. Broken. A pack of hralcins; the one had gone back for reinforcements. A touch too much stress on the binding somehow. The spell broken, and now all of them loose, hunting. Hunting *him*. But he hadn't been in his body. So they couldn't find him. But they had found something else to hold them until he returned Freelorn. Freelorn's people. Downstairs. Defenseless.

He tried to stand again, and it didn't work. Too much drug. Out of it too suddenly. His body disobeyed him, and responded to his commands with vengeful stabs of pain. He pushed it anyway. The screaming was louder, voices terrified beyond understanding. He refused to let his body's punishments stop him. There was a little light now, sickly, the light of the Moon almost gone down. Against the wall was a dim gray blot, the only thing he could really see. He made a hand go out, despite shrieking protests from his head and arm and aching body, and took hold of the thing. It swayed in his grasp. The other hand, now. He gripped the object hard, and wrenched himself to a sitting position next to it.

If his voice could have found his throat, he would have screamed. It was the sword, sharpened that morning, and it cut into his hands in icy lines of pain, and the blood flowed. But he had no time, no time for the pain, and he struggled to stand, using the sword as a prop. He moved his hands feebly to the unsharpened tang, where the hilt would go, and pushed himself up, and somehow managed to stand. His legs wobbled under him as if they belonged to a body he had owned in a former life. He made his feet move. He went to the door.

The stairs were dark, and Herewiss fell and stumbled down them, using the sword as a cane, caroming

off the walls with force enough to bruise bones—
though he couldn't feel the blows much through the
shell of fire which the drug had made of his body.
The cries of men in terror were closer now. They mingled with that awful lusting hunger-howl and were
nearly lost in it, faint against it as against the laughter
of Death. As Herewiss came to the landing at the foot
of the stairs, very faintly he could see some kind of
light coming from the main hall, a fitful light, coming
in stutters and flashes. With every flash the hralcins
screeched louder in frustration and rage. *Segnbora!* he
thought, *she's holding them off with the light until I
can get there. But what can I do? Nothing but Flame
would do anything*—

He reeled against the wall to rest his blazing body
for a second, and the answer spoke itself to him in his
brother's voice. (It'll turn in your hand unless you acquit yourself of my "murder.")

He stumbled away from the wall and went on again,
shuffling, hurrying, pushing himself through the
pain. The light before him grew brighter as he approached the hall, but the flashes were becoming
shorter and shorter. *Segnbora spoke of choosing when
to listen to the voices of the dead—and when you can
choose freely, and not be driven by them, you're free
to find out who you really are*—

And the voice spoke again in the back of his mind,
saying, (There's neither lying nor deception, back of
the *Door*—)

He couldn't *lie,* Herewiss thought through the effort of making his body work. *He was telling the
truth. He* was! *I* didn't—

He came to the doorway of the hall, and stood there,
trembling with fear and effort, taking in the scene.
There was little sound from the people in the hall
now. They were crowded together in one corner, huddled together with closed or averted eyes. Before them
stood Segnbora, arms upraised, shaking terribly, but
with a look of final commitment on her face as she

summoned the Flame from the depths of her, brilliant and impotent. As Herewiss watched, supporting himself on the bloody sword, she called the light out of herself again. But this time there was no starflower, no burst of blue: only a rather bright light, quickly gone.

In that light he could see the huge things she was holding off, as they backed away a bit. They reached out with twisted limbs, black talons raked the air like the combed claws of insects. Even through their banshee wail the sound of sheathed fangs moving hungrily in hidden mouths could still be heard. The light seemed to refuse to touch them, glancing off hide the color of night with no stars—though there were baleful glitters from where their eyes could have been, reflections the color of gray-green stormlight on poisoned ice. The air in the room was bitter cold, and smelled of rust and acid.

The light flickered out, and the hralcins moved in again for their meal.

Herewiss staggered in, into the thick darkness. Well, maybe *this* was what he was for. The hralcins had come after him: he would give himself to them, and they would feed on his soul and go away, satisfied. His friends would escape. He found himself suddenly glad of those few precious moments with his brother, however painful they had been. After the hralcins were through with him, there would be nothing. No silent shore, no sea of light, no rebirth ever; only terrible pain, and then the end of things. But if this was going to be the last expression of his existence, he would do it *right*. He drew himself up straight, though it hurt, and lifted up the sword. Almost he smiled: it was so good to face his fears at last—!

"Here I am, you sons of bitches!" he yelled. *"Come and get me!"*

The howling paused for a moment, as if in confusion—and then, to Herewiss' utter horror, resumed again. They were not interested. They had found other game; they would take the souls of Freelorn and his people, and then later have Herewiss at their leisure.

"No," he breathed. "No—"

"Herewiss!" two voices cried at once, and there was the light again, but only a shadow of itself, pallid and exhausted. Segnbora held up her arms with fists clenched, as if she were trying to hold onto the light by main force, while her eyes searched the shadows for Herewiss. Freelorn stood apart from her, grimfaced and terrified. His sword was naked in his hand: a useless gesture, but one that described him in full. *That man walked the land of the dead with me unafraid,* Herewiss thought, *and here he is facing down things that'll drink him up, blood and soul together, and he's afraid, and still he defies—!*

The light died out, for the last time. The hralcins howled, and moved in—

The hall exploded into fire, an awful blaze of white-hot outrage. Freelorn and Segnbora and the others crowded further back into the corner as Sunspark flowered between them and the hralcins, its fires raging upward in a terrible blinding column until they reached the ceiling and turned back on themselves, the downhanging branches of a tree of flames. The hralcins backed away again.

"Sunspark," Herewiss cried, the sound of his shout hurting his head, "Spark, no, *don't*—"

The hralcins were already sliding closer again. (Herewiss,) it said, lashing out at them with great gouts of fire, (he loves you. And you love him, more than you do me, I dare say. How shall I stand by and allow him to be taken from you? And then afterwards these things would take you too—) Its thoughts were casual on the surface, almost humorous, but beneath them Herewiss could hear its terror for him.

"Spark—"

It went up in so unbearable a glare that Herewiss had to close his eyes, but before he did he saw that the hralcins were still moving closer. (They don't seem to be responding as well to this,) it said conversationally, while beneath the thoughts all its self sang with fear. (I think—)

There was a sudden shocked silence. Herewiss opened his eyes again to see one of the hralcins reach out and somehow tear the pillar of fire in two, hug a great tattered blaze of light to itself with its misshapen forelimbs, suck it dry, kill the light. The other hralcins moved in for the rest, tore at the light, fed, consumed it, darkness fell—

"SUNSPAAAAAARK!"

The hralcins howled like the Shadow's hounds, and moved in again. And through the howling, Herewiss heard Freelorn scream.

The scream entered into Herewiss and burned behind his eyes, ran through his veins in a storm of fire and filled him as the drug had filled him with himself. He needed his Name. There was no time any more. He threw the door open, and looked. Time froze in him. No, *he* froze it—

All his life he had thought of time as being flat, like a plane. It was the world that was three-dimensional. A moment had seemed to have an edge sharp enough to slice a finger on, and by the time he summoned up the self-awareness and desire to try balancing on such a razor's edge, the moment was past already, and he was teetering on the next one.

Now, though, he found himself poised there, effortlessly, in the exact middle of a moment. And since he was truly *still* for the first time in his life, he perceived his Name. He looked sideways down it, or along it, or into it—there were no words to properly express the spatial relationships implicit within its structure. Its strands stretched outward forever, and inward forever, flung out to eternity and yet curling back and meeting themselves again, making a whole. A scintillating, dazzling latticework of moments past and moments future, of Herewiss-that-was and Herewiss-that-would-be,

284

all entwined, all coexisting; a timeweb, a selfweb, himself at its heart.

He looked up and down its length, and *saw*. Down there, root and heart and anchor-point of the weave, the night of his conception. Elinádren his mother, and Hearn his father, tangled sweetly together in the act of love. After some time of sleeping together for the sheer fun of the sharing, they were making an amazing discovery; that each of them was finding the other's delight more joyous than his or her own—and not just while in bed. The long comfortable friendship of the Lord's son and the Rodmistress who worked with him had come to fruition; they had become lovers; and now that they were in love indeed, their Names were beginning to match in places. He could see the two brilliant Name-weaves tangling through one another, and where they touched and met and melded, they blazed white-hot with joy. It was as if someone had cast out a net of silver and drawn in a catch of stars.

Herewiss' soul, existing in timelessness, saw that bright network and was entranced by it; the joystars were beacons that drew him in. He wanted that kind of joy, of love, wanted to be part of it, to share the joy with someone else that way. And as he watched, Elinádren exploded in ecstatic fulfillment, and her Fire ran searing through the glittering weave, igniting the joystars into unbearable blinding brilliance, setting free for a bare few moments the spark of Hearn's suppressed Flame, which swept down like wildfire to meet hers. Their two commingled souls burned starblue, and Herewiss, overwhelmed by an ecstasy of light and promised joy, dove inward, furled his wings, and blazed into oneness with them as *they* were one; started to be born again. . . .

And other occurrences, later ones. Being held in his father's arms, carried home half-asleep after his presentation at the Forest Altars; three years old. "Oh," Hearn's voice whispering to Elinádren, who walked beside them with her arm through Hearn's, moving quietly through green twilight, "oh, Eli, he's going to be something special."

And another one over there, watching his mother make it rain to stave off what seemed an incipient dry spell. He was six years old. Watching her stand there in the field, garlanded with meadowsweet to invoke the Mother of Rains, seeing her uplift a Rod burning with the Fire and call the rainclouds to her with Flame and poetry. He watched the sky darken into curdled contrasts, clouds violet and orange and storm-green, watched her bring the lightning-licked water thundering down, and a great desire to control the things of the world rose up in him. He got up from the grass, soaking wet, and went to hold onto Elinádren's skirts, and said, "Mommy, I'll do that when I grow up too."

And yet another, when he was out camping in the grasslands east of the Wood, and he woke up and stretched in the morning to find the grass-snake coiled in the blankets with him, and heard its warning hiss: eleven years old. He knew it could kill him; and he knew he could probably kill it, for his knife was close to hand and he was fast. But he remembered Hearn saying, "Don't *ever* kill unless you must!"—and he lifted up the blankets slowly and then rolled out, and from beneath them the grass-snake streaked out like a bright green lash laid over the ground, and was gone, as frightened of him as he had been of it. *I guess you can do without killing,* he thought. *Always, from now on, I'll try—*

There were thousands more moments like that, each one of which had made him part of what he was, each linked to all the moments before and all the moments after, making the bright complete framework that was his Name. And each act or decision had a shadow, a phantom link behind it—sprung from his deeds, yet independent of them somehow—another Name, shadowing itself in multiple reflections, reaching out into depths he could not fully comprehend—

Her name. The Goddess'. Of course.

No wonder She wanted to free me. And no wonder She wanted my Name. Not power, nothing so simple. It is part of Hers. Her Name is the sound of all Names everywhere. And with the knowledge of my Name, She will win ever so slight a victory against the Death. There will be more of Her than there was; the sure knowledge of what I am at this moment in time will make me immortal in a way that will surpass and outlast even the cycles of death and rebirth, even the great Death of everything that is.

If I accept myself—

Herewiss stood there in the midst of the blazing brilliance of the weave, hearing words long forgotten as well as ones that had never been spoken, tasting joys he had ceased to allow himself and pains he had shut away, and also feeling with wonder the textures of things that hadn't happened yet, silks and thorns and winds laden with sunheat like molten silver— Whether the drug was still working in him, he wasn't sure; but futures spun out ahead of him from the base-framework of his Name, numberless probabilities. Some of them were so faint and unlikely that he could hardly perceive them at all; some were almost as clear as things that had become actuality. Some of these were dark with his death, and some almost as dark with his life; one burned blue with the Fire, and he looked closely at it, saw himself almost lost in light, rippling with Flame that streamed from him like a cloak in the wind. And that future was ready to start in the next moment, when he let time start happening again. But there was still a gap in the information, he didn't know how to get there from here—

Yes I do.

Herewiss looked forward along all the futures, and back down his past, weighing the brights and darks of them, and accepted them for his.

And knew his Name.

And knew the Name of his fear.

His Flame, of course. There it lay, dying indeed, but still the strongest thing about him, the strongest part of him. How long, now, had he been trying to control it, to use it like a hammer on the anvil of the world? The blue Flame was not something to be used in that fashion. He had been trying to keep it apart from him, where it would not be a threat to his control of himself. If he wanted it, *really* wanted it, he was going to have to take hold of it and merge himself with the Fire, give up the control, yield himself wholly and forever.

It was going to hurt. The fires of the forge, of a star's core, of an elemental's heart would be nothing compared to this.

So be it. There's no more time. I've got to do it.

He had been trying to make the Fire his.

He reached out and embraced it, and made it *him*.

Pain, incredible pain for which the anguished screaming of a whole dying world seemed insufficient expression. He hung on, grasped, held, *was* fire—and then time began to reassert itself, the pain mixing with the sound of Freelorn's scream, feeding on it, blending, changing, anger, incandescent blue anger, raging like the Goddess' wrath—hands, surely burned off, eyes transfixed by spears of blue-white fury, too much, too much power, has to go somewhere, forward, moments moving, forward, terror, rage, *forward*, Freelorn—!

—staggering forward, carrying the half-finished sword in his hand, and a murderous freight of rage within him, burning under his skin like the red-hot heart of a coal under its white ash. No anger he had ever summoned had been this potent, it was devouring him from within, he was fire, like Sunspark, *ah, Sunspark, loved, gone, dear one!*—and he sobbed, his own fires consuming him now, fury, horror, revenge, he tried to treat them as a sorcery, shaping them, directing them, scorching himself with them, weaving them—

—something stumbled into the firefield he was making, no, that he *was,* for it was *he* and he *it*; *that's the secret, isn't it—not trying to use a tool, but being one with it—who uses their hand to do something? It does it*—a something, no, not really—a not-something; it had no name, nor even any life; and it sensed his sudden incredible upsurge of life, of selfness—*they* sensed him, and were closing in, for such a feed as they had never had in all their centuries. *Well, let them try. They are not alive, so it's all right to kill them—disassemble would be a better word, actually; see, a break here, at this linkage, and here, quite simple; I know what I'm for and they can't say as much—now the hard part,* push—

If Freelorn's scream had terrified him, the ones that came now were worse, but Herewiss shut them out. He stood still, clenching hard on his sword, on himself, his eyes squeezed shut. Outside of him he perceived a terrible turbulence and upset, a maelstrom of freed forces that shook the air inside his lungs and battered at the thoughts inside his head. But he felt sure that if he looked at see what was happening, something might go wrong. He urged the anger on, feeding it with his fears, pouring it out. It pushed through his pores as if he were sweating molten metal. His skin would have melted too were it not already charred into a blackened shell. The burning had rooted itself deep in him, his bones glowed like iron in the forge. His heart raced, its rhythm staggering in pain, every beat an explosion of sparks and burnt blood. But still he pushed, fanned the fire, breathed it hotter, pushed, *pushed*—

The hralcins keened and screeched up to the top of the range of hearing, a multiple cry of agony and excruciating fright. The sound hurt the ears, piercing them unbearably, boring inward to the brain—

—and then it stopped.

*   *   *

Herewiss opened his eyes. The hall was empty, except for the hralcins' horrible smell and a faint brief echo of their last despairing cry. Slowly, Freelorn's people began to come out of the corner. Segnbora slumped down into an exhausted heap on the floor, and wept with frustration and fear. Herewiss stood where he was, holding himself straight, and Freelorn came and put his arms around him. Freelorn was shaking terribly.

"Lorn," Herewiss said.

Freelorn held him, just held him hard for a few moments, and then reached up a trembling hand to Herewiss' face, brushing away the tears and sweat. Herewiss caught at that hand, bowed his head over it, pressed his lips to it. "Lorn," he said again, his heart clenching like a fist in a last spasm of fear. "Are you all right, did it hurt you at all—"

"No, no, it just touched me." Freelorn laughed, a weak, shaky chuckle. "You know how I am about gooey things—"

"You were justified, I think. . . ." He held Freelorn's hand tightly against him, and swayed slightly; his voice was soft and slurred with fatigue. "Lorn, it's awfully bright in here for Moonset . . . is Segnbora—"

"Ohh—oh, *Herewiss*—"

There was such a strange tone to Freelorn's voice that Herewiss glanced down to see what he was looking at. It took a while before it registered, before he really saw the bright blue Flame that licked around him like an aura, curling down his arm and flowing through and about the blade of the half-finished sword in runnels the color of summer sky. And even then, all he could find the strength to do was to slip his free arm around his friend, as much from the need for support as from love.

TEN

*After even the fieriest sunset comes
the Twilight; and in the Twilight,
anything is rather more than less
likely to happen.*

Gnomics, 14

Herewiss woke up all at once, as if his mind had opened a door and stepped through. He sat up, and glanced at the shadows outside to tell the time. It was nearly noon. Beside him Freelorn lay curled up, having stolen all the blankets as usual, and snored like a whole pride of lions.

He leaned against the wall for a few minutes and just felt the Fire within him. It was freed now, it was *him* now, no longer bound into a tight controlled package at the bottom of his self. It ran all through him, warm as blood, no longer urgent, but calm and glad. There was time to do the things that had to be done. All the time in the world.

The sword lay beside him, among the cushions, and he looked at it and smiled. If he had shed blood on it—and he checked his hands, finding only Flame-healed scars there—then the blood had burnt off, for the metal was bright and unstained. The steel had acquired an odd blue sheen, as if even indoors it was reflecting the memory of the morning sky.

He reached down, picked it up. At his touch it flared up brilliantly, a bar of blue-white light like the core of a star, hammered and forged. Thin bright tongues of the Flame strained away from it and curled back again. Herewiss' smile dimmed as the sight recalled to him another image, that of a bright torn veil of fire arching away from some star, daring the darkness—and then fallen, consumed, gone forever into the greater brilliance.

Spark, he thought, *oh my dear loved.* He leaned his head back against the wall and began to weep. The sword's light blazed up with his pain. *My sweet firechild, my hungry piece of the Sun. You always were good at doing the impossible, but this time you outdid yourself. You went and got killed.* The sobbing began to rack him. *And for my sake. The only man in history to have a fire elemental fall in love with him, and it loves me so well that it dies for me. Oh, damn, damn, damn—!*

He cried and cried for what seemed forever, the sword clutched in his hands, its Flame trembling and wavering with his sobs. *So now what? There's nothing left to bury—and what kind of a tree do you plant for a fire elemental, anyhow? Maybe it would be more appropriate to start a brush fire—oh, dammit straight to Darkness! I make my peace with a guilt, and not an hour later I have a grief just as bad to replace it! One more empty place inside me—and I'll never be able to so much as light a campfire again without being reminded of just how empty it is! I always knew that you have to accept the pain at the end of love to make the loving complete—but this, this is harder than I thought— Oh, Mother of Everything, why her—why him—why my sweet little Sunspark? Why, why . . .*

Eventually he ran dry of tears, and even the great heaving sobs that shook him grew less—his chest ached too much to sustain them. He scrubbed at his face with one hand—he still could not bring himself to let go of the sword—and fell to running his fingertips up and down the water-cool metal of the blade, the rhythm of his stroking being occasionally broken by a leftover sob or choke. *This whole thing hasn't gone the way it should, and now is no exception. I thought*

292

it would be all joy, that it would feel good at the end—and look at me. And I never dreamed that there would be such a price to pay. Or even that I wouldn't be the only one paying it. Herewiss shook his head slowly. *She asked me what I would be willing to pay. If I'd known then what I know now, I wonder if I'd have been so sure of myself.*

"Goddess, Herewiss," came a grumble from within the pile of blankets, "how come you have this crazy preference for rooms with eastern exposures? Anyone who gets up this early has to have something wrong with his—" Freelorn's head and shoulders and arms emerged from under the covers; he stretched and turned over, and saw. "Oh," he said. "Ohh—" —and sat up, shedding blankets in all directions, reached over and took Herewiss in his arms, hugged him tightly enough to bruise ribs, kissed him hard, hugged him again. Herewiss hugged back, one-armed. His underhearing was alive as it had never been before, and the blaze of triumph and joy that his loved was radiating made him smile. It was a strange feeling; after all the crying, he felt as if his face might crack.

"You've got it," Freelorn was saying. "You've *got* it—"

"It looks that way."

"But, Goddess, it's so long," Freelorn said, propping himself up against the wall beside Herewiss. "You're going to—hey, my face is—you've been crying—?!"

"I've been—I've—oh, Dark, I thought I was, was *done*—oh, *Lorn*—"

"No, no, it's all right. Come here, then. Come on. There—let it out." Freelorn took Herewiss in his arms, holding him tight, and Herewiss buried his face against Freelorn's shoulder and wept anew. "You've had a hell of a night, go ahead and let it out—"

"It's muh, muh, m—" (more than that. And why am I trying to talk? I can make anyone hear me now. Whether they have the talent or not.)

"Sweet Goddess above us," Freelorn said in amazement. "So that's how it feels."

(Yes. But, Lorn, poor Sunspark—!)

Freelorn was shocked into silence as Herewiss gave him the image of Sunspark's Name without words.

(And it's gone, it *died*, it wasn't supposed to be *able* to die and it *died*—)

Herewiss said nothing more for a long time, but only sobbed, and Freelorn held him close and wondered. When after a while the sobs started to die down, and Herewiss gulped and choked and started to control himself again, Freelorn sighed and made himself smile.

"I was saying," he said conversationally, "that you're going to have to put a bastard broadsword's hilt on that thing if you expect to be able to handle it. It's four feet long easily."

"I—uh—no." Herewiss sat up straight again, wiped at his eyes and got his breath back. "Not at all. See, look—" He stood up, and taking the sword one-handed, Herewiss cut and parried and thrust till the air whistled and the sword left trails of blue Fire behind it. "It's like an arm, it's almost weightless. Not quite; the balance is a little heavy toward the point." He held the sword out at arm's length, point up, eyeing it with a critical smile. "Possibly my error at the forge—or possibly the sword itself is impatient. But whatever, it's no problem to handle."

"Looks like it has a nice edge."

"Nice! This sword could shave the wind and not leave a whisker. In fact—" Herewiss looked around the room for something to try it on. "In *fact*—" He moved toward the grindstone, grinning with wicked merriment.

"Are you going to—Dusty, you're, you've got to be—"

Herewiss took the sword two-handed, swung it up behind his head, felt a wild joy as the Flame ran up through his arms and into the blade, poised, waiting.

He brought it sweeping down hard, channeling the Fire down into the striking fulcrum of the sword, as he had been taught to channel the force of his arms. The blade struck the grindstone and clove it in two, kept on going and smote through the oak framework, kept on going and finally struck the floor, where it left a slit as if a knife had been stuck in a cheese. The grindstone smashed in pieces to the floor, leaving no mark on the shining gray surface.

Herewiss stood up straight, turned and grinned at Freelorn.

"Show-off," Freelorn said, grinning back.

"Have I ever denied it? Lorn, I'm ripe, serves me right for sleeping in my clothes. Come on, let's take a bath."

"There's hardly enough water in your cistern for that—"

Herewiss drew himself up to his full height. "*That,*" he said smugly, "can be fixed . . ."

By afternoon it had rained four times, once with a mad magnificence of thunder, and lightning like fireworks; and the knobby barren sage around the hold was in bloom a month early. Freelorn's people were walking around with grins almost wide enough to match Herewiss'. Despite the terror, they had been present at a miracle, or something that could pass for one, and they were also relishing the prospect of seeing Freelorn back on his throne again, escorted there by Herewiss' Flame.

For a while that afternoon Herewiss sat down in the great hall, one arm around Freelorn and the other hand holding the sword across his knees, answering all the questions about how it felt and where the hralcins had come from and what had happened to Sunspark and what Herewiss was going to do now. When Segnbora asked that one, Herewiss looked sidewise at Freelorn and smiled.

"How much did you say you got, Lorn?"

"Eight thousand."

"Mmm. We could bribe a lot of people with that."

"Or hire a lot of soldiers."

"Lorn, I'd still rather sidestep that solution. When you're King again, your people will bless your name for taking Throne and Stave without bloodshed. And with this—" he rapped one knuckle against Freelorn's skull—"and this—" he lifted up the sword—"we should be able to work something out. But as soon as you people are ready, maybe in a few days, when we're all rested, we'll start heading west. The Arlenes have been without a child of the Lion's line for six years now, and the effects are beginning to show. It's time something was done about it."

He got up, and they stood with him, nodding and murmuring agreement. "I have a few things to take care of," he said to them all, "so I'll see you around dinnertime. Is there enough of that deer left?"

"We'll get another," Dritt said, and smiled. "This is too important an occasion for leftovers."

They headed for the door, Segnbora walking slowly behind the rest of them. She looked very tired. Herewiss glanced at Freelorn, and Lorn nodded and went off to the back of the hall to be busy elsewhere for a moment.

"Segnbora—"

She turned as Herewiss came up behind her. "Mm?" she said. She held herself proudly erect, as usual, with her hand on her sword-hilt. It wouldn't have fooled anyone, with or without underhearing.

He reached out, took that terribly capable-looking hand in his and raised it to his lips. "It was a valiant gesture," he said, "even though it didn't work for long. You gave all you had to give, and you bought me the time I needed, one way or the other. Without you we would have all been someone's dinner last night."

She smiled at him, but her eyes were still very very tired. "I see what you're saying, Herewiss," she said.

"Thank you." He started to let go of her hand, but she bespoke him suddenly, in a clear warm voice that sounded more like Segnbora than she did herself. (But though I'm sorry for myself, I'm as sorry for you. You may be fooling the rest of them, even Freelorn perhaps, but not me. Somehow or other, my perceptions tell me, you've paid more for your Power than you'd thought to. And worse than that, though you have the Fire indeed, you also still have all your problems. A new grief to replace your old one, a king to put on his throne without any sure idea of how to do it—and, worst of all, no real idea of what you yourself will do when you're finished with that.)

He stared at her, too incredulous to really hear the compassion in her voice.

She was still smiling faintly. (They really pushed us at Nhàirēdi,) she said. (Too hard, I think. See you later.)

She turned, and went outside.

Herewiss walked slowly back to Freelorn, looking sober, and Freelorn nodded and slipped his arms around Herewiss again. "It does seem a shame about her," he said.

"Yeah."

"You never did tell me if this ridiculous chunk of steel had a name."

"Oh, it has," Herewiss said, smiling again, holding the sword up before him. "I haven't done the whole blood-and-four-elements business to it yet—well, actually, it's had the blood—but whatever. Its name is Khávrinen."

"Mmph. Trust you to go for something obscure."

"No, it's in the original Brightwood dialect of Darthene, a few hundred years removed from Nhàired. You could render it as HarrowHeart."

"Mmmm . . ."

"I mean, really, Lorn. Was ever heart harrowed as mine was last night?"

297

"If it was," Freelorn said with a slow smile, "I'm sure that whoever wrote the ballad about it divorced the emotion from the reality somewhat."

They stood smiling at one another, and Freelorn reached up, took Herewiss' face between his hands, pulled it down, and kissed him long and passionately.

"We've been all over you all day," he said. "I'm going out with them so you can have some time by yourself."

"You know," Herewiss said, "I think I love you."

"And I, you," Freelorn said, and reluctantly—with a longing backward look—hurried out after his people.

The first thing Herewiss did when he got back to the tower room was find the old spear he had carried with him on all his travels since Herelaf's death. Khávrinen made short work of it, and Herewiss threw the splintered remains out the window, chuckling all the while.

The second thing he did was to send word to Hearn about what had happened, while he rooted around in the room for the materials necessary to finish the sword. *The Wardress should be in the Wood this time of month, with the full Moon just past,* he thought. (Kerim!) he called, digging around in his chest for the sword-fittings he'd been saving.

(What? What? Who's that?)

(It's Herewiss, Lord Hearn's son—)

(Impossible! I smell Flame!)

(Impossible?) Herewiss laughed. (I'll show you impossible!) He bound sight into the linkage between them, and held Khávrinen before his eyes, pushing Flame into it. The sword blazed like a blue noon.

(Dear Mother of Everything—)

(She is that, every bit of it,) Herewiss agreed. (Kerim, will you give my father a message?)

(Why . . . why, surely, but Herewiss, how, how . . .)

(Say to Hearn that his son sends him greetings, and

bids him know that the Phoenix is risen again, though the fire is blue this time. Say also to him that the name of my focus is Khávrinen. Will you do that?)

(Certainly, but Herewiss—)

(I'll let you have a look at it when I get back to the Wood,) he said. (Be nice to your students, Kerim.)

(But—)

Herewiss cut the contact and found the sword-fittings. (Spark,) he said, (I'm going to need—)

He fell silent. A pillar of fire, torn, devoured, gone, and only a dark space where a bright lance of flame had defied the long night.

"Oh," he said, very quietly. "Ohh . . ."

He sighed, a sigh with tears in it, and straightened up, regarding the sword-fittings. Gold though they might be, they weren't any good. Khávrinen's metal was as alive as he was, but this stuff was dead. To fasten such onto the sword would be like hanging a corpse around someone's neck. (Khávrinen,) he said, (if you were a bit shorter in the blade, a foot or so, there'd be enough metal along with the extra in the tang to make a respectable hilt and crosspieces—)

He pushed Power into the sword again, and beneath his hands he felt metal flow, though there was no heat. Khávrinen cloaked itself in Fire, possibly self-conscious about changing form in front of him. When the light died down, Herewiss examined it again. The sword had grown itself a severely plain crosspiece, hardly more than a slim bar of steel, as well as a textured grip and a concave disc-shaped pommel, and for good measure had carved a fuller down the length of its blade. It had not, however, changed its balance. Herewiss held it in the air and smiled at it—

—and felt something stir in the corner by the window—

He whirled. *Dammit to Darkness,* he thought, *some power coming to test me already? I thought I was entitled to at least* one *day's rest—*

It was faint and weak-feeling, a troubling of the air in the corner, looking like the heat-shimmer above a pavement—

—brightening—

—a wobbling, wavering, exhausted column of fire— Herewiss froze, not even breathing.

(Hello, loved,) said the pale blaze in the corner.

(SUNSPARK!!!!)

It smiled at him in slow tired patterns of fire. (Half a moment,) it said. (Let me enflesh—)

At the end of a few seconds it was standing there in the dear familiar red roan shape, and Herewiss had his arms around its neck and was hugging it hard. "Sunspark, Sunspark, where have you *been?*" he cried out, leaking tears.

(Coming back,) it said. (This dying,) it added, butting its head up against Herewiss' chest, (it is very interesting. I really must try it again some time.)

(But Spark, those things ate *souls*—!!)

(So they did. It was uncomfortable. Though I dare say I gave them a fair case of indigestion. —How long have I been gone?)

(Hardly a day—)

(It seemed longer,) the elemental said, very wearily. (I had some trouble finding my way in the dark. Though I seemed to hear someone calling my Name over this way—)

Herewiss rested his head between Sunspark's ears, his cheek against the golden mane. (Thank You,) he said. (Thank You.)

(It was nothing,) Sunspark said absently. (How did you manage to survive, by the way?)

Herewiss straightened up, unlaced his arms from around its neck and showed it Khávrinen, gripped in his hand.

(I see. Your focus indeed. And you're changed, too,) Sunspark said, regarding him out of its golden eyes. (If I ran into you in the middle of nowhere now, I would know you are a relative. You, too, are fire.)

(Well, and a few other things,) Herewiss said. (Sunspark, what you did last night—)

(I would do again,) it said. (You are my loved. And anyway, shall I dare less than you?)

Herewiss put his arms around Sunspark's neck again, gathered it close, and wept like a child.

Later, back in the hold, Freelorn and his people were sitting around the firepit, pledging one another in great drafts of Narchaerid and rr'Damas and Jaráldit wines. that Sunspark had filched for them. Herewiss, however, sat crosslegged in the dust about half a mile from the hold, looking at the Moon and stars. Khávrinen was laid across his knees.

(Hearn was right all the time,) he was saying to the night. (Always he used to tell me, "When you're praying, don't *beg* the Goddess. What mother can stand hearing her children whine at her? Talk to Her, tell Her what's on your mind. You'll *always* get answers back. Lie to Her and you'll get lies back—but tell Her the truth and you'll find solutions." And he was right. There *is* a part of each of us that is part of You—I just never really saw it until last night—and though it speaks in one's own voice, there is no mistaking the source of the answer.)

Your father is a wise man, the reply drifted back after a while.

Herewiss nodded.

(Herelaf wouldn't tell me what he was for,) he said. (There can, of course, be no deception on that last Shore—and he *did* tell me that he might not have been finished. Which leaves me with a conclusion that I find a little frightening. Was he trying to tell me that what he was *for*—was specifically to be my brother, to die on the end of my sword—and so to begin the events that ended in last night? To make me into what I am now? Was that it?)

The silence drifted around him for a long time.

(It's not an answer that I like,) he said.

It is the answers we dislike the most, came the reply, *that usually have the most truth to them.*

(But, Mother, it isn't *fair!* Not to him, not to me—)

He knew what the answer was going to be. It was spoken with a little smile, a sad one. *Who ever said anything was fair, son of Mine? That's My fault, and every time I hear that cry, it goes straight through Me. But next time. Next time—*

He nodded, sighed. (I'm sorry. Mother, I really feel guilty about complaining. I have so very much; the Fire, my Name . . . and Yours too. That's what I'm *for*—to find Your Name, as much as to find mine.)

That's a start.

(You're looking too,) he said in sudden realization. (But it is through we who live that You look. And when all who live find their Names, and all the other pieces of Yours—)

Silence. A star fell.

Herewiss smiled. (My life had been so pointed toward one thing, that I guess I panicked—I was afraid there would be nothing left for me to do. Béorgan's mistake. . . . But if this is true, if I am for seeking out Your Name wherever it is to be found, and freeing it, I'm going to be awfully busy. This is a big world. . . .)

He ran the fingers of one hand up and down Khávriñen's blade again. (Mother, mightn't You have chosen better for the first man to have Flame in all these years? The Fire won't lessen my flaws—they'll get bigger, if anything. And even with all this Power—and I know I have much more than the average Rodmistress—can I really change the world that much, will I really be worth it? There's so little time, so little of me—)

That, and the voice came firmly as that of a mother taking a sharp knife away from a child, that *evaluation I reserve for Myself. By the common conception of it, humankind doesn't consider something "worth it" unless they get their investment back, preferably with a profit. By this criterion, most of the Universe is "not worth it." But I know—as do all the others who care—* and the voice smiled at Herewiss—*that it is often necessary to give and give and not get back in any way save the knowledge that the worlds are better for it. Freelorn is right, in that respect. Béaneth was right. Béorgan the doomed was right, so were Earn and Héalhra and all the others. They* knew *they were doomed, but they did the right thing anyway, trying to make the world a little better.*

The voice sighed. *Valiant absurdity, lost causes, such things may be doomed to incompletion and failure of one kind or another, but they are none of them "wasted." Judge these things by whether they will prolong the Universe's life, or bring joy to what I made, and that is their worth. All things must die, but I will not scatter My poor botched creation like a child kicking over a misbuilt sand castle. I will make it work the best I can.*

Herewiss nodded.

(What shall I do now?) he asked.

You're asking Me? Herewiss could feel a grin stirring somewhere. *What would I do?*

He grinned back. (Share the gift. Defy the Death.)

The answer was silence.

Herewiss stood up and was silent in return for a while as he gazed up at the stars. High above him burned the Moon, chill and silver in the quiet. Down the gray length of the sword, the blue Fire flowed and rippled in the stillness.

Wordlessly, he told the stars and She Who watched his inner Name. It surged in him like fire, and made him blaze with sheer joy, just to say it.

As he did, across the western sky there burned a line of fire, slow and silent. Then another fell, but closer, and another, trails of brilliance all around him, falling stars like rain in summer—burning blue, a storm of starfire, beating on the silver desert. At the white heart of the downpour Herewiss waited, hardly breathing, as he watched the bright rain fall.

Slowly, then, the starfall lessened, passing like a sudden shower—fewer stars and fewer falling, here and there a single stardrop. One last one, vivid blue like Flame, and then the sky was still.

Herewiss breathed out, smiling. "I'll keep Your secret," he said.

He slipped Khávrinen through his belt, and went back to the hold, and Freelorn.